Recompense
Book 1

A King for Scotland

Jay Anderson

Dercon Publishers—Giddings, TX
ISBN: 979-8-9897372-0-8
eBook ISBN: 979-8-9897372-1-5
Library of Congress Control Number: 2024900065
Title: *Recompense: Book 1: A King for Scotland*
Author: Jay Anderson
Digital distribution | 2024
Paperback | 2024

Dedication

Where do I begin? This project began as a whim—a desire, at 60 years young, to create a different world. Thanks to God as the words came – with minimal effort. Thanks to my dear wife of 40 years – as she allowed me to work all day, and then write into the evening – not exactly an attentive husband. Thanks to my son, Connor Anderson, for giving me the drive to write a book, even as he began to write his own. A special thanks to both of my sons – Derek and Connor. Their personalities and namesakes – The McAndrew Brothers – are who the main characters are modeled after. They motivated me to create them in their image – as I could not think of more fitting models with honor and character to fit what was needed to make the book work. Thanks to Jewel Pierce – who read the manuscript as I wrote – and would text me wondering where the next chapter was and why it was taking me so long to complete as he wished to know what was next in the story. Thank you to Andrew Quintana and John Heine – who continually encouraged me to keep the story going. Thank you to Keith Williamson – who inspired me to create "Lord Keith Lamont" – who has become a considerable part of the story. There are so many to thank – and even if your name is not mentioned – please know that I am forever humbled and appreciate you more than you will ever know. Finally – to Scotland. Home of my ancestors… may you be forever free and steadfast in your fight against tyranny! "Alba gu bràth!"

Chapter 1
Beginning

He gazed up at the canvas tent that had been his "home" for far too long. This was Sergeant Major Ian McKenzie's 5th tour of duty, his 3rd in Afghanistan. He stared at the brown stains that could barely be picked out against the tan material. It was 0400, but he had been awake for an hour. His knee ached from the shrapnel he took in Kandahar. His mouth was dry, like the outside of his tent, coated in a thin layer of dust. His whole body had been covered in that muck since he had arrived. No matter how much you washed, it seemed to stick to you—you tasted it. It was palpable.

McKenzie got up from his cot to make some coffee. It was instant coffee, but it did the job. He winced as he gulped it down. Swallowing this vile imitation made him miss the coffee his translator used to make. They had lost him to an RPG attack last month and hadn't found a replacement he trusted. It was a senseless death. They all were. The Sergeant Major kept asking himself why he and his men were there. How did an attack in America land him in the desert, barely knowing friend from foe?

He looked down at his watch to see if he had time for another cup... out of the corner of his eye... he saw her. The painting from memory he had painted of his sweet Annie. Twenty-five years they'd been married. So much of the time, she'd done it alone. A smile crossed his face as he thought of the "look" she would give him if he offered her this "coffee"?

Well... thoughts of that would have to wait. The briefing for their next mission was in thirty Minutes. If he left now, he might have ten minutes to speak to the Colonel before it started. He closed his eyes... winced a bit, and then shook his head. Something didn't feel right.

Colonel James Alexander, in Her Majesty's service for twenty-eight years, had been up hours before. He was 6'2" tall, 190 lbs., a pure unadulterated warrior. He was tough as nails because he had to be. He knew if his men saw him as soft, it would all go to hell quickly. He was as decisive as he was strong. He was not a risk-taker by nature, but he knew the strength and caliber of the men under his command. He also knew that this damn war was getting old.

So far, he had lost three of his Majors, damn good men, and friends as well. Three Hundred seven of the best and brightest men he had ever led into combat. His eyes moistened... the lump in his throat that had been there for the last seven months returned... the hardest by far was Sergeant Nathaniel Alexander... father to three of his grandchildren... he was in the barracks sleeping when those cowardly bastards got him with the mortar. You couldn't even find enough to bury. That's why he had no problem calling in air support when he needed to take those bastards to their Allah.

He chomped on his cigar. He looked up, and for a minute... he was home in Nairn. He could smell her... He knew every line... every wrinkle... every curve... Elizabeth had been so angry when he requested command in Afghanistan. She knew damn well that he could have any command he wanted. He could coast his way to retirement. But how could he? His family was going to war in Afghanistan! How the hell could he stay home when they needed him? How could he make it through a day not knowing if his training had prepared them for this? How could he? His throat was dry... his eyes were not... and his thoughts trailed off... Of course... none of that mattered after Nathaniel. She divorced him a month after his funeral. She wouldn't even look at him – let alone speak to him. Didn't she realize his heart was broken, too? Apparently not... sigh...

"Pull yourself together, man! Your boys need you now more than ever! It will be a few days of hell until we get through what is coming tomorrow."

For the last few months, their mission has been to support the Afghan Military. True, some were Taliban in disguise, some were cowards that ran at the first sign of resistance... some didn't even know which end of the rifle was the business end. But one thing was for certain: many of those men were tough in their own right. They wanted their country back and were willing to fight and die to do so.

"So, here we are in Merry Fucking Marjah. We have been here since February 2010, and it's April? It's already getting hot. It'll be over 40 in another month or so." He kept looking at the map and the red dots that indicated the Taliban. "How are there so many after all these years of getting their asses handed to them? I'm ready to finish this."

He was so lost in his thoughts that he didn't hear Sergeant Major McKenzie enter the room. He looked over and smiled. They had been through Hell and back together many times, from barroom brawls to heavily outnumbered hand-to-hand "we're not going to make it out of here" situations. He wouldn't like what he had to say, but he usually didn't anyway. Alexander knew he could count on Mac to get the job done.

"Good morning, Mac," was the conversation starter.

"Morning, Boss," was the typical response. But something in Mac's eyes concerned him.

"What are you thinking, Mac? You look like hell this morning."

Hesitantly, Mac shared his thoughts. "Well, Boss, I got a bad feeling now."

"Now, wait a damn second!" Alexander stated firmly. "The last time you said that nearly got us killed in Fallujah!"

Mac laughed at that. "Well, there was a good reason for that feeling, now wasn't there? But there's something that doesn't feel right about now. Something in the air. Hell, I don't know! It just doesn't feel right!"

Colonel Alexander had learned a long time ago to trust the Sergeant Major's instincts. He would have to let him brood for a while and then get his opinion on the matter. But he had to narrow it down to take some action on those "instincts."

"So, what are you feeling, Mac?"

McKenzie narrowed his eyes. "That's the fucking hard part, Boss. I've never felt anything like this in my life. It's like the air feels different. All I know is that whatever the orders are, we damn sure better be ready for anything!"

"Well, the Brass must be expecting the same. We just got our gear, enough to arm Her Majesty's whole damn Infantry, and that's just for our Regiment."

"You know what tomorrow is, don't you?" Mac asked, and of course, that meant a history lesson was to follow. "I'll make it easy... 16th April?"

"And?" The Colonel asked.

"Damn, Boss... 246 years ago tomorrow, the Brits whipped us in Culloden."

"16th April 1746," Mac answered. "And here we are... fighting for the Queen in a godforsaken country, helping another gain their independence from a tyrannical government. Talk about fucking tragic irony?"

"Careful, Mac. You know better than to talk like that. Talk like that could get you in deep shit, and you know it," the Colonel warned.

"Aye," Mac said. "But you know you feel it too!" Colonel Alexander could only nod silently in agreement.

There was a quiet knock on the door. That would be Major Derek McAndrew with his brother, Captain Connor McAndrew, by his side. They commanded the Delta Company of the 4th Battalion, Royal Regiment of Scotland. The Colonel usually didn't allow siblings to be in the same company, but damn, these boys made a hell of a team. Their company would be taking the lead.

The Colonel said, "Come in," and true to form, the Major and Captain entered the room and saluted smartly. "Good morning, gentlemen. Glad to see you. Are the officers ready?"

"Aye, sir," they said in unison.

"Very well, then. Let's get this party started, shall we?"

The Colonel, the Sergeant Major, the Major, and the Captain proceeded to the room. Captain McAndrew opened the door and stated loudly, "Attention!" The air was suddenly electric as everyone rose in unison and snapped to attention, saluting the "Old Man," as they called him.

The Colonel paused for a moment and did something unusual. He stopped in front of each man and saluted them individually. They were his family. They were "his" boys. They would be fighting and dying by his orders tomorrow. He wanted each of them to know how important they were to him personally. Who the hell knew what tomorrow would bring? Especially after what Mac had told him?

"All right, gentlemen. Let's get down to business. The Afghanis are taking a bit too long to retake Marjah. Along with a rather large NATO contingent, we have been tasked with getting this done in the next week. Even the Americans are coming into the fray with full air support. Our task will be to flank the Taliban, coming in from the west side of Marjah. Major McAndrew, your company will be leading the regiment," the Colonel explained, motioning to the map. "NATO will be coming in from the east, the Afghanis from the north. The Americans will provide a squadron of Apaches and a couple of AC-130s to assist us and mop up any Taliban that decide to head south. A lot of this will involve door-knocking. You know how those bloody bastards like to greet us at the door. We'll use overwhelming firepower to get their attention and eliminate the threat. I want each of your men armed and ready to unleash Armageddon. I want those bastards to meet Allah tomorrow, not us. If any building hints of hostility, I want it turned into ash. Is that Understood?"

"Aye, sir," they all stated in unison.

"The 4th Battalion will let the Taliban know they made a terrible tactical decision engaging us here and now."

Sergeant Major McKenzie then took over the conversation. "As the Colonel said, Major McAndrew, first of all, I will ride to this dance with you. So, Delta Company will take the lead. Charlie Company, you're next, one Click back, followed by Bravo and Alpha working jointly. You're hitting where the bulk of the Taliban harassment is coming from. The attack will commence precisely at 0200 tomorrow morning. Keep your drones and radios up. I don't want any surprises. We'll have a couple of Apaches providing close air support. Don't shoot at the Yanks; they're here to help," he added to break the tension. "Major McAndrew, where we will be attacking, is close to their command-and-control center. We will find and take out their leadership. Gentlemen, the fighting is expected to be heavier than usual. I want you to bring every damn thing with you in preparation. The Afghanis will start a distraction at 0100 tomorrow. We head out at 0130. Each company commander needs to brief their men by 0730 today. Any manpower or equipment concerns need to be addressed by 1000 this morning. Any questions?"

Captain McAndrew stood up and asked, "Are there any rules of engagement we need to be concerned with? Or do we do what's necessary?"

Colonel Alexander stepped in. "I'll take this, Captain McAndrew. This is a quote from the General himself: 'You are to dispatch those bastards to Allah by any means necessary.' I will add this, though—be on the lookout for civilians. Try to minimize their casualties as much as possible."

"Aye, sir. With prejudice?" Captain McAndrew asked.

"Extreme prejudice," was the reply.

Chapter 2
Preparation

0730: Delta Company Briefing

Major Derek McAndrew was on his 3rd deployment to Afghanistan. It better be his last, he laughed to himself. He has another bairn to feed and support every time he goes home - 9 months later, like clockwork. But damn…. His wife is a sight to behold! How can he help it? He's just a man? She's the only bit of comfort in this life. Leaving her was getting more difficult when it was time to go… but he's done this for 20 years. It's all he knows.

McAndrew is 5'10", weighs 190 lbs., and is built like a rock. His workouts terrorize all but his brother. He was trained as a mechanical engineer at the University - but found a new love when he joined the Highlanders. His brothers… everyone. A family that no one else would ever understand. They fought… they bled… they died together—a genuine "Band of Brothers," as they say.

His brother… Captain Connor McAndrew was a different animal altogether. He was 6'2" tall, 180 lbs. of sheer muscle. He also went to the University and became a Mechanical Engineer. He's been a soldier for eight years. And though he would admit it to no one - he enjoyed working with Derek. They did complement each other. That Yin and Yang thing. Their Da was damn sure proud of the lot.

Like his brother - they both love explosives and firearms. They can build a firearm out of virtually anything. Hand-to-hand combat - especially with knives - they excel. Fearless… but daft in his own way. He would say something to get you to laugh - especially when you would be called out for doing so. But also, like his brother… his leadership skills commanded respect from his officers - to peers — and those under his command.

Major McAndrew was ready to get the bloody hell out of Afghanistan and wanted to be home. To say it is hot here is a colossal understatement. It's April, and hit 35 degrees already. What the Hell is that? And the dust? It gets into everything. Trying to keep weapons clean is a continuous challenge.

Well… it's 0715. "Connor… I mean the Captain… damn… why is it so difficult to see that little shit as a Captain - and a damn good one at that?" "I guess it's because I remember Dangleberry in diapers." He chuckled. Now, there's no one he would rather have as his second in command. Anyway - he should have the lads together by now.

Sergeant Major McKenzie and Major McAndrew strode into the outside of the barracks. Captain McAndrew shouted! "Attention!" Everyone jumped to attention. Everyone knew something big was coming soon. The tension was so thick you could cut it with a sgian-dubh. With the grim look on both - the Major and the Sergeant Major's faces - the company was instantly on point - understanding the seriousness of what was to come.

Major McAndrew said, "At Ease." Everyone relaxed physically… but mentally, it was a different story. This wasn't their first time. They had been through these many times… from Kandahar forward. The majority just wanted to get this done and get back home.

Major McAndrew took center stage. "All right gentlemen… I'm sure you realize that we're not having our daily brief. Tomorrow - we will not be operating in a supportive role for the Afghans. We are going to engage in an offensive movement to eliminate the Taliban from Marjah."

"We have been assigned to take out their command-and-control centers. Here is the map of the city. Our target is 22 klicks South, 2 klicks East, and roughly 500 sq meters. SU 125 461. Artillery support will be non-existent here. As usual - the bastards are packed around the Hospital. We're taking the Jackals and the Mastiffs in. I want them loaded with ammo and enough Ration Packs for a week. The temperatures will be 35-40 most of the week. It's going to be hot. Water is key to all you Jocks. Get with your Fire Team Leader. He'll set you right."

"Company C will hit the grid 2 Klicks north of us and proceed East. Companies A & B will be 2 Klicks North of C and head East. The Afghan National Army (ANA) will start north and push South. The rest of NATO is coming in from the East and headed West. We're leaving the South open, hoping they go out the back door.

They'll be introduced to American Air Power and Allah shortly after that. McAndrew has the Company Assignments."

As Captain McAndrew stepped to the front - his usual jovial personality was unexpectedly somber. "All right, Lads - listen up. You each know your place. We've been here before. Lieutenant MacLeod - You and your platoons are getting us there. We have 10 Jackal 2s and 14 Mastiffs at our disposal. 2 Mastiffs will carry ammo, ordnance, and our Rations…. Understand this… I'll be highly irritated if you lose my dinner," he said lightheartedly. "Seriously - every spare Centimeter of extra space will carry supplies. We're carrying enough supplies for a week - but we should be done before. Your Platoons will also be tasked with fire support.

"Lieutenant Gordon - we need two squadrons for Signal - including drones when we have daylight. Two Squads for Support."

"Lieutenant Ross - you're doing the heavy lifting again. You have the Riflemen and the EODs…. If the bastards don't open the door for you - I'm sure you'll encourage them?" Connor said with a grin.

Ross's men shouted, "Aye, Sir!" And shouted a Battle Cry that made the ground tremble! Then the entire Company collectively roared as they began a Hielan' Coo… Warriors all - ready for the battle to come!

The Sergeant Major grinned as he walked to the front of his lads. "All right, lads - settle down. Here's what we're doing: The Lieutenants will get with their Platoons for individual assignments after our little get-together. We Mount up at 0100. We head out at 0130. We need to be on-site in Battle Formation headed East by 0200. The Jackals will lead the way in introducing ourselves. We'll have contact with their perimeter shortly after that. It's our job to take out their command and control. Consider every building directly East of the Hospital - including the Hospital to be hostile. We'll have to open every door in that hospital to clear out the vermin."

"Once daylight is here - I want the drones in the air. Intelligence says every building East and Southeast of the hospital is hostile. I'm betting they've planted some surprises along the way - so keep your bloody head in the game."

"It's 0900. I want everything packed up and buttoned up at 1600. You need to sleep before we head out in the morning."

"Any questions?" He shouted. There were none. These men were experienced warriors…. McKenzie thought to himself, "There is nowhere on earth he would rather be…than right here… right now… preparing the way of the warrior." "Dismissed!" he shouted.

The lads - in unison…stood to attention…and yelled again! "Alba gu bràth!" Their ancestors would be proud.

Chapter 3
Reflection

"God, what a day!" the Major said to himself. The men were all veterans - but damn! Did he have to make every decision for them? Connor was in the tent with him... sweat also poured off of him. "The Bastard" ... "I need to quit calling him that... My mum and da were married... but still! Was he working out before combat? Has he lost his mind? Even I'm not that much of a masochist!" "Connor... go get the Officers. Time for a smoke - a few stories and a wee dram of what's not allowed nor would ever be tolerated in this beautiful oasis."

Captain McAndrew went to get the Sergeant Major and the Lieutenants. Their routine before combat was as predictable as this scorching heat. Good cigars... some good stories... and good Scotch. Of course, it's illegal here... but only if you get caught - he grinned. Not once have they even been wounded since doing this ritual. It's a warrior ritual older than the Picts. Thankfully, there are no drums and dancing - especially since Derek can't dance!

Suddenly, Colonel Alexander showed up... the officers stiffened a bit. The Colonel smiled and pulled out a bottle of Talisker, 25-Year-Old Scotch!

The Colonel said, "I've been saving this for a rainy day.... Since it never bloody rains here... now seemed to be a good time."

Everyone smiled at that.

The Colonel continued, "I know not what tomorrow will bring - but this I want you to know." ... his voice quivered a bit, and a tear ran down his face... "You're the best group of mates I've ever had the privilege to serve with." He poured each of his officers a shot... "To my comrades in arms who have stood faithfully by my side, I raise my glass. Here's to the countless moments of laughter, the unwavering support, and the camaraderie that has made our journey all the more meaningful. We have learned each other's strengths, weaknesses, and dreams, woven together through shared experiences."

The Colonel continued, "May the fires of our friendship continue to burn bright, lighting the way as we face whatever lies ahead. Let us toast to the unbreakable unity that binds us, for in this regiment, we have found colleagues and a second family. To absent friends, cherished memories, and the enduring spirit of camaraderie that defines the Royal Highlanders Regiment. Cheers!"

All returned the "Cheers!" …. Not one gulped down the shot, however! Dear God… 25-year-old Scotch must be savored! Lightning would strike you dead to do otherwise!

The amber liquid touched their lips, and they inhaled deeply. Slowly, the delicate nuances and warmth splashed over their tongues as it went down their throats. "Dear Lord of Heaven… nature's very nectar," said the Sergeant Major… "That's the best thing I ever drank."

The Colonel laughed… "I know. Right?" …. And everyone agreed. The Colonel then lifted the bottle and showed them the half remaining… "and when you get back - we'll drink a toast to kicking the Taliban's arses out of this little bastion of paradise. Aye?"

"Aye, sir," they all heartily agreed.

The enlisted men had their rituals as well. They knew damn well that some would not make it back. This time - for whatever reason - seemed even more likely not to end well. They felt it. They all did. So most - wrote letters. Some could call home and speak with mothers… fathers… wives and children. All cheery, like there was no concern… but they knew. They all knew. That was the risk of being in the Regiment, of being in this war in this fucking country. They knew. They accepted it. What they could control - they would. What would come - would come.

Sergeant Josh Douglas. A beast of a man. His men would follow him to hell and back - though he was hard as hell on them. 6'4" tall. A behemoth. He could rip off your head for looking at him wrong! Men follow courage into battle. Douglas is the man to get them there. The Sergeant's Platoon had a little surprise for him. Unbeknownst to him… they had concocted a Still! They had been gathering and bottling it for several months. Of course, they bottled it in 2-litre Coca-Cola bottles - but hey… beggars can't be choosers now - can they?

They gathered the bottles and shouted to the Sergeant. His eyes twinkled with delight when he saw those "Bottles of Coke!" One offered the bottle to Sergeant Douglas. He took a considerable draw… Damn! That had a bite! He grimaced a bit. He wiped his mouth with his arm and exclaimed, "That'll knock the tits off your mum!" They all laughed at that… and the Sergeant passed it around. He did warn them not to get drunk. The Taliban would love to meet them with a hangover the next day… but then again… A fucking pissed-off, hungover Scotsman? That might win the battle quickly!

The Sergeant Major made his rounds. They needed to see him, and he knew it. They needed his reassurance… they needed his laughter… they needed his even temperament and confidence. Tomorrow will come, and the fates be damned. With the Sergeant Major - they all knew they stood a better chance of getting home.

He walked up to the last platoon.

Then it happened. Someone brought out the pipes. Usually, you hear a couple of Reels or Jigs - a few snappy tunes to get you in the mood. But not today… not today. What the actual Hell?!?! Amazing Grace? Really? A lump more prominent than a cricket ball leaped into his throat. A tear came out of his right eye - unannounced and unapologetic. He looked at the men. Even Douglas - you could tell he felt it. How many men had he buried while listening to that song? He loved it… experienced it… He knew it, yet hated it just the same. He was jovial… now the darkness set in. That feeling he had yesterday hit him right between the eyes… he knew they also felt it. Something does not feel right. Not at all. Perhaps he should write a letter to his Annie as well.

An early dinner and early to bed. Tomorrow is going to be here soon. Everyone that could - was asleep by 1800. Everyone was asleep by 1900… and then it happened… precisely at 1937… everyone in Delta Company… was there… Culloden… a dream… a shared dream… an old man… a Clan Chief… a Stuart… in Gaelic… In an old, grizzled voice… ancient… full of an ache that can only be felt… "Lads…. I know ye can hear and see me… Look at me Tartan… I'm a Stuart. We need you, lads. Your future depends on it. We need you…. nnnnnnnoooooooooowwwwww…. And his voice and face trailed off…And then it was over. Everyone. Every single man in Delta Company heard it… saw it… woke up at the exact time with a start…. And remembered.

Chapter 4
Radiance

At 2130, the officers' alarms went off, but they were not asleep. Neither were any of the other men in the Company. Their thoughts were deep regarding the dream. What the devil did it mean? None knew that they had all dreamt the same dream. Sleep escaped them, so as if in a trance, they all got up at precisely the same time. Preparation for the operation was automatic. Most of everything was taken care of the day before. They all realized that in a couple of hours, it would not matter. Combat and survival would be all that was in their minds then. Maybe that would be a good thing.

Sergeant Major McKenzie felt haunted. He felt like he knew that man. He could see him out of the corner of his eye. He started and shouted to himself. "F O C U S! You have a battle to fight. Men to lead. You will not permit yourself to think about this… this… apparition any further. Nnnnnnnnnooooooooowwwwww." He shivered. "NO! Fuck you. I'll not play your game."

The Sergeant Major quickly got dressed and ready for action. He was locked and loaded, 152 lbs. of gear. Besides the stiffness in his knee, he carried it with ease. What a dream! Maybe the Major will help me forget about it for now.

The Sergeant Major got to the Major's tent as the Major came out. "Sir!" He saluted.

The Major half-heartedly returned the salute. "You alright, sir?"

"Mac… I had this dream…"

"Wait, what? What was it about?" Mac asked cautiously.

"I saw this old clan chief, a Stuart," the Major started.

"What did you say?" Mac asked.

"It was this old clan chief…"

Mac got a chill… He told the Major, "I did too, sir."

"That's not possible," said the Major.

At that moment, the Captain arrived. "Bloody hell, I had this dream!"

Both the Major and Sergeant Major stared at him in disbelief. "Was it about an old Stuart Clan Chief?"

"Aye," stated the Captain. "How'd you know?"

They both said, "We did too!"

The Major declared, "We don't have time to think about it. We gotta get our boys ready for a fight. We'll have to talk about this when we get back."

They all nodded in agreement.

They never expected everyone to be geared up and ready to go. EVERYONE. It was eerily quiet. No one said a word. They were afraid to speak. The apparition might return.

Then one spoke… "Lads… I had this dream that scared me nigh unto death! I dreamt about an old Stuart Clan Chief!"

Then everyone erupted. It was discovered that everyone had the same dream. Everyone was troubled. And though they had been through too much to be superstitious, this one was too damn close!

The Sergeant Major shouted them all down. "QUIET! NOW!!!" "ATTENTION!" Muscle memory kicked in as lips were closed, and they snapped to attention. "Yes, we all had the same dream. I do not know what it means - even as you don't. The timing is bad - because we want to discuss it. But we cannot. We have a mission! Is that clear?!"

"Aye, sir," they said in unison.

"Do ya all wanna die?!"

"No, sir!" they shouted back.

"Then get your fucking head screwed on straight! If you do not stay focused - the Taliban will send you home in a body bag! Do ya want that?!"

"No, sir!" they yelled again in agreement.

"Then get your gear and saddle up! We will discuss this when we get back!"

Everything erupted as mission focus returned. In the distance, the thunder of the 155s and 105s started the diversion. It's 0100! The Afghans better be convincing! Damn! We better hurry, was the collective thought now.

Each man, fully armed and ready, moved to their assigned positions. Everyone turned on their Night Vision Goggles - NVGs.

The Jackals and the Mastiffs would run dark at full speed with no lights on. Not even a cigarette.

The 10 Jackals and 14 Mastiffs were loaded to maximum capacity. The Major, The Captain, and then the Sergeant Major were in each of the First three Mastiffs. They were with the Riflemen. They were going to be upfront with their boys. It was 0115. All engines were started.

Hearts were hammering, breathing intensified, and prayers for those who prayed were going up, even from those who did not pray. It's 0130… and they were off!

The first Jackal howled out of the gates at 0131, and the last Mastiff was out at 0133. In 20 minutes, they'll hit the southernmost part of the grid and turn due East. The road has been hit by everything from small arms fire to large IEDs. It's definitely not an interstate. Every bone-jarring pothole wreaked havoc on the comfort, and the riders questioned the marriage of their driver's mums to their dads!

Two minutes to the eastward pivot. Tracer fire! Fuck, they know we're coming. Then it happened. A light, brighter than the sun, a radiance began to envelop the first Jackal, and then covered them all. The light blinded everyone wearing the NVGs! The drivers slammed on their brakes as chaos reigned. Bullets began to hit the vehicles in the front.

The occupants of the Jackals felt it first. Everything shot straight up in the sky. The light was so bright it was thought the Taliban had gone nuclear. It was seen from the space station. The subsequent shockwaves utterly destroyed the two kilometers and the entire command and control operations of the Taliban. The 4th Battalion - Delta Company became sudden heroes, then they were gone. All of them, all of their vehicles, without a trace!

The Colonel was watching in real-time. When he realized that he had lost an entire company, he felt weak… he felt sick. At daylight, he would send a convoy to figure out what the hell happened. In the meantime, that remaining bottle of Scotch would never be drunk. Overwhelming sadness hit the Colonel before the blinding rage replaced it. Those bastards would pay!

The Highlanders felt their guts implode. They tumbled for what felt like days. Then, mercifully, they all passed out.

Chapter 5
Disoriented

Major McAndrew weakly opened the driver's side door to the Mastiff and fell to the ground. He was dizzy and disoriented. "Where the hell am I?" He staggered and fell to the ground, where he began to violently wretch until he thought surely his insides were coming up too. He got up on all fours and attempted to stand, but his vertigo prevented that. He stood upright for a moment before blacking out once again.

When he awoke, he saw Connor standing over him, looking like death warmed over. "What the Hell happened?" he asked.

"I have no idea," Connor replied.

"Do you have any idea where we are?" Derek asked.

"No clue," was Connor's response. "It looks like everyone is responding the way we are. They are at least moving. It looks like we all got severe vertigo from radiation? Hell, if I know." Connor steadied himself as he felt another round of nausea come close to erupting.

Sergeant Major McKenzie came staggering around the corner. He stopped momentarily, bent over, and took a deep breath. Resilience then kicked in. He'd never felt that bad, even after combat. When his heart beat, his head hurt. But he would not let his men see him like this. He slowly stood up and finally didn't feel a wave of nausea. Water. That's what he needed. He made his way to his pack and grabbed his canteen. Slowly, methodically, he raised his canteen and took a swallow. He held it in his mouth and swished it around before swallowing. Yes. That's right. Now, take another. He did just that and felt the spinning slow. Deep breath. Water. Deep breath. Water. He stood there for 20 minutes. He shook his head and poured some water over his head, took his hand, and rubbed it on his face. Much better.

McKenzie found the Major sitting with his back against a tree. "What the Hell?!" Mac hadn't seen a tree that big since he had been home. His eyes focused, and he looked at his surroundings for the first time. They were in a forest? How? They didn't have fauna like this in Afghanistan. He looked at the Major, who looked much worse than he felt. "Well, sir... Have we figured out where the Hell we are?"

The Major looked at the Sergeant Major with that "Hell if I know" look in his eyes. "I haven't a damn clue, Mac. When everyone comes around - we'll have to send out a couple of teams of scouts. In the meantime - we need to build a camp with a perimeter. We don't need the Taliban to sneak up on us... if there are even any here."

"I want to be one of those scouts," the Sergeant Major stated.

"No doubt," grinned the Major. He knew that already.

Mac looked at the Major, and it clicked. Something about this tied into the dream. He didn't know how - but he knew it did.

The Sergeant Major bent over and offered the Major a hand. "We need to check on our men, sir."

"Aye," the major said. "No time like the present, I suppose. Let me get some water first. I feel like I swallowed the Afghan desert!" He took a deep drink, and his head began to clear. He looked down at the Captain. "Get your arse up, brother. We got work to do."

"Aye... let's do this."

Connor grabbed his canteen. The Major looked at both of his Officers and directed them. "Go check on your men in your Mastiff. Get them over to this tree. If any can help - get them to start bringing the men up here. We need to get a head count and devise a plan." With that - the orders were given... action took over worry.

When the Major got to his Mastiff, he saw all but one of the men moving around. The one that looked like death warmed over was awake. The Major spoke to him. "All right, lad... you're gonna be fine." The major reached out and pulled him upright.

The Corporal let out a moan. "Sorry Major.... I'm feeling a bit dizzy still." He fell back on the seat again.

"I understand, Corporal. But I need you to get up. You'll feel better." The Major pulled him up again and got him out of the Mastiff.

The Corporal took a deep breath and bent over.

"There ya go, lad. That's better. All right - listen up, men. I want you to - start moving up to the Jackals. Help the men there. Get everyone to come to the clearing by that big Oak tree."

"Aye, sir." They stated and started moving slowly - to their objective… the next vehicle and that Oak.

Sergeant Major and Captain McAndrew had much the same response. Slowly but surely, the men gathered together.

"This is taking too long," the Major told himself - though it had been less than an hour. He could tell it was close to noon. It was cool and damp. This was not Afghanistan. But where were they? How did they get there? "Don't overthink, lad - one step at a time."

Finally - everyone was by the Oak tree. Small talk had started. It was easy to see that the effects of whatever happened were fading. Everyone was staring at their surroundings. For whatever reason - they felt comfortable there. Almost like they belonged. It felt like home.

The Major got up. He knew they would look to him for answers, and he had no idea. But he knew he had 150 men to organize and care for. So, it begins. "We have to set up camp before it's dark. We have no idea where we are or if there are hostiles - so we have to plan for it."

"I want a perimeter 100 meters out with this Oak tree as the center. Lieutenant MacLeod - I want you to get our equipment set around our perimeter. I want you to clear out the camp. I have no idea how long we'll be here. We need eight latrines dug as well. I also want an inventory. If nothing was damaged getting here - we should be supplied enough to get us to where we need to go."

"Aye, Sir." The men set off to do as instructed.

"Lieutenant Ross - your men are the sentries. Split your platoon into three squadrons. I want one squadron in the Jackals for fire support should we need them. I want the other Squadron separated into two-man patrols - one-half of the Squad at 250 meters and the other at 500 meters. I want the other third to make a bed in the Mastiffs. Each squad will get four hours to sleep and rotate accordingly."

"Aye, sir," they formed together to discuss their duties.

"Captain McAndrew and Sergeant Major McKenzie. I want you to gather the remaining men in the platoon. Find water. We'll need it. Then I want you to get some rations, and I want you to get some shut-eye. Tomorrow, you'll be finding out where the Hell we are. Grab the drones, see if you can find anything, and determine where to go tomorrow. I tried to pull up a GPS. There's none to be had."

"Everyone - keep your gear on and your weapons about you. If the Taliban are here - they won't catch us flat-footed. No fires tonight. We'll be eating rations. All right, let's get this done." With that - everyone was set to task.

19

Chapter 6
Apprehension

10 April 1746

“Aye! I saw it and heard it! I swear to the Highest that it was brighter than the sun! And the booming noise made my entire house shake to the foundations! Everyone in town is talking about it. I heard Lord Granard’s and some of the Church’s windows were blasted out, too!”

“You know where it came from?”

“Aye, Culloden Wood. Aye, I do. The Devil himself must have been there! I doubt the Faeries could’ve done that!”

“On top of that, I heard Bonnie Prince Charlie is headed this way! That’s all we need is to have Duke William Augustus come here looking for him!”

That was the type of conversation heard all through the town. Apprehension, fear, and excitement all tied together like a knot on a string.

The taverns had been running a brisk business the night before. Most of the talk had been about the Jacobites and how the Scots had been beating the Duke. The Prince seemed to be outfoxing the Duke in every battle and skirmish. Maybe there was a chance, then!

“Aye. But you know Lord Granard is on the fence. He’ll be on whichever side is winning, you know.”

As the night wore on, the lively chatter in the tavern continued to swirl around the two prevailing concerns of the day - the strange occurrence at Culloden Wood and the potential arrival of Bonnie Prince Charlie. Patrons huddled around dimly lit tables, fervently sharing their opinions and speculations.

“Did you see the way the ground shook?” one man exclaimed, his eyes wide with excitement. “I’ve never seen such a sight in me life! ‘Twas like the heavens themselves were angry!”

"Aye, and they say the windows at Lord Granard's estate were blown to bits," added another, taking a swig of his ale. "Surely a sign of the Almighty's wrath upon us!"

Amidst the talk of the mysterious event, the looming possibility of Bonnie Prince Charlie's arrival weighed heavily on everyone's minds. A group of men gathered near the hearth, their faces illuminated by the dancing flames.

"What if the Prince comes to rally his supporters here?" one man pondered, stroking his beard thoughtfully. "Are we ready to stand with him against the Duke's forces?"

"Aye, he's been proving himself on the battlefield, hasn't he?" another replied. "If he's smart, he'll rally enough clans and make a stand!"

"But what if the Duke's men find out? They'd tear this town apart looking for him," a cautious voice interjected.

The atmosphere in the tavern shifted from excitement to trepidation as the potential consequences of the Prince's arrival sank in. The sound of clinking glasses and the hum of conversation continued, but a sense of unease hung in the air.

In another corner of the tavern, a group of serving maids exchanged hushed whispers as they refilled the ale of their ever-thirsty patrons.

"Have you heard about the strange lights and sounds at Culloden Wood, Mary?" one of them asked.

"Aye, lass, I did," Mary replied. "Folk says 'tis the work of the faeries, or maybe even the spirits of our ancestors come back to warn us."

"Superstitious nonsense!" scoffed a giant of a man nearby. "It was probably just some natural event. Nothin' to fret about."

As the night progressed, the discussions grew more animated, with each tale of the strange event at Culloden Wood becoming more incredible than the last.

"I heard that the fairies were having a grand celebration, and that's what caused the bright light!" one man exclaimed, waving his arms dramatically.

"A celebration, eh?" chuckled another. "Maybe they were rejoicing over the Jacobites' victories!"

A few patrons shared amused glances at the fanciful tales, finding some respite in humor amidst the uncertainty surrounding their town.

The tavern keeper, a weathered and wise-looking man, moved between the tables, refilling tankards and joining in the discussions when he had a moment to spare. "Mary and Anne - get your arses to work. You can gossip another time."

"I've seen my fair share of strange happenings in these lands," he said, wiping down the bar. "But this one takes the cake. 'Tis as if the very earth and sky conspired together to stir our souls."

The conversations in the tavern ebbed and flowed well into the night, each tale becoming more embellished and exaggerated than the last. As the hours waned, the crowds drifted away. All knew - things were about to change. For the better or worse - only God would know how and to what extent.

Chapter 7
Reconnaissance

11 April 1746

Sergeant Major McKenzie gazed at the moonlight while warming himself by the fire. He could smell the oak burning, but it was funny - he didn't remember making the fire. The venison roasting over the flames smelled heavenly, reminiscent of his Da and childhood. And then, he saw him—the Clan Chief from his dreams. He jumped with a start!

"Ya look like ya saw a ghost, Lad... relax. We have much to discuss. You have many questions - but until we meet - you'll have to trust me. In the meantime, sit your arse down and get ready for the best thing ya ever ate." The grizzled chief was preparing the backstrap of an Elk. McKenzie looked around, and suddenly, the large fire had reduced to coals. The back strap had been skewered, and he could see the juices glistening on the meat, hearing the sizzle as they dripped onto the coals. He was suddenly starving. The Chief cut a slice with his Dirk and held it to McKenzie. McKenzie bit down, and the juices exploded in his mouth. His eyes opened in amazement! Beyond a shadow of a doubt, it was the best he had ever eaten. The Chief cut off a significant portion and offered it to McKenzie, who took it hungrily.

The Chief took his portion and sat on a rock opposite him. Quietly, they enjoyed the meal together. Finally, the meal was over.

The Chief began the conversation, "I am Sir John Stuart of Grandtully. Your men are here because of me. You are an answer to my prayers. You are here to fulfill your destiny. You and your men will forever change the world - for us now, in the ridding of tyranny. But the future world will be better because of what you and your mates will do moving forward. You will meet me later... but this is all for now. It is time for you to awaken to find out where you really are."

"Wait! I have questions! Don't go!" And the dark faded to dawn.

Sergeant McKenzie awakened with a start. "What the bloody hell is this?" He was troubled. He had dreams like this in the past - but this was so bloody real it was unnerving. He felt like he could have touched the old man... and the Venison! My god, that was lovely!

He was still in his combat gear, his firearm right beside him. For whatever reason, he believed the Taliban would no longer be a concern. He got up to relieve himself. There would be no coffee this morning. He closed his eyes and inhaled deeply. The air smelled so clean. His senses were alive again as he tried to take it all in. He still wondered where they were... but now he wondered if a time element was involved as well? And Annie! He wanted to call her. He. Wanted. Her.

He knew the order of business this morning was to find answers. They ran the drones yesterday. They found a couple of streams that looked promising for water. There was much wildlife, so food would not be a problem should it come to that. There was a herd of Elk two clicks to the Northwest if the numbers were anywhere close to right on the drones.

There were a couple of towns. The biggest was around eight clicks to the Southwest. But back to the drones... none of the GPS tracking systems worked. That meant they had to keep a visual on the drone or lose it. So long-distance recon from the air was all but impossible.

Much to everyone's chagrin, no cell phone had any signal. It's like the signal capability did not even exist. It was amusing watching the youngsters trying to make them work and finally giving up in utter frustration. Why does that make me happy? He asked himself with a grin...

He started towards the Major. I'm sure he found sleeping in the Mastiff as much fun as I. He could see the progress in the camp moving forward. The layout would've made Caesar proud. Every aspect was detailed - in order - and defensible. They only needed a wall around them to make it more secure. There were plenty of trees to build it... however, no axes were available to cut them down.

Major McAndrew was standing outside his Mastiff... makeshift HQ, and tent. He looked none the worse for wear. How the hell did he do that? In the middle of God knows where. He looked the poster boy for all that was right with the Highlanders! He was a damn fine officer. The only one his equal was the Colonel.

Oh, the Colonel! He's gotta be tearing up Marjah and Afghanistan looking for the lost company!

"Good Morning, Major."

"Good morning, Mac," was the reply.

"You got any sense of where we are or what happened?"

Mac thought about the dream. He wasn't going to tell the Major about that yet. "No, sir. I don't. I only know this looks, smells, and feels like home," Mac said.

"Aye," said the Major. "It sure does. But there's no way we could be home. Not even close!"

"Aye... I suppose," came the answer. "But it feels right. A damn sight better than Afghanistan!"

Captain McAndrew came strolling in - none the worse for wear. He had a smile on his face as he started eating his ration pack for breakfast. "Good morning, lads! Are ya ready for our adventure today? Mac! Ya look off today! Where's your sense of adventure?"

"Alright Mac. Ya got that look. What the hell are ya thinking about?"

"What do ya think, sir? We have no idea where we are... what the potential enemy could be... where our FOB is - even if there is one... our radios only work on our traffic.... GPS is MIA... cell phones don't work... how long will our rations last... what the hell our inventory is... which reminds me."

"Major... has Lieutenant MacLeod completed the inventory?" The Sergeant Major asked.

"No - he hasn't. I told him this morning that I want it by 1600 today."

"Good," said the Sergeant Major. "I'll feel a lot better with that information known. I'm thankful we didn't lose anyone."

"Aye, me too," reflected the Major.

"Anyway - I want you to get Lieutenant Gordon and his Platoon together, then separate into four squads to recon the small towns. I don't want any contact with them. I want actionable intelligence on which we can plan. Understood?"

"Understood, sir."

The Captain and Sergeant Major saw Lieutenant Gordon and headed over. The Captain said, "Lieutenant Gordon - get your platoon together. Split them into four squads. I will lead one. The Sergeant Major will lead another. One will be your command, and I want Sergeant Douglas commanding the other. Full battle gear. I want a drone with each squad. Bring your NVGs in case we don't get home before dark. I want three radios per squad. Meet me here at 0830. Make sure the men have a ration before we go. Don't know what we can scavenge or not? Fill your canteens, too. Questions?"

Sergeant Major McKenzie put this out there, too, "The Major said no contact with the natives. We'll use cover there and back. We don't have GPS, so we must go old school. From the looks of the drone coverage that we could make out - there is a large body of water Northwest of here. I'm guessing less than two clicks. Lieutenant- I want your squad to go there, follow the coastline until 1500, and return to the base. Douglas - You head due south - use your drones and look for targets of opportunity. There's a town less than four clicks Southwest of here. The Captain and I will take our squads in that direction. I want everyone back in base by 1900. Is that clear?"

"Aye, sir."

At 0830 - the platoon split into squads. The officers gathered for one more time before heading out. McAndrew and McKenzie's Squads headed out almost directly West. There was a bend in the creek up ahead they would follow that went toward the village. Gordon headed Northwest. The forest was thick here, which gave good cover. Douglas headed due south. He decided he would get to the forest's edge before bringing out the drone. He damn sure didn't want to lose it.

Douglas and the squad reached the edge almost four clicks south of the FOB. He got the drone out and put it to flight. On his iPad, he was able to navigate and see at the same time. He took it about seventy-five meters high and started his search. "There," he pointed to the team. It looked like a large homestead. Several men were working in the fields. You could see some children running about. A little to the East, he could see a smaller homestead. That would be the one to recon if the goal was info without being seen. Besides, the woods went almost to what appeared to be a barn. "That'll do," he told his men. He brought the drone back and started toward the smaller farm.

When they got to the smaller farm - there was no one there. He left a sentry in the front and back that could radio him if someone were coming. He checked the door and was surprised that there was no lock available. He stepped in gingerly and was surprised to find a dirt floor. He'd have to do something about his tracks in the dirt before he left.

This was a quiet, simple one-bedroom home. There was no modern kitchen and no loo... there was a large fireplace with cooking utensils. He couldn't see any electrical outlets or anything modern. There was a simple bed in the bedroom. Pipes and a fiddle.... He thought to himself, "We're definitely not in Afghanistan!" He saw a Kilt and plaids on a dress... he jumped. That was Clan Macintosh! His brother had married one!

He heard the radio. "Sergeant! A couple is coming down the road in a Horse and Buggy!!! We need to go now!"

He brushed the dirt quickly, sprinted out the back door, and headed to the woods. That's when he heard them. Two Collies used to tend sheep got their scent and started after them. The farmer and his wife thought it was rabbits and let them go without concern.

The Sergeant and his squad made it to the woods. The dogs were on their scent. He could hear them a few hundred meters away. Douglas was praying they would stop. He had no desire to kill the farmer's dogs - but kill them he would if need be. There was a creek up ahead. Maybe they could throw the Collies off their trail... the men jumped in. They got to the other side and started sprinting to the Camp... the barking slowed... and then stopped altogether. The farmer had called the dogs home, and they had obeyed. "That was too damn close," he said under his breath. With that, he and his men headed back to the base.

Gordon and his men found the body of water, as the Sergeant Major had said. There had been a couple of small farms they skirted around. They wanted to get their feeling of the body of water and a greater context of where they were. Besides, the one farm they tried to sneak up on had big dogs that barked incessantly. It would be hard to sneak up on that bastard. "Sure hope that's not the way everywhere." He got out his drone and took it up to one hundred meters. "Damn! That body of water is large. It looks like it goes to the ocean. I don't know where we are - but it damn sure ain't Afghanistan," he said to his squad. "There are several homesteads close to the water. Let's see if we can get close enough to hear someone."

They came across two men and their sons working with sheep. They each had dogs, and they started bragging about their dogs to each other. That's when it dawned on the Lieutenant.... They were speaking Gaelic... but wait?!?! How?!? He had to get closer. He pulled out his binoculars... they were wearing Kilts! They had dirks and swords on as well!

"It's time for us to head back, lads. I'm feeling a bit daft. How the bloody hell can we be in Scotland? Surely, I'm dreaming!" He took some photos with his phone to show the Major. "Let's go, lads!"

McAndrew and McKenzie - with their squads followed the creek. They heard horses neigh... dogs bark... and cows coo.... Damn, they sounded so familiar. They pulled out their drone and let it fly.... The town was less than two clicks away. They had stuck to the forest but now had to decide their path. They were close to a road. McAndrew ran the drone while the Sergeant Major pulled out his binoculars. McAndrew was commenting on the lush green ... he saw men and women working ... he saw hogs – well, they definitely were NOT in Afghanistan... In the meantime - The Sergeant Major was scanning the horizon.... And they both saw it... "No fucking way!" Exclaimed McAndrew.

The Sergeant Major said, "This can't be!"

McAndrew shouted, "Do you see it?!?!"

"Aye, sir! I do!" .... The big hairy beast... the Highland Cow! Here?!?! But how?!?! How can it be?!?! A screenshot from the drone confirmed their vision was good - it just didn't make sense!

McAndrew gathered his wits about him before he lost the drone. He then began to look closer... he could see kilts! "Dear Mary... Mother of Jesus! We're home!" But wait... he looked closer... something didn't look like what he expected to see. He asked the Sergeant Major to look at his 1 o'clock position. He did so... three men were sitting on their horses talking... they had Tricorn hats!

"One man is wearing a cravat tied neatly in a bow; his waistcoat and breeches are a dark hunter green. He is wearing a long-sleeved white linen shirt. He has knee-high riding boots... with a sword buckled to his waist."

"The second man is wearing a tricorn hat - but it is a dark brown - matching his waistcoat. He, too, has a white linen shirt with a sword around his waist."

"The third man looks a bit older. He is wearing a Forbes kilt if I see it right from this distance… He has a white linen shirt and a black Tricorn hat... Riding boots and a sword about the waist as well!"

McKenzie was incredulously describing it to McAndrew. Now, they were both perplexed. He and McAndrew decided to scout out a small house close to the woods. Perhaps they could get close enough to hear something. It would have to be dark or close to it. The Major would be angry - but they would return later than 1900.

The two men returned to their squads and told them to return to Camp. "Let the Major know where we are now and that there will not be any Taliban. We'll get back as soon as we can," said Connor.

The squad headed back. McAndrew and McKenzie made their way over to the old farmhouse. They saw two older women preparing to enter what was probably their home. They wore floral print dresses and had their hair in a bun. They pulled off their bonnets… let out their hair… stretched long and hard. It had been a hard day… but the garden meant life or death to them. Neither felt like making dinner, but it had to be done to sustain their strength for another day.

Margaret looked at her younger sister Sarah… "I think we are indeed making progress… but I'm not afraid to say I'm nearly worn out!"

"Aye - me too," said Sarah. "I'm thinking stew for dinner - does that sound good to you?"

"Aye. At this point - give me a carrot, and we can call it a day!" They both laughed. It would be more than a carrot, they knew… Both husbands had died last year during a clan war. It had been a struggle ever since. They both felt the grief now. It ached deep in their souls... but live they would. They each had grandchildren to live for - at least for a while.

McAndrew and McKenzie began to inch toward their residence. They kept expecting a dog - but fortunately, none were there. As the darkness began to creep in - they stationed themselves behind a wall that led to a root cellar. They could overhear their conversation. It was in Gaelic… dear God, it sounded like music to their ears. The women began talking about the troubles. About the Jacobite rebellion and Bonnie Prince Charlie!!! What the actual hell?!!!

Sarah reminded Margaret they would go to Inverness on the morrow to get supplies. And finally, they heard it... the date... when Margaret asked her sister what the next day was.... April 12, 1746. APRIL 12, 17fucking46!!!!!

McKenzie was suddenly transported to that same fire, and the Chief was awaiting him. "You're the historian. You know what that means?"

"Aye. I do. The Battle of Culloden is four days from tomorrow," said McKenzie weakly.

"Exactly." Then, the chief was gone.

"McKenzie... McKenzie... MCKENZIE!" McAndrew slapped him on his face and finally got his attention. "Where the Hell did you go? We must get back. NOW!"

"Aye, sir," offered McKenzie weakly...

They both knew where they were... but more importantly - when... They both took off at a run. They figured it was five clicks back to Camp. Thankfully, they had night vision. They could run safely and get back quicker. And run they did.

Chapter 8
Realization

The Captain and Sergeant Major rushed into camp at 2000. The Major was furious - but relieved. It showed on his face.

"Have you lost your minds, you two? Staying out there by yourselves with no backup? What in the world were you thinking?" he barked.

Both officers were panting, but they stood at attention, understanding the necessity of maintaining discipline even in these peculiar circumstances.

"Sir!" they exclaimed in unison. "We need to speak with you privately, sir. Right now!" Captain McAndrew insisted.

"It's urgent, sir," added the Sergeant Major.

Major McAndrew scrutinized the two men. He knew these officers well; one of them was his brother. He sensed there must be a good reason for their delay, and he decided to grant them a private audience. He realized that discipline among the ranks was still essential, perhaps now more than ever.

"Very well," said the Major. "At ease." They walked to the outskirts of the camp and ventured a bit further into the woods. The Major could see the tension on their faces.

"I've debriefed the others," the Major mentioned, "and they've come up with some far-fetched notions. Gordon seems to believe we're in Scotland!"

Captain McAndrew decided to break the news, "Well, sir, we are... in Scotland."

"What?" the Major exclaimed, startled.

"Yes, Derek, that's the good news." Connor whispered to his brother, "But... there's more. Tomorrow is April 12... 1746!"

"That can't be!" the Major shouted.

"Derek, look at these pictures we took today." They showed him the photographs of Highland cows, men on horseback, and other evidence of their strange surroundings. The Major examined the photographs in silence, his face revealing a mix of disbelief and shock. He leaned against a tree, overwhelmed by the revelation.

"How are we going to tell the men? And what about our families?" he mused aloud. Never seeing his wife and children again weighed heavily on him. He refused to break down, to show weakness. He needed to be strong for his men, who depended on his leadership.

Mac also confronted his own emotions. He thought about his wife, Annie, and the world he had left behind. Strength, not grief, was his only option now. The world they had entered was vastly different, with different rules, beliefs, and severe punishments for transgressions. Even something as basic as the measurement system had changed. They used the English system here, not the metric system.

Captain McAndrew mentioned the next pressing issue, "So, when do we tell the men? The Battle of Culloden is only four days away."

The Sergeant Major revealed more of his experience, "I haven't had the chance to mention it yet, but I saw the Clan Chieftain, just as you did. He told me that our company was an answer to his prayers." Mac recounted everything he said, every detail of the conversation to them. The officers listened attentively.

McKenzie continued, "During that encounter, he told me I was the historian." I realized the Battle of Culloden was only four days away. When I told him, he said, 'exactly,' and then vanished."

The Major took charge of the conversation, "It's getting late. We've been at this for hours. You know, rumors have started circulating. We need to rest and gather our thoughts. We'll meet again at 0600 to plan our next steps. I want to convene with the officers at 0730, and 0900 - we'll address the entire company. It's important to remember as it stands – we have no legal authority over them. We'll have to discuss this further tomorrow. Agreed?"

"Agreed," they replied in unison.

The three officers returned to the camp where the men had built fires to keep warm. It was a chilly, damp evening, and their spirits were dampened too. The Major addressed the men, his sense of responsibility weighing heavily on him.

"I know you've all been talking about what you've seen. We're still trying to make sense of it ourselves. Here's how we're going to handle it," the Major began. "At 0730, all officers will meet at the oak tree. At 0900, we will gather as a company. We have a lot to discuss and many decisions to make. This won't be easy, but we're Highlanders, and we've come this far. We'll face whatever challenges lie ahead. In one hour, I want all fires extinguished. Sergeant Douglas select 16 sentries in pairs, 4 hours each on duty. Maintain a 250-meter perimeter. Remember, there are questions without answers. We'll share all we know tomorrow. Goodnight, lads!"

Chapter 9
Resolution

The Major looked at his watch… 2130. He knew Sleep would not come easy - if it did at all. If this is their new world - there will be much to learn. Things that would not have been taught in their schoolbooks. He knew that many traditions are handed down. As well as stories and tales from the past. These folks - his ancestors - would be highly pious. Though some would be the opposite. Learning who to trust. Knowing some would lust for the power they would wield during this time frame. Thanks be to God; we all know Gaelic. There might be nuances and grammar differences - but communication would be easily doable.

What about the Battle that is coming? He remembered his history. Bonnie Prince Charlie. A Stuart that, by rights - should have been King instead of the Hanovers from Germany. From the Hanovers came the Windsors - Queen Elizabeth. Ahhh… the Queen. What about his vows? She's hundreds of years away. His vow would no longer be valid.

He thought back to his cadet days…when he said his Vow after the OTC - Officer Training Course. He smiled to himself. A 24-year-old Buck ready to take command and make a bloody difference. He could see himself as he said, "I, Derek Jason McAndrew, pledge my unwavering allegiance to Queen Elizabeth and her heirs. With a steadfast heart, I shall defend her crown and her realm from all foes, placing duty above self, and honor above all else. As a guardian of the realm, I vow to follow the orders of my superiors faithfully, serving with valor and integrity. So, help me, God." His parents were so proud … though his mum was apprehensive. He didn't know who cried the most - his mum or da! His heart began to ache - would he ever see them again? Or, with this timeline - would they even exist? And his wife and children?!?! How do you come to terms with any of this nightmare?

Fifteen years later… and a dilemma he never trained for. He knew instinctively that they all needed to stay together to make it. With their firepower - they have the strongest military in the world. It could make them all wealthy or destroy them all. And in four fucking days - THE battle that defined Scotland and the United Kingdom was to be fought. Here.

Fuuuuuuuccccccckkkkk. That is too surreal. What should we do? Our vows say we fight for the King. Wisdom would probably dictate we stay out of it. My heart says it is time for recompense. I know damn well what the Sergeant Major would say! That made him smile.

How would his company take this? Hell! How am I going to take this? And what about technology? I know the Steam Engine was invented in the late 1600s. In 1746, there would be some improvements – but it would be almost one hundred years before the Industrial Revolution. We could do that in a few years - just with what we know! Scotland would be the most powerful nation on the planet!

The Sergeant Major was emotionally all over the place - which pissed him off. That was so unlike him. But how do you make a decision? How do you exercise your intellect when this is impossible? And he thought about Annie… He was eighteen and a Private, right out of Basic Training. And she was a Brit?!?! His mum was so angry! "There are millions of Scots, and you pick a Brit?!?!" Blonde hair… shoulder length… her eyes were the bluest he had ever seen. The first time she looked at him… she pierced his soul. He had met her in Leeds while he was on R&R. 1982…. He and his mates went to Merrion Centre. How would he know the moment would change his life forever? She had asked him to dance. His mates had razzed him about that for months after… "The only reason she asked you is because you didn't have the balls to ask her yourself!" He smiled. The first time they kissed - she had his heart and didn't even know it. They exchanged addresses.

Little did he know that the Falklands a few months later would be where he met the Colonel when he was but a Lieutenant… and the first time he would go to combat… where he killed his first man. It took time to get over that. He nearly quit because of it. Now, it's of no significance. How fucking tragic is that if you think about it?

He and Annie wrote back and forth. It would be two years before he saw her again. He decided right then and there when he saw her - he would have his ring, and she would be his! He telephoned her when he was on leave and got to town. He met her at her flat. He knocked gently. He intended to get on his knee and propose right there. She created a problem when she opened the door, leaped into his arms, and smothered him with her kiss…. He held her and carried her into the flat while their lips embraced. He had almost forgotten what he had come there for - he was so entranced… but he forced himself to stop…. he gently set her down on the couch… he got down on one knee and pulled out a ring… the Diamond was small. Only a one-fifth carat… and before he could even get the question out, she said, "Yes!" … the most amazingly utterly beautiful word he had ever heard! And then they made love. Fierce. Intense. Passionate…. They were married the next day. Ah, lad… these will be dangerous thoughts now! And a tear fell.

Ok. Enough of the emotion. What do we do now? There was definitely strength in numbers. Do we get involved in the Battle? For me, that's an easy question. The Windsors weren't even Brits! They were Huns! How do we govern our troops? What about money? Supplies? Food? Clothing? Room and board? All of the basics? A fucking infection can kill ya here! All of these questions and no fucking answers. That's not the way things are supposed to be. That's not how I operate! And ammo and taking care of our firearms? Then, he fell into a fitful sleep.

The Chieftain was there. They were in a tent where officers would meet to discuss battle plans. There was a bottle of whiskey. The Chieftain poured a dram for the Sergeant Major. McKenzie looked across where a mirror stood…. There he was… wearing a Kilt with the McKenzie colors… a fine white linen shirt…. a sporran… he pulled the dirk from his sheath and gasped… it was engraved with his family crest and motto… "Luceo Non Uro," Latin for "I shine, not burn."

"Ya don't have one yet, Lord McKenzie - but ye shall."

"Lord McKenzie? What the devil are ye talking about?" Questioned McKenzie.

"You will see soon enough lad… you now know why you and your company are here. You know the difference you are going to make in my world. I hope to be able to show you and your men - the difference you are going to make in your world as well."

The Sergeant Major drank the loveliest Scotch he had ever had… and fell into a deep sleep.

Captain McAndrew felt the tension from his brother and his own as well. He could feel things in a way that only his mum understood. Derek and Da had none of that. Sometimes, he thought it was more of a curse than a blessing. But sometimes, the insights he had were invaluable.

Was he concerned about where and especially "when" they were? Of course. He wasn't daft. But he felt like this would be home. He believed it was going to be "home" for all. Of course, he didn't have a wife or children in his old world to worry about. He asked this question quietly to himself… "Alright God. I know you know what you're doing. A little hint and a lot of wisdom would be highly appreciated on this end… because I have no bloody clue what we'll be doing tomorrow."

How are the men going to react? Are there any that won't believe or stay with the group? We must keep the command structure in place until after Culloden. Funny - he believed this to be a foregone conclusion. They were going to fight and beat the shite out of the Brits. They were going to throw everything they knew out of the window completely. But why else would they be there?

So first, we have to convince the officers… then we have to convince the troops. Of course, that'll be easy if we actually get involved in Culloden and see the Redcoats!

Connor was the first to sleep and the first to awaken. He looked at his watch… 0430. He got up to go to the loo. He would not be able to return to sleep. He decided to walk by the creek. He looked and saw the moon. It wasn't full - but it was close. That's when he saw it… an Albino Elk…the most fantastic animal he had ever seen! It stood... stretched… and looked him in the eye. He felt… almost unnerved… yet… it was hard to describe. He felt a shiver run down his spine. He began to breathe rhythmically… he could feel an inner peace and strength begin to develop. He inhaled deeply…Yesssss…. He was home.

The tension was felt throughout the camp. Small discussions emanated from the Lieutenants to the privates. Was it fear? Wonder? A quiet desperation to be with loved ones?

Lieutenant Ross, Gordon, and MacLeod spoke in hushed tones. Ross started, "I know we're home... but something's amiss. I can feel it."

Gordon was the practical one... yet stated, "Aye. You're right on that - no doubt. If we were truly home, we could call our families now. We would already be having a reunion!"

MacLeod interjected, "Something tells me there's much more to this than we know. There's something that brought us here for a reason. Ya know, we're gonna have to be steadfast for the men? I almost wish it were 0700 now. I'm ready to find this thing out now and get ready for it!"

They all agreed. None of them were the superstitious types... but the nearly full moon had them thinking a million thoughts - and none were good. Gordon finally blurted out - "It's the not knowing that is bothering me. A few days ago, we were preparing for a battle with the Taliban. How the bloody hell did we get here?!?!"

A few Sergeants and Corporals were having the same kind of discussions. All want to know the details instead of the suspicions. If they're in Scotland, why can't they just find a town and call the Regimental Commanders to get them? They all agreed that right now, they would rather be fighting the Taliban than this god-forsaken uncertainty. They each ached for their families and their friends in their own way.

The Privates... were the youngest and the least experienced. All felt their worry. Loved ones missed. Fear... doubt... concern. The uncertainty made for an uncomfortable partner. Sleep would be hard in coming - answers. That's what they thought they wanted. Tomorrow will have them all questioning everything around them.

One by one... a quiet resolve began to make its presence known. They were Highlanders. They have fought... bled ... and some have died. They damn sure wouldn't give up now. Besides... the Major, the Captain... and the Sergeant Major had gotten them all out of worse situations than this. A fitful sleep finally came as exhaustion finally took its toll.

Chapter 10
Resolved

It was 0530. A full 30 minutes until he met with Connor and McKenzie. He had not always been a praying man - especially with all the death and destruction he had seen. But he stepped away from where they were to meet. He got on his knees. Quietly, he bowed his head. "Heavenly Father, you know me better than I know myself. You know the future better than I know the past. You- above all - know why we are here. Now. I'm asking you, Father… to give me wisdom. Please help me to know and to do thy Will in this and all situations to come. Please help me to lead my men as you would lead them. Father, I am asking you to protect my men as you give us all courage and the strength to do thy Will. Amen."

0600: The Major, the Captain, and the Sergeant Major met together. It was decision time. You could see in their faces that none slept well. Today would be a brand-new day… for everyone. Today, they must accept their circumstances and figure out how to move forward. Today, they meet… define… determine… and shape their destiny. Today, they must understand and come to grips with the fact their world no longer exists to them… that will be the most sobering and challenging part of this journey to acknowledge and wrap their heads around.

The Major started… "All right, gents. You've had all night to think about our predicament and how we should proceed. I need your input now."

Connor answered, "Derek… we have no choice but to speak the truth. Four days from today is Culloden… We must decide what we will do and plan for the battle if we will engage. We must hunt and feed our men before the Brits and the Prince arrive. We are far enough from the battlefield that we should not have any intrusion- but we need to be prepared in case."

McKenzie said, "Aye. You're right. You both know that no other army can defeat us if we have ammo and fuel. We could be a mercenary force working with the Prince - though not directly under his command - until he understands modern warfare. If we stay cohesive - we will change the future for the better."

"Point taken," stated the Major. "I agree. We need to stay cohesive as a force if for no other reason - than to increase our value. I also agree - we must tell the truth to our troops. We must be able to answer their questions or tell them we do not know. The hard part, as you all know... will be understanding that none of our loved ones are," He hesitated – only for a second ... "Here." At this point – there are three choices: 1. Do nothing, 2. Fight the Scots 3. Fight and beat the British here and now.... Thoughts?"

The Captain stood smartly at attention. "Sir. I think we engage the British here and now." His jaw was set, and he had a look of determination that his brother had never seen before. It surprised the Major and the Sergeant Major.

McKenzie smiled... "Damn straight, sir. Engage the British here and now!"

Derek smiled... "Well - the first part was easy. We agree then."

0700: 30 minutes before all of the officers were to meet - the Sergeants and Lieutenants were already there. The Major noticed and motioned them forward. "I'm guessing you would like to get this done as well?"

"Aye, sir." They stated in unison.

"Alrighty then. As you all know - we are currently in Scotland. By the best available knowledge- we are in Culloden Wood. Not too far from Inverness."

"Excuse me, sir," interrupted Sergeant Edward Bruce... "I've been to Culloden Wood, and that's not far from Inverness. We should hear traffic noise... city noises... and it's not near as big as this wood is."

"Aye," agreed the Major. "I've been there too. But this is where the confusion sets in... You remember that bright light before we got here?"

"Well, of course I do," said Bruce. "What does that have to do with it?"

"That's a good question, Sergeant. We think it was a time warp of some type. We don't know for sure - but that's what it looks like now." The Major hesitated... "I know you've seen all of the pictures now. Correct?"

"Aye, sir." Stated Bruce.

"Did you Pay attention to the clothing being worn?"

"Yes, sir. I did."

"Did anything seem peculiar to you?" asked the Major.

"The clothing looked old, sir," said the Sergeant.

"Did you notice the Swords?" asked the Major.

"Aye, sir. I did."

"When was the last time you saw anyone with Swords?"

"Never sir. At least not wearing them in public. Especially on a horse."

"Precisely!" Exclaimed the Major.

"Sergeant Major!"

"Yessir," McKenzie responded.

"I want you to tell the officers the date you overheard from the sisters." Ordered the Major.

McKenzie said, "Today is April 12."

"When?" asked the Major.

"April 12, 1746, sir."

"What did you just say?" asked Sergeant Douglas.

"April 12, 1746, Sergeant. Four days before the Battle of Culloden! And we are in Culloden Wood!" said McKenzie.

Everyone erupted all at once. The Captain thought to himself… "This is going to be a bloody long day."

The Sergeant Major stepped in. "QUIET!" Immediately, there was a hush. The Sergeant Major didn't yell often. It was as if he fired for effect! "There's a possibility we could be wrong. About Scotland? No. You know we're home as well as I. The date we feel is certain - though that could be wrong. If it is wrong - then on April 15 - neither the British Army nor the Scottish Army will show up here. Are ye willing to see what happens? Or are ye gonna keep flapping your bloody lips and getting nowhere?!?!"

No one had seen the Sergeant Major this incensed in some time. He was the one that kept his wits about him when the shit did hit the fan. This silenced everyone. The Sergeant Major continued. "Lads – none of this makes sense to us as well. None of us knows what or why any of this has happened. All we know is that it has. We'll have to figure out what to do moving forward – and it will take leadership to get it done. You all need to understand that WE are the only family WE have right now. We must be wise and make the right decision to move forward in this new world. We must make the best of it – or it will all be for nothing. We must have a united front for the men to follow until this bloody thing is figured out. It will take you to silence their fears – even if you still have your own. Are ye prepared to do that? And - If you're not a praying man – God only knows that I have not been... now would be a good time to start?"

They all said "Aye" individually...until it got to Sergeant Douglas. Eventually – he agreed. And he sat down quietly.

The Major then stood and said quietly... "Here's the primary question we must ask ourselves if this timeline is indeed what we believe it to be. I will ask you the same way I asked the Captain and the Sergeant Major: We must stay cohesive as a force for no other reason than to increase our value. We must tell the truth to our troops. We must answer their questions or to honestly tell them we don't know. The hard part, as you all know... will be coming to the understanding that none of our loved ones are here. But we can make a difference in a significant way moving forward. As I see it - we have three choices: 1. Do nothing 2. Fight for the British 3. Fight for our ancestors and beat the British here and now.... Thoughts?"

Douglas stood up and said, "Sir, I've served with you for a long time. You've never led me wrong... and I can't see ya doing so now. I'm on board. We'll know on the 15th if you're right or mistaken. We know where and when the two armies assembled. If you're right sir? I say we beat the Redcoats this time. What do ya say, lads?" Every officer looked at the Sergeant... then at each of their officers... and nodded in agreement. If these are the cards they've been dealt, so be it.

The Major looked at Connor. "Now for the big test," he said under his breath. Connor knew for sure he was right on the money with this one.

0900

The troops had all gathered by 0845. At 0900, All of the officers came together. They wanted to show unity. The Sergeant Major said, "Attention!" Everyone snapped to attention. It was unexpected- but carried out dutifully.

The Major said, "At ease... please sit down." The men all sat on the ground. You could feel the nervous apprehension in the air.

"I'm sure there have been many rumors. Some of those rumors may be true. I will be honest with you, lads, this situation is one none of us have dealt with before. We don't know if anyone has ever had to deal with this before. Here is what we know or at least have a theory concerning: 1. It appears that bright light created a rip In space/time. We're not sure how, but it transported us here. The rumors you've heard about us being in Scotland are correct." There was an excitement brewing - the Major had to calm it down. "2. Herein lies the problem. You recall I said it was a rip in Space/time, correct? Well - I'm not a physics guy… but it looks like we've gone back in time."

Several men said, "Would you repeat that sir?" ….

"Aye," the Major said. "We are not in our current time. It appears we've gone backward in time."

"How far sir?" Well - there was the question. That didn't take long. "Today is Saturday, Lads…. Saturday, April 12…. 1746."

"Will you repeat that, sir?" A Private asked.

"Aye," said the Major. "April 12, 1746. If we're right - we are in Culloden Wood, and the Battle of Culloden is in four days."

What was not expected by the officers is what occurred next…. Quiet. Warily quiet. That's when they saw him. They all nearly jumped out of their skins! The Stuart Chieftain in his Stuart Tartan Kilt… a white linen shirt… Leather boots that went above his calf… he had a sporran… a dirk… he was dressed in his finest. He appeared out of bloody nowhere and scared the be-Jesus out of the lot of them.

"Relax lads. You've all seen me before right before you got home. This is a profound moment. You have a lot of questions. Hopefully, this will answer most for you. You are all here by destiny… not by choice. You will have a decision to make. When you initially hear this, you will think it is to benefit my time. You are about to find out that it helps your time even more.

I am Sir John Stuart of Grandtully. We will meet in person on another day. So, let's get this out and over with… You are in Culloden Wood. The date is April 12, 1746. In 4 days, the Battle of Culloden takes place, and the road to your future begins. So, you'll need to stop blaming your leadership. They were here along for the ride as well. Understand this… Every One of you are here because you are essential to righting this wrong that is to take place."

It was deathly quiet. No one stirred. They were totally mesmerized by the grizzled old man.

"So, you know how your history shows this battle and that the Hanovers keep their crown at our expense. You know your time past... I'm going to tell you your future."

"In 2011 – Fukushima, Japan, has a 9.0 earthquake that floods a nuclear reactor - which will spew out radiation, destroying your oceans. Egypt, Libya, and other nations in the Middle East will burn in protest. After that – terrorism will increase, mass shootings will rise, and gun control will become more pronounced. Donald Trump will actually become the President of the United States. The World Economic Forum, The World Health Organization, and the United Nations will push for a global government."

"In November of 2019 in Wuhan, China - A virus pandemic goes global. Every pretense of individual freedom is gone for everyone's safety. Individuals are forced to take an untested vaccine to travel or even to work. Every movement you make will be tracked and traced. In February of 2022 - Russia will invade Ukraine... In 2023 - Central Banks will develop a digital programable currency - where if you decide to go against the political narrative - your money will be turned off. You won't have access to your own money. The war in Ukraine will escalate. NATO and the US will declare war on Russia and China. On April 16, 2026 - there will be a global nuclear war. Life will almost cease to exist. Every single thing that you have ever fought for will be obliterated. None of you will survive."

He spoke with authority... he spoke of things that he had no business knowing... he made it plain... he made it understandable... he made it personal.

To say that you could hear a pin drop is simply an understatement. Everyone was thinking of their individual lives... those that they loved... gone in only a few years.

"So, the Major has given your leadership three choices.... Major McAndrew- it is time for you also to give these choices to your men. I hope I have helped you see why this decision is important."

With that... he vanished.

Major McAndrew- once he got his wits about him... stood front and center... "We need to stay together as a cohesive unit. We have the strongest military in the world right now - though our ammo is limited. As I see it - we have three choices: 1. Do nothing while our ancestors bleed the ground and Butcher Cumberland does his work 2. Fight for the British and make it worse... or 3. Fight for our ancestors and beat the British here and now- and perhaps profoundly change what could be the destruction of all we know and love in the future."

To a man - they all got up and agreed they would follow the Major... and defeat the British in Culloden.

Never in his life had the Major felt so proud and grateful for these men... his brothers... never had the weight of this responsibility felt so heavy.

Chapter 11
Readiness

"All right, men! We have come to a decision. Now, we must focus on readiness. We will have to prepare our equipment and put together a battle plan. MacLeod! I want that inventory of our armaments in 15 minutes!"

"Aye, Sir!"

This is more like it! Action! God, he loved this. Strategy. Planning. He had never lost a combat role. This damn sure would not be his first. So much is riding on this! And this is just the beginning…. And a tactical plan was coming together in his mind. Strategic planning - especially in combat situations- had been his specialty. Connor has kicked around a few good ideas as well. We'll see where it leads.

"Sergeant Major!"

"Sir!" exclaimed the Sergeant Major.

"Pick out the Mastiff in the best shape. It will be our temporary headquarters. Then get all of the Lieutenants… we are going to build our tactical group."

"Aye, sir!" Mac responded.

One of the things that Mac admired was the decisiveness of the Major. Once an objective was decided upon - the decisions flowed from the Major. He was indeed in his element now. He knew how to lead. He knew how to allow others to complete their job without micromanaging them. Once the Major had taken over the Company - they had not lost an engagement, and their casualties were 20% of what the nearest company in the entire Regiment recorded. He loved his men, and they adored him.

He found what he was looking for. The Mastiff looked brand new - like it had not seen any combat. "That'll do nicely," he thought to himself. He got on the loudspeaker, "Lieutenants Ross, Gordon, and MacLeod! Meet the Major at the Oak!"

Mac cranked up the Mastiff and headed towards the oak. He reminded himself that they would have to go easy on the Diesel. It's not like he can go to Inverness and fill up at a Petrol Station! They'll have to come up with a solution for that. They can't waste a bloody thing!

This Mastiff was large enough to stand in. It will also make a good HQ and the Major's quarters - at least temporarily.

Major McAndrew, Captain McAndrew, Lieutenants Ross, Gordon, MacLeod, and Sergeant Major McKenzie were in attendance.

The Major said… this is somewhat ironic - but it fits…. "From William Shakespeare:

"We few, we happy few, we band of brothers.

For he to-day that sheds his blood with me

Shall be my brother; be he ne'er so vile,

This day shall gentle his condition.

And gentlemen in England now-a-bed

Shall think themselves accurs'd they were not here,

And hold their manhoods cheap while any speaks

That fought with us upon Saint Crispin's day."

They all laughed… the Major continued - "Gentlemen - I am honored that we are in this together. We have no idea how this will run its course - but we have indeed wandered into the impossible. We will change the hands of time. Let's pray it is for the better."

"Alright, MacLeod - Let's have it. First of all - was any equipment damaged in transit?"

"No sir - they're small dents - probably from the incoming fire before we left."

"Very well then. Give us your report."

The Lieutenant began:

"10 Jackal 2's - almost at total fuel capacity - roughly 160 liters in each - 1600 liters total

Each Jackal 2 carried 2 GPMGs (General Purpose Machine Gun) with 7.62mm rounds - 3,000 rounds per jackal - 30,000 rounds. Thirty thousand extra rounds for a total of 60,000 7.62s.

14 Mastiffs - same - almost 380 liters in each - roughly 5300 liters total

Each Mastiff has the Browning Heavy Duty Machine Gun - 50 caliber. Six hundred rounds per Mastiff - 8,400 total rounds plus 8,400 additional rounds for a total of 16,800 - 50 Cal rounds.

We have 150 Highlanders.

Each has their rifle - The L85A2- 5.56 caliber. There are 1000 rounds per Highlander for a total of 150,000 rounds.

M203 (Grenade Launcher) - 25

300 - High Explosive 40 mm

100- Smoke 40 mm

Each Highlander has their Sidearm - the Browning Hi-Power 9mm - 200 rounds per Highlander for 30,000 rounds.

6 - AIAW sniper rifles - 338 Lapua Magnum - 6000 total rounds

500- Offensive Grenades- L109A1 HE

500- Frag Grenades - L109A2

10 - 81 mm Mortars - 1000 High Explosive Mortar Rounds

500 Kilos of C-4 and all that entails.

We've been limiting our rations to one per man per day. We still have 2700 ration packs.

Compared to the Brits… we have them outgunned with only the 9mm."

"Thank you, Lieutenant. We will have to maximize casualties while minimizing the use of our stores. We need to have an Operational name. I have an idea- tell me what you think. How about Operation Recompense?"

Connor stood up and gave a resounding, "Hell Yes!"

Everyone heartily agreed.

"I'm glad you think so, Connor," said the Major - "Because you're the one leading them to battle on this."

Connor gave Derek a High-Five. "It's about bloody time!" he exclaimed.

The Sergeant Major stepped in. "Alright," he said…. We know the Brits come from the East, and the Scots come from the West. They started their formation at about 12, and the battle commenced with artillery from the Brits around 1 pm. It was over before 2 pm. We also know it will be cold, dreary, and wet. So, we need to plan for that as well."

"From what I understand- the formation was typically British - except in this battle, the artillery was in front of the infantry to prevent the routes they had received from the Scottish charges before this battle. You would have the Calvary and Dragoons flanking each side …. The infantry was in the middle, with the Artillery in the front. It was estimated there were 9-12 3 lb. Guns positioned in front of the infantry. 9-12 men manned each gun. Prince William Augustus, The Duke of Cumberland (who became known as the Butcher of Cumberland after the Battle of Culloden), and his staff were roughly 200 meters behind the front lines."

"The Scots lines were mostly infantry. The center line was the shock troops. The flanks were those better armed. Further out was the Calvary. They had artillery, too - but the guns, for the most part, were left out of the fray. Prince Charles believed in the invincibility of the Scottish charge. As we know - Bonnie Prince Charlie let the British guns pack too big of a punch before they charged - and the rest is history."

Captain McAndrew asked, "How many personnel were in the Artillery?"

Mac said, "9-12 per gun. 9-12 guns. Low side - a little less than 100. High side - maybe 144."

Connor pulled out his notepad and wrote approximate units. So, he drew 12 guns in front of a big rectangle he labeled infantry. "So, each gun would be separated by 3-5 meters?"

"Aye," said Mac. "That would be about right."

"So, we're talking maybe 80 meters across?"

"Correct again, sir," said McKenzie.

"Let's use the 81's. Ten, maybe twelve of the high explosive rounds will take them out. It'll damn sure let everyone know we're in town!" Connor said with a grin.

They all liked the plan. Connor continued, "Mac - tell me about the Calvary and the Dragoons." Mac added to Connor's notes: "There were approximately 4,000-4,500 men on horse. Probably close to split evenly on each flank."

"What if we do this?" as he drew the Scots across the battle lines. "We take 3 Jackals on each flank and have them neutralize the Calvary and the Dragoons? The 7.62 GPMGs would have them neutralized in less than 2 minutes. But I have a special prize for the Butcher of Cumberland - I think we start this fray with the first shot having a sniper take out the Duke and then the snipers taking out the rest of the Command Structure."

"So basically – in less than 5 minutes – we have eliminated the Command Structure – the entire Officer Corp, their calvary, AND their guns. We can have one Platoon taking out individual Infantry. Two platoons will proceed to the rear to prevent anyone from getting away and the news reaching the true Pretender. Then I say we let the Prince and his men finish the rest of the infantry. That way, the Prince can get credit for the victory, and we can save ammunition."

The Major got a smile on his face… His little brother had put together a damn good plan. Everyone but the Brits win, and we barely put a dent in our ammo supplies. "I like it. But here's the deal – there can be no survivors. If there are – they must be prisoners without access to the King. I have a long-term plan to put the Prince on the Throne… but we have to win this first – and Old George must be wondering what the bloody hell has happened to his Duke and their army."

"What about the camp followers?" Added Lt. Ross.

"Camp Followers?" asked the Major.

"Yes, sir," Lt. Ross continued. "Camp followers were civilians from Prostitutes to Wives to Merchants, Cooks, Blacksmiths, etc. They followed these missions and supplied necessary goods and services to the officers and their troops."

"I don't want to kill a bunch of Civilians. Either we capture and imprison them – or perhaps they can provide their wares to the Scots? We will have to let the Prince decide. I guess we will have to send a Platoon to gather them together. The bottom line is that no one gets away," stated the Major.

"Ok, Sergeant Major… Who were the Commanders of the British? Besides the Duke of Cumberland?" asked the Major.

"Lieutenant General Henry Hawley, Lieutenant Colonel Sir Robert Rich, Colonel Howard, Major General Bland, Major General Huske, and Colonel Munro."

The Captain asked, "Did they have distinguishing uniforms or any other way to tell them apart from the other men?"

"Yes sir," said the Sergeant Major. "The Officers could be distinguished by their Red Coats, Tricorn Hats, Swords and Hangers, Sashes, and Gorgets. Anything ornate would be a good inidicator."

"In total," added the Sergeant Major - "there would probably be 200-400 officers above the rank of Corporal in the field."

The Major added, "Our Riflemen will seek after them while our Ancestors finish the rest … Now tell me the Leadership of the Scots."

The Sergeant Major Started, "John Campbell, the 4th Earl of Loudoun: He was a prominent supporter of the government forces and commanded the government troops during the battle."

"I'd forgotten about that. A lot of Scots fought for the Brits." stated the Major.

The Major then addressed them all… "We know both armies arrived the day before to prepare for the fight. The Battle began on April 16 – at around 1 pm. We'll let them have their ceremony and line up before we enter the field of battle."

The Major mulled everything over for a while. It was still early on April 12…their world changed rapidly. The first order of business was to feed the troops.

"Ross …. I want you to get some drones and three squads. Find some game, and we'll have us a BBQ. All of you get with the men and see who knows how to cook wild game for a big crowd over an open fire. Unfortunately - no spices. We'll get what we get! Three Large Elk could feed us all. Remind the men to aim carefully." Ordered the Major.

The Major continued, "Tomorrow morning - we're going to have a peek at the battlefield. I want us to meet here at 0600. Anyone not involved with the hunt should be checking out their equipment and getting battle-ready. We'll finalize the battle plans tomorrow, and you can debrief your platoons. On the 14th, we'll put out double the guards if the history books were wrong, and they decide to knock on our door."

Chapter 12
Hunt

1500 Sergeants Douglas, Bruce, and Stewart, with six privates, were responsible for the hunt. Douglas considered himself a Scottish Redneck. As the song says, "A Country Boy Will Survive." He once boasted that you could put him butt naked on the isle of Sky for six months - he would come back fully clothed and will have gained weight in the meantime! The 5.56 wasn't the perfect ammo for an Elk Hunt - but if you make the right shot - the animal will fall every time.

Each Sergeant got a drone and two privates... the bragging started, and the wagers were on.

Then there was a surprise. Who decided to show up? The Major, the Captain, and the Sergeant Major.

Connor asked, "Well... how much are you losers going to give us for getting the first Elk?"

"Well," said Sergeant Stewart. "We don't know what the currency is like - but we figure there's gonna be at least Copper, Silver, or Gold Coins out there. I guess you can give us each a Silver Coin too."

"Alright then," said the Sergeant Major. "The first one in with an Elk wins the pot. Does that sound good to you? Of course, it'll have to be after we get the money coming in. I'm sure our paper money is worthless here," he grinned. "Be sure you lasses point that thing in the right direction. Do you still remember how to pull a trigger? Or do we need to show you how again?"

Well, that did it. The competitive spirit lightened the mood. The drones were up looking for a herd.

The first one to get an indication of a large Elk was Sergeant Stewart. 5'10" and 180 lbs., with a redhead and a beard to match. Congenial in every way - but competitive to a T. They had found a sizable heard of Elk that were two clicks to the South. They started a double-time march.

Sergeant Bruce and his team saw some elk and wild boar a little to his Northeast. His mouth watered at the thought of a Boar on a spit... Sergeant Bruce was pretty much a loner before he joined the Highlanders. His da had left home when he was but a bairn. His mom did her best - but couldn't make it. He was given to her brother to raise. That bastard could go to Hell for all he cared. He didn't know what infuriated him more... the drunkenness or the beatings.... But enough of that. He had an Elk to hunt and money to be made. Besides... he was with his mates. He and Sergeant Douglas had become the best of friends. He had taught him to hunt... live in the wild... and get over the bitterness. Douglas would never understand that he had probably saved his life. "Focus, lad... ye can't let them bastards beat you now- can ya?"

Douglas? Well, he had a plan. There was a great water source just to the north. It wouldn't be too long until dusk. He was betting from the look of the beach, which had animal tracks everywhere - is where the trophy would reside. If he played his cards right, he and his team would surely be the winner.

The officers already had a site picked out. They weren't daft. About a click to the East - they had already seen several. The proliferation of Wildlife was so much more than any of them had ever seen. This felt good. It was just getting away with the men to enjoy an afternoon hunt and provide some competition. He heard genuine laughter. It was good to hear - especially since the full ramifications of where and when they were have not yet had time to be processed.

Sergeant Stewart had lost the herd when they got to where they should have been. But the tracks were obvious. Track them they would.

Bruce and his men were closing in on their prey. It was a boar. It's not overly large. But it would be delicious smoked... his men stopped ... Bruce took aim... slowly... exhaled, and squeezed the trigger. Just as he did - the damn thing got spooked and jumped and took off running. Private McDonald had him in his sites as well. He pulled the trigger and got him in the ear. Perfect shot. The Boar squealed, fell to his knees, and then fell over. "Damn McDonald! Bloody good shot!"

"Thank you, sir," said McDonald.

"Alright, boys - we'll leave this here a bit. We aren't too far from those Elk. We can't let them beat us in!" They spread out, walked 400 meters - and then saw them!

Douglas and his men had already seen a few cow elk and their young. But that's not what they wanted. They wanted bragging rights - not just a quick meal. They had heard someone fire a shot already – followed by one in succession. "Probably Bruce," he chuckled. "I betcha he missed too!" And there he was... the most enormous Bull Elk he had ever seen. The Bull had shed his antlers - but Douglas knew it was what he sought. He motioned for his men to stop. They didn't see him initially, so Douglas pointed him out. He aimed... exhaled slowly... and squeezed the trigger. The Elk took off running. "Damn!" said Douglas. "I know I got him." He did. But not where he wanted. They would have to track him.

Derek was at the controls of the Drone when he had an idea. "Hey lads - I have an idea. There's a Bull... it looks to be about 500 meters to the East. Watch this..." The men gathered around the screen. The Bull wasn't overly large... but the largest Elk wasn't the prize. Getting the first Elk in won the pot. The Major deftly maneuvered the drone to the rear of the Elk and buzzed it. The effect was just what the Major wanted. It spooked the Elk. The Elk began running right towards them. The men all hid behind the trees. They got the Bull to within 50 meters, and the Major pulled away the drone. The Bull stopped running and flared its nostrils in complete irritation to the drone that harassed him. Mac and Connor had him in their sites. 1-2-3... squeeze the trigger... and exactly as planned. They had their Elk. "You do know we now gotta carry this bastard over a kilometer?" said the Major.

"True," said Mac. "But showing them youngsters who are their betters is worth the backache tomorrow!" They fashioned a Sledge with the wood and boughs to drag the Elk to where they needed to go. They rolled the Elk onto it when it was fashioned and started pulling it back to camp.

Stewart tracked... but it wasn't Elk. It was Red Deer. He wasn't going to argue. They shot two big bucks. They, too, realized they had to get them back - but it was still early, and they would not be without. Everyone will eat well tonight.

Bruce and his team saw the Elk and started towards them... then something spooked them. Damn! "Well, boys - looks like we got the boar and not much else. Let's get back so it'll get cooked! I can already taste him!"

Douglas and his team? They got their quarry all right... but it grazed his lungs and missed his heart. You could see the blood, so they started tracking. It took two full hours and two more shots to knock him down. But damn!!! He was huge! They found an extensive branch and used some vines to tie him to it so they could carry him to camp. It was getting dark, so they double-timed it in.

The first team in was the Major's. It only took them an hour to make it in with an Elk. They were the winners. Bruce's team came in next with the Boar. Stewart was next with his deer, and finally Douglas and his men... exhausted a full hour behind the rest - he came in with the Colossal Elk! He lost the bet - but he took the bragging rights regardless.

Douglas and Stewart got their knives and began to skin and gut dinner. There was eager anticipation with the entire company.

The Cooks for the evening would be Ferguson and McIntyre. They had spent the day foraging. They found a host of wild garlic and thyme. They splayed the meat like the Argentinians do... and got the fire hot. Dinner would be late - but no one cared. This was a feast for the ages.

Once the fire was going and the coals were suitable - the meat was raised into its position after being sliced with the garlic and thyme being introduced liberally. The boar was placed on a rotisserie over coals. You could hear the fat sizzle as it melted into the fire.

Around 1900 - it was ready. Every man in the company was there salivating. The intoxicating smell of meat and fire and smoke made their stomachs rumble. Those rations had not been enough!

Before they could eat - the Major got up to talk to his men. "Alright, lads - I'll make this short and sweet... I'm starving, so I know you all are as well! First of all - thanks to everyone for making this happen. We are indeed a family now. And Douglas! Are you sure what ya brought wasn't a Cow or Moose?!?! I've never seen an Elk of such size. Too bad there's no consolation prize for the largest animal!" Everyone laughed. "Especially since it was the old men that beat ya!" ... this time, the laughter was from the gut - you could feel it... it was good ...it was necessary. "Finally - thanks to the cooks... Ferguson and McIntyre! Is there anyone that would like to say Grace for the bounty we are about to eat?" Where did that come from? Hmmm. But it felt right, and everyone agreed.

A quiet voice from the back said, "I would, sir." It was Corporal Ryan Keith.

"Very well," said the Major. Corporal Keith began, "Heavenly Father, we come humbly before you. We thank you for this mighty bounty. We thank you for men who have become brothers. We know that you have a purpose for us being here. I pray that you will be honored and glorified by what we think or do. In your name, we pray…. Amen." In unison - they all said, "Amen." Some men crossed themselves… some did not. But you could feel this… this knit… this bond… tighten even more.

"Let's eat! I'm bloody starving! I never thought the Major would be so kind as to stop flapping his lips so we could eat!" said the Captain with a grin. Everyone laughed.

The Major, the Captain, and the Sergeant Major got the first taste since they had brought the first game in. The old Ration plates came in handy as they piled on each -the Elk, Deer, and Wild Boar. The Major took a bite of the Boar… "Dear Lord in Heaven- I've never tasted anything so grand!!!" And he meant it… the meat melted in his mouth.

The Captain and the Sergeant Major took a bite… their eyes widened! "Aye!" Was all the Captain could manage to get out of his mouth…

"Oh My God!" Exclaimed McKenzie!

Then the feast began earnestly as each man was served until they could eat no more… which is good… there wasn't much left!

Smaller fires cropped up as small groups of men gathered around the fire… to talk… brag… reminisce… to voice their fears in their own way.

The Major, Captain, and the Sergeant Major did the same. They had a fire and started talking about old war stories… stories about when they were young… Like when Derek talked about tormenting Connor whenever possible! And beating the drums so loud to drive Connor crazy. Connor told a story of how his da had talked him into using an air horn to scare Derek… unfortunately it scared the devil out of Mum too, and both he and his da got into trouble.

Story after story came out, and they all laughed until their sides hurt… then it got deathly quiet as each began to think deeply about their own lives.

The Sergeant Major had received a call. Annie was so excited… she was pregnant with their first child… or so she thought. Her periods had stopped, and she was beginning to show… but this call was from the hospital. It was not what they thought. She had cancer in her Uterus. If they left it as it was - she would surely die. The surgery happened. They were heartbroken. Children were no longer an option. On the way home - they were quiet. He didn't know what to say - so he said nothing… at once, in a quivering voice… she broke down sobbing… "I am Soooooooo sorry!!!" "I'm no longer a woman! I can't give you children!"

He immediately pulled over. He parked on the side of the road. He exited the car in the rain… walked over to her side and opened the door. He commanded her to "Look at me!" She wailed… she couldn't.

She said, "If you want to leave me…I'll understand!"

He was on his knees in front of her… he grabbed her face with both hands…. "LOOK AT ME!" "Woman! Do ye no understand? I married YOU. For YOU. Not just for children. I will never ever leave you… for as long as you would have me! And that's a promise!" She collapsed in his arms… he held her until she stopped crying… then they went home. And now he's here?

The Major was deep in his own thoughts. He thought about his youngest son… who he would never see. His oldest son - Grant…. almost 15…He looked most like his Da – but his temperament was like his brother, Connor… which is why the little shit was always in trouble… that made Him smile…his looks… her passion, and his stubbornness. Then he thought of Nicole. An American there for college. He had never seen anyone so beautiful. It was a whirlwind romance. In 8 weeks, they were married. And then life got in the way, and he was called to duty. He had been gone so much lately. The last time home had been hard. Nicole acted so angry towards him. At first, he responded in kind. Didn't she realize he was doing the best he could? He didn't start the bloody War! Once he realized the real reason behind her anger… he approached it differently. Maybe when it was time to re-enlist, he could get a home assignment for a while. Or maybe he could give it up altogether. But what now?

Are they even alive? If so, is he now presumed missing? How the bloody hell do you come to grips with this?

Connor, too, was lost in his own thoughts. For whatever reason - he could feel himself being tugged more to the reality of here rather than the life he left behind. Yes... he would have to figure out locations without a GPS... that made him smile.... But the women surely weren't batshit crazy here? How the bloody devil would you find a wife here? He did know she would want a family. She would want land, and a farm life is a given. Well... God only knows.

The fires began to dim. 0600 would come early - and the Major wanted to see the battlefield. He needed to make sure the plan would work. It's not like the Jackals could get on the highway and drive. They had to ensure they could get out of the forest to the battlefield.

Well... As uncertain as the future was... and how far away their old life lay... they were here... now... and home this would be unless God changed his mind.

Chapter 13
Skull Bowl

14 April 1746 - 0700

It was getting closer. The anonymity was about to be gone forever. A whole new world was about to be unveiled. Everyone knew it. Everyone avoided it. You could taste the apprehension. Not from the battle to come… but after. How would anyone adapt to a life they had never known? The friends and family going into this new world were their brothers…. Their brothers in arms… their brothers bought by blood and honor.

The Major could feel the nervous energy. He fully understood it. Everyone there was a professional in his craft. Everyone had been briefed Ad Nauseam. In Afghanistan, one could play basketball, lift weights, or throw a baseball - hell - even run to get rid of that nervous energy. Could he come up with some game or exercise to get the men moving … without breaking their skulls in the process? We don't have a ball… there's a meadow not far from here…. Maybe run? No. All this was running through the Major's head… and then he saw them. The skulls from the animals they had eaten. Someone had thrown them in the fire to cook the meat off, and the skulls remained.

What if he used the skulls like some sort of ball? Rugby? Oh hell no. We have no infirmary. Football? It's hard to kick a skull around. What if we played something like Canadian or American football? We could hand off the skull and even pass it like a ball. Maybe have small teams of touch? Maybe at the squad level?

He got the Captain and the Sergeant Major and told him of his thoughts. That might work. They had felt it too. It felt like a cannon about to blow. This might work.

They pulled out the skulls. The big Elk was too big. The deer, The boar, and even the small elk would all work.

So… the three came up with the rules of the game:

Rules:
- Each platoon has four squads - three platoons are twelve squads.
- two end zones twenty-five meters apart.
- The game starts with one team kicking off by throwing the skull to the other team, and the receiving team tries to advance it towards the opposite end zone.
- The ball carrier can run with the skull or pass it to a teammate.
- The defending team tries to intercept the passes or tag the ball carrier to stop the advance.
- Once a player is tagged, they must release the skull immediately.
- The skull can only be passed laterally or backward, not forward (similar to rugby rules).
- If the skull is dropped or fumbled, it becomes a turnover, and the other team gains possession.
- Scoring: When a team successfully carries or passes the skull into the opposing team's end zone, they score a point. Three points is a win and advance.
- No one can get bloody hurt.

They gathered the skulls together and called all the men to follow them to the clearing.

When they got to the clearing, they asked everyone to sit down. For effect, the Major set the skulls at his feet. It quieted down quickly. "All right, lads - you are all wound up tighter than a bloody drum. So, we're gonna fix that problem. We're gonna play a game that me, the Captain, and the Sergeant Major pulled out of our arse with what we had available. This will be The Game of Skulls." The Major reviewed the rules, and the men were excited to play.

"Lieutenants Ross, MacLeod, and Gordon - split your men into squads of twelve men each. Your Sergeants will be the Captains of each of your teams. You'll be the referees."

While the men were dividing up, the fields and goals were put together. The clearing was large enough for four teams to play at once.

And the banter talking began almost immediately... and the Officers smiled. This is what they needed.

Sergeants Douglas's and Stewart's squads and Sergeants Fraser's and Campbell's squads were the first to begin play.

The Major heard the intense banter between Douglas's and Stewart's men and realized they would be the ones to watch.

Douglas's team won the toss. Douglas chose to receive. Stewart told Douglas to get ready - the skull was coming to him because Stewart said, "My Nana can run faster than you!"

Douglas taunted back, "I bet your Nana could run you twats over as well!"

The skull was tossed, and Douglas received it. He started running. Stewart almost got him when Douglas pitched back to McDougall. He was almost tagged, but he pitched it to Alexander. Alexander was tagged. Alexander then pitched it to Douglas, who got a block from Cameron, and he scored! "Bet your Nana couldn't do that!" Exclaimed Douglas.

They traded sides, and it was time for Stewart's team to receive. Douglas backed up and threw that bloody skull like a Rugby Ball! McPherson had to run backward to catch the thing. Alexander caught him as soon as he caught the skull. The teams lined up. McPherson tossed it to Stewart, who was about to get tagged. He tossed it back when McDougall intercepted it and ran it back for a score. Two to Zero. Douglas hollered at Stewart, "Ya ready to quit yet?"

Stewart yelled back, "We just let ya score. Couldn't have a big old crybaby over there getting whipped!"

After changing sides, Douglas threw the skull. Stewart's team was ready this time. Stewart caught the skull and advanced with six men in front blocking for him. He almost scored when Douglas reached behind and tagged him. Stewart had the skull and tossed it back to McPherson, who tossed it to Grant. The blockers were in front, and Grant scored! Two to One.

Stewart threw the skull to Douglas again. Douglas tripped and was falling. He tossed it mid-air to Cameron... but McPherson intercepted and ran it back for a score. Two to Two! The next team that scores wins!

McPherson threw the skull back to the far goal. Cameron ran to pick it up. He was the fastest in the team. He started running around the edge of the field. Stewart had him in his sights ... Cameron threw it back to Douglas, who immediately tossed it back to

Cameron again…. Grant intercepted! He was at full speed when Douglas tagged him. Grant tossed it back to Stewart, who tried to sweep around to the left. Douglas was NOT going to let him score! He gained on him and was about to tag him when Stewart fumbled the skull. Cameron reached down, picked it up and ran full speed until he scored!!! Three to Two: Douglas over Stewart!

The games continued throughout the day. Douglas's team won the Championship, and everyone knew it. Douglas strutted around like a gamecock! Everyone enjoyed the diversion. There were two minor injuries: a twisted ankle and a sprained elbow. The Major was not happy, but the injured would heal. It just meant they would have guard duty at the camp on the sixteenth unless they healed quickly.

Chapter 14
Committed

15 April 1746

O600: The Major woke up with a start. Today is the 15th. Tomorrow is the day. History changes tomorrow, and our lives will begin anew. And suddenly, he felt old. This was a new weight of command he had not felt before. He genuinely believed he was making the right decisions. The ramifications of those decisions have never reverberated as far or deep as they are right now. It's a juxtaposition when you consider how important an insignificant battle like Culloden cascaded to significance in a historically literal context especially if you consider that an entirely different monarch and their descendants will be on the throne.

I know what led to the Windsor's. Elizabeth was a force to be reckoned with in her own right. But could we have done better with the Stuarts? They did have a better claim to the Throne. They were Stuart's after all.

The wars with France are continuing today. The American Revolution is supposed to happen in 30 years. What happens if we modernize the Military and the economy of Scotland? We could defeat the French - bypass the French and Indian Wars… what if we could keep America in the fold? Get America to keep their act together and avoid the American Civil War? Will we be allowed to guide the King… he is so young. We could bring the Industrial Revolution to our country an entire half-century sooner. Scotland could be the business hub of the entire planet! There's so much that we could accomplish if allowed to do so.

But there are so many opportunities for failure. Superstition… jealousy… envy… duplicity… all of those things are potential pitfalls we must overcome. The Lords of this time were so damn bloody stubborn. If Scotland had ever unified - the Brits would never have been able to defeat us. Now we have the technological edge that all of the Scottish Lords will have to listen. But once again - some of their loyalties will need to be questioned.

As a mercenary team - we will have to have strict Justice. We cannot become a belligerent force here. We have the power now, but our ammunition is limited. We'll have to utilize all of our talents moving forward to be able to resupply. We must win the new King's trust without him fearing our power. The whole lot of them are a damned suspicious bunch. Then, if we win that trust - who will try to undermine that trust out of fear or jealousy? It will be a political tightrope for sure. I pray we are up to the task.

"Well… time to rise and shine," the Major said to himself. Connor and Mac came walking up. The Major acknowledged them, "Good morning, Lads. Are ya ready for what's coming? We're gonna have to be more subdued and diligent today. The Brits and the Scots will be here this afternoon. I don't want anyone to see or know we're here."

"Agreed," said Mac. "You did good yesterday, boss. You don't hear that enough. The Lads will be talking about that for generations." He added with a smile.

The Major smiled and then said," When it gets dark, I want us to put on our NVGs and go have a look. Maybe we can gather some intel to help us out tomorrow. We also need to gather the men and discuss the times we're living in. The customs, though similar, will be different too. I'm sure there are Blasphemy laws, and most crimes will have a severe penalty. Executions for theft or even punishments for pre-marital sex. Our boys must behave like they've never had to before."

Connor said, "I hadn't thought of that. We need to talk about that for sure. Even simple things like medical issues. The way doctors treat things is different as well. You are damn sure don't want to get an infection or surgery - as there was no anesthesia!"

"There's much to learn," said Mac. "Even learning to farm and be a Herder. Not many tractors around. Maybe we can invent one?"

"I have some ideas about that," interjected the Major. "But the first thing we must do is figure out how to take care of our firearms and resupply our ammo. We have so much talent here - we'll take the bloody world by storm!!!"

"Absolutely! I have some ideas about firearms for the Scots. But first, we must get the gunpowder right. That black powder won't help much with our arms. You know - we can "invent" a lot to make things more modern," said Connor. "We could be the Rockefellers before it's all over. We have to use wisdom."

"Let's go check on the Lads," said the Major. The camp was a bit more subdued today. One thing these officers knew was their men. They didn't ask any questions regarding their upcoming mission. Each man in the Company knew what was expected of them. They would be more than prepared. "Well, Connor- have you made up a speech for the highly esteemed Duke of Cumberland and his loyal subjects?"

"Indeed, I have sir. I'm quite sure he'll object to the overall theme that will be discussed. I'm thinking of allowing him to surrender- even after I call him something that will make him question the fidelity of his parents!" Even Mac smiled at that.

The officers went throughout the camp. The men were in various stages of preparation... cleaning their firearms... checking magazines and loads for the umpteenth time... There was a distinct difference this time. They had an unbridled confidence. What they were going to do mattered. If not to them personally - it damn sure did to their ancestors. Some of them realized their seventh or eighth great- grandfather would be on the field of battle tomorrow. They had heard stories of those that were murdered by the Brits. That Scottish Nationalism passion was being sparked anew. They knew this was the beginning of a new world.

After checking on their men, the officers also went their own way. They had their responsibilities to meet. And they would be ready.

The Captain was going to need twenty-four men for his six jackals. Douglas and Bruce and their squads are the men that Connor chose. He went to check on their work in getting everything prepared. They decided to go with the Belt Fed ammo. It was faster to load than drums and had a higher capacity. Seven belts per GPMG with room for the men was more challenging than anticipated. But Douglas and Bruce had everything squared away. "I wish we would've had a trial run before tomorrow," Douglas said.

"Agreed," said the Captain. "The Major would have none of it. Secrecy and stealth are the primary tools we need to accomplish what we wish."

Douglas agreed - but he still didn't like the fact they would be running it blind.

The Major made an announcement. "Alright, Lads - It's about 1800. Let's get our rations. I have something we need to talk about. Get them and meet me at the oak."

Everyone got their rations and headed to the oak. The nervous energy from the day before was gone. It was determination now... that steel spine prepared to deal the worst to our foes. Let the future be what it will be... righting a centuries-old wrong was worth it all.

There would be no fires tonight. There would be no celebration. There would be no yelling or anything where their sounds could travel to their enemies' ears.

The Major stood up and got everyone's attention. "Alright, Lads... you each know your portion of the battle plan tomorrow. Lieutenant Gordon - your platoon will be the sentries. Four sets of two on a four-hour rotation. I want them to wear the NVGs. No one is to make it to our camp. No one."

"Aye, sir," said Lieutenant Gordon.

"Alright, men - listen up and pay attention. As you well know, the battle tomorrow is the easy part. After that, and we've made ourselves public - we must fit in here. With the knowledge we each possess, there will be many opportunities to benefit in huge ways. However - there are many risks as well. The laws and rules will be different than anything we have ever experienced. Blasphemy laws are on their books. Hangings for theft and simple crimes are punished harshly. Don't even think about Premarital sex - as that could be a crime as well. There are blood and clan feuds. Things we may not even be aware of. Caution and discretion are the better part of Valor. If you behave like you did in Afghanistan- there should be no problems. Really pay attention to your language- especially around women. We will all have to learn the rules for our new lives. Any questions?" None were asked, and none were expected. They had a job to do, and they were prepared.

At 1930- Derek, Connor, and Mac met up for their incursion into the enemy's camp. They were armed - in full gear with the NVGs. They started in the direction of the Brits - roughly two clicks away. It was cloudy, cool, and damp. Perfect to avoid being seen. Especially knowing there would be guards, sentries, pickets, and patrols in the enemy's camp.

They got to the edge of the British camp at 2030. They came across a couple of intoxicated patrols. They listened to their impaired speech. It was difficult to understand - but it meant they were ready to defeat the Scots once and for all. And something about buggering that pretty Prince.

Fires were burning, the rum was flowing… there was no worry for the Scots. Only contempt. They were in for a rude surprise tomorrow.

They made their way to the Scottish Camp. You could feel the total difference between the camps. The Scots were tired, cold, and hungry. They just wanted to get the battle over and get home.

"Hang in there, boys," said Mac under his breath. Help is coming.

Then this beautiful young Lass strode to the middle of the camp, and she started to sing… it was… it was? A lament? Even the Brits hushed to hear her haunting voice as it pierced your very soul.

She started singing, "You Give Us No Choice" in Gaelic…

Chuala mi 'm pailtinn o'n chùil bhan,

Chan eil againn nar beatha ach bròn

Tha ar deòir mar an drùchd a' caoidh

Tha thu air beatha ar gaisgeach a ghabhail

Dh'fhàg thu sinn gun dad ach pian

Ach sabaid nì sinn

Chan eil thu a' toirt roghainn dhuinn

Agus mas e bàsachadh a h-uile rud as urrainn dhuinn a choileanadh

An uairsin is e bàsachadh an dearbh rud a nì sinn

In English, it translates to:

We have nothing in our lives but sadness.

Our tears are as the morning dew.

You have taken the lives of our brave.

You have left us with nothing but pain.

But fight we will do.

You give us no choice.

And if dying is all that we can achieve

Then dying is exactly what we will do.

Connor held his breath… it was the most beautiful sound he had ever heard. He decided right then and there that he would meet this woman and make her his wife if available.

Derek looked at Connor. He knew that look. "Are ya daft man? The night before a battle that will change the course of history, and you're thinking with your other brain?!?!" He started chuckling as they made their way back to camp. But Connor knew… this time, he definitely knew.

Chapter 15
Culloden

Derek fell asleep quickly. He slept soundly… until 0400. He woke up with a start. His heart was pounding in his chest like a sledgehammer. His head was filled with doubts. Are we doing the right thing? Was the Chieftain guiding us down the right path? Were they going to be substituting one tyrant for another? Men were going to die that did not before. Men were going to live that died before. Was he playing God?!?!

He broke out in a sweat. Anxiety? What the bloody hell? … He had never experienced that before… he was drawn… unmistakably… inexplicably… to his knees… "Lord… I have felt so confident that we were doing the right thing. Are we? I am crying out to you for your guidance. I'm just a man. I can't see or know what you do. What was your plan in bringing us here if not to take this action? Dear Lord in Heaven, I pray for your wisdom… for your comfort… for your peace. Lord, please lead us down the path you have laid for us. Let there be no confusion. We are committed to this destiny. If it is not your Will - then let it change. I am only committed to what you would have me committed to. Protect my men. Let this be your decision. Let this be according to your Will. In Jesus' name … Amen."

That's when he felt it. He heard thunder, and it resonated in his soul. He felt a peace that he had not had since childhood. The sledgehammer in his chest ceased. He knew. He was committed.

He heard a light knock on the door of the Mastiff… it was Connor. Connor opened the door and saw Derek on his knees. He smiled. "You felt it too then?" asked Connor.

Derek smiled back… "Ya know it, wee bro."

"I'd like to gather the men one last time before we go to kick some Brit's arse." Derek smiled again. Connor left to gather the men. "How did it get to be 0800? Where did the time go?"

The men gathered by the Oak. Their gathering place…. For only a week, yet it seemed like a lifetime. He wondered about what he was going to say… but he decided he would give his men an "out." If this was of God - it should be a resounding "yes" one way or the other.

As the men were gathering… he stood there and looked at them in a way that had never done so before. These men were his brothers. He would die for any of them, and he honestly believed they would do the same for him. He was lost in his thoughts when a Private walked up to him. Derek knew him. He knew everyone. But he didn't know Private Sinclair that well.

Sinclair approached Derek and told him, "We are here for this purpose. There's no need to doubt."

The Major almost lost his balance. "What did you say?"

Sinclair reiterated, "Don't doubt."

How could he have known?

"I don't know why I told you that, sir… I just felt that I needed to let you know that you don't need to doubt. That's all I got!"

The Major grabbed his hand and thanked him sincerely… "You have no idea how much I needed to hear that!"

The men were all gathered by the Oak. The Major stood before his men… and his family and said, "Alright, Lads. You know where and when we are. You know what is supposed to happen today. You know what we intend to do. Even those injured in the Skull Bowl have made a somewhat miraculous recovery in order to be with us today. But I realized that I was presumptuous. The Highlander Regiment you committed to is hundreds of years in the future. Your vows are no longer valid. You do not have to follow this path. I am telling you that you have the right to decide - not to do this. If you choose to stay here - it will all be well, and no one will think the worst for that decision. So, I want to see a show of hands for all that are committed in the action we are taking."

Immediately - every single hand went up in a flash. Every. Single. Hand. They were all committed to what the day would bring. They were committed to each other.

"Very well then. Go over the plans with your COs one more time. Check all of your equipment one more time. We leave for Culloden Moor in an hour. Our snipers are already there. Check your coms. Let's do this.…"

"To Scotland! To Scotland!" they repeated. Then, each went to their assignments. They had a battle to prepare for!

Connor said, "Nice speech. I'm not guessing you spent a lot of time writing it?" he chuckled.

Derek laughed as well… "Well, not exactly." Speaking of speeches - have you decided what to say before you start shooting things?"

"Aye… I've thought about it. I'll probably just wing it…" Connor mischievously smiled.

Derek looked at his younger brother and the man that he had become. He could not be prouder.

Connor saluted his brother and was off.

Derek once again checked all of his equipment. He would be with the riflemen at the edge of the wood. He wasn't going to let Connor whip the Brits by himself!

Damn. It was wet, dreary, and cold. Though his uniform was designed for the desert - it functioned admirably when it was cool as well. They will have to get used to Kilts and the required attire of the time as they move forward. Since the weather was far from ideal - they decided to move in earlier. They left at 1030. They moved quietly and were not in any hurry. They had scouted where they would set up to take on the British without being seen. He would radio Connor when it was time for the Jackals.

They could hear the drums when they got about a Kilometer away from the battlefield. That would be how the regiments and companies would move to their formations. You could hear two distinct cadences - one for the British and one for the Scots. He wished he would've pressed Connor more about what he planned to say… "I guess I'll hear soon enough." He mumbled to himself.

The Mortar crews left the Company to set up in their assigned area.

The Company got to the edge of the wood. They all stood in amazement as they watched both sides prepare. It was like watching a re-enactment. Except this was real.

It was 1230. The Major could see they were getting close to beginning the battle. He radioed Connor and told him to come.

The Jackals roared to life. Connor could feel the adrenaline rush beginning like it always did before combat. This time, he wasn't apprehensive. He was eager to do this and make the wrongs right.

Now… what the bloody devil was he going to say? He quietly laughed… Derek would be pissed if he knew that he had no idea what he was going to say and was, indeed… going to wing it!

MacDuff and his fellow spotter and snipers had been there long before daybreak. He positioned himself in the trees. He wanted a clear shot at the Butcher… He felt his cause was noble… to rid the world of such a man was undoubtedly the right decision. The Butcher had killed many of his ancestors… men who walked the ground below him. Not this time. The bastard would get his due today!

The Major and the Sergeant Major got their men into position. He had radio contact with MacLeod and Ross. They were in position in the rear. They were to advance when the first shots were fired.

That's when heard them. The Jackals were almost here. The drums were still beating and directing the men into their final position. Looks like the timing will be perfect. The drums ceased. It was about time. You could hear the orders from each perspective side being yelled to finalize their formations. The guns would be firing soon….

That's when the Jackals made their appearance. They came lumbering between the two combatants, as Connor had described. Three Jackals on each Flank. He could see Connor…. What the bloody devil was he going to say?

The PA system was designed to be loud enough to disperse mobs… I guess we'll see how well they work here.

At first - Connor decided to address the Scots. He opened up in Gaelic and said, "Fathers and Sons of Scotland! We are a Scottish Regiment here on your behalf because of the prayers of Sir John Stuart of Grandtully! For whatever reason, the Almighty chose us to answer his prayer! Because of this - you can expect a lot of noise and considerable heartache for the enemy. Do not fear! We are Jacobites like you! Tonight… your bellies will be full, and you will sleep soundly… This is a day for the ages! One you will tell your children and grandchildren… that today - the destruction of tyranny begins…The true Pretender is in London! A Stuart will be on the throne soon enough!" With that - the Scots - who were initially terrified of the obnoxiously loud, horseless carriages… erupted in cheers.

In French, Connor addressed the Prince: "Prince Charles, I am Captain Connor McAndrew, and we are indeed an answer to prayer from Sir John Stuart. He is the reason we are here. Sire… we will do our best to help you take back your throne. Today, it is imperative that there be no quarter given - or you must imprison anyone who survives. For no one can tell the Usurper what you see here today. Sire… please use your monocular and observe the Duke."

In English, The Captain's voice clearly changed. "Good afternoon, Duke of Cumberland. I am Captain Connor McAndrew. You, sir, are trespassing on our land. And even though you are a vile contemptible arrogant ass, as a gentleman, I will give you thirty seconds to surrender to your rightful King unconditionally. If you do not do so - you will be the first to die today." Connor told Hamish… "On My Mark … take him out. No headshot. We have to be able to identify him."

Unceremoniously, the Duke stuck his middle finger at Connor. "Very well then… Hamish… take the shot. Right after he pulls the trigger, I want the snipers to take out the rest of the officer Corp."

The Major commanded, "#1 Mortar… send one down range." …

There was a "BOOM" you could hear from a distance. The Major watched as it came into view. "Perfect! On The Captain's Orders… Fire for effect!" Connor instructed the mortars to engage as planned. Five seconds after the first detonates - the Jackals will engage."

Prince Charles lifted his monocular to watch the Duke. He was so far away - how could this bragging Scotsman take him down? He had to be over a half-mile away!

Hamish slowed his breathing. He had the Duke in his sights. He breathed in gently… he reverently placed the cartridge into the open chamber and gently pushed it home. "Round Chambered sir!." The bolt is closed. The round is now snug into the chamber. "Target acquired…Engaging now sir." He breathed in one more time…exhaled one half out and held his breath… his finger deftly on the trigger. He pulled the trigger gently, and the shell moved down range. At nearly one thousand meters per second - it took less than a second for the .338 Lapua Magnum shell to reach its target.

The Duke was bringing his finger down as he looked toward his aid… as the shell and its dreadful impact came into contact. His body position to Hamish was to the side. The shell pierced the Duke just beneath the right armpit. It went between the 2nd and third rib, instantly breaking them both. The shell then punctured his right lung and eviscerated his heart - like Jello. It continued on its trajectory through his left lung, the 4th rib on his left side and finally hit the thigh of his aid. His expression went from surprise... to shock... to pain... to blank before he collapsed off of his horse. He was dead before he hit the ground.

The Prince jumped! He looked again! That was impossible! Then... all... Fucking All of the command officers were lying on the ground! How?!?! There's no fucking way!!!!

"BOOM! BOOM! BOOM! BOOM! BOOM!" The first five mortars directed at the cannons were on their way. Each aimed with clockwork precision from the loaders acting as Forward Observers (FOs) had their lasers aimed precisely where they were supposed to land. There were twelve guns with twelve men per crew. The first shell exploded with cruel efficiency just behind the second Cannon. The crews of the first through the third cannon were hit with shrapnel and a blast wave that finished what the shrapnel did not. This continued behind the fifth, the seventh, the ninth, and the eleventh Cannon. All men were dead in seconds.

The second mortar rounds were aimed behind the infantry. BOOM! BOOM! BOOM! BOOM! BOOM! ... the same results. The same effects. This time to men at the rear - not expecting to be engaged! Blood... guts... the smell ... the cries of anguish... chaos everywhere!

But more was coming. Just before the mortars hit - Connor and eleven other Operators opened up with the Machine Guns. Their targets? The flanks. The Calvary. The Dragoons!

There was an estimated 2250 Calvary on the left flank and the same - but Dragoons on the right flank. During the melee, everyone on the British side tried to flee or fight. Some brought their firearms to bear, only to be hit before they could fire a shot.

The 6 Jackals were set up with three on each side. Their targets were those on horseback. The first focused on the left, the second on the middle, and the third on the right. Six Hundred rounds of 7.62 mm copper-encased lead rounds at 2,850 feet per second - fired every minute.

Connor was on the left flank of the Dragoons when his men opened fire. The thunderous drums of war spewed their demons of death. He concentrated fire on that left flank. The Moor shook like the epicenter of an earthquake. The belt-fed ammo had two hundred rounds. His loader was kept busy. Every 30 seconds - it was time to reload.

Blood… guts…fear…fury… the best that Britain had to offer breathed their last as they were silenced forever by the Highland Warriors. Between the Jackals… all 4500 men and 1500 horses were dead in 2 minutes of hell on earth.

The Scottish Highlanders viewed this total annihilation in a mix of revulsion and reverence. There was fear, awe, and exhilaration. The Prince… though elated at the destruction of his enemies, had concern and apprehension as well. His ambition grew a bit. Perhaps Europe and Emperor could lay in his future? Hmmm… that was an exciting thought.

The British Infantry was in trouble as well. The Highland Riflemen had been picking off their officers… one by one until only the Privates and Corporals remained. Out of the roughly 9500 British Army that began the day, there were less than 4000 remaining.

Captain McAndrew ordered a Cease Fire. No one dared to move. He then addressed the Highlanders. He started with the Prince in French… "Sire. You are to be King. We cannot finish this battle that is in front of you. You must do so. You must be credited with the win." The Prince looked at him and nodded in agreement.

The Captain spoke in Gaelic: "Lords, Chieftains, and my brothers in arms… these men before you offered no quarter. We have done our part. Now we offer the field to be finished by you. Please do not desecrate the body of the Duke. We may need it in the future. Are you ready to finish this?"

There was a tumultuous roar as by the hundreds, then by the thousands… the Scots charged. The Prince with Saber raised joined them as well. The rest of the British Army had no chance. None were given the chance to surrender. All were sacrificed to atone for the sins of their fathers against the Scottish people. The bloodlust would not be silenced until the last British soldier fell.

Chapter 16
Aftermath

The entire battle lasted but 30 minutes. 9567 British Soldiers breathed their last as the Scots had their way.

The Major began to make his way to the field. His first thought was to save as much material as possible. While the Scottish army finished the Brits - he had the Riflemen pick up every bit of brass they could find. Someday, they will have to produce more ammo. Who knew what they would need?

The Major started calculating what was expended today. The Riflemen had used maybe a half clip each. The Mortars only used ten rounds. The Machine guns used at most eight thousand rounds. Their power and influence, for now - depended on their firepower.

When the Major got to the middle of the field - he was met by the Captain and the Sergeant Major. They all had a mixture of the adrenaline rush waning, thankfulness that this part was over… relief that none of their men could have been injured… and the smile of a successful campaign.

Connor ran to his brother and hugged him. Derek smiled at his brother. "Ya did good out there, lad. Impressive speeches for pulling them out of your arse!"

Derek knew… he always knew!

Connor laughed. "Aye. I did pull them out of my arse, but they damn sure worked!"

"Aye. They did. You're off the cuff remarks are gonna bite you in the arse someday!" said Derek.

"Ahhh - yes… I'm sure! But not today!" said Connor with a twinkle in his eyes.

"Major!" Lieutenant MacLeod yelled.

The Major turned his head. "Aye."

The Lieutenant ran up to the Major. "Sir! I have the camp followers. Lieutenant Ross and I split up. We had to kill 20 Brits protecting the paymaster's chest. I have never seen so much gold in my life! When the Brits were dispatched as quickly as we were able to do… it's amazing how the men and women decided compliance was a wonderful idea! Anyway - we flanked the army right after the fighting started. We thought once the Scots came - it might be difficult to protect them."

"Good idea," agreed the Major.

Lieutenant Ross and his men soon came to the clearing.

"Report," said the Major.

"Aye, sir," said Ross. "After MacLeod left with the Camp Followers, we heard the fireworks from the front and took cover. About ten minutes into the battle, we saw individual Brits running from the front. They were dispatched immediately- as per your orders. We got three or four hundred before the Scots came running through, and we let them know we were on their side. That's when we made it up front. I'm sure this isn't how our history books showed Culloden!" He said with a grin.

"Any wounded or injured?" asked the Major.

"Yes sir," said Ross. "Private Mackintosh received a nasty bruise. It appears one of the Brits was able to fire at him. The .75 ball hit him right in the chest. The Body Armor protected him, but it's gonna leave a huge bruise. He said the man was going to bayonet him, when he pulled out his pistol and changed the outcome. I'm sure the Brit was rather surprised by that change of events. A couple of bumps and bruises. Nonetheless for wear, however."

"Very well. Get with MacLeod. I want a roll call to know if we have any injuries."

Ross saluted. "Yes, sir," and was on his way.

"Connor!" The Major yelled! "Get the Jackals off of the fields and into the woods. No one needs to understand anything about them yet. We need to conserve fuel as well."

Just as Connor started to depart - a group of men on horseback came in their direction. One man stood out on a White Stallion. That, of course, was the Prince. The Major and the Captain knew the proper etiquette and bowed to the Prince.

"Well, gentlemen… you've made a day, haven't you?" The Prince said in Gaelic with a smile. "John told me to expect a surprise. I can't say that you are what I expected. You and your officers will dine with me tonight. I will expect you in my dining tent at six."

"Sire- we have nothing to wear. We only have our uniforms," said the Major.

"Nothing to worry about, gentlemen. Sir John Stuart had already made the arrangements. That is why I have you coming to my dinner tent at six. Supper will be at 730. Oh... I expect the paymaster's chest to be turned in as well. Whatever is in there - you may split with your men. Is thirty percent fair?"

"Yes, Sire," said the Major. "That is more than generous."

"How many men do you have?"

"We have one hundred and fifty, Sire."

The Prince marveled at the sheer amount of destruction such a small force created. "Very Well. We now have an overabundance of fine, well-trained horses. Your men will each be given one and an extra for backup. Nothing but the best, of course."

"Thank you, Sire, we are eternally grateful. Oh! We have the Camp followers with us. They will soon be your subjects... We thought you would better understand what to do with them. They cannot get back to the king until you are the King," said the Captain.

"No... it is I that am eternally grateful. We have much to discuss tonight. I shall send some men to procure your prisoners, sir," said the Prince. "Be on time at six. Bring your men to camp as well. They will be treated as the heroes they are. Let's give them a chance to meet the ones whose lives they saved up close and personal." And with that - he was gone.

Connor got onto the Jackal, as did the Major, and picked up the Sergeant Major on the way. So tonight - they would dine with a future King who - according to their history - left Scotland dressed as a woman.

The men were tired but content. It was, by far - the easiest battle they had ever fought. Why did it feel so utterly gut-wrenching? They all knew that no matter the outcome of whether or not the Prince became King - their world just changed.

Chapter 17
Alliance

Everyone was back at camp. Fully satisfied at the way the day had turned out. It was only 3 pm. The Major, the Captain, and the Sergeant Major gathered the men together. The Major started, "Men… my brothers… today was about as perfect as a day could be from a Military standpoint… but the next battle - and there will be many… will be unpredictable. We won't have the past to draw from to make them as lopsided as this was. We can't become cocky. We must be forever vigilant. That being said … you kicked the bloody Butcher's Arse today! That's much to be proud of!"

"Now! We have been invited to dine with the future King and to get to know the men you fought with today… our ancestors!" The Major was interrupted by cheers.

"Lieutenants Ross, Gordon, and MacLeod… we need at least ten men to be on guard duty while we are gone. Though I believe that we can trust our Prince - we would be wise to protect all we have," said the Major. "See if we have volunteers. If not, you will have to pick them. Ross and Gordon - I know you are not much of an advocate of royalty - but you have been requested to dine with us and the Prince tonight - so don't think you can volunteer your way out of this!" Everyone who knew laughed at this remark.

The Sergeant Major chimed in…" Lads - I know not what our future holds. Whether we will stay here - or be guided back to our time. My gut tells me to make this our home. Don't be surprised by what you are offered. Many will be eternally grateful- some may resent their opportunity for heroism. Be as it is… it would be best if you were wary of too much whiskey. You must keep quiet about where and when we are from. So please keep your wits about you when you are with these other men tonight. If anyone asks you about your past… you can tell them that you will tell all when you are allowed to do so."

The Captain said, "By the way, Lads - we're going to get to split a good portion of the paymaster's chest with the Prince. We will also get at least two horses each from the British defeat. So, as the Sergeant Major said - keep your wits about you. I want every man to carry your service pistol and two extra magazines - just in case you need them. In the meantime - you may want to try to wash off a bit. You can give out your names. Perhaps you can meet your ancestor clans and get at least a family kilt for good measure? Ye may want to take a nap as well! It's probably going to be a long night."

Everyone liked that idea!

The officers later discussed the treasure chest and how to distribute the funds. The plan was to give the Prince his portion when they got to the Prince's camp. "That's right," thought the Major. We will have to split the money fairly. Historically, the booty would be split by Rank - with a substantial portion going to the already wealthy officers. Of course - in this world - the officers will be expected to live a more expensive lifestyle because of their rank. Perhaps we can do that to a certain extent. The Major then got the Captain, the Sergeant Major, and the Lieutenants together.

"Gentlemen," said the Major. We will need to split the proceeds based on rank. Here are my thoughts… tell me what you think:

Connor, Mac, and I will get 400 Guineas each. The Lieutenants will get 350 Guineas each. The Sergeants will receive 300 Guineas each. We'll keep 1000 Guineas in our treasury. The balance will be split with the men. Thoughts?"

"None? We're all in agreement then?"

"Aye!"

"We will need to pick a paymaster then," said Derek.

The Major continued, "I want one man from each Platoon to act as the Paymaster - exceedingly trustworthy men - preferably with some finance or banking background. We need two from each Platoon to act as guards. We need a Sergeant to be in charge of all this."

They wrapped everything up, realizing it would soon be time to go to the Prince's tent. They all went to the creek and attempted to bathe with what they had available. Unfortunately - there was no washing their uniform yet. Perhaps one of the camp followers could come with them to do their laundry?

It was agreed that all men except those who volunteered for guard duty would be at the Prince's camp at 630.

At five - they were off: The Major, the Captain, the Sergeant Major, and Lieutenants MacLeod, Ross, and Gordon. You could sense an almost awe of them as they approached the camp. That would have to stop. They will have to know that everyone is indeed quite human. Once the training process begins - it will become evident enough.

Those that were on guard duty escorted them smartly to the Dining Tent. They walked in and were greeted by a woman in the service to the Prince. She was raven-haired and carried herself with authority. Probably not someone to trifle with!

Her eyes pierced his as she spoke in Gaelic, "Ahhh," she said with a smile - "You are on time! I am Fiona McDowell - - you may address me as Fiona. I am the Lady-In-Waiting to Prince Charles. You will get to know me well over the next few months. That being said - when we go inside, there is a table with clothing and all of what you will need to attend tonight's Supper - as well as some everyday clothes so that you may get your other clothing washed. There are six different tables. Go to the one with your name on it. Sir John Stuart was precise about what we would have upon your arrival. You will have thirty minutes to make yourself presentable to Prince Charles. I will see you, gentlemen, then."

Connor wasted no time, however. "Fiona... last night I heard a young woman sing the most beautiful haunting song I have ever heard."

Fiona smiled, and her eyes lit up. "So, you fancied our Lady Mary Forbes, did you?"

Connor didn't know why, but he blushed.

"Well," said Fiona, "Lady Forbes is not married... but it will take a lot to win over her father... but you are a cute one... you never know."

With that - all of the men laughed at Connor's expense. Connor smiled - they could laugh all they wished... but now he knew he had a chance.

Fiona pulled back the entrance to the tent, and the men went inside. They each found their name and rank. The tables went from the lowest to the highest rank. In that order, the lieutenants were Gordon, MacLeod, Ross-Sergeant Major Ian McKenzie, Captain Connor McAndrew, and Major Derek McAndrew. There was a water basin to wash.... And as the men began to inspect their tables -

there was a stunned silence - then eager excitement as they realized the significance of what was on each table. Each table had their family Tartan as a Kilt- a formal one - which would be worn on this night - and an informal one for every day. There was a dirk with their family's motto… two white linen shirts… and a Claymore! Exquisitely crafted. The scabbard once again had their name and family motto upon it.

They had little time to appreciate this beauty - but had to dress quickly for their dinner with the Prince. This hit Mac rather more intensely… for he had been here before. He looked at his sword… "Lord Ian McKenzie" was etched with precision upon the blade. He gasped. He looked in the mirror in front of him… he had seen this man… this man in the mirror before in his dreams.

Connor and Derek knew the value on the table in front of them. It told them the Prince knew of their arrival months before. All of this took a great deal of time and effort to produce. They washed the mud and sweat off them with this exquisitely made linen washcloth and toweled off with a towel.

It had been so long - but they knew the order. The first thing on was the shirt… this wasn't linen! They had an additional shirt besides the two linen shirts. This was Silk! It was the same sky blue that matched their kilt! Next came the Kilt. The Kilt was made of wool, as were the socks. They wicked away moisture and helped you stay dry in this ever-changing climate. The sporran and the Sgian Dubh, or small dagger were next. Then, of course, the Ghillie Brogues, or shoes tied above the ankles…. And they fit!!! They each had a jacket that fit as well! How?!?! Then they saw their Claymore… to say it was beautifully made was such an understatement… and etched into the Blades were "Lord McAndrew." Well, this was indeed a surprise.

Everyone was dressed in their finest. Everyone had Lord etched into their blades. They knew this dinner would be life-changing and that they would be observed down to the smallest detail. That didn't suit Connor. He preferred harsh truth over a phony display. But the military had taught him the value of politics as well. Tonight, they would make lifetime friends or lifetime enemies….

Fiona opened the tent flap and walked right in, acting like she swooned at the sight of the dashing men before her. "Alright, gentlemen… I have neither the time nor patience to teach you the proper royal and noble etiquette. I am sure any sins committed this night will be forgiven by the day's events. Prince Charles is young… impetuous… incredibly charming, and immensely inquisitive. Expect hundreds of questions. If you do not know - be truthful. There will be Chieftains as well. Some are great men with honor and integrity. Some are questionable by my judgment. We will have that conversation another time. Are you ready, Gentlemen?" she asked.

"Yes, ma'am," they all replied.

She escorted them to the main tent. There were roughly twenty men in attendance besides them:

Prince Charles Edward Stuart (Bonnie Prince Charlie): the grandson of King James II of England and VII of Scotland and had the rightful claim to the Throne.

George Murray: A Duke of Atholl and a military commander - friend and confidant of the Prince.

William Gordon, Viscount of Kenmure

John Drummond, Earl of Melfort

Lord John Murray: Brother of the Duke of Atholl, he was a skilled military commander and strategist.

John O'Sullivan: An Irish officer who was "Secretary of State to Francis Edward Stuart.."

Cameron of Lochiel: Known as "Gentle Lochiel," he was the chief of the Clan Cameron.

MacDonald of Clan Ranald: Clan Chief

When the men walked into the tent… they were met with thunderous applause. This they did not expect. They were soldiers performing their duty.

The six chairs for them were right next to the Prince. Mac knew some of those Lords would be upset that they had been given a preferential seat. Interestingly, Duke Murray and his brother, Lord Murray, were the only others seated with them at the Prince's table. Mac was pretty happy they knew the tartans of the Nobles at this dinner.

Derek and Connor, with Lieutenant MacLeod, were immediately on the right of the Prince. In that order, Mac, Lieutenant Gordon, and Ross were on the right. Next came the Murray's. Mac stared in amazement at the Murray's. George Murray would have gone into exile, while the Viscount would have been executed in the other timeline.

The Prince was announced and strode in with such confidence… it was easy to show him the deference that was his due.

In very accented Gaelic, the Prince introduced each of the men who were the guests of honor. As each man stood… the applause and shouts of appreciation would begin. After the introductions - everyone was invited to sit as dinner would begin immediately. "But before we start- please stand up and introduce yourselves to these gentlemen. Moving forward, they will have much to work on, and we will need your continued support and diligence to accomplish the goals that we have set."

Duke Murray began with a brief introduction, followed by Viscount Gordon…. Then Earl Drummond. This continued quickly through the ranks. Those who were the adult children sat silently.

The Prince simply wanted to get through this tedious formality and talk to his guests. He knew how important the game was, however, and it continued.

Finally!!! The food would be here soon! Then they could talk!

The first course was Pottage - a thick stew with some flatbread. The meat was venison. It smelled heavenly! Connor and Derek enjoyed the hearty stew. They could have made a meal from that alone! But of course - for Royalty, that would not suffice!

The second course was roast Pig and more Venison. These were served with potatoes, carrots, and turnips with a salad. All roasted to perfection.

The dessert was fruit and honeyed nuts. It's quite good as well. All they needed was cigars and some good whiskey? Don't know if they had cigars… but whiskey would be nice. Probably not, though… too common for Royalty? Connor laughed to himself.

Instead… it was Port and wine. Everyone at the table received glasses while the Prince poured. Everyone knew the small talk and conviviality were over, and the real talk would begin.

The rest of the Company had arrived at a far different celebration. When they arrived, there was a bit of confusion - until the Jacobites realized that these were the men that saved their asses that day. Malcolm McDonald yelled at the top of his lungs, "Boys… they're here!!!" The rowdy crowd quieted as they came into the encampment. Then, all at once… it was as if they were celebrating the return of a long-lost loved one... they ran towards them and clamored to hug and congratulate them.

Fires were raging all over the camp to cook the horses that had been killed in battle. There was no wine or port - nor fancy serving dishes. These were men who had lived a hard life. They lived hard. They fought hard. They loved hard. The meat was pulled off and eaten by hand. The drink was cheap ale, or whiskey poured into their canteens and passed around for all to share.

The men started introducing themselves. It was realized shortly that every one of the Highlander Regiment names was represented there at Culloden. Once that was determined- every one of the Scots returned to their camp and brought out an extra Kilt - so the Regiment could get out of their well-used clothing into a Kilt. It was much more their style and definitely to their liking.

After their meal - each of the Regimental members drifted to their Ancestors. Some had built a family tree with that company and followed those leaves to the men before them. But that was something that had to be handled delicately. The men had been told not to mention anything about the future. Of course, possibly burning at the stake for witchcraft was a pretty good motivator for keeping one's mouth shut. They had all been told to say, "You will know all when I'm allowed to tell you."

Next came the pipes, drums, and dancing... and don't forget the drinking. The strangers to this new universe drank some - but knew better than to get drunk and lose their wits.

Suddenly, this Giant of a man stood with a huge smile on his face... mixed with a look of determination... Angus MacLeod was his name. He had long red hair and a beard that went to the middle of his chest. "So, Lads... You're mighty handy with your toys in defeating your enemies.... But I want to know if any of you can fight? Or do you have to let others fight for ya if your weapon doesn't work? Do you have anyone with the balls to take me on? It was quiet for a moment... Corporal James McDonough stood. Angus burst out in laughter. You see- the Corporal was 5'6" tall and, at best, 165 lbs. Angus was at least 6'4" and 285 lbs. "Son... you may want to leave this to the men?"

Corporal McDonough said, "What? Are you afraid of getting your arse whipped by the likes of me?"

Angus' eyes flashed in anger. "Well, come on then, you little shit. I don't want none of your men to get upset when I bend you over and whip your little arse!"

The Corporal just smiled - and waived him forward. At that point - Sergeant Josh Douglas stood up. Angus liked that. At least he would be on equal footing. Instead - 'Josh asked him if he had a Dirk.

"Of course… why do you ask?"

Josh smiled. "Because you're gonna need it."

"Are ya serious?" Angus mused.

"Ya damn straight I am. He's gonna have you down and out in less than 5 minutes."

With that statement - the side bets began…. And Angus wondered if he may have just made a terrible decision.

The two men squared up in the firelight. After the Sergeant insisted on Angus using his Dirk - he pulled it out with a menacing glare in his eyes. They went around each other to size each other up. Suddenly, the Corporal had the Dirk out of Angus's hand and threw it in a tree over 10 yards away, only two inches above the head of the man leaning against that oak. The Corporal then looked at Angus and said, "Let's get down to business."

Using Mai Tai, he kicked his knees hard twice, then gave the big Scotsman a dead leg with his heel, causing Angus to come down on one knee. James then jumped and kicked Angus right in the forehead. He went crashing down. Then it was time for Brazilian Ju-Jitsu. He rolled onto his arm and quickly got it in an arm bar. Angus knew that his arm was about to break. He was able to pick him off of the ground and was going to slam him against a tree. The Corporal repositioned himself into a figure four position on Angus's neck. The big man fought admirably for a minute before losing consciousness. He fell to his knees, and James squeezed harder - until Angus was flat on the ground, unconscious. There was silence in the entire camp - and then an uproar as all congratulated the Corporal for beating the most formidable man in his clan.

A family member got some Ale and poured it on the face of Angus. Angus jumped… "What the bloody hell just happened?" he asked.

A man from the back said, "You got your ass handed to ye lad. In less than two minutes!" Everyone laughed. The Corporal offered him a hand to get up. Angus accepted. Then, gave him a rowdy smack on the back. "Well, you little Shit - I guess that proves ye can fight if one of those weapons does stop working. That's good to know. From now on I'll be taking ye with me to the tavern as backup!"

The Prince was getting impatient. There was so much more that he wished to discuss- but there were too many ears listening to what he had to say and needed to hear.

All of a sudden - you could hear the gurgle of a slit throat and six armed men with pistols and blades charged into the tent. Assassins! They saw the Prince. One raised his pistol - but before a shot could be fired - Derek had taken him and two others with his pistol. Mac and Connor entered the fray. Mac grabbed the sword from one of the men and stabbed him deftly through the heart. Connor pulled his Claymore and cut the hand off of one of the men aiming at the Prince. Mac and Connor each had slashed gaping wounds into the intruder. The only survivor was dying fast from blood loss. Mac made a tourniquet and stopped the bleeding. This one would need to be questioned.

Needless to say - the evening was going to be cut short. The Prince was seething. The audacity to try to assassinate him in his own camp? He had his officers come to take this man and to question him. The Prince wanted to know who had hired these men and would know the answer!

However- he thought... he now knew the loyalty of these strangers. Their loyalty will be tested, he thought. And the pistol the Major used? What a wonder! Three shots in a row!

The Prince quietly told the Major to be in his tent at 8 am. He wanted to speak alone to the Major, the Captain, and the Sergeant Major. He would have his talk... ask his questions... and be prepared to take care of the so-called King in London.

Chapter 18
Chatter

That night… news of the tremendous victory by Prince Charles had already reached Inverness. The Tavern in Inverness was packed with those trying to learn the latest news of the battle at Culloden Moor. The patrons were excited and relieved as the locals gathered to celebrate the victory at the Battle of Culloden. Laughter and chatter filled the air as they exchanged stories and shared pints of ale.

Seated at a corner table, Duncan raised his tankard and shouted, "To the Prince and the Highlanders!!! The heroes of the day!"

The men around him cheered, clinking their tankards together. "Aye, here's to 'em! May they bring us more victories!" someone shouted.

As the night wore on, Mary and Anne - the serving maids moved gracefully among the tables, their laughter and friendly banter adding to the festive atmosphere.

"Ye've got quite a tale to tell, don't ye?" one serving maid, Mary, asked a group of men who had just returned from the battlefield.

"Aye, that we do," replied James Grant with a grin. "It was a sight to see, lass. The Redcoats didn't have a chance! Every one of those poor bastards lay lifeless on the moor tonight! Even the Duke died today!"

Mary leaned in, her eyes wide with curiosity. "And what of the Prince? Did ye catch a glimpse of him?"

"Ah, we did," another soldier chimed in. "He was there, leading the charge. A true leader he is! He raised his sword in the air… led the charge… and rallied us to finish off the Brits, and this other Highlander - Connor McAndrew started it all by taking out the guns and Calvary!"

"Did ya say the Duke died?" Robert yelled from the back.

"Aye," said Ewan - who had been on the front lines. "The very first shot. I saw the bastard fall from his horse right before the leadership fell from theirs. Then there were these terrific blasts that took out the big guns. Then these guns that the Captain brought took out the whole Calvary and the Dragoons in less than five minutes!"

Over by the bar, the tavern owner, Malcolm, wiped a glass clean, poured a Patron another round, and listened to the conversations with a contented smile. "Are ya sure you haven't had too much to drink, lad? Less than five minutes seems like a stretch!"

Ewan came back. "No, barkeep - I've only had a couple of pints… did ya not hear the guns from here?"

"Aye," said the Tavern Owner. "I heard the big blasts here as well. Then the sounds of drums for a few minutes- then it all stopped."

Ewan said, "Listen, Barkeep - them drums was their guns. It was the damnedest thing I ever saw. I nearly shite myself!"

"Well… I dunno who or how we won - but it's a good day for Scotland, it is," he mused to a customer seated next to him.

The customer nodded in agreement. "The clans may have been divided, but a victory like this might just bring them together."

Malcolm's gaze shifted to a group of men huddled around a table, deep in conversation. "Aye, the clans have been through enough strife. They've seen the power of leadership today. None of the bastards can beat us if we'll stop fighting each other!"

At the nearby table, Ewan leaned in and said, "Did ye hear that the clans might rally behind the Prince now? With such a resounding defeat of the British, they'll see the hope we have for a free Scotland."

"Aye, Ewan, tis true," John added. "They'll remember what we achieved today and see we can stand together against the bastards."

As the evening continued, the atmosphere in the pub grew livelier. Stories of bravery and camaraderie flowed freely, mingling with the sounds of clinking tankards and cheerful laughter. And some talk about these new guns that sprayed death on the enemy!

Malcolm looked around the room, a grin on his face. "It's rare to see everyone so full of spirit and hope. I know we can do better than the rot in London!"

"Aye, Malcolm, let's drink to that," Duncan said, raising his tankard. "To the Prince and the Highlanders! The only ones with balls big enough to take on the Brits!"

"To a free Scotland!" Malcolm declared, and the men raised their tankards in agreement.

Even Mary and Anne joined the celebration, dancing and singing along with the men, their skirts swirling as they moved.

As the night went on, the conversations shifted from concerns about the clans to plans for the future. At one minute, the ebb and flow of conversation would give hope to all… only to be dashed with thoughts of retribution. The Prince had to win – otherwise, there would be hell to pay! But that was for another day. Tonight, in the Tavern - it was the Highlanders that were victorious. The air was filled with an air of renewed determination and confidence.

And so, in the warm glow of the pub's lanterns and the company of friends and neighbors, the Scots took and regarded their win with a mixture of pride, joy, and a newfound sense of unity. The distant echoes of battle and the unfamiliar roars of these new weapons had initially sparked curiosity and apprehension among the townspeople. However, as the news spread and rumors exaggerated the valiant efforts of their clansmen, a collective sense of optimism began to take hold. With their glasses raised high, they toasted to the victory that had been achieved by the Prince and his brave warriors, celebrating the triumph over the British forces and the hope of a Stuart restoration.

Chapter 19
Confidential

Promptly at 8 am, the Major, the Captain, and the Sergeant Major stood outside the Prince's tent. Fiona opened the tent and offered a warm smile. "Ah – perfect. You are here just in time for breakfast. We have some oatcakes with honey and some smoked venison. Is that acceptable to you, gentlemen?"

Everyone smiled and said, "Yes, ma'am."

Fiona said, "I thought that would be the case. It is being prepared. In the meantime, you may come into the Prince's makeshift Drawing Room.

The men walked into the tent into the Drawing Room. They were indeed surprised. There were several luxurious furnishings- a desk and a table to sit. The Prince was reading a parchment. He looked up and smiled at the men as they entered. The men bowed before the Prince. The Prince gave a slight nod. "Gentlemen! I am so glad you are here. First and foremost – thank you for saving my life last night. I didn't get a chance to do so under the rather unexpected circumstances. Your quick action and daring stopped what could have been a rather bad outcome for what had been an excellent evening. Unfortunately, the prisoner that we had died before we could question him. No one appears to know any of the involved scoundrels."

"You are quite welcome, Your Highness. Unfortunately, we have become rather used to reacting to unexpected violence," said the Major. "Sire, we are inexperienced with dealing with Royalty and this environment entirely. We are soldiers. We can be crass and disrespectful at times – usually in jest. May I ask you to forgive us in advance and let us know if something is amiss as we begin learning the proper etiquette?"

"The Prince smiled, "Why, of course, Lord McAndrew. Perhaps we can disregard this etiquette as time moves forward?"

Several servants walked in with breakfast. "Oatcakes, honey, and some smoked Venison, Your Highness." "Excellent!" exclaimed the Prince. "It smells heavenly!" Platefuls of Oatcakes, smoked venison, a few small fruits, and a container of honey were served for all.

The Prince was served first, followed by the Major, the Captain, and then the Sergeant Major. "Rank is everything," thought the Captain.

The Prince began the conversation. "We have much to discuss today. I expect you to be honest with me with any questions I have, any concerns you have, or any advice you may give this day. This conversation is expected to stay in total privacy. Sir John Stuart has already updated me on several items. He will be meeting us on the Morrow. I count on him for a great deal. As you know and shall see – there is a great deal of mystery with him. That said, I know that the Major was born in the 1980s and, I believe, in 1994 for Lord Connor McAndrew. I believe that you were born in Aberdeen? Is that correct?"

Cautiously, they both said, "Yes, Your Highness."

And you "Lord McKenzie, were born in 1964 in Dingwall?"

"That is also correct, your Highness," said McKenzie. "Those dates just do not resonate with me. I cannot even fathom 1800 – let alone 2010 – the year you were in Afghanistan. Unfortunately, that is about all that I know. Except that it was endowed by God to have you here to assist us in this cause," said the Prince.

"Well, Your Highness," said Connor with a broad smile, "1746 doesn't necessarily resonate with us either!" Even the Prince chuckled at that.

The Prince started rather matter-of-factly. "I would like to give the men a week or two to rest, gather more clans into the fold, and then move directly to London. No one can stop us with your amount of firepower."

"Ah, Your Highness, you are probably correct. But I would strongly recommend against that course of action," said the Major.

"And your reasoning is why?" asked the Prince.

"Well, Your Highness," continued the Major – we have tremendous firepower. But it is not without limits. We have a limited amount of ammunition available. If the battle is large – and we expect it to be so – then we could run out – which would have disastrous consequences. Even our gunpowder will not be developed in over 100 years. We know how to develop that now, but it will take time, especially in the needed quantities. And then the actual shells must also be produced and manufactured."

The Major then pulled out his pistol and removed the clip and the shell that was in the chamber. "Your Highness, this is the pistol that I used last night. Look at the ammunition." As he handed the Prince the 9mm shell. "Your Highness – this holds the shell like the musket ball and the gunpowder used to propel the shell. Here is the casing, and here is a shell. I removed one this morning to show them to you."

"Fascinating," said the Prince. "So – do you have men with the required knowledge to do much of this work to make this happen?"

"Yes, Your Highness, we do… and so much more," said the Major. "My brother and I are both Mechanical Engineers – there is much that we could do. Sire – All 150 of us are either University or field-trained in many disciplines – it would boggle your mind. If you wish to do so – Scotland could become the unrivaled World Superpower. The wealthiest nation on the planet. But it will take time."

"How much time would you think?" asked the Prince.

"Your Highness – to be able for us to resupply our ammunition with a concerted effort – I would estimate 6-9 months."

"That is only to provide you with ammunition?" asked the Prince.

"Part of that, of course. But you know as well as I that the current throne holder will send a huge army to try to defeat you and punish the Scots for even supporting you. I would not be surprised to see an army of 100,000 or more invading our country. Even with our weapons, I am not sure we could defeat that many."

"Which is why we need to invade now. Before they can gather those forces." Stressed the Prince.

"Sire, let me ask you a few questions. First of all – think of this. I initially said that we could give no quarter to those invaders because we did not want the current king to find out any information regarding what had occurred. That secrecy is vital to getting your throne. So – now to the questions. How quickly can the current muskets be loaded and fired by Britain's highly trained professional soldiers?"

"The best that I have ever seen are between 3-4 shots per minute," said the Prince.

"What is their range and their accuracy?" asked the Major.

"Perhaps 50-75 yards," answered the Prince.

"Now imagine a firearm that could shoot six shots per minute accurately to 200-400 yards?" asked the Major.

"Yesterday morning, I would have laughed at even a possibility – until I saw the Duke fall. I can imagine. There is no other military in the world has that capability," said the Prince.

"That is the total truth. Now imagine if we could produce 1,000 – 10,000 of these weapons before the King invades, along with the amount of ammunition necessary to defeat the army that would come to invade Scotland. Especially if the King has no idea what we have these at our disposal?" asked the Major.

"The entire army would be defeated as they were today," said the Prince.

"Precisely," said the Major. "How much easier would it be to march into London as the reigning monarch?"

"Much," stated the Prince.

"But this won't be easy to construct," said the Major.

"Then what would you suggest?" asked the Prince.

"Since there was no opportunity for any communication with London, it will take months for them to know what has happened. I would guess that it will take at least three months for London to have a complete understanding that the Army sent here has been eradicated – including his son. It will take another 3-6 months to gather an overwhelming force to march to Scotland. With Winter coming then – he may wish to wait until Spring to invade. So, we have six months to maybe a year to let them build their force and send them here.

"Ok," said the Prince. "That is indeed plausible. I will grant you that. So, what would you suggest?"

"First of all,' said the Major, "You need to be crowned King of Scotland. Now. I'm guessing there are still holdouts and those who support the British Monarch. Word of your overwhelming victory must be given to every Clan Chief in Scotland. We need to have unanimity. You have 12 cannons, thousands of extra muskets from the British, thousands of extra horses and supplies – plus the 70,000 Guineas to help fund some things. Sire, is there someone well respected among the Clans who was neutral and did not take a side in this conflict?

"Clan Lamont is a well-respected clan that refused to take sides. The Chieftain is Lord Keith Lamont. I met him once to garner his support, and he politely declined. He said he would not use arms against me or the London Usurper. He might be a possibility. Why?"

"Well, Sire – Once he discovers your victory – perhaps he may be more inclined to be one to negotiate between the Lords and the Chieftains to get you the Scottish Crown. Sire – you know much more about the politics than I do. But it would be best if you got the Scottish Crown first. Once you obtain the Crown and the London King comes to attack you – you will be justified by the entire world in defeating him and taking his crown. If I remember correctly – Lord Forbes was, at best, lukewarm in his support of you. I dunno if bringing him to the battlefield and showing him the devastation wrought upon the British might give him reason to throw his full support behind you?" asked the Major.

"I have already sent for him. He is to meet me here at 10 am. Why?" asked the King.

"He has a lot of resources that are probably available in Inverness. We must begin modernizing and arming the Scots in preparation for the battle. We also need to begin to train the men as a proper Scottish Army. We have to begin becoming Scottish – not just a member of a clan – but of something larger – a member of a nation. Sergeant Major McKenzie would be ideal in training your men to become soldiers. If we can professionally train them with the arms that will be coming - we can have you on the throne in a few months. We need to start with Forbes now and then send someone to Lord Lamont so that he can see the future and help you negotiate your crown," said the Major.

"It will take a lot to get the men trained, Sire," said McKenzie. "I know that we are going into Spring. Men will need to plant soon to take care of their families. If you become King – you can order 10% of the men in the country to become your soldiers and the other 90% to plant and take care of their farms for them. If we can get 100,000 men trained and armed – no army in the world could take them. Especially with us as support."

"This is what I want then. I want you to work on a preliminary plan to get this started. Lord John Stuart will be here on the morrow. I would like you to return with your plan and meet with us both tomorrow at 9 am. I may have Lord Forbes there as well. Would you bring that firearm that killed the Duke along with the man who made that shot tomorrow? If you have that and can have some demonstration, perhaps we can get Lord Forbes on board, and he can start the process of what you may need in Inverness," said the King.

"Ah… Lord Connor McAndrew, you have been silent this entire meeting. Do you have anything to say?" said the Prince. "Aye, Sire – I do. Everything that my brother, Lord McAndrew, has said is true. There may be a way to generate a gun that can fire almost as fast as the one that I was operating. The mechanics are quite simple. As Lord McAndrew said, we must first develop the necessary gunpowder to do the job. They called it smokeless gunpowder. I also know that the British were beginning to use steel in their muskets at that time. We will need those muskets to get started in making your new firearms. Oh – would it be possible for our men to have some of the tents captured from the British? Our men have not had much to sleep in since we arrived. Also – you may wish to save the newer muskets made from steel. I have an idea that will allow us to use those and make rather rapid changes that could be implemented soon. And Sire, one last thing… if you could put in a good word for me to Lord Forbes – I would like to meet his daughter – the one that sang two nights ago!" Exclaimed Connor.

The Prince busted out laughing. "Well, I see – the desires of men have not changed to your time period. That is good to see. Yes, Lord McAndrew – if given the opportunity, I will see if the opportunity to play matchmaker arises! I will indeed introduce the two of you. Whether you sink or swim may well be up to you. Gentlemen – you have given me food for thought. My first inclination is still to march on London. But that being said, I will await the council of Lord John Stuart on the morrow. Lord McKenzie. I would speak to you a minute?"

"Privately, Sire?"

"Yes, Privately," said the Prince.

The other men left the tent, leaving McKenzie and the Prince alone in the room. "Lord McKenzie," said the Prince.

"Yes, Your Highness," answered McKenzie.

"You are the Sergeant Major. Correct?"

"Yes, Your Highness."

"You are responsible for everything from training to Security to disciplining the infantry. Correct?"

"Yes, Your Highness."

"I know that you had dreams regarding Lord John Stuart. That he was able to speak with you in your dreams."

"Again, Yes, Your Highness. It is as you say," said McKenzie.

"Lord Stuart said to trust you completely. You would also be honest and blunt–and I should listen to you – and the McAndrew Brothers. I would like to have you on my Council," said the Prince.

"Your Highness – I am truly honored. But to be honest – until you are on your throne – the best place that I can serve you is in the military with my lads and training yours. Once you are King of the United Kingdom, perhaps we can revisit this, if acceptable to you, Your Highness."

"Actually, no, Lord McKenzie – that is unacceptable to me. That being said, however, I will acquiesce to your wishes – for now. We shall indeed see what the future holds," said the Prince.

"Thank you, Your Highness." Lord McKenzie bowed gracefully and left the tent. "I'll be damned," mused Mac. "I just turned down a job from a Prince and future King!"

The Major saw Mac coming down with a smile, so he asked him what had happened. Mac explained, and once they got to the edge of the encampment, everyone erupted in laughter.

Chapter 20
Striker

"Alright gentlemen, the Prince wants a plan by in the morning," said the Major. "At least the basics."

"The hard part is working with what we assume are the technical limitations," said Connor. "Our history books may not be on point to reality."

Mac kicked in, "That's a good point. Let's talk about priorities for us and military strength overall."

"Ours is easy – resupply. But some of our weapons – like the grenades and the mortars – we may not be able to any time soon. We have to guard those and use them only when necessary," Derek said.

Of course, everyone agreed.

"I think the 5.56 and the 7.62 will be the most needed replacement. The 50 Cal. will be used sparingly. We might need to come up with more of the Sniper Rounds."

"So, the first order of business is gunpowder. Black powder won't cut it. For the ingredients – we need Potassium Nitrate, Charcoal, and Sulfur. For the Potassium Nitrate, the best place would be caves and bat guano. The Charcoal, of course, is easy. Willow, Alder, or Dogwood would probably be the best for the Charcoal. We will have to get with someone to find out about the Sulfur. I think they called it Brimstone now. If I remember correctly – it's about 75% Potassium Nitrate, 15% Charcoal, and 10% Sulphur," Derek said.

The Sergeant Major interjected, "We can probably develop molds for the lead for the shells. We'll need to develop a method for electrolysis to get the copper for the shell's exterior. Brass is readily available for the casing. We must determine the best way to form it into the casing, maybe some lathe? But then again, we might have to use brass. The mass will not be like lead – but with the increase in the velocity – that might make up a good bit of the difference. We'll have to see what would work the best in the least amount of time – and still not damage our weapons.."

"We will also need to develop a Primer of some sort. Sealing, crimping, and the rest. If we could mass produce that – that could be huge," said Connor. "We need to be able to clean our weapons as well. We don't have large stocks to maintain the firearms that we have. Maybe there is mineral oil – or something along that line? I know they had that capability – though we might have to develop a distillation process to make it purer."

Derek brought this up. "We're forgetting the Elephant in the room. We need fuel for the Jackals and the Mastiffs. We could use horses to get the vehicles there – but it would be much better if we could drive."

"Biodiesel. Biodiesel from Animal Fats, Vegetable fats... something along that line. We would have to "Invent" the process. I feel pretty sure we can get all of that done in a relatively short period. So, it's doable," said Mac.

"Now, what about a firearm for the Clans?" said Derek.

Connor said, "The steel musket barrels will help. What if we developed a bolt-action rifle? Probably make it in a single caliber – like maybe the 7.62. That way, we get the shells for our GPMGs and theirs as well."

"I thought about that. If we had more time – I would like that. We could develop a magazine and have 6-8 shells per load…. But… developing the action is going to take some time. We might be able to get a few of those developed – but I don't know if we could get the numbers we need," said Mac.

Derek said, "Connor – do you remember the first firearm we shot?"

"Well of course," said Connor. "It was Da's single-shot American-made 410 shotgun. It was a Break Action. I miss that shotgun. We killed a lot of squirrels and rabbits with that old shotgun!"

"What if we did that with a rifle? It would only be a single shot – but 4-6 shots per minute shooting it accurately for 300 yards would be a game changer," said Derek. "God, I wish we had our tools. I guess we will have to, once again - make our own."

Mac then brought this up. "You know, the Steam Engine was first developed in 1712 – it was more of a pump used to pump water from coal mines. It was not a feasible source for the Industrial Revolution at that time. It was in the 1760s when it began to take off with the

Textile Industry. We can invent and develop all that – including steam-powered trains!"

"We just need to survive the rest of this war and maintain the favor of the Prince," said Connor.

"Ok, lads, I think we have a start. From a military standpoint – we need to be able to train these men. I am afraid The battle will be much bigger than anyone can imagine. We need to get Lord Lamont on board. I think the first test will be Lord Forbes. I am also interested in meeting Lord Stuart. I wonder if he looks like anything we saw in our dreams?"

"It's still early in the day. Let's send Gordon, Ross, and their platoons to pick up the tents and whatever furnishings that may come with them. Maybe they could also get a musket or two for us to look at. We'll probably need to pick up the horses and get everyone used to riding. That should be hilarious! I'm glad we learned to ride, Connor. Though it's been a while – I wouldn't be afraid of jumping on one," said Derek.

Lieutenants Ross and Gordon came to the Major. "You asked for us, sir?"

The Major answered, "Yes, I did. The Prince said that we could have tents for our men. Grab your platoons. Look at the size of the tents. I think that the majority were for 8-10 soldiers. We're bigger. Get one for every six men. I want one that will double as a command tent. Borrow some wagons. Throw that "Lord" Title at them if any give you grief! Also – see if you can scavenge a musket or two from the Brits. We need the ones made from steel. Get Sergeant Douglas and ask him to meet me here."

"Aye, sir," said the two Lieutenants.

A few minutes later, Sergeant Douglas appeared by the Oak. "You asked for me sir?"

"Yes," answered Derek. "Please grab a handful of men for a hunting party. We will need to do this daily. Would you like to be in charge of that mission – or should I get Bruce?" he said with a knowing smile.

"Do I really need to answer that question?" Douglas said with a smile. "I may need to have Bruce, though, so I can beat his ass daily. It would be nice to have enough to buy some land!"

"You sir, are incorrigible Douglas!" said The Captain.

"Which is why you love me!" Smiled Douglas. He left to put together his team.

"Gentlemen," said Derek to Connor and Mac, "What say we go to the battlefield and then to the camp and get a better feel for those we would lead? We must dress accordingly with our blades and our Brownings. Bring a couple of magazines, and meet me here in 15 minutes. Perhaps we could get a horse while we are there? In the meantime, we can get a little run-in for the exercise."

The men met by the Oak. This was still so surreal. To be here. Now. So much has happened in the last week. Has it only been a week since we arrived?

Connor just realized it had been a week since he had his cell phone. The thought of it seemed almost alien now. How had he felt so attached to it before? His thoughts wandered to his past and thoughts of his future. He smiled despite himself and wondered if a Lady Forbes would play a prominent part in his future. But that will be after the war is over. This Hanoverian King will not go quietly. And we have to be able to influence the Prince to make better decisions...to get to know his subjects. Maybe give them some rights like what are in the American Constitution. Of course, he knew Nobility would not accept all of the Bill of Rights. But it would be a good thing if something could be fashioned to resemble the Bill of Rights. I suppose we shall see.

It took 30 minutes to get there on foot at a brisk pace. The first thing that hit you was the stench. Of course, with that many that lost their lives – the smell would be horrendous. The crows were there by the thousands! You could see those pilfering from the dead and preparing some mass burial. They went down to see if there were any muskets or materials they could use in their design plans for the modernization of Scotland. Most of the valuable materials had already been removed from the battle site. They did find a basket-hilted sword that someone had missed, and YES! They found a steel musket that had not been picked up yet. They took their newfound treasure and headed to the Prince's Camp.

Once there, they strode off to meet the men. At first, they were ignored by those getting on with their day. Then, someone noticed the McAndrew and McKenzie Tartans and asked them if they were on the battlefield. Then the crowds started. Handshakes, hugs, and then whiskey started to come about. Of course, none of the officers would get intoxicated in front of the men. They just wanted to shake their hand and get a feel for the caliber of the men they hoped to lead.

Questions, of course, led to their Jackals and firearms. Their answers were vague and were put into the context of the "You'll know more in due time" – and deflected into thoughts, hopes, and dreams from the men they would one day lead into battle. Upon initial inspection – besides being a bit leaner – they were very much like their Delta Company. Initially, they went into combat because their Lord or Chieftain had required it. They were not asked their opinion. But once battles began to be won – they were cautiously optimistic. And now – after that last battle and the new weapons on their side – they were ready to move on, beat the real Pretender in London…, and hopefully make a better life for themselves and their families. They were eager to take the battle to the enemy. They were tired of always being on defense.

They went by the Prince's tent to let him know they had been there and what they had discovered – and that the men and their loyalty was definitely behind the Prince. The Prince insisted they stay for dinner – even though they were not dressed for the occasion.

"Ahhh…Finally! I am going to meet you, lads, in person," said a familiar voice. This voice, however, came from the mouth of someone who did not look familiar. "What lads? You don't recognize the voice?" This was not an old Chieftain. This man was robust in his mid-thirties, at best. He was 5'9" tall – considering the average height was 5'5" –quite tall. He was slender, clean-shaven, and red-haired, with it in a ponytail. Far from the grizzled old chieftain, they anticipated meeting!

"Sir John Stuart?" asked McKenzie.

"Aye – tis me," said Lord Stuart.

All three men began to laugh…a little at first – then full-blown, side-splitting laughter.

"Well," said Lord Stuart. "I don't know whether to laugh with you or to be offended?"

Major McAndrew said, "Please do not be offended, Lord Stuart! You do know that we thought you were an apparition? The grizzled old Chieftain scared us all nigh unto death! It is only right and reasonable that you be who you are!" Everyone then reached out to shake the hands of the man who led them down this path. It was as if they met an old dear friend.

The Prince sat back and observed. There is much more to these men than even he was aware of. There will be much to learn from them indeed. The Prince called for his Servant and told him to prepare for three more gentlemen for dinner. "We will have just us this afternoon, as all the Lords are with their men. It's more to my liking. Does Roast Elk and roast vegetables sound acceptable?"

"Indeed, Your Highness. We are grateful to be able to dine with you, Sire," said the Captain. "How did the meeting with Lord Forbes go today?"

"Oh," said the Prince with a grin. "I see that Lord Connor McAndrew can be a bit impetuous?"

Connor blushed. "Your Highness, I meant no insult. Please forgive me."

"No insult was taken, Lord McAndrew. I know the primary reason you are asking. Does it have something to do with Lady Mary Forbes?"

The way that Connor smiled – nothing needed to be said.

"Ah, Lord McAndrew – are you smitten with someone you have not seen? Why! I believe that you are?" said the Prince. Everyone joined the Prince in laughter at Lord Connor McAndrew's expense! "Should I be coy? Or should I be direct?"

"Please, Your Highness – be direct," said Lord Connor McAndrew. "Will I be able to meet her?"

"Ah – if it were that easy. You will have to meet the father first. You may have a chance if you can pass the initial test with him. Having a Prince for a benefactor does help a bit in this 'Situation'?" The Prince smiled sincerely. "You will meet him tomorrow."

Lord Connor McAndrew was at once excited and petrified at the same time! He was also relieved when all were notified that dinner was ready.

As expected, the meal was divine. The Roast Elk had Juniper Berries, Thyme, and Rosemary – with Black Pepper to top it off. Several Roast Root Vegetables were made simply with Salt and Pepper, and more of the honeyed nuts were sprinkled on a fresh toast bread with honey drizzled on as well.

The talk was small talk. The Prince wanted to get to know his latest subjects. He conversed easily. There was no air of superiority.

He asked questions and learned that he indeed liked the McAndrew Brothers as well as Lord McKenzie. Duty was all to these men. He knew he could trust them with his life. That was the most significant revelation. He could be himself. God, what an unusual action that was! Lord Stuart was flawless in his assessment of these men.

Finally, the meal was over. The Prince asked Lord McAndrew to show his weapon to Lord Stuart. He also wanted to see the way the gun loaded more closely. How it automatically loaded from that small box in the handle was a total surprise to him. He was also still surprised by the deadly effect of those small shells compared to the size of the musket balls.

The Prince invited Lord Derek McAndrew to bring his men and move into the camp with the rest of the men. "Your Highness, that will eventually happen. However, I would still like to keep as much information about what we have secret as long as possible. You and Lord Stuart are more than welcome to visit our camp on the morrow if you would like to do so. I would like it only to be the two of you if possible. If we could get horses for the three of us – we could escort you there and back. We could have a full military escort if you would prefer that as well?"

"I think that I would enjoy that. What say you, Lord Stuart?" asked the Prince. "As far as an escort is concerned, you three are sufficient for me – especially if you bring your long guns."

"After seeing the firearm that I just saw – I would like to see what else is available to build our future," said Lord Stuart. "Gentlemen – I know you did not ask any questions regarding how you got here. We will have that conversation – but now is not that time."

Lord McKenzie responded, "Indeed, sir. I would also like to hear that story, as the rest of us would, too."

"What time would you like us to be here to ride to our camp?" asked Lord Derek McAndrew.

"Oh, that reminds me," said the Prince. He looked over to his servant and told him to get the Master of Horse to get three prime stallions fully saddled and outfitted for his guests. "These stallions are bred for Nobility. They are my gift to you for saving my life. Lord Forbes will be here for dinner at noon. I want to visit your camp at eight on the morrow. Get here by 7, and we can break our fast."

Lord Derek McAndrew continued, "First of all, Your Highness – the gift is not necessary. We were performing our duty."

"So, you would insult your Prince by refusing a gift from the heart?" asked the Prince.

Lord Derek McAndrew's eyes grew wide in astonishment. The Prince's eyes sparkled mischievously, and he smiled. Lord McAndrew breathed a sigh of relief as he understood it was a jest.

"Lord Derek McAndrew – you are correct. You did your duty. It was a response based on my Title – I intend to show you that I was worth that action. Not by giving you a horse – though a fine one – but by proving that I will be a King worth supporting. So – the gift still stands – because I wish it. Was there more?" asked the Prince.

"Well," said Lord Derek McAndrew, "Your breakfast will indeed be better than we can provide for ourselves. We will be here at 7 am sharp."

The Prince continued, "Also, I was speaking with Lord John Stuart- We decided between us that your men can throw quite a punch. How would you like to be called the 'Striker Brigade'?"

"Well, Your Highness – we're not quite a Brigade strong with only 150 under our command," said Lord McKenzie.

"True," said the Prince. But you are more powerful than any Brigade on the planet."

"Very well, Sire – the Striker Brigade it is!" said Lord Derek McAndrew.

The Master of Horse entered the tent. "Your Highness, please see if you approve of our choice for these gentlemen."

The Prince led the way from the tent. The sun was beginning to lower on the horizon. There were only a couple of hours left of daylight. He nodded his head in approval to the Master of Horse. "Nicely done sir. I fully approve."

The men exited the tent, looked at the Stallions before them, and all gasped collectively. None had seen such majestic animals—three black stallions, saddles, and all that went with it. Lord Connor McAndrew stepped up and grabbed the reigns of one of the Stallions. The horse started to pull back from Connor. He reached up and gently stroked its nose. He extended his hand so the horse could learn his scent. He then pulled the reigns tighter and whispered. "Hello there, Lad... we will get along famously." He stroked the head, and the Stallion leaned in towards him. Connor then stroked the length of his back. He scratched behind his ears, and the stallion nuzzled back. He pulled the reigns, put his left foot into the stirrup, and climbed on. He spoke gently to him the entire time. This felt so right. His heart skipped a beat. "Your Highness – you have no idea how grateful I am for this gift. I will truly never forget this."

The Prince nodded his approval. The other men did the same with their steeds. It was natural for all three. They would have to make a corral or Picket Lines when they returned to camp. They thanked the Prince again, promised they would see him in the morning – and were off.

Once out of the camp – the men became boys. It started as a trot. It was exhilarating. Hearts began to pump with excitement. The sound of the hoofs digging into the earth… the stallions felt that and began to gallop slowly without even being coaxed. These animals were built for speed. They felt the intoxicating need for freedom … the urge… the compulsion to gallop … the race was on!

Derek took the initial lead. He had gotten a full length ahead when Mac and Connor began to catch up. This is what freedom felt like. The wind flowed through their manes… the thump of each step echoed through the meadow as the distance mounted… the stride lengthened. Connor took the lead. Then Mac. Then Derek. The men laughed – giddy as schoolchildren. The responsibility of command was lost – if only for an instant. It was evident that each man knew how to ride. The speed was almost identical… except for Connor's steed. He was indeed the fastest, and Connor began to take the lead. The entry into the forest to their camp was just ahead. It was the gloaming period… when the sun kissed the horizon – radiating… painting their forest as an artist with a brush – knowing which color to express the joy of the moment. The men pulled on their reigns to slow their steeds. They would take no chances with their charge. They walked the horses until they got into camp.

They heard laughter and banter in the distance as they got closer to camp. When they got to the clearing, they were pleasantly surprised. All of the tents were up. Fires were roaring, and the smell of roast meat mingled with the smell of the burning oak. They realized that it had been some time since they had eaten. The Sentries waived them through. They dismounted and tied the mounts to trees a distance from the fire. They had no desire to spook the new members of their family!

Lieutenant Gordon and Ross looked up and smiled at the three as they walked to the fire. "It will be at least an hour before supper is ready. Sergeant Douglas and his men outdid themselves. Three large sows, an elk, and two red deer. We managed to get some salt from camp, some mighty fine ale, and even a liter or two of Scotch!" He then whispered, "We put that in your tent for later! Would you like to see our temporary home?"

"Absolutely," said Mac…and Ross took them around the camp. Not only did they have tents – they had put in pine straw for bedding. It would not be a mattress by any stretch of the imagination, but it would have some comforts to keep them dry should it rain.

Gordon said, "We saved the best for last." They walked towards the oak in the center of the camp. There were two officers and one command tent – I think it was the Dukes! "We found the furnishings -even beds for you three! – though it did take a while. Once the Highlanders realized what we were doing – they bent over backward to help us get fully outfitted. We now have cooking utensils, eating utensils, plates, and a few other supplies courtesy of King George himself! There are even some writing materials – though I don't know how easy it will be to write on parchment with a bloody feather! Even lanterns! And… we found six of the steel muskets used by the Redcoats."

"Ya did good lads! Thank you! You have no idea how much this is appreciated," said the Major. "Having the muskets will go a long way towards figuring out how to modernize the Scots somewhat. Furthermore, I don't know when we will be moving. I think this will be a fine home until we move."

The Major looked back at Connor and Mac. "Well – I suppose we have a home and command tent – at least for now. At least we have something presentable for the man that will be King tomorrow! Well, Gentlemen – we have horses to attend to and then Supper to eat!"

"Horses?" Questioned Ross.

"Aye," said the Sergeant Major. "Gifts from the Prince."

"Can I see them sir? We have a horse farm at home. I would love the chance to care for the animals. It would at least feel like a bit of home," said Ross.

"That would be more than acceptable," said the Major. They went to get the animals – who were munching on the grass where they were tied. Ross asked if they had been watered. Of course, that had not been the case. Ross looked at them with an accusing look. "We were going to water them – but then we got sidetracked. Let us take off the saddles and stow them in our tents. You can probably get some rope to make a picket line for them until we can build some corral. Make it close to the creek. There is plenty for them to eat, and being able to drink from the creek would be a bonus."

"Aye, Sir, "said Ross. "I will also see if I can find a brush to brush them down. This has to be some royal line. I have never seen finer stallions! You should be proud!"

"We indeed are," said Connor… "more than anyone will know."

"Let's go get supper," said the Major. "I'm famished!"

They all began to move towards the group of men. The Sergeant Major expressed his thanks to all for setting up camp. "This may be home a while, lads. We need to take good care of it. We also need to be prepared for tomorrow. The Prince will be coming to our camp, so there will be no hangovers tonight! Think of it as an inspection tomorrow at 0830. Incidentally, the Prince has come up with a name for us. He said that we collectively packed a punch to the enemy. So, because of that – he has named us the 'Striker Battalion.' Why 'Striker Battalion'? Because we hit harder than any battalion on the planet!" The men cheered!

"Let's eat! I'm starved!" said Lord Derek McAndrew.

The men got in line for dinner. The Officers got in line with the rest of the men to get a feel for the morale. They listened more than talked. Small talk abounded between the men and the officers. Keeping morale up would be a challenge. Homesickness would be difficult with missed loved ones and the familiar. One thing that helped morale was hiring several washerwomen and cooks to take care of some of the men's immediate needs. Lord Forbes had recommended these folks for the men. They were probably spies – but much of what they had available was not readily visible. In the meantime, there was someone to do the Laundry and cook the meals for his men.

It was easy to see that a couple of the women who were cooks would become mother figures to these lads. There may need to be discussions with them on delicate subjects. They will probably already know that instinctively – but it never hurt to be adequately prepared. It is truly amazing what 2 Guineas a month would purchase. A damn sight more than at home!

One of the noticeable things was the potential for boredom. Boredom is dangerous. It allows you to think. Lord McKenzie knew all too well that thoughts could bring loneliness and despair. How he missed his Annie.

As the men talked, Lord McKenzie heard talks of home, childhood shenanigans, and mum's cooking…the hardest was talks regarding wives, girlfriends, or children. Knowing the probability, they would never see them again. That was in the back of every man's mind. After the Prince makes his visit – it will be essential to have the men come up with meaningful tasks. Ways to utilize their skills and make a difference in the lives that surrounded them. Not just the immediate military needs but also to expand their thinking about the possibilities after the war to determine the rightful king.

Chapter 21
Restricted

That night – Derek, Connor, and Mac did something they had not done in months – if not years. They slept soundly. No dreams. No thoughts. No concerns. No worries. No fears. Blissful, blessed sleep.

The first one up was Derek. He glanced at his watch. It was 0600. Snap! He had to get up! He had fallen asleep in his Kilt… in a bed! A Bed. Oh my God, it had felt so good! He had gotten so used to a cot or the ground – this was indeed a luxury he could get used to. He stuck his head in Connor's tent – "Hey, you little shit! Get your arse out of bed! We need to leave in 15 minutes!"

He had to do the same thing for Mac. That was highly unusual.

The men rushed to get to their horses – and to their surprise and delight, they were saddled and ready to go. Ross came around the corner – "You better take better care of them today! You don't want to piss off Lord Ross in the care of such fine specimens of horse, now, do ya?" Everyone smiled at him and expressed their thanks for getting them ready.

With that – they climbed onto the stallions and were quickly off to see the Prince, and that promised breakfast! When they got to the camp, it was precisely 7 am… Fiona gave them a stern look. Connor gulped… something about her put the fear of God in him. He did not want to make her angry. They were ushered into the tent.

All of the Sudden – Mac stopped in his tracks. That smell. That delightful, amazingly, wonderful aroma he thought he would never smell again… C O F F E E!!! His eyes perked right up! "Oh, Your Highness!" Mac exclaimed! He stammered… "You… You… You have coffee?!?"

The Prince said, "Why, of course, sir – we may not be from your time period – but we are civilized! Besides… we like the way it makes one feel!"

"Aye, your Highness. As do I," said Derek.

"Well then," said the Prince. "Perhaps we should have a cup before we break our fast!"

"Yes, please!" asked Mac.

The Servants prepared cups for them all. The Prince liked his with Cream, Cinnamon, and sugar. What was noticed is that the sugar was not white as the men were accustomed to. It was brown – interesting. They were crystallized from Cane Sugar. It almost had a brown sugar flavor with the presence of molasses. Derek, Connor, and Mac wanted their coffee black - which surprised the Prince. The Prince noticed the smile on each of the men's faces when they had taken their first drink. These men like simple pleasures. That is the benefit of living life surrounded by the horror of constant war. Simple things have colossal meaning.

"Well, Lads. Let's eat! I am rather hungry!" said the Prince.

His cooks had prepared a simple but luxurious feast. Blood Sausage, Duck eggs, scones, with apples and honey. Truly delicious. After small talk, the breakfast was rather rushed. The future King and Lord Stuart were ready to see what their allies brought to the table.

The Master of Horse brought the horses for all. He informed Lord McKenzie and Lords McAndrew that their stallions had been fed and manicured while they ate. Everyone mounted up and headed out of camp. It was not a leisurely ride – since the Prince had an appointment with Lord Forbes at noon…but it wasn't rushed either. It was a beautiful spring day, with the sun tantalizing the abundant wildflowers and showing them off for the world to see. The colors! So vivid! It was a feast for the senses.

The mood was relaxed. Even the pretense of being a Prince was coming down a bit. He called others by their proper name – not by their title. All the men riding at the time appreciated that more than anything. These men had earned the trust of the Prince – even in so short a period of time. All hoped this would become a trusted friendship – more than the strained Ruler over the ruled.

They approached the edge of the forest. Mac had placed a few men at the edge to ensure the Prince safely made it. He nodded in their direction and stopped the Prince. "Your Highness! I would like you to look into the woods and ask if you see anything."

The Prince stopped and looked deeply into the woods. He looked up, down, near and far – and saw nothing. "Mac – I don't see anything but the forest. I am afraid you will have to enlighten me," said the Prince.

"Men! Reveal yourselves!" said McKenzie. Instantly, 20 men came out into the open. One had only been 20 feet from the Prince – and the Prince had not seen him.

That surprised the Prince, who was instantly prepared to have his stallion running in the other direction. He had the presence of mind to keep from spurring his horse to flee. He was a little irritated – but realized this was part of the ability of the men he wished to have as a part of his team.

"Your Highness! I apologize – I had no desire or plan to startle you!" said McKenzie.

The Prince relaxed and smiled. "Ah, Lord McKenzie – it is one of the hazards of being Royalty. Sometimes those you wish to be a friend become a foe!" Everyone noticed that the formality had returned with the presence of the men and acted accordingly.

"Your Highness," said Connor. "Please dismount. We have something to show you!" Connor then became Captain McAndrew… "Sergeant Douglas!"

"Yes sir, Captain… er… I mean 'Lord McAndrew,'" said the Sergeant. This brought a smile to the Prince.

"Please bring me the iPad."

"Yes Sir," … Damn, he thought…he did it again. This Royalty Nobility bullshit was going to be hard to navigate! He handed over the iPad to the Captain.

Lord McAndrew got in front of the Prince. "Please look at this, Your Highness."

The Prince looked at the screen. He could see what the drone saw – high above the treetops. Captain McAndrew was an expert drone flyer – he flew just above the trees and then took it high enough to see Inverness in the distance. He then brought the machine down to treetop level and brought it to them. The Prince was enraptured by what he saw. He even saw himself through the lens of the camera on the drone.

All of a sudden, something buzzed in the air. The horses began to act nervously, especially as the drone got closer. Since the Captain didn't want to spook the horses, he landed the drone about 50 feet away. He walked over and showed the drone to the Prince.

"This…this…this seems like witchcraft! How can you make this thing obey you?" stuttered the Prince.

"Please relax, Your Highness. This is but a machine – like a clock. It does what it is told because we hold the mechanism in that screen that Lord Connor McAndrew is holding," said Derek. "We have to be careful with this – but would you like to control it for a bit? Please excuse me if I have to take the controls from you – we don't want it to crash or go beyond our range."

"May I?" asked the Prince.

"Absolutely, "Said Derek.

He retrieved the pad and started the drone. He had it rise above the ground and showed the Prince the controls. He then guided the drone out of the forest into the clearing. The Prince then assumed control.

It took the Prince a minute – but soon, he had mastered the basic skills. He took it up well over 300 feet above the ground – where it became a speck above them that could not be heard. He then had it dive down toward the ground. Derek thought he would have to take the controls away from the Prince when the drone suddenly stopped 5' above the ground. The Prince then slowly had the drone turn around to stare at them. He brought the drone within 10 feet of them and gently landed it on the ground. Everyone erupted in cheers, which made the Prince jump as he focused on the flight. Then everyone laughed – including the Prince.

"Well done, Sire!" Exclaimed Sir John Stuart. "Well, Done!"

The Prince understood what this meant – the enemy could not hide!

Lord Connor McAndrew explained, "We must be very careful with these. We only have a few. It takes a rechargeable battery to make this function. Currently, we have to use our Jackals to have them charge. That will be one of the things we will have to formulate using the technology from here – to make that work."

"A rechargeable battery?" asked the Prince.

"Yes, Your Highness," said Connor. "Each of these drones has a power source. Are you familiar with electricity and how it works?"

"No, Lord McAndrew – I'm afraid I am not," said the Prince.

"Imagine an oil lantern, Your Highness," said Connor. "The light is what you see. What fuels that light – is the lamp. This drone operates on electricity like a tiny bolt of lightning. And just like that lamp – when it is out of oil – it will not provide light. If the drone is out of electricity – it cannot fly."

"If you wish to return to Lord Forbes, Your Highness – we must proceed to the camp. The drone will show us where the enemy is, but the weapons will defeat our enemy. We have much to show you, Your Highness," said Derek.

"Very Well, Lord McAndrew, let's proceed," said the Prince.

Everyone remounted and moved on towards the camp.

When the Prince arrived, everyone stood and saluted him, and applause erupted. The Prince got off of his stallion and began to clap his hands. "It is I that should Thank you. Understand this, gentlemen – when all this is over – you will be richly rewarded. I owe you more than you can ever imagine!" stated the Prince. Everyone then bowed accordingly.

"Your Highness," said Mac. "Here is something that I would like to show you first. Here are each of the shells that our weapons use:

9mm – for our Pistol

5.56mm – for our Rifle

7.62 for our GPMG – and what we want to make as a caliber for the rifles we discussed previously.

Now, the heavy firepower:

.338 Lapua Magnum – Our Sniper Rifle

50 Caliber for another of our machine guns

81 MM Mortar Round

Grenades

Plastic Explosive – if we wish to bring down a bridge or building."

Mac took over, "Your Highness, we are now going to show you each of the weapons and explain when we used them during the battle."

"Here is the AWL L115A3 – which fires the .338 Lapua Magnum. This is the Firearm that dispatched the Duke and his Officers." Mac showed the Prince the Bolt Action and how to aim the weapon.

The Prince said, "I expected this to weigh much more – especially because of the range. How far away from the target is it accurate?"

"The shot that our sniper took was close to 1000 yards. It is accurate, up to 1,600 yards, depending on the conditions. If highly skilled and all of the stars align – one may hit a target close to 2,000 yards," said Mac. "Our snipers are that good."

"That's almost a bloody mile!" Exclaimed the Prince.

"Aye, Sire," said Mac. "There are not many places to hide if our snipers have you in their sites and range."

"This is our work-horse. It is SA80. The effective range is over 400 yards. The maximum range would be around 600 yards. Would you like to fire it, Your Highness?" asked Mac.

"Are you sure it would be safe here?" asked the Prince.

"Absolutely, "said Mac. "Watch what I do and where I aim. I will walk you through it. Watch me first. After I fire, I will give you each step." Mac picked up the firearm, checked the Magazine – which was loaded, and charged the weapon. Then Mac said, "Your Highness. Do you see that tree – the Oak tree just to the left of the Pine? It's close to 400 yards away. Now, look at the second branch on the right of the tree. Captain McAndrew – will you be so kind as to give the Prince your Binoculars?"

Connor gave the Prince the Binoculars – and showed him how to use them. The binoculars excited the Prince greatly – especially when Connor showed him how to adjust the binoculars to give him a clear view! "Those are AMAZING!" Exclaimed the Prince!

Mac showed the Prince the Rifle. "Your Highness – this is the Safety. It prevents the firearm from accidentally discharging. When not in use – you should always have the Safety engaged. I have disengaged the Safety so it is prepared to fire. To acquire the target, I will look through this SUSAT Scope. Now – look at that tree, the second branch." Mac inhaled, then exhaled. He inhaled a half breath and held it. He acquired the target and fired the shot. The Prince was stunned when the branch snapped a split second later and flew backward!

"That is truly astonishing!" said the Prince.

After Mac cleared the weapon and removed the magazine - Mac gave the Prince the Firearm. "This is so light!" said the Prince.

"Correct Sire. These are built for what we would call. Close Quarter Combat." We would use these to go into a building against a determined enemy with equally powerful firearms – but they are also effective at a longer range. Are you ready, Sire?"

"I suppose," said the Prince.

"Okay. The First step is to prepare the Rifle. Get a feel for it. Go ahead and put it to your shoulder, look through the scope, and tell me what you think," said Mac.

The Prince picked it up and did as Mac directed. He looked into the scope and was again astonished at the optics in such a small device.

"Is that comfortable?" asked Mac.

"Yes," said the Prince.

"Now load the magazine just as I showed you. Make sure it clicks. Good. Now Charge the Weapon. Pull this back and release it. The shell is now prepared for you to fire. Please do not aim this at anything that you do not wish to die – ever. Once again, Sire – good. You're a natural," said Mac.

The Prince smiled at that and aimed as he was directed. Mac then told him to turn off the safety – which he did. He asked the Prince if he had a target. The Prince told Mac that he decided to aim at the middle of the tree – so that maybe he would at least hit something.

Mac then instructed the Prince to take a deep breath and exhale. Then, take a half breath in and pull the trigger easily. Mac, in turn, looked through the Binoculars. The Prince did as directed. He pulled the trigger. He thought that he hit the tree. But he wasn't sure. Mac saw it hit, not quite where intended – but in the Pine just to the right of the oak. Mac explained where the Prince hit. The Prince laughed. "Well, the fact that I hit something excites me!" Mac had the Prince clear the firearm, remove the Magazine, and put the safety back on.

The Prince exclaimed, "Once we have more of these bullets, as you called them – you will have to show me how to be a better marksman!"

"Indeed, I will," said Mac.

"Now, Your Highness, we will move on to the Mortar. This removed the guns for the British. He held up the Mortar Round and showed the Prince how the shell was dropped into the Mortar and that the explosive propellant sent the shell down range. The Prince remembered the explosions around the cannon – and shivered. He would not have wanted to be on the receiving end!

You, of course, have seen how the pistol works and how it can also be an effective weapon in close-quarters combat.

"Now, Sire, Let's look at the Jackals and the Mastiffs," said Connor.

"The what?" asked the Prince.

"The Jackals and The Mastiffs," said Connor.

"Well, Lord Connor McAndrew, "said the Prince. "I know what a Jackal and a Mastiff are. I don't need to see them. I want to see the weapon that dispatched the Calvary and Dragoons."

Connor laughed, "That's where I am taking you, Sire. Follow Me."

The men walked to where the Jackals and the Mastiffs were parked.

"That's what I want to see!" Exclaimed the Prince.

Connor smiled, "This is the Jackal Two Sire. That Behemoth over there is the Mastiff."

"Ahhh," said the Prince.

Connor opened the door so that the Prince could see inside. He asked the Prince to get in and sit down. Connor started it, which caused the Prince to Jump. Connor smiled again. "Hold on, Sire, I will take you on a quick ride." Connor put in gear and began to accelerate. There was initially fear on the Prince's face – and then it became exhilaration. Connor didn't go far – only a mile or so- then turned around and returned to the camp.

Once parked, Connor got on top of where the GPMG was located. He showed the Prince the basics – but explained that they would not fire the shot in the Prince's hand. They did not want to waste a single cartridge. "The effective range for this, Your Highness, is 600-800 yards. The maximum range is close to 2,000 yards. It fires 10 of these per second if we open them up. We generally want to fire around 200 rounds per minute to avoid overheating and for better accuracy."

"Now, this is the Beast," said Mac. The Prince was escorted to the Mastiff. The Prince saw the front, and then they opened up what could be for carrying supplies or bringing troops to the front lines for combat. It is designed to be able to take getting shot. I think the London Pretender has a 42-pounder at his disposal. This can move through just about anything and protect our troops in the process. What makes it the beast, however, is this." Mac handed the Prince the 50 Cal BMG shell. "The effective range for this is 1800-2000 yards. It could sink or at least disable anything in the Fleet. We must be very discerning with this – as we don't have any ammunition to waste. It can also fire ten rounds per second. Of course, we are more prudent with this when in combat," said Mac.

"I am going to ask you what may seem to be an absurd question. Do your enemies have these weapons to use against you?" asked the Prince.

"Yes, Sire, and some are much more deadly than we have here," said Derek.

"My Lord! How does anyone survive your battles?" asked the Prince.

"Usually, for every weapon, there is some defense against them. But many have no way to defend against. If they are used – you are likely to die."

"That is what nightmares would be made of, I would think," said the Prince.

"That Your Highness… is a colossal understatement," said Derek. "Our battles are intense. The only way to win is to control the skies."

"Control the Skies?" asked the Prince.

Sir John Stuart interrupted. "Sire, we must get back to camp. You will barely make your meeting with Lord Forbes."

"Before we leave, Your Highness," said Derek. He held up a musket and the 7.62 mm shell. "Here is our idea to modernize the firearm capability quickly for our troops." He held the musket and acted like it was a break-action firearm. "Imagine Your Highness, where you. Break open the barrel, insert the shell, and fire. It would have an effective range of at least 300 yards and be accurate. With Practice, 5-6 shots per minute would be quite doable."

"Could we do that with our current technology?" asked the Prince.

"I believe so, Your Highness," said Derek. "But it is something that we would need to get into production quickly. If we can come up with the shell and casing – AND get the production facilities up quickly – I think we could have a realistic goal of 10,000 of these when it is time to meet the strength of the Pretender when he invades."

"Damn," said the Prince. "I have so many questions. I guess it will have to wait. In the meantime – Lord Connor McAndrew. I want you to meet me in your best dress at my tent at 130 pm – where you will have the honor of meeting Lord Forbes!"

"Wait," said Connor. "What?!?!"

The Prince smiled. For whatever reason – he enjoyed making Lord Connor McAndrew a bit uncomfortable. He is fearless on the battlefield – yet uncomfortable in other ways. Almost like a brother,

I would think. He chuckled to himself as he said, "Yes. Lord Connor McAndrew. Lord James Forbes, The 17th Lord Forbes, 6th Baronet of Pitsligo, actually seeks your presence. I have told him all about you, I'm afraid."

Connor paled. "Like what, Your Highness?"

"Oh my, Lord McAndrew – you shall indeed see. Alright, your Lordships, I am afraid we must be off," said the Prince.

Everyone except for Lord Connor McAndrew mounted their horses to escort the Prince back. He needed to bathe and prepare to look his best if he had any chance with Lady Mary Forbes. "This is so unlike me," thought Connor. I've not even seen her. She could be ugly as sin for all I know. And if that is the case – how the bloody Hell will I get out of this mess?

They reached the Prince's Camp just after 11. That gave the time for the Prince to freshen up to meet his charge. He hated having to play the game with the Nobles. But he knew he could not win the Crown without them. How he wished he could trust them to be honest instead of trying to play the political game constantly. I get it – everyone wants to expand their wealth and influence. I know that some who would give me an oath of fealty – would sell me to the highest bidder if it came to it.

Derek and McKenzie decided to ride back to camp. They had quite the day. As they were riding, Derek stopped. "Mac, did you notice anything about Sir John Stuart today?"

"Aye, I did. He was strangely quiet and not interested in anything we had to show. It was like he had seen it all before," said McKenzie.

"That's how I felt as well. Something about him is way beyond what we know or have been told. I feel like I can trust him. But there is something that I can't figure out about him," said Derek.

"Agreed. I feel the same," said Mac.

"Well,," said Derek. "Let's be off. We need to make sure Connor is presentable." They both smiled at that and headed to camp.

Chapter 22
Forbes

When they got to camp – Connor was all dressed up and preparing to leave. He was in his saddle. Derek looked at his brother. His hair was growing longer, and he was showing a beard. He was getting leaner because of their diet. But his countenance had changed entirely. He was… happier. More comfortable in his skin. He carried himself with an air of authority. He had to admit he was proud of the little shit. His mum and da would be overjoyed. To think their bairns had grown to be Lords? That still was hard to accept.

"Damn, Connor. You almost look presentable!" Smiled Derek. "Whatever you do, you little shit – don't embarrass us. We have to live here now!" he chided.

Connor remarked, "You haven't yet – so I feel pretty confident that I will be acceptable. By the way – you do realize I'm like 4" taller than you. You need to come up with something better than 'you little Shit.'"

"So, have you prepared a speech yet?" asked Derek.

"Just like I always do!" was Connor's reply.

"You are armed?" asked Derek.

"Of course," said Connor.

"Very well then," said Derek. "Don't shoot Lord Forbes! Good Luck."

With that, Connor rolled his eyes and was off, and Derek and Mac returned to camp.

In the meantime, Lord Forbes, Prince Charles, and Lord Stuart were discussing strategy. They discussed getting Lord Keith Lamont as a negotiator with the other clans. It was decided that Prince Charles would need to be named the King of Scotland first. That would light a fire under the King to invade. That would probably involve the recall of most of the France Contingent. The War of Austrian Succession was creating a mess in Europe. Everyone wanted their share of the Hapsburg lands. Perhaps they could create an alliance with King Louis XV. The Prince had met him several times. He was the epitome of arrogance, in his opinion. But his global stature and strength could not be denied, especially since his Navy was the only one, except for the Dutch or Spanish, that could effectively counter the British Navy.

Lord Forbes – who was not a supporter of the Prince – was becoming one day by day - despite the Prince being a staunch Roman Catholic. He was firm in his belief system. Some would say overly so… but damn it… right was right. This young man may deserve to be on the throne. He did have, by birth, a stronger claim than King George. Perhaps the real Pretender was in London.

Forbes was 5'9" tall. His wavy black hair was in a "queue" – tied back like a ponytail with an expensive silk ribbon. Although in his upper 30s, the weight of responsibility made him look older.

"So, Your Highness, You had quite a bit of time to meet with our newfound allies in arms?" asked Lord Forbes.

"I'm growing quite fond of them. They are men with a high devotion to duty. They have already protected me twice – during the Battle of Culloden – and the assassination attempt. Their capabilities, I believe, will indeed make me King of Great Britain – and more if conditions are favorable. Lord Forbes – you would not believe their capabilities. I believe they can make Scotland the strongest country in the world within a few years. And whoever can generate their plans and help them build what they can build – would be among the wealthiest men in Scotland. Does that at least interest you, Lord Forbes?" asked the Prince.

"Why, of course, Your Highness. But being right and just is as important," said Lord Forbes.

The Prince smiled – he knew he was full of shite… But it would take a lot of nobles to get on board to fund these projects. He damn sure didn't want to use the Rothschilds. They had far too much power as far as he was concerned. If he could abolish the banks – he would do so. That alone would fund his requirements. All of this – this risk of taking his throne – must be from those he would rule. The masses would put him on the throne – and he would be beholding to none.

"Now, Your Highness, would you tell me of this Lord Connor McAndrew, who would like to meet my daughter?" asked Lord Forbes.

"Well, you know of his courage. You heard about it on Culloden Moor. He was fearless when speaking or fighting the enemy. He graduated from the University. He appears to be quite intelligent," said the Prince.

"Tell me of his family. You realize how important family is today," said Lord Forbes.

"He is of the Clan Anderson, as you well know. I know nothing of his immediate family. What I do know is this – if he continues down his current path and I do indeed become King – he and his brother will both be Earls with sizeable estates," said the Prince.

That revelation startled Lord Forbes – but he liked that part of the equation. So, his Mary – who will be 19 in February – should probably meet this man. "I suppose it is Providence that I didn't marry her off earlier," he thought.

Connor arrived at the Prince's tent. How the bloody hell had a man like him ever reached this point – where he would be groveling before a "Lord" to meet a daughter that he had never met before? Again…what the hell was he thinking? "But... I guess I'm too far in to back off now!" He got off his horse and gave the reigns to the Master of Horse. His stallion would be well-fed and brushed. He would be glad when he had a home where he could do that as well. But he knew that it would be a while before that occurred.

Lady Fiona met him at the Tent and smiled. "Are you Ready, Lord McAndrew?" She patted him on the back to encourage him.

"I suppose I am as ready as ever," Connor said nervously.

"Very well then," said Lady Fiona. He approached the tent and announced the arrival of Lord Connor McAndrew. She escorted him in.

The Prince looked at him and smiled. Lord Forbes looked at him and scowled. "What the hell is that all about?" thought Connor. Connor bowed to the Prince, nodded to Lord Forbes, and smiled. The smile was not returned. Connor gulped. The Prince smiled. Then, to make it even more awkward – no one began the conversation, making an awkward silence for only a few seconds – but it felt like hours.

Finally – the Prince, out of mercy perhaps, began to speak. "Lord Forbes. May I present Lord Connor McAndrew from Aberdeen? Lord Forbes briefly nodded to acknowledge Lord McAndrew. "Lord McAndrew – May I present Lord James Forbes, The 17th Lord Forbes, 6th Baronet of Pitsligo." Lord McAndrew nodded to Acknowledge Lord Forbes.

Lord Forbes stared directly into Lord McAndrew's eyes and said, "Lord McAndrew. I am a direct man and will get directly to the point. I understand you wish to meet my daughter, Lady Mary Forbes, with a possible interest in courting her. Simply because you heard her sing the night before Culloden? Why on earth would I even consider such a thing? What have you even to offer? And don't say undying love. Love gets old and wrinkly and won't keep her fed or happy. So again. What the bloody devil do you have to offer?"

What was Connor's response? He started laughing. Hard. He was bent over laughing so hard. He had to stop to breathe. Of course, Lord Forbes was not quite so amused. He became offended and thought he would have to duel with him on the spot. When Connor got his breath. "Lord Forbes. Please do not be offended. There is no offense meant or given. My da told me that I would meet my future Father-In-Law – and he said he would be tough as nails – and try to intimidate me thoroughly. Lord Forbes – You have no reason, based on current circumstances, to even think of allowing your daughter to be wed to me possibly. I am not wealthy; I own no estates as of yet. So – do you want to know why you should encourage the relationship and eventual wedding? Your Highness, do you have any paper? Something lighter than parchment?"

This intrigued the Prince – "Lady Fiona, would you bring a piece of paper for Lord McAndrew?" Lady Fiona went to her writing desk and brought a piece of paper – made from Linen. It was light and durable.

"Thank you, Lady Fiona. Now watch." With that, Connor deftly began to fold the paper. One corner folded down. Then another. Fold in the middle. Fold the wings. He picked up his paper plane.

By now, the Prince and Lord Forbes were both intrigued.

Connor then asked the Prince and Lord Forbes to step outside. They did so. Connor determined which direction the wind was blowing. He threw it with the wind. Both the Prince and Lord Forbes shouted in utter amazement! The damn thing was flying. That paper

was FLYING! How the bloody hell?!?! Connor saw their reaction –
and smiled. Something he pulled out of his arse again… Thank you
Lord! Connor went and gathered the paper airplane and stepped back
into the tent with the Prince and Lord Forbes – who were still
astonished.

Connor began, "Lord Forbes… what you get is what's in my head.
Not just in my head – but with 150 other men - we will build a
nation that the world envies and would not even contemplate
attacking or trying to intimidate. You will have more wealth than
you imagine – if only part of my ideas come to fruition. You will
have "Me," a man of honor and integrity who will treat your
daughter as a Princess and protect her honor, reputation, and life
with my own. I swear it – so help me, God."

Silence. That's what Connor heard. Both men who listened…
were moved. They could not – nor would say a word.

After a few minutes – Lord Forbes spoke up," Lord McAndrew,
when you first walked in here – I thought you a buffoon. I was
prepared and almost bound by honor to duel you here and now. I
sincerely apologize, sir. I was wrong. You will meet Lady Mary and
me tomorrow for dinner at my home. I expect you at 1130. I will
send an aid to meet you at Prince Charles' tent at 1030 to escort you
to my home. It will be a small affair. If Lady Mary decides that you
should court – you will have my blessing. If Prince Charles becomes
King Charles – I will consider marriage. If he does not – then it
probably will not matter. If we are still alive – we will be shipped off
to the Colonies as paupers. Understood?"

With that – Connor offered his hand to Lord Forbes – who took it
– and smiled.

"There now," said the Prince. "See! That wasn't difficult – now
was it!" All gave smiles.

After Connor left – Derek and Mac called the men together. They
were going to have to put together a think tank. Ways to begin the
process of modernizing Scotland. Yes, they would have to
modernize the Military – but also – by the relationship with the
Prince – perhaps there could be an input of rights for the individual.
Developing the infrastructure to help with health and simple things
like indoor plumbing. Water treatment. Electricity. Things that are
easy to take for granted in the world he came from. They needed to
better understand how many engineers were a part of the group.

What about craftsmen? What about the trades? Even some of the young will have skills that could be immensely valuable here.

We have 150 men in total. Almost half have a University degree – even if earned in the service. Most of those are engineering – which is what we need. How many are mechanics – if not professionally – then as a hobby? How many are scientists or mathematicians? We should have them all as part of our group. All of those skill sets will be vitally important moving forward. We have to be able to adapt to the current technology and then modify and modernize it as well. This will be an ongoing process. Logistics… Lord – all of it. We will need to build an entire infrastructure! It's almost overwhelming. We can't do it all – we must train the tradesmen here—the firearms, the ammunition, and the Biodiesel.

Mac got the troops by the Oak. Derek went on to discuss the possibilities as well as the challenges. He wanted this to be an open forum to get the wheels turning. He wished he had a white-erase board!

"Men," said Derek, "As you know. We are going to be tasked to complete a lot of modernization projects. Afghanistan did an amazing job of training us to be ingenious in applying local technology to accomplish miraculous results. The problem is, though – we don't have a logistics channel to get what we may be lacking. We must improvise and think outside the box in ways we never dreamed of. I will have to get a better grip on what skill sets we have among us. I had a general idea of college graduates but will need specifics. I need to know who among you are engineers. How many are tradesmen? How many are mechanics – either trained – or just a hobby? Medical concerns – keeping us healthy in a challenging environment – all while preparing to train a brand-new army while developing arms and training methods to teach those without any education."

Derek Continued. "Ideally, these will be the skill sets that we need and that I believe we have among us:

"Engineers and Inventors. Everything that we know is a wonderous invention here. We'll need Blacksmiths and Metallurgists. Working with ancient tools will be difficult – unless you have those skills. Most of us are munitions experts. We must figure out how to develop our ammunition and a firearm that can be mass-produced. Medics and Surgeons. We have two doctors among us, as well as Medics. What you know is by far superior to current knowledge. You will have to be careful – so that you don't get accused of witchcraft – which is still a thing, gentlemen. Carpenters and builders. Mechanics and Machinists. Mechanically – all that I know that is available would be steam-powered. Perhaps we can do some water-powered projects as well. We must figure out how to convert and use that steam power. We'll need Scientists, Mathematicians, and Agricultural experts. Communication and strategy experts. The need is great, and the opportunities are as well."

"The future that we knew is gone. We have the opportunity to make things so much better. We have to be smart about what and how we direct this adventure. You will be tempted by offers from those in power – because they want more wealth and power. I am asking you to commit to us as a team. Maybe not for life – but at least until the War ends and the Prince is King. If we do that, gentlemen – we will have more wealth, honor, and appreciation than we can even begin to consider."

"I want you to spend tonight thinking about your particular skill sets. Even hobbies can make a huge addition to what we can offer. Every Platoon Sergeant – I want you to get with your platoon. Get me a list of each specialty so we can gameplan this and present it to the Prince. Questions? Seeing none. All officers, meet me tomorrow by the Oak at 0900."

Connor got back to camp a little after four. Derek and Mac got with him to discuss what he missed and to find out how it went with Lord Forbes. When they heard what transpired – especially with Connor breaking down and laughing at Lord Forbes… Derek had a few words, "Connor, Sometimes you are a dumbass. But I gotta admit – the airplane was a pretty good idea. I sincerely hope this Lady Mary isn't 5'2" and 175 Kilos!" They all laughed at that.

Everything was discussed at the beginning of the planning process. They needed to get everyone on board and plugged into the overall strategy. Sergeant Douglas and his hunting party should be back soon. Who knew what dinner would be tonight?

Chapter 23
Insight

The night was uneventful…Spring is rolling in with life and optimism abounding in all of God's creation… and beginning to raise its head in all surrounding the Prince. The Prince did something this night that he had never done before. Lord John Stuart was the only one he would trust with such an action. What was the plan? To go to a Tavern in Inverness. To get a feel for who would be his subjects – not just Nobility – but the people. He was able to get "Commoner" clothes and borrowed horses that were beneath his station. Fortunately – they were relatively docile beasts and did as commanded. He traded in his Gold Sovereigns to have Coppers and Shillings. That would be all he needed this night.

He had rules he had to follow. Some he remembered as a youth when he played this game often. Before they found out, some of his best friends were the commoner boys close to his Estate. He smiled, remembering the games he had played and the relationships that he had built.

He and Lord Stuart were dressed as Merchantmen. Not lower class – but not wealthy either. That seemed the best way to travel. They did not want to attract attention. They were there to observe.

The Tavern was busy when they arrived. Mary, the Serving Girl, was rather brusque in getting them seated. You could tell she was rushed. Once she delivered her six tankards of ale to another table – she came to take their order. "Well, love, what can I get you – besides myself? As you can tell – I'm a bit busy tonight. Our Ale is the best in town, and the stew is more tender than I," she said with a suggestive smile.

"An Ale and the stew it is then," said Lord Stuart.

"And for you? My… your eyes are as blue as the sky! I bet you're a heartbreaker, love!" said Mary with a twinkle in her eyes. That immediately made the Prince blush – which caused an even bigger smile from the raucous serving girl.

"I'll have the same," said the Prince. "Thank you."

"Manners. Too?" gushed Mary. "You might need to leave before I get off and have my way with you." Which elicited another round of blushing and more laughter from Mary.

She went to get their order. In the meantime, John and the Prince listened to those around them.

"I hear the Prince wiped out all of the bloody bastards – that none but the camp followers survived. If that's true, maybe the clans will stop fighting each other and beat the Redcoats!" said Angus.

"Some say it was supernatural," said Abigail. "That some of those poor souls' parts had evaporated, leaving only their blood and guts!"

William scoffed, "Nonsense Woman! Have you never seen a canon and what it can do to a man? I can tell you it ain't for the faint of heart!"

"Who the bloody hell cares? We'll just be trading one form of bondage for another!" said another, and several others agreed. "It seems the more power they get – the more they want – and it always costs us!" This created a lot of agreed sentiment.

"Well, we at least got a chance if there's a Stuart on the throne!" Everyone agreed with that statement. "Besides – it's the greedy Lords that do us in!"

"Shut Up Shamus! You want to be hung up by your balls?" Everyone laughed at that.

"But he's a Pope lover! You know what happened the last time!" said one.

"Aye – he is, but the real Pretender in London is a Protestant – and what good did that get us?" said another.

Mary brought up the Ale and the Stew. Everything in the Prince made him want to turn up his nose at what was presented to him – for no other reason than it was meant for a commoner. Come on, man! These people you would rule. You must learn them and lead them. He smelled the mystery meat stew… and damn! It smelled good. It was amazing! He might need to bring that cook on board when he had the crown! Mary brought them a refill of ale and some Barley Bread. It, too, was satisfying. "I still love those eyes…" Mary murmured.

"You know that when the King hears his son has died – there will be retribution?" James said.

"The bastards will have to beat Bonnie Prince Charlie first!" The room erupted in support and agreement.

That is what the Prince needed to hear. He needed to hear the people – the commoners – supporting his push for the throne.

Lord John Stuart rose then. "Here's a Toast then… To Bonnie Prince Charlie and his continued success!"

The crowd yelled back in agreement. The Prince and Lord Stuart raised their mugs, smiled, and drank deeply. They paid Mary… and the Prince left her a Gold Sovereign – where none but her would see it.

Time to head back to camp!

When Mary cleaned the table… she saw the flash of Gold. She picked it up and took it by the fire. When she saw what it was… she felt weak in the knees. She started crying. This would feed her family for a long time. She needed to thank these men – especially the one with the blue eyes… but alas…they were gone. But she would never forget those eyes…

The Prince promised himself that night that he would never forget those who make the nation work. The Commoner. The Peasant. Somehow, he would make their lives at least a bit easier. He swore it.

Chapter 24
Liaison

Connor got up in a rather cheery mood. Of course, today, he would meet his future wife. He knew it. He went to Derek's tent. He was in a pretty chipper mood as well. Of course – again – the sun was shining – and it wasn't an Afghanistan burn your ass to ash kind of day!

"Good morning, brother!" said Connor.

"Back atcha," said Derek. "Of course, you'll be gone when I could use you today."

"Well, I have a wife to meet. You can build the entire planet's future without me today!" Connor said with a smile.

Derek returned the smile. "Enjoy your tart for today. Though she may one day be your bride, we need Lord Forbes's favor right now. He holds the Key to Inverness and us beginning the process of modernization. If you – through your dull wit and attempt to charm can accomplish anything – his favor, is it."

"Point taken. I guess my charm and dazzling good looks will have to cover the gaps?" Joked Connor as he gave Derek a playful shove.

Derek stopped for a minute. "You do realize it was less than two weeks ago, and we were in Afghanistan getting ready for a helluva fight?"

"Aye – this still seems so surreal," said Connor.

Derek remarked, "That's because it bloody well is!"

"Well, I wonder what Lenora fashioned for breakfast today?"

"Looks like Porridge and Corn Cakes. Not the same meal as with the Prince – but it'll do. Especially with the fresh butter and honey!" said Connor.

The fast was broken, and bellies were full. Connor had to go his way and prepare to meet the Steward for Lord Forbes at Prince Charles' tent.

Derek needed to meet with Mac to prepare for the process of planning the future. Damn – that sounded rather daunting. But it is the truth! "We need to know our full talent pool and then get them thinking out of the box," thought Derek.

Connor sought out the new Horse master that the Prince had provided. He had also supplied everything needed to take care of the Stallions properly. He needed to come up with a name for his Stallion. All at once, he knew it – it would be Shadow Bane –dark and formidable – a good combination.

As he walked to the makeshift stable, the Horse Master exited his tent. "Ah, good morning to you, Lord McAndrew."

"And Good Morning to you, sir. I will need to leave here in an hour. Would you be so kind as to get Shadow Bane ready for a ride?" asked Connor.

"Shadow Bane? I like it, My Lord. A noble name for a noble beast!" said the Horse Master.

"If I remember correctly – your name is Robert McCloud. Is that correct? And you are from Ireland?" asked Connor.

"Yes, My Lord. To both," answered Robert.

"Where in Ireland?" asked Connor.

"A Baile beag – Swords. It's close to Dublin, My Lord," said Robert.

Connor began, "You will learn that neither my brother nor I are too formal in our words or actions. Would you mind if I called you Robert? You may have to put up with us for quite some time!"

"I would be quite honored," said Robert.

"Would you be so kind as to get some oats that I can give Shadow Bane so that I can introduce him to his name?" asked Connor.

"Indeed, my Lord. It would be my pleasure," said Robert.

As he had done nightly, he went to his Stallion and offered him his oats. The Horse nuzzled close to Connor. "Shadow Bane – that is your name now. We shall be a part of many adventures together!" He patted him and scratched his ears.

Well, enough of that. He had to get ready to meet his future wife! Connor headed to the creek. He would bathe at least and look presentable. The water was bloody cold. It was a lovely day – but still only April. "It's good that Lady Mary can't see my privates now! It's shriveled up from the cold!"

From there, he went to his tent. The Washerwoman had cleaned his best clothing that he had – an Anderson Tartan and a Blue Silk Shirt. He donned them and put his sword on. He looked the part of a

Scottish Lord. Next, he armed himself. His 9 mm and three magazines. He didn't know why – but knew instinctively that was simply a pragmatic way of thinking. He looked at his watch – it was almost 10. He went over to gather Shadow Bane – and mounted up. It was going to be a beautiful day.

He arrived at the Prince's tent at 1115. He was early, though Lord Forbes' Steward was still there waiting. The Prince walked over and appraised him. "Well," he said, "If I were a woman – I might find you at least tolerable!" and smiled with a twinkle in his eye.

"Thank you, Your Highness," said Connor. "I guess we best be off!" they were on their way. They headed Southwest from the Camp.

The Steward was silent and very business-like. Connor gathered that was probably that way with most. He was not a fan of being that way. He would have to endure it for now.

He asked the Steward how far Lord Forbes's Estate was and how long it would take them. The Steward answered that it was roughly 2.5 miles away, that they should be there by 1215, and that dinner would be at 1 pm sharp.

They had only gotten a little over a mile on the road to the Estate when they noticed six men riding towards them. Connor made his pistol more accessible and clicked off the safety.

When the men approached, one addressed them, "Ahhh, my Lords – it's a mighty fine Spring day."

Connor answered, "Indeed it is."

"I hate to ruin it for you," said the band leader.

"Oh?" queried Connor.

"You see, My Lord. The times are hard," he started.

"I'm sure they have been. Unfortunately, I am on a time schedule, and we must go," said Connor.

"I'm sure you are, indeed. But I'm afraid you're going to be rather late," he said.

"Oh, I have enough time as long as I leave now," said Connor.

The man and the others pulled their pistols.

"I was really hoping you weren't going to do that. You're really making a terrible mistake," said Connor.

"I am the Steward for Lord Forbes – don't make this mistake," said Robert. "My Lord won't stand for this so close to his Estate."

The men laughed. "You see, Gentlemen, with what you have in your purses and that steed of yours – we will fare quite nicely," said the leader.

Out of the blue, Shadow Bane reached up and bit the man on his thigh. Connor took the queue and pulled his pistol. He shot the leader in his chest and ducked behind him as he fell. His compatriots all fired their pistols from bucking horses – to no avail. They reached for their swords but did not know what was coming.

The Steward pulled his pistol and calmly shot one of the band right beneath his left eye. The man collapsed to the ground. He grabbed his sword and prepared to fight the man closest to him. He raised his sword to deflect the attack - when the man's sword was able to give him a gash on his right leg.

Connor shot the man in the neck, where he collapsed suddenly. Three more men were left. Connor brought his pistol up and shot two of the men who were brandishing their swords towards him. Both shots were in the chest, with an additional headshot in one of them.

When the lone highwayman saw he was the only one left, he turned to flee. Connor shot him in his right shoulder blade, and the man fell to the ground. He then turned to check on Robert.

Robert had placed his vest over the wound and said that he would be okay. "How did you do that?" asked Robert.

"Do what?" asked Connor.

"Shoot so many with your pistol?"

"I will show you later, Robert. Are you ok? Can you ride?" asked Connor.

"Yes, My Lord." It's not severe.

They heard the highwayman who was wounded cry out in pain. Connor got off of his horse – after giving Shadow Bane a hug and a promise of a treat after he bit the bastard that would rob them.

He checked the pulses of the men on the ground. Only one survived. Connor rolled the man over and smiled at him. "I tried to warn ya, ya stupid bastard." He punched him and knocked him out for good measure.

Robert said, "I sincerely hate to ask you this, my Lord. But could you throw him over his horse, get the other horses, and bring them?"

"Why?" asked Connor. Someone will find them and can probably use the horses. Your Lord doesn't need them." He decided to check their pockets and relieve them of their purses. Between the six of them, there were 52 pounds and 11 shillings. He promptly gave the money to Robert.

"What are you doing, My Lord?" asked Robert.

"Rewarding a man's bravery," said Connor. "You very well could have saved my life by the brilliant shot that you made."

"Sir! It's not necessary. You are in my charge!" exclaimed Robert.

"Oh, I am sure of it. Consider it a gift, then," said Connor.

"Thank you, My Lord. That is a very generous gift!"

"You are indeed welcome, sir!" said Connor. "Now, do I really need to put that bastard over a horse and bring the others?"

"Yes, My Lord. Especially since we are going to be late. That is the one thing that angers Lord Forbes. We need to soften the edge. I think your incapacitating these criminals will be very much appreciated. We had heard that there was a problem with highwaymen. You seem to have eradicated a few!"

Connor gathered the horses and threw the groaning man on his horse. He tied his hands to his feet so that he wouldn't be able to get loose or fall off of the horse. And he got blood on his kilt and shirt!!! "The Son of a Bitch bled on me!" he exclaimed. "I'm sure Lady Mary will appreciate that as well?"

Robert laughed. Bravery is always appreciated.

They were on their way. Connor kept it at a Canter, ensuring his unwanted guest would feel every bump.

They arrived at the Estate. Lord Forbes met him there with his brows furrowed. He had been angry, alright. The Steward explained all that happened. Lord Forbes' face went from anger… to surprise… to shock as the story unfolded. Robert faltered as he got off of his horse. He was pale, and then he passed out.

Connor jumped off of his horse to offer medical assistance. He knew how to treat battlefield wounds. He pulled the vest off of the wound and saw that it had been a sizeable wound on his thigh. There had been considerable blood loss – but it was a muscle that would heal, provided it was stitched up and didn't become infected.

Lord Forbes shouted to his servant, "Go get the Doctor!"

Connor explained there was no need that he could treat him.

Lord Forbes started to object. This was not just a servant – but a dear friend. Connor insisted, and Lord Forbes acquiesced. They took Robert to a bedroom.

Connor asked Lord Forbes if he had whiskey, a needle, and silk thread. These were brought to him immediately. Connor poured a good amount of whiskey into the wound. Robert groaned.

Connor said, "I know that hurts, lad. I'll have you fixed up in a jiffy."

Connor got the needle and coated it, his hands, and the thread with the whiskey. He curved the needle and deftly began to stitch the leg. He then asked if they had Comfrey and Tallow with a mortar and pestle to make a poultice. "Do you have White Willow Bark?" Yes – they had that as well. Excellent. He added that to the poultice to ease inflammation. He put it on the wound liberally and used clean linen strips as bandages. He was finished.

Connor promptly reached down and took a large draw from the whiskey. Lord Forbes had watched all in utter amazement – then laughed when Connor took the drink.

"I think that was well deserved!" he exclaimed.

"We're not quite finished, My Lord," Connor continued. "We have another to contend with – that wounded highwayman on his horse."

"Indeed, we do," said Lord Forbes angrily. He called for a few select servants to meet him in the courtyard, where the horses and highwayman remained. "Cut him down and yank the bastard off of his horse."

The servants did so. The man fell on his head and then onto his back – moaning as he did so. Lord Forbes asked Connor, "Is this a bastard that tried to rob you?"

"Yes, My Lord," affirmed Connor.

"Do you swear it?" Lord Forbes asked.

"Yes, My Lord," said Connor.

"Very well then. My punishment then is that this man will be hung by the neck until he is dead…now."

The verdict was given. The sentence was executed as One of the servants got a rope and threw one end over a large tree. A hangman's noose was fashioned and put over the man's head. The other end was tied to the man's saddle horn on his horse. He was coherent enough to understand what was happening and tried to resist. It accomplished little. The men got the horse to begin walking. At first, the man was drug by the horse by his neck slowly. The man began to struggle – but his wounded shoulder made the attempt almost laughable and yet pitiful at the same time. He would gasp for air as he was pulled closer to the tree. Finally, the horse pulled the rope taught. He was pulled to a standing position and finally began to swing. He used his good arm to try to pull off the noose. Once he was in position, the men tied the other end of the rope around the tree and watched him struggle to breathe…to maintain what was left of his miserable life. His face began to change colors…from red… to crimson…to gray as the last of his life gave way to the inevitable.

Once the spectacle was over, he was cut down and unceremoniously thrown into a field for the birds to eat out of sight of Castle Forbes.

Lord Forbes looked at Connor. "Well, my young Lord McAndrew – you have had a day!"

"Yes, My Lord – that is a huge understatement! And my clothing! Bloodstained and ruined! I'm afraid I will not make much of an impression on Lady Mary!" said Connor.

"You do look rather … strained?" He smiled. "Ah, My Lord McAndrew – Lady Mary has already seen you – at your worst, it would seem. And against my better judgment – she seems intrigued by you. Let's do this, My Lord. I have some clothing that will fit you. Perhaps you can bathe and clean up a bit – and see what you think of what we can provide? I am sure you are probably famished after your adventure today?"

"Yes, My Lord – to all. I would be honored and eternally grateful to clean up and sup with you and your family today. It is still somewhat early? I can't believe that it is only 2 pm. I would say that quite a lot had occurred over the last 2 hours!"

The servants rushed to make a bath. And Lord Forbes was true to his word. He indeed did have clothing for the young Lord to wear. The first thing that caught his eye – was the Light Blue silk coat! Silk?!?! A darker silk vest made it stand out. The Breeches were the exact light blue Silk. The shirt – was the finest fabric he had ever felt. It was also silk – but the whitest white he had ever seen. The stockings were white, and there were these leather shoes with large buckles that were black – and they shined – he could see his reflection in the shoe staring back at him in disbelief! He did have one problem, though – the damned Cravat. It was a Dark Blue, light blue, and white plaid pattern. He knew it was a precursor to the tie… but how the bloody hell do you tie it? Fortunately, one of the servants smiled at his bewilderment and asked him if he needed assistance. Connor eagerly accepted his assistance – and by 0230 – he was ready to present himself and meet Lady Mary. He sure did not want to screw this up!

It was announced that he was ready and came down the extravagant stairway. He walked over to Lord Forbes and thanked him for his generosity. Lord Forbes told Connor that his clothing had been washed and should be dry when he was ready to leave. At this point, Connor thanked him again. He also announced that he had sent a servant to the Prince to let him tell Lord Derek McAndrew – that he would be spending the night. There was too much to discuss.

Lord Forbes said, "Well, I know you didn't come to see me! Shall we go make the introduction?"

"Yes, My Lord," said Connor enthusiastically.

Connor was escorted to the drawing room. Lord Forbes had spared no expense. This room was exquisite. Connor was sure that a King would feel quite comfortable in this environment. He felt a bit intimidated. Lord Forbes then introduced him to his wife… Lady Mary Keith Forbes. Connor bowed and thanked her for her hospitality in allowing him to dine with the family.

Lady Forbes let him know how delighted she was to have him there. She also expressed her delight that he had been there to assist their Steward in defeating the dreadful Highwaymen.

And then… he saw her!

Standing before him was the most beautiful woman he had ever seen. He was already in love and didn't know how to process it. He wanted to drink in the vision that was in front of him. She stood about 5'2", maybe 5'3" – and maybe 110 pounds. Her hair was raven black with curls that framed her cream-colored face with a bit of rose blush to accent – that went to the middle of her shoulders. She had a diamond tiara in her hair – but it was her eyes – the bluest eyes he had ever seen. He was instantly lost in them.

He noticed she wore an emerald green dress with a white bodice – the Forbes colors. Pearls that encircled her neck and touched the top of her breasts brought a delicate touch of grace. She noticed how deeply he was looking into her eyes… her soul, really…and began to blush.

Lord Forbes said, "Lord Connor McAndrew, may I have the pleasure of introducing my daughter, Lady Mary Forbes, to you. Connor bowed deeply, gently grabbed her right hand, and kissed it gently.

"Finally!" Connor told Lady Mary, "I have wanted to meet you since I heard you sing on the Culloden Battlefield. Your voice graces my heart even still. It is indeed my pleasure to finally meet you!"

Lady Mary was almost speechless. "You heard me? You listened to me sing Lord McAndrew?"

"Indeed, My Lady. The Angels graced Culloden. My heart became eternally yours," said Connor.

"Lord McAndrew… you honor me. I am truly at a loss for words," said Lady Mary.

"Excellent!" said Lord Forbes. "I am famished! I am sure Lord McAndrew is, as well! We should at least let him get some nourishment before he faints from the exertions from today!" Lord Forbes smiled earnestly… and led them all to the dining room.

The guests went into the dining room. They were met by a small chamber of musicians who would entertain them while they dined.

Connor was overwhelmed by the dining room. Fine China and Crystal flourished. A Crystal Chandelier made the light sparkle throughout the room. The table settings were immaculate. Candles were added for an additional touch.

First of the faire were the Hor d'oeuvres: Smoked Salmon, Cheese, Caviar, and Canapes. Fine wines began to be served for all. The small talk began. Connor was seated to the right of Lady Mary. He could smell her perfume – a cinnamon, clove, vanilla scent. He noticed the small things. The texture of her voice as she spoke. She would laugh and tuck her hair behind her ears – pulling him into her as she cast her spell upon him. She asked him to tell the tale of the highwaymen and then what had happened in Culloden. He was careful with his words as he wove the tale.

She had heard how he had addressed them all – first in Gaelic, then French for the Prince, and then in English for the Duke. Lord Forbes had not heard the tale, so Connor was asked to tell the tale for all to hear. Then, the second course was served: A rich Lobster Bisque. Connor could have made a meal from the soup alone! But he knew more courses were coming and did not want to insult his benefactor and future father-in-law!

Connor spoke of his words – and yes – it was as she described. He attempted to be modest – but Lord Forbes would have none of that! "I heard from the Prince that you and your men obliterated the Cannon and the Calvary. All of a sudden, he felt rather uncomfortable. He performed his duty. Not for fame or ambition – but because it was his duty. He expressed that opinion… and won the heart of the future father-in-law as well. Lady Forbes began a series of conversations – regarding his take on the Prince… what he thought of their home… Culloden Wood… Make conversation… but he felt like it was an "audition."

The next course was Dover Sole with a light brown sauce with a strong hint of black pepper. It was cooked perfectly. He was finally able to have a conversation with Lady Mary. What were her hopes and dreams? What were the things that she enjoyed? What did she wish to do or become as time moved forward? She began to open her heart in a way she had never done before. She did express her hopes. She wanted to be able to travel and have an adventure with whoever would be her husband. She wanted children – lots of them. She wanted to enjoy simple things –quiet conversation and children's laughter.

Next came the main course. Prime Rib encrusted with black peppercorn and salt. Truffles in mashed potatoes, roasted vegetables, and a salad with edible flowers with a delicate vinaigrette. More wine – this from France. Connor was no longer paying attention to anything or anyone else in the room. He was enraptured with Lady Mary… and her with him.

Now for dessert… A Trifle, several pastries, and tarts. The Trifle was made with a sponge cake, a custard, and fresh blueberries topped with a whipped cream. That is what Connor asked for, and he received a large piece cut by Lady Forbes herself. "Well, maybe I charmed her as well!" Thought Connor. A Claret accompanied the dessert. Absolute heaven! The meal had taken several hours! It seemed only as minutes.

Lord Forbes then announced that the men would retire to his study to talk. Of course, that meant talking politics, smoking a cigar, and drinking some scotch. Lady Mary seemed disappointed but accepted that it was part of the ritual. On the good side, though – was that she could talk to her mother about Lord McAndrew... even she was surprised and somewhat confused about how she felt about this young man.

The ladies retired to the parlor. That is where they could talk. As soon as they sat down, Lady Forbes asked her servant for some Cherry Brandy. Lady Mary thought that sounded quite nice as well. The drinks were served, and the conversation erupted from both parties.

Lady Forbes said... "Oh my love... I think that he is smitten. What do you think? How do you feel?"

"Mum... I cannot even describe how I feel! I expected to be somewhat disinterested, especially after his exploits from today. I anticipated he would be arrogant... but he was not! I think he had my heart after saying I had his after I sang to our boys in Culloden!"

"He seems to have several skills... But I wonder if he is too good to be true?" asked Lady Forbes.

"Mother! Did you see how he looked at me? Did you see his eyes? And when he spoke to me... he actually listened to what I had to say! He wanted my opinion! I am flushed just thinking of him now as we speak!" exclaimed Lady Mary.

"You don't say!" teased her mother.

Meanwhile – in the study. Lord Forbes pulled out his best Scotch and poured heavily for Lord McAndrew. He wanted to see how the young man handled his liquor. He pulled out cigars from Virginia. "Alright, young man – it appears you may have won my daughter's heart. You have won my attention. What do you think that it will take to win this crown for our dear Prince?"

"Where do I begin?" asked Connor. "First of all – thank you so much for your hospitality today. Besides my afternoon encounter, I cannot remember a day as good as today. Second – the Scotch and Cigar? Good sir! Those are to die for!' Connor continued, "Lord Forbes, your daughter already has my heart. I did not lie or exaggerate when I made that declaration to her. And finally... to win the crown? I believe much...but it can be overcome. All of the obstacles can be overcome."

"How would you overcome these 'obstacles'?" asked Lord Forbes.

"Before I begin, I must ask you a question, My Lord."

"Please do," said Lord Forbes.

"How much do you know about us, My Lord?" Queried Connor cautiously.

"The Prince told me that you and your men were from the future – though he would not specify much about it. He had mentioned that it was Lord Stuart that had made the arrangements – that's about all that I know," said Lord Forbes.

Connor pulled out his pistol and showed it to Lord Forbes. He removed the magazine, then the chambered shell. "This, My Lord, is the weapon I used in my struggle with the Highwaymen today." Connor pulled out the shell and showed Lord Forbes how to extract a shell and load the pistol. He also explained that he had 13 Rounds in his double-stacked magazine.

Lord Forbes' eyes grew wide. Connor then explained that the gunpowder was actually in the shell…how a rifled barrel worked, and how it improved the range and the accuracy. Connor asked if Lord Forbes had seen the Duke fall. He had not. Connor explained that the kill shot came from over 1000 yards away. This was almost too much.

Then Connor talked about his and Derek's grand plan. "Imagine, My Lord… this scenario. Do you remember how we eliminated the Calvary? Well, imagine this – the shells that we used there – are being produced by the thousands here. Do you have a musket that I can see to show you?"

Lord Forbes retrieved his musket. Connor took the musket and acted as if it were a breakaway shotgun. "Imagine if you could have the musket "Breakaway" come apart close to the stock." He then grabbed one of his 9mm shells and continued… "Once it is apart – you put in the shell, then close it back together– and you are ready to shoot at least 200-400 yards accurately. How much of an advantage do you think that would be? Especially if we had 10,000 of those rifles, and they could be fired at a rate of 4-6 per minute. How long would it take for the British to be defeated? Even if we could only make 1,000? Along with our equipment?"

Stunned silence.

Connor continued, "Here is what we think needs to happen to move the Brits where we want them. We need the Prince to become the King of Scotland. That information will slowly get to the King. He will have no idea what happened to the Duke and those men. That will put much doubt into his and his General's planning. He must call back thousands of troops from France and the War of Austrian Ascension. We need him to attack who will be King Charles openly. We would have the respect of the world when they are defeated. I could see 100,000 men invading Scotland. I want to steer him to Falkirk and defeat them there. From a logistical standpoint – getting here with sufficient troops and supplies will be difficult. He will want to try to quash our rebellion, so he must heavily arm and fortify his troops. It could be spring next year before he gets his troops here. By Fall – with your help – we could have at least 1000 rifles… by Spring next year – we should have at least 10,000 of the weapons we need to defeat him soundly. I would like it to be the same as Culloden. Either no quarter given – or prisoners taken and held until the war is over – with no word getting back to the King. We have to keep him off of his normal expectations. We need to keep him unbalanced and unsure of how to move forward. Thoughts?"

Silence again… then, "He'd be fucked, and King Charles of Scotland – would be King of the British Isles! I'll be a Son of A Bitch, Lord McAndrew! You got me thinking we could do this?!?!?"

"That's the point, My Lord. But we will need you and the other Nobles to make it happen," said Connor.

"What can I do?" asked Lord Forbes.

"We need credibility with the other Nobles. We will need you to help us gather the best and brightest artisans, blacksmiths, and metallurgists to make this happen. We could use Chemists and Alchemists – and we will need to construct the facilities to get everything started. We are going to teach you some 20th-century technology in the process. My Lord… Scotland will never be the same. We will be a global world power. No one will be able to defeat us…. For decades. I could even see France or Spain invading when King Charles of Scotland became the King of the British Isles. They will think us weak. That will be a bad decision. We will then have the moral authority to attack them in their home countries…and once we have applied our abilities – we will also be the dominant power on the seas," said Connor.

"Done," said Lord Forbes. "I just want to have my hands in all the new technology you will develop. If it is as I believe it will be – a small percentage will dominate every asset I own."

"Okay, Lord McAndrew. You have my permission to court and wed my daughter when she feels ready to do so. You have proven your value. But understand this, sir – if you hurt my daughter – especially physically abuse her – she has my heart as a father. I will kill you dead, sir. Do we have an understanding?" Lord Forbes' face turned to stone as he said this.

"Yes, My Lord. I fully understand. Your daughter will never lack nor be injured by me. Our families will grow together as Scotland grows!" said Connor.

With that, they toasted another glass of fine Scotch. Hands shook…the deal was made. The future was brighter than Connor's wildest hopes had been before the day began.

"Come," said Lord Forbes.

Connor did so without question. He followed Lord Forbes to the Parlor. He opened the door, and his wife and Lady Mary were slightly startled. Lord Forbes asked his daughter directly:" Do you wish to see this man again?"

Lady Mary looked at Lord McAndrew and said, "Father… I want nothing more."

"Very well, daughter. I have told Lord McAndrew that he may have your hand in marriage when and if you are prepared for him to do so. The decision will be solely yours. If you decide to kick his arse out the door – you may do so. You will be the sole decision-maker in this matter. Is that understood?"

Lady Mary ran to her father – kissed him on his cheek, hugged him, and thanked him for his blessing. This was about to get really interesting, she thought!

She then walked slowly to Lord Connor McAndrew…curtsied ever so politely… walked up to him… her nose right in front of his… "Are you ready for this, Lord Connor McAndrew?"

"More than you will ever know, My Lady," said Connor.

Lady Mary then wrapped her arms around his neck… and gave him a long kiss. She stood back, looked him in the eye, and said, "My Lord, you are all I have ever dreamed… and more. May we wed soon! I will talk to my Mum… and we'll make the arrangements – if that suits you?"

Connor looked at his now fiancé. "That is more than I could've ever hoped for!"

They hugged tightly – until Lord Forbes cleared his throat – and Lady Mary backed away.

"Can this even be real?" thought Connor to himself. He would marry her – just as he believed when he heard her in Culloden!

Chapter 25
Groundwork

While Connor left for what would be an adventurous day, Derek and Mac would have their hands full as well. The Officers met to discuss what had occurred and where they were in their planning process.

Out of the 150 men of Delta Company, there were 42 Engineers:
12 Mechanical Engineers
10 Civil Engineers
7 Electrical Engineers
3 Aerospace Engineers
3 Petroleum Engineers
7 Chemical Engineers
There were also:
10 Metallurgists
10 Gunsmiths
14 Carpenters
8 Doctors/PAs/Nurses (Medics)
8 Farmers
6 Herders
12 Mechanics
9 Teachers
12 Munitions/Explosive Technicians
9 Oilfield Drillers/Workers
10 Machinists

Of Course, most of these men had other skill sets as well. But we now have to focus on our major priorities, thought Derek.

So together, the Officers came up with the primary focus points to concentrate on for now:
1.   Gun Powder
     a.   Bat Guano
     b.   Sulfur

       c.   Charcoal
2.   Replace ammo – focus on 7.62 mm.
       a.   Brass
       b.   Lead (?)
       c.   Copper plating – need to develop plating. (?)
3.   Develop primers.
4.   Develop Loaders.
5.   Develop Welding
6.   Develop New firearms for Scots.
7.   Develop Biodiesel.
8.   Water Filtration/Hygiene factors to prevent disease.
9.   Develop Boot Camp for Highlanders

Derek liked the planning process. Execution was going to be a challenge. He hoped Connor was convincing Lord Forbes to come to their cause. He knew Connor thought he needed a wife… He understood – but he hoped he was thinking with the right brain. This was too important to screw up. Getting all of the above right would ensure the defeat of the British.

He and the officers agreed this would be a good start. Once they met with Lord Forbes and other wealthy nobles, it would be easy to convey the message. He wanted to avoid bankers at all costs. Investors had to be thoroughly convinced and ready to pledge fealty to who would be the new King. Maybe allow others once the next large contingent of British are defeated.

The officers agreed that they would need to draw a lot of the plans. Either using parchment or linen paper would probably work the best. They would need to get with the Prince and the Nobles in Culloden and convince them to continue with what would be a year or two long venture – but would ensure their victory.

Derek got up in front of Mac, Ross, Gordon, and MacLeod. "Alright, lads – I think we have a decent gameplan – with the primary needs going forward. It will take a lot of money to get this started. We must bring the wealthy Lords to the same conclusion to help get this kicked off. Hopefully, we can get them and all of Inverness involved. It will take a major infrastructure rebuilding and truly innovative thinking to make this work. We need to bring those Lords here, do what we did for the Prince, and show them what we can do. I'm pretty excited about the process. Based on the capabilities of our men – with what raw resources are available – we should be able to complete all of the tasks required to take on and defeat a major invasion."

Derek continued, trying to get a feel for what everyone was thinking. "I believe that we have three basic items to focus on, which encompasses the nine items we discussed: 1. Ammo, 2. Firearms, and 3 Miscellaneous items. Ross: I want you in charge of the ammunition. MacLeod: I want you in charge of firearm development and Gordon – You and your team will be in charge of the company's innovation team. Of course, input from all of you into each division is encouraged. Look for gaps that need to be closed. Look for shortcomings that can be improved upon. Don't get stuck on any one way of doing anything. We must be creative. You each have a list of each man's different skill sets at his disposal. Pick them out for your teams. I don't care about rank. I care about skills. Mac and I will see if we can meet here with Prince Charles, Lord Murray, Lord Forbes, and Lord John Stuart."

"The sooner we get this started, the more will be able to get done. I would like to have Inverness as our HQ. We will probably need those carpenters soon to start the construction to get these things built. Put your teams together. I want them to work on these projects in 24 hours – even if it's just discussing plans. Dismissed," said Derek.

Derek and Mac went to get their horses to see the Prince… Damn – being able to use a Cell phone would come in handy right now. This having to go everywhere to communicate is a pain in the ass. We might have to set up a radio with the Prince to stay in touch without riding everywhere. He started laughing to himself – as he thought of the scare it would probably give the Prince the first time he heard one!

At least with the Horse Master – it was a quick process in getting them saddled and being able to get on the way…but Derek did have to admit – it felt good riding. The weight of the world was off his shoulders as he rode "Riogh"- Monarch in Gaelic – that is what he decided would be the name of his steed. A Monarch was what they were fighting for, after all.

They got to the Prince's Tent – and when the Prince heard them speaking to Fiona – he called for them to come in. Lord Murray was with him, trying to discuss the future. "Your timing is quite advantageous," said the Prince.

Mac and Derek dismounted and went into the tent, bowing before the Prince and giving a nod to Lord Murray. They were equals after all. Lord Murray nodded back in respect.

Out of curiosity – the Prince asked them, "Well -what have you been up to since yesterday?"

Mac answered, "Your Highness, we have been determining our troops' intellectual and skill levels. We know their military skill sets, but we need to be able to utilize their skills with what we will need moving forward, from ammunition and what that entails… to a suitable firearm that can be produced quickly for the Highlanders… to miscellaneous items like fuel for our equipment. This requires a large jump in the current technology available… which means an investment. Probably a substantial investment – which is why we are here, Your Highness."

"Lord Murray and I were discussing just the thing. I fully understand the need to produce what we need for the Military right now. But once I am King – is that something that we can do that will benefit everyone in Great Britain?"

"Your Highness," answered Derek. "There are huge techniques that can also move from military production to civilian production. We can improve textile production, home and building construction, infrastructure development… there is so much, Your Highness! I can't even begin to tell you the benefits that will benefit our Country – even in reducing illness. But we can't do it by ourselves. We will need Alchemists, Chemists, blacksmiths, Metal Workers, Gunsmiths… We could use the entire town of Inverness to get this started!"

Lord Murray quipped, "Lord McAndrew – I can appreciate your enthusiasm – and I can also appreciate the military strength that you now occupy – but this seems like quite the exaggeration, don't you think?"

"Not at all, Lord Murray," said Derek. "Here is what I propose, under strict secrecy, however. We want the honor of Your Highness, Lord Murray, of course, as well as The Duke of Perth, Lord James Drummond; The Earl of Kilmarnock, Lord William Boyd; The Duke of Gordon, Lord George Gordon; Lord David Ogilvy, and of course, The 3rd Earl of Granard, Lord George Forbes – to come to our camp so that we can show some of what we will be able to do if we have their backing. We will have to be extremely careful with our ammunition – but there is so much more than the military aspects of what we can produce if we work together. The opportunity for products to be produced and shipped globally is another enticing part of what we can offer if given the chance. The potential wealth from the exports alone is staggering.”

Derek began, “This is a change of subject – but it will give you an idea of our potential using what is available. Is there a cave with bats nearby? I seem to remember there are several close to Inverness?”

Lord Murray laughed. “Yes, My Lord, that is a dramatic change of subject. But there are several caves of which I am aware. Those are evil places, sir.”

“Not necessarily, My Lord. Believe it or not – there is much that can benefit from a cave – and one that we need for our gunpowder to work in our cartridges. We need Potassium Nitrate – a lot of it. Bat Guano is an excellent source for producing it. We will also need Sulfur and charcoal to make it work.”

“Interesting,” said Lord Murray.

The Prince interjected, “You will be amazed, Lord Murray. Trust me. Lord McAndrew – I will work with those that you have requested. These are men who can be trusted. They also have a business mind, knowledge, and connections to make good things happen. Our men have been resting and recovering for almost a week. We will need to either send them home to plant and take care of their farms - or be able to provide for them.”

“Here’s a thought, Your Highness – and I am sure that you would need to have this discussion with those that supplied those men first – send them home for now so they can plant. It will take time before we are ready for them – but as long as we know they can come in time for us to train them in their new weapons and some military tactics and orders – as well as fighting – then it might work for them as well,” said Mac.

“Your Highness, would you be acceptable for technology over 200 years distant to be in your tent?” asked Derek.

The Prince laughed. “Well, Lord McAndrew – I suppose it would depend on what it does?”

"Imagine, Your Highness, us being able to communicate from our camp to your tent? Instantaneously? Being able to talk with you directly with what we call a 'Radio.'"

"It sounds a bit unnerving. I would at least entertain the thought. I suppose we will see," said the Prince. "Go get your camp ready for guests tomorrow. You will have your chance."

"Your Highness—I sincerely hope it is more than a chance. Their support may determine if you can get the crown or not. If we can't re-supply – we cannot guarantee the crown," said Derek.

With that – the meeting was over. Derek and Mac went to get their horses to head back to Camp Striker. "Well, Mac… what do you think?" asked Derek.

"We made headway. We need to be able to show off a bit – but we have to be careful with our assets. They need to see the power of the 50 Cal and the Mortars – perhaps a grenade and a grenade launcher. The Drones as well," said Mac.

"I wonder how Connor is doing with Forbes. I hope he is taking care of the primary focus, not just Lady Mary." Derek Laughed.

Just before they left – Derek heard his name being called. "Lord McAndrew!" He spun Riogh around to face the person who addressed him.

"Lord McAndrew – I am Malcolm Sinclair – the Household Steward for Lord Forbes."

Derek looked concerned. "Is everything okay? Is Lord McAndrew okay?"

"Yes, My Lord," said Malcolm. "He is fine. He did have quite the day, however. Six Highwaymen accosted him on the way to Lord Forbes' Estate – which he and Steward Robert McCloud dispatched. However, that is not why I am here, My Lord. I am here to inform you that your brother, Lord McAndrew, will stay the night at Lord Forbes' Estate. Since the assault occurred, it took quite some time to get the day back on track. I am sure that you can appreciate that?"

"Leave it to my brother to add excitement to an ordinarily uneventful day!" said Derek. "But he is okay? He was well received?"

"Indeed, he was, Lord McAndrew. Steward McCloud was wounded, and Lord Connor McAndrew stitched him right up. I think Lady Mary was also quite impressed!" gleamed Steward Sinclair.

"Was that all then?" asked Derek.

"Yes, My Lord," said Steward Sinclair.

"Would you be so kind as to pass a word privately to Lord McAndrew if you have the opportunity?" asked Derek.

"My Lord," said Malcolm.

"Please let Lord McAndrew know that I fully understand that love has no time constraint and can be limitless in its possibilities – that I will need to have him get his arse out of bed early – because there is much work to be done. We will have a lot of important visitors to camp tomorrow," said Derek.

"Should I quote you, My Lord?" asked Malcolm with a smile.

"Indeed, Steward Malcolm Sinclair. And you have my permission to embellish with more personal profanity if you wish. He is my brother, after all. He would expect no less?" Derek said with a smile.

Steward Malcolm Sinclair left, leaving Derek and Mac to return to the Camp. They had a lot to prepare for tomorrow.

Chapter 26
Sealed

It was time for bed. Before being escorted to his bed chamber, Steward Malcolm Sinclair came to Connor with a message from his brother - Lord Derek McAndrew. "Please let Lord McAndrew know that I fully understand that love has no time constraint and can be limitless in its possibilities – that I will need to have him get his lazy arse out of bed early – because there is much work to be done. We will have a lot of important visitors to camp tomorrow." Connor laughed and asked him to wake him at 8 in the morning. The servant said he would make sure that it happened.

"Connor expected to be escorted to his room to prepare for bed. He had no night shirt – which is what he expected would be required for him to get ready for bed. A servant escorted him to his bed chamber, where he was given a water basin, and a nightshirt was laid on the bed before him. He had several candles lighting up the room. Though he could not see it as well as he could see in the daylight hours – he felt the silk sheets. This would be the most comfortable sleep he had ever had. And Lord knows he needed it. It had indeed been a day. It had been the worst and the best in only a six-hour span of time!

He looked around and saw a chamber pot in his room. Thank goodness! He was not quite sure what he would do to relieve himself! He washed himself, used the chamber pot, and put on his nightshirt. He had just laid down when he heard a light knock at his door. He opened the door, and a servant looked at him and said, "Come with me, My Lord."

Connor shrugged his shoulders and left with the servant. He approached another bedroom. Lord Forbes was outside the door. "Alright, young man. You are officially engaged to my daughter – but you have only had a minor conversation from today. We have a custom called bundling – where you will be allowed to share the same bed as my daughter tonight. There will be a board in between the two of you. This is for CONVERSATION ONLY – am I clear? I am expecting you to be a man of honor with my daughter. You will have time for intimacy once you are married. If I find out that you have dishonored my daughter – I will personally slit your throat. Is that understood?"

Connor gulped. He knew Lord Forbes was serious. He would behave himself. He swore on his honor! But to be able to speak to her privately! I'm exhausted... but a little sleep deprivation is a small price to pay.

Connor's heart picked up its pace. Was he actually nervous? Really? What the Hell is that all about? He was so glad he went to the bathroom before he was escorted in. That would've been a bit awkward. Of course – Lord Forbes in the room did not make it any easier.

There were many candles and a couple of lanterns to light the bedroom. Lady Mary was standing in a nightgown, smiling and blushing simultaneously. Connor was trying not to be excited – especially in front of Lord Forbes and his wife, Lady Forbes. Lord Forbes unceremoniously pulled the covers back. Connor was having a hard time keeping from laughing uproariously at the discomfort this entire situation was heaping upon his future father-in-law. "For me?" smiled Connor. Lord Forbes scowled. He was not amused. That made it even more laughable and more challenging to contain. Connor got into bed. As Lord Forbes began to step back – Connor said – for whatever reason... this just came out... "Aren't you going to tuck me in?"

That was all it took. Lady Forbes burst into laughter. As did Lady Mary. It was all Lord Forbes could do to keep from unceremoniously punching Connor in the mouth. At this time, Lady Forbes was bent over laughing as she saw her husband's uncomfortable frustration with this entire situation. Finally – with the absurdity of it all...even Lord Forbes cracked a smile.

"Alright, My Lord Connor McAndrew. We have an agreement – and I expect you to abide by that agreement. As you can tell, I am not at all happy with this situation, and I only reluctantly agreed. My comment to you before you came into this room still stands. You WILL be a gentleman to my daughter. Agreed?" stated Lord Forbes firmly.

"Agreed, My Lord. I will be a gentleman. Tonight is for talking," said Lord McAndrew.

With that, Lanterns and most of the candles were removed. And the talking began. Connor was reticent about giving all of his information to his bride-to-be. He would talk more about the future as they began to speak to each other from the heart. Connor actually asked her thoughts and opinions on not only Prince Charles and the Jacobite Rebellion but also about global affairs. He was beginning to understand that Lady Mary was well-educated. He even spoke of trade, farming, and animal husbandry. There was not much that he asked – that she was not well-versed in.

Lady Mary was totally shocked. Never in her life had any man asked her opinion. Lord McAndrew not only asked – but then challenged her thoughts and assumptions. In her 19 years of life – she had never had a more stimulating conversation.

Lady Mary asked Connor questions as well. She would get frustrated when he answered with a question – but she also saw that he was leading her down a path where the answers would have to be limited until she knew him better and he trusted her more.

Finally, the better part of the day began to defeat Connor's desire to continue the conversation. He looked at his watch, and it was almost 3 am… Of Course, Lady Mary wanted to see the watch. She was mesmerized. She could read it in the dark? What kind of sorcery was this? Connor explained how the watch worked and that it was purely mechanical – not witchcraft.

When Connor began to snore softly during a break in the conversation, Lady Mary decided to take advantage of the situation. He was going to be her husband, after all. She stood up and removed her gown. She tiptoed over to where Connor was sleeping and pulled back his covers. She climbed into bed next to him and started to kiss him. At first- Connor was startled and jumped back a bit. Then he realized it was Lady Mary next to him… and she was naked. He began to kiss her back in earnest as he grabbed her and pulled her to him. Then he stopped.

At first, Lady Mary was puzzled. Why did he stop? It was apparent that he felt it as much as she. He got out of bed and picked Lady Mary up. He told her how very much he wanted her – but he had given his word of honor to her father. What kind of a man would he be if he broke his word while sleeping beneath the roof of the man who had consented to allow him to marry Lady Mary? He had her stand up, held her briefly, and kissed her deeply. He then put her nightshirt back on her. She didn't like it – but she understood. And though Connor may not have been aware of it – what he did and how he acted towards her had installed a bond that would not easily be broken. He could have had her easily – yet his word of honor meant something; her father would greatly value that when she spoke with him about the incident. In the meantime, both agreed that it was time to go to sleep.

Connor woke with a start. The sun was rising. He reached up to feel Mary over their centerboard, realizing she was already up and had left the bedroom. He arose as well. He remembered the message from Derek. He went to his room and put on the kilt he had worn the day before. It had been hand-washed, and all the stains had been removed from the kilt and his silk shirt.

He walked to the dining room and was greeted by the smell of a large breakfast. Bacon, eggs, Corncakes, honey…some smoked meats, cheese, and COFFEE! Yes! It was hot, fresh, and tasted amazing. Lord only knew how much he needed the caffeine this morning!

He looked over and saw Lord Forbes – and he was staring back at him – and actually smiled. "Good Morning, Lord McAndrew. I trust you slept well?"

"Indeed, I did, Lord Forbes. Your daughter is quite enchanting, and you, sir – have educated her extremely well," said Connor.

"I'm glad you see that, sir. I'm also glad that I do not have to slit your throat this morning. It would have made for a rough beginning of the day." Lord Forbes Chuckled.

"I would have to agree with that as well, My Lord," said Connor with a smile.

"You sir, are a man of honor, my young Lord McAndrew. I am to let you know – Prince Charles summoned us this morning. We are to go to your camp. Your brother and Lord McKenzie have some things planned for us today," said Lord Forbes.

Lord Forbes sent his servant to get the Horse Master so their horses would be ready. Connor asked if they were to meet the Prince at the Prince's Tent or go straight to the camp. Lord Forbes said that he was instructed to meet the Prince at the camp and only to bring Connor. "I am sure the Prince needs us to open our purses to fund this venture with promises to repay with ownership stakes, gold, or land once he has the crown.”

“That makes perfect sense to me,” said Connor.

They mounted their stallions and began towards the Striker camp. The weather looked like a possibility of rain. At first, the prospect wasn’t appealing to Connor – it dawned on him that poor weather would make it easier to appeal to the Noblemen since Black Powder was so undependable in poor weather conditions. Our firearms operate well in any weather condition – extreme heat or cold can be problematic – but the rain in this weather would not be a detriment to our firearms.

It was only 30 minutes to their camp by horseback. Connor saw the sentries – whereas Lord Forbes was oblivious. Connor felt secure with them patrolling the area.

They entered the camp and saw Derek and Mac working feverishly to prepare everything for their display. The Prince must have supplied a few tables to show their wares. Though Connor understood the need for the Nobility, it still didn’t prevent him from feeling like a high-priced prostitute, selling his wares to the highest bidder.

Derek walked up to the pair, as did the Horse master and his helper, to take care of the horses.

The men dismounted. Derek walked to Lord Forbes, “My Lord Forbes – it is so good to see you again. Welcome, My Lord, to our humble abode.”

“I am delighted to be here, Lord McAndrew. I am anticipating quite the spectacle, My Lord.” Derek appeared somewhat concerned with that statement and was relieved when he saw Lord Forbes smile. “You must relax, My Lord, I am already convinced – despite your brother’s somewhat dull wittedness…” Lord Forbes’s eyes lit up, and he and Derek laughed at Connor’s expense.

“To be honest, Lord Derek McAndrew - he had me when he flew a paper – I think he called it an ‘Airplane’? Additionally, how he handled a group of highwaymen and treated my daughter.”

Derek laughed and looked at Connor, “Well, it appears you were quite busy in 24 hours!”

Connor laughed… “Just making it up as I go, brother! Incidentally, I am now engaged, sir.”

Derek's eyes were raised. That was interesting. Hopefully, it is for all the right reasons, thought Derek. Lord Forbes was a strong ally… but would be a disastrous enemy.

With that, some whistles were coming from the East. That meant the other guests would be coming around the corner soon. And sure enough, they were coming over the hill and headed down to the camp.

What was difficult was treating the Prince with the deference that is expected. Familiarity is a gift full of dangerous opportunities for the too-familiar remark or statement. They had to be careful – there must be no hint of favoritism – but only of a relationship built on pragmatism.

"Welcome to our Camp, Your Highness and My Lords. You are now and always welcome here. Before we begin, may I remind you that our men are unfamiliar with addressing those with Nobility. I ask you please to give us your indulgence. If anything is said or insinuated that could offend – please understand – that no insult is intended," said Lord McKenzie.

Everyone nodded in agreement.

"Also, My Lords – we will be using a minimal amount of our ammunition. We will guard what we have jealously until we can produce the ammunition we need." Explained Mac.

Eight men – would determine their immediate plans and set their course. Derek didn't like those few who had so much of an influence – but this is the world they lived in. Of course, these men were willing to sacrifice everything to support the Prince before they knew they would have a shot at overcoming the English. Courage was not lacking. Let's hope they have an even better business acumen.

There was a clearing roughly 2000 yards in diameter. There was a table at the edge of the clearing. Each weapon to be demonstrated was on the table, except for the 50-caliber weapon attached to the top of the Mastiff with a gunner on board.

The weapons that would be demonstrated were a 50-caliber machine gun, a grenade launcher, a grenade, a mortar, and a bit of plastic explosives. Each of the Lords would be given a ride in the Mastiff. On the table was a set of binoculars for each of the men, as well as an iPad and a drone.

Each of the participants made themselves ready and steeled themselves. They had no idea what to expect.

The Mastiff came rumbling into position. Each of the men was told to look at the far tree line. There was a prominent target that could be seen. They were told the distance was almost 2000 yards to the other side. They were instructed to watch and to be prepared for a loud "Bang" as the machine gun was aimed – and prepared to fire. All at once, the countdown was given… "BOOM!" the Lords watched and then saw in amazement that the shot had reached the target and hit close to the Bullseye. Everyone was astonished. Especially the man that had made the shot. Aiming the Machine Gun on the Mastiff to that level of precision – while not impossible – is a challenge.

Next was the 81 mm. It was already in position. The Lords were asked to cover their ears and to watch the target they had just witnessed. The round was fired – and the target disappeared – followed by a large "Boom!" seconds later. The Lords – and the Prince gasped.

Next – came the grenade launcher. Its effective range was roughly 300 yards. The crew had built a target for all to see. They were warned about the shot to come… "THUMP!" … it wasn't that loud. The explosion was not that loud either, but they could see the fragments impacting the target through the binoculars.

Next was the hand grenade. They were assigned a place behind a temporary wall. They were told how the grenade worked and were shown where to stand and to cover their ears. "Grenade away!" The man who threw the grenade turned away, covered his ears, and felt the concussion from the grenade. They were able to walk over to the target and saw the effect of all of the fragments – and each thought of the horror of these weapons being aimed towards them… they shuddered in their own way.

They were then asked to look at a large tree roughly 1000 yards away. It was an oak - probably 40' tall and at least 24" in diameter. Derek radioed the Combat Engineer, "Remove the tree on my order."

"Aye, sir," came the reply. That action startled all there.

"Where the bloody hell did that voice come from?" queried Lord Murray.

Derek smiled. That's the reaction he wanted. "From my radio, Lord Murray. This would be a device that I would like to produce eventually – but that will be after Prince Charles is King. This, Your Highness, is what I mentioned to you earlier. It's set up a bit differently – but it would allow me to communicate with you from our camp to yours. But now, Your Highness and My Lords, please observe the tree."

Derek picked up his radio. "Combat Engineer… On my Mark… Three… Two… One… EXECUTE!"

At first… there was a low "thud" … almost imperceptible to the ears. Something you could feel… From this distance, one could see the tree shudder… then in an instant, it was enveloped by fire, smoke, dirt…, and a blinding flash of destruction as it consumed the once mighty oak… Then, the noise and the shockwave startled all in attendance. As the smoke cleared – all were stunned into silence… where once that mighty oak had stood… nothing remained.

"Your Highness, and My Lords – that is all the ammunition we shall use today. However, I want you each to be able to use the Rifles that each of our men carry into combat. Once again – these will be able to be developed – or at least something similar – but it will take much more time. We have an idea for something far superior to the British Smooth Bore Musket. I will show a drawing of what we propose. Lord McKenzie, please provide our guest with one of our Rifles."

Lord McKenzie provided each with a Rifle. He then stood at the front with one in his capable hands. He instructed those in attendance on the overall capabilities of the Rifle. He then discussed how to handle the weapon safely. Each of the Rifles had three shells in the magazine. There were targets 100 yards away. McKenzie raised his rifle and hit the bullseye. He then encouraged everyone to do the same. He instructed them to aim and pull the trigger when they were prepared to do so.

Prince Charles – already accustomed to the Rifle, pulled it up and fired his three shots. Each one hit the target – one was close to a Bullseye. Everyone was astounded…including the Prince. The other Lords aimed their rifles and slowly pulled the triggers tentatively. Then again, and then the final time. Each felt an adrenaline rush. This was enjoyable! They all had smiles on their faces when Mac approached them all. He instructed them on clearing the chamber to ensure it was no longer loaded and how to safely stow the firearm.

Mac, Derek, and Connor left the Noble class for a few minutes to talk among themselves. After a few minutes, Connor addressed them, "Your Highness, and My Lords, may I ask you to climb aboard our Mastiff. We will take you to the location of the targets so that you can better assess the destructive power of each of the firearms presented."

The Prince was first, then was followed by the rest. Connor, Derek, and Mac were the last ones in the vehicle. Each of the Lords and the Prince – some of the most powerful men in the nation – became as children when the vehicle began to move. Their excitement filled the air once the initial fear and trepidation had passed.

The first stop was the 50-cal target. You could see the target had been pierced… from 2000 yards away. Everyone shook their heads in dismay. Lord Drummond asked, "How the bloody hell can anyone fight and survive such carnage?" The question remained unanswered.

The next stop was the 81 mm target site – It was explained to the audience that the mortar they had heard was over a mile from the target when it was fired. When they got to the target site – what was pointed out to everyone was the fragments – the shrapnel that could be seen piercing through the leaves of trees…but it was the hole! Several feet deep! Terrifyingly effective. No doubt.

The next stop was the tree. Oh, My Lord! What a wretched sight. The hole was deep, and the stump of what was left had been blown dozens of yards from its original position. The stump looked like it was ripped from hell and left there for all to see as a reminder. It was still smoking. It was blackened. It was charred. The power here felt unnerving.

Everyone was silent on the way back as they had a thousand thoughts flying in multiple directions simultaneously. The crown for Prince Charles was assured. Of that – they had no doubt. They would have to figure out how to govern the country once it was theirs.

When they arrived at their starting point, Derek asked the Prince if he would come forward. The Prince saw the drone and smiled. Of course, Lord McAndrew would save the best for last.

"Your Highness, I am sure you remember this device?" asked Derek.

"Indeed, I do, My Lord. I have wanted to experience this flying machine again since you allowed me to fly it the last time," said the Prince.

"Would you like to demonstrate for our illustrious Lords the capabilities of this machine?" asked Derek.

The Prince smiled. "I thought, My Lord, that you would never ask."

The Prince picked up the iPad and started the drone. The Lords jumped a bit - but observing the Prince was elated rather than terrified – they stood their ground, not wanting their actions to be seen as cowardice in front of their Liege Lord.

The motors began to hum as the blades began to spin. It began to hover – then the Prince throttled it up. Everyone was asked to gather around the iPad and watch. They were surprised to see themselves from the air as the drone hovered over them. The Prince began to take it higher, and the expanse of the area they saw was almost surreal. This is what the birds must see as they take flight. They could see the other camp from that height, and as the Prince went higher, they could see Inverness! This was… astounding! Finally, the Prince brought the drone down to around 10 feet high. The drone was about two hundred feet from the men hovering. Then a mischievous grin came across the Prince's face… he turned the drone towards his position and made it fly towards them... faster… and faster – when it passed directly overhead, Lord Murray jumped to the ground to get out of the way.

Of course, the drone was too high to hit anyone – but it was too close for Lord Murray's comfort. It brought laughter from all and an embarrassed smile from Lord Murray. Derek reached down and offered him a hand. He stood up and awkwardly wiped the dirt away from his clothing. At that point, the Prince hovered the drone and gently landed it safely on the ground.

Derek suggested that they retire to continue this conversation in his tent. Everyone loaded into the Mastiff and was taken to the tent. The Prince provided wine, bread, and cheese for all.

Derek stated the obvious to all, "You do know that King George will invade once he discovers that his son was not only soundly defeated – but died in battle as well. Imagine we had drones up to see his battle plan in real-time – as it happens. What kind of advantage will that give us?"

Lord Drummond quipped… "Immense."

Derek continued, "You know why you were asked to be here. We have a tremendous amount of firepower, as you have seen. If it were unleashed all at once, no country could withstand that amount of firepower. Prince Charles has mentioned that we should invade now, surprise our enemy, defeat them, and take the crown. Perhaps he is right. But it would take many of our limited resources to do so. If there are 100,000 men, we must fight to win the Crown – we may not have enough to be entirely successful."

Derek continued, "What if we were to develop some of the characteristics into weapons for our Scottish Army – and defeat them here? First, it will take him some time to learn that his army was defeated. Once he learns that his entire army was eliminated, he will be angry at first, and then he will be pragmatic. He will not be impulsive and rush to assemble an army that could be defeated again. The problem for him, though, is the War of Ascension in Europe now. His seasoned military and commanders are there. At best, logistically – if everything were to work well for him – it would be Winter before he could consider attacking. He won't, however, because the Winters are harsh and difficult to fight in a foreign war with no internal support. I would bet my life that he will not be able to fully bring an attack on our nation until spring at best or summer if we are fortunate."

Everyone agreed with that assessment.

"So, what do we do to prepare?" asked Lord Forbes.

"We build these – at least 10,000 of them." Derek brought out a drawing of a rifle. It was a breakaway action rifle using the 7.62mm cartridge. Derek pulled out the cartridge and showed it to the men. He then asked them the same question he asked the Prince, "What is the effective range of the smooth bore muskets that the British Infantry use? How many shots per minute can the expert marksmen fire?"

Lord Forbes stated, "50-75 yards. The best rate of fire? Probably 3 per minute."

"Precisely," said Connor. "Now imagine our men having 10,000 Rifles that range 200-400 yards and can fire accurately at a rate of 4-6 per minute. What would that do to our enemy?"

"They would be decimated. No army could withstand that onslaught," said Lord Gordon.

Connor continued, "That would be the plan – with your help. But here are other issues to consider: The gunpowder that is currently being used will not work for our firearms. And look at the ammunition. Have you ever seen any of this type? The gunpowder is in the shell, allowing it to be fired in the rain. We can make the gunpowder necessary, and with current technology – we believe we can develop what will be necessary to produce what we need to make Scotland the strongest military in the world."

Derek then took over, "We know that it is time for planting for our men for food for their families. Perhaps the men should go home knowing they will be called up after harvest to begin to train with the new weapons and tactics we will use going forward. Lord Forbes, you are highly respected and greatly influence Inverness. We can probably utilize almost the entire town to build what we need."

Derek continued, "We fully understand the desire to move to London and take the Crown now. After much prayerful consideration, I hope you will consider what we have to say – though we do not profess to have the political prowess you have with your experience. Take the Scottish Crown first by becoming the King of Scotland – that gives you global legitimacy. Once you have that, we can pool the nation's resources to prepare for a springtime invasion. When King George invades –you will have a global legitimacy in protecting your crown – and then seizing the crown from the head of the usurper."

Prince Charles stepped in, "Alright, My Lords, you have seen the tools that we have in front of us. This is so much bigger than anything that I had ever hoped it would be. We can transform the entire world. These men have so much to offer; I sincerely hope we can band together to transform Scotland and, by doing so – transform the world. What say you?"

Lord Murray was the first to speak, "These weapons are terrifying – I hope once they are used – they will no longer be necessary. That being said, Your Highness, I am fully in agreement. I was with you when there was no hope. How can I not be with you when the Crown is all but yours now? And – even though I would prefer to make a charge to London and win this now – Lord Derek McAndrew makes perfect sense. If we are pragmatic and do this with the world watching – we can be on the right side of history. Especially as the trade with our new products begins to open up.”

Lord Forbes then chimed in, “Before I begin, I wish to make an announcement – Lord Connor McAndrew will be marrying my daughter, Lady Mary, in the next couple of weeks. You must know this, My Lords, so there is no perceived conflict of interest. I am totally on board with this arrangement. I also agree with Crowning Prince Charles to be the lawful King of Scotland. What Lord Derek McAndrew has said makes total sense from a global political perspective. My Lords, we must begin to think more about why we joined this cause in the first place. We will need someone to help negotiate this process that was neutral through all of this – and I know just the man… Lord Keith Lamont. He’s no fan of the Campbells, which would align him closer to our cause. He has wisely chosen neutrality – but because of this – if we can win him to our cause – that would make moving forward easier.”

“Very well, we are all in agreement?” asked the Prince. Everyone nodded. “We will need to form a Business Venture to do this properly. I want to be able to add others as we move forward so that all who enter on our side will benefit from what we produce. How about the “Royal Scotland Manufacturing Consortium”? I want to keep it simple as I believe there will be many opportunities in various ventures as this progresses. Thoughts?”

Connor added, “Your Highness and My Lords, the possibilities moving forward are larger than any of us in this tent. We must get the Crown first. How can we engage Lord Keith Lamont, and how can we do this sooner rather than later?”

“I know him well. He is stubborn – but he loves Scotland. He will need to know that we will win beyond a shadow of a doubt – as he knows that a loss will bring retribution. He will need to know the level of commitment. Here is a thought – Lord Connor McAndrew and I can make the trip in a few days – it’s roughly 100 miles to Inveraray. We can take a few weapons that will show him the superiority that we currently have. We must also take something from the Duke to prove that we won. Perhaps his signet ring? We also will need to send runners to all of the clans to announce the total defeat of Cumberland and his army due to the leadership of Prince Charles. This will take time – but it would be nice to have you crowned King of Scotland before the end of the Summer. We can then enter into treaties and alliances to assist – especially with a large Navy such as the Dutch, Spain, and France. France would probably become an ally to piss off the current King," said Lord Forbes.

The Prince pulled out the signet ring from his pocket. "I keep it and always will as a souvenir to the folly of the Duke. I will part with it for a few days for this venture. Lords Derek and Connor McAndrew – how do you feel about this idea?"

"I don't particularly like the idea – as I can use Lord Connor McAndrew here, and it will be more difficult without him – however, I fully understand the benefit of having him there with you to add credibility to the entire situation. I guess it is up to Lord Connor McAndrew?"

Connor said, "I am more than willing. It would be an honor." Connor then developed a mischievous grin. "Are you sure it is for the greater good of Scotland, My Lord Forbes? Or to avoid the preparation for a wedding and to keep me away from Lady Mary in the process?"

Lord Forbes smiled as well. "My Lords, that thought never crossed my mind… but now that you mention it… I believe that is an ingenious idea."

Everyone laughed – especially at the prospect of Lord Connor McAndrew on the trail for at least a week with Lord Forbes?

"Very well, Your Highness, we will be off on the morrow," said Lord Forbes. Lord McAndrew, I would suggest bringing that pistol of yours with back-up ammunition and a rifle or two with additional ammunition. We will have a dozen men with us when we leave. Lord Connor McAndrew – it would appear that I am stuck with you again tonight?"

"Well, Lords Derek and Connor McAndrew and Lord Ian McKenzie, you have met with success with your endeavor. We are in agreement and committed to however this resolves itself. Is there anything else that needs to be discussed?" asked the Prince.

"No, Your Highness. As the company is formed and developed, I would like The Strikers to be listed as a single entity in partnership with this venture. It is going to take all of my team and all of their expertise to make this happen. I want them all to be rewarded handsomely for their hard work and dedication – wait until the invention of the locomotive…," said Derek.

"What is a locomotive?" asked the Prince.

"Imagine a wagon that can transport hundreds of people and thousands of tons of supplies – all at once!" said Mac. "Gentlemen – you have no idea what will happen and the wealth that will rain down on Scotland like a Biblical flood!"

"Your Highness, Would you like to be the one to tell the men that they may return home to plant and to be prepared to return where ordered when the harvest is complete?" asked Lord Gordon.

"I would be honored to do so, My Lord. Lord McAndrew, could I use your device to make me louder so that all may hear me speak?" asked the Prince.

"Yes, Your Highness. You will need to speak from one of our Jackals. We have a megaphone that can be used for smaller groups – but for thousands – the Jackal will perform admirably as you saw on the battlefield," said Mac. "Would you like to ride back to camp in one? I am sure someone can lead your stallion back as well."

"That sounds delightful!" said the Prince excitedly.

"Your Highness, would you mind if we bring a radio to your tent to communicate with you immediately?" asked Derek.

"Please," said the Prince. "I will need you to show me how to use it. I do have a question. As much as I trust you, some conversations must be kept private."

"I fully understand, Your Highness. The only way you will hear us or us hear you is if you wish it," said Mac.

"Very well," said the Prince. "Please bring it, set it up, and we will try it tonight."

Everything was in the tent – including the antennae and a battery to keep it charged. They also pulled an auxiliary battery for backup. They realized they would have to come up with a way to develop electricity. They were going to need it. Possibly, the steam engines could be turned into steam generators. There is so much that needs to be developed and will be once the war is over. However, first things first. Prince Charles Stuart must become King! Thought Derek.

They all decided they wished to ride in the Mastiff. That meant that several men would have to bring the horses back to camp. Derek decided to make it an adventure. It was less than five miles to the Prince's Camp – but it took over an hour to get there by horseback because of the terrain. This was going to be a rough ride – but with the Mastiff and the Jackal – they could make it quicker than anything that these Nobles would have ever had the opportunity to experience.

They took off. The Jackal could hit eighty mph, while the Mastiff could reach sixty mph. The Prince and Derek were in the Jackal. Derek was driving. He told the Prince, "Hold on, Your Highness!." Derek floored it. It's good that everyone was buckled up – it was rough as Hell. The Prince was turning a couple of shades of white. There was a wagon trail. Derek got it up to seventy mph before reaching a sharp curve to the right. He skidded into the turn and then floored it again! The Prince asked them how fast they were going. Derek told him they got up to seventy mph, and he was trying to find a place to get it up to eighty mph. Top speed. He found it. He dropped a gear and floored it... seventy... seventy-four... seventy-six... seventy-eight .... eighty! Oh Shit... dead end coming! Derek slammed on the brakes and had to apply sketchy braking and turns to keep from hitting the trees. The Prince was delighted! This was faster than anyone in Great Britain had ever been!

"Derek! Were you endangering the life of a Sovereign?" Jested the Prince.

"Not at all, Your Highness. I was showing him how to live!" shouted Derek.

"For whatever reason – that resonated with the Prince. He must learn how to 'live.' He had never been so terrified – yet electrified at the same time. He would get one, or something like it, for personal use. Perhaps one day Scotland can build something like this!"

They rolled into the camp. The Mastiff a few minutes later. Mac had taken the hint and also gave the Lords an exciting ride. Lord Gordon was visibly shaken!

These vehicles gathered a lot of attention. Derek got onto the PA and, in Gaelic, asked for everyone to come immediately to where they were. The Prince had an announcement to make.

Derek said, "Your Highness – I know you will dismiss the men to go home to attend to their families. Might I suggest that you ask for volunteers who may wish to stay and assist as we plan and move forward with the construction – perhaps hint that they will be able to be a part of history? Another consideration is that those who stay can be trained first to go through our new boot camp in preparation for the battle."

"That's a good idea, My Lord. We will need all that may choose to do so," said the Prince.

After the men had gathered, the Prince began, "My Lords, Gentlemen, Friends, Patriots... before I begin – I want to take this time to thank you humbly. Thank you for your trust. Thank you for your courage. Because of you, I am standing before you, not a firing squad!" Everyone laughed at that. "Here is our situation. You know as well as I that this is not over yet. More battles will come, but it will be time before George can come to grips with his total defeat and then mount a counter-offensive and march on Scotland. In the meantime – I plan to become the King of Scotland." As soon as he said that – thousands of men erupted in cheers. He continued, "That, of course, as you know, takes time and negotiations with the Nobles."

"Fuck the Nobles!" came a cry from the rear. There were lots of smiles and laughter that could not be contained. One thing for sure – is that this attested to the popularity of the Prince.

The Prince smiled at that and continued, "You have bravely served your call to duty. Now, I would like to present you with two options moving forward... One: You may go home. Plant your fields. Take care of your livestock. Spend time with your family. However, your service will again be required in October after the harvest – as we prepare for what we expect to be an invasion from George. As you saw at Culloden – we have an advantage. But you have no idea how much more we have planned to move forward. The second option is this: Stay. Stay and help. Stay and make history. You will be the first to see the many innovations that will change our nation forever. I want you and your Lords to understand this... this is YOUR choice. I plan to be YOUR King. There are many things that I have been thinking that will be necessary to ensure you and your families are taken care of as well. Your choice will need to be made tonight. It would be best if you told your commanders your decision so that we can determine how many of you will remain. For those that decide to go...I wish you Godspeed and a bountiful harvest. For those that wish to stay and change the course of history – you have our eternal gratitude!"

"Nice Speech, Your Highness," said Mac. "I have two requests."

"Name them, My Lord," said the Prince.

"First, we need to get your radio hooked up and operational. And Second.... SUPPER! I am famished!" said Mac.

The Prince looked at him and said to all, "I agree to both!"

It took some time to get the radio with the battery hooked up. Mac was an excellent instructor in showing how the radio worked. Where to hold the Microphone… Basic upkeep... Etc. It was rigged – but it should work for the short term.

Supper was next. It was a small gathering, and everyone was relieved it would be an intimate Supper. Excellent food... excellent company... and the food and wine, as always – was delicious.

Chapter 27
Onset

Connor and Lord Forbes made it to his Estate by four in the afternoon. Lord Forbes hit the ground running. He had his Steward, Malcolm Sinclair, rushing to organize who would go, packing tents, other supplies, and provisions. He would be up most of the night preparing everything to be ready for his Master. Lord Forbes told him the plan was to leave at 7 a.m. and that they would be gone for at least ten days. That let him know what to put together. Lord Forbes also let Steward Sinclair know that Lord McAndrew would have his own tent and would need his own personal Steward moving forward. He smiled at this, knowing that Lord McAndrew would be very uncomfortable with that situation – but he also knew that Lord McAndrew would have to get used to it since that was his new station in life. It would be up to Steward Sinclair to pick out someone who would be a good fit for his new Master. He had just the right person in mind. Colin Grant. He would be perfect. He was honest, trustworthy, young, had a great sense of humor – and could teach young McAndrew what it meant to be a Lord and how to conduct himself. He would do it himself – that would be an incredible ride… but alas – his allegiance was with Lord Forbes.

Lord Forbes had told him to plan for a dozen to go with him and Lord McAndrew. Since Lord Forbes's personal Steward was still recovering, that meant that this would be up to him to attend to. Two weeks in a saddle and sleeping on the ground sounded about as much fun as running naked through briars – but duty over comfort. That meant ten additional men who were comfortable in arms and, of course, a cook– they would be the Lord's personal bodyguard. Lord McAndrew was going to have to get used to that idea as well… but the lad did a pretty good job of taking care of himself. Well, Shite… that meant he had to get his things ready to go as well. He laughed to himself. He had almost 25 years in service to Forbes, and the one thing that you can count on is the unexpected!

Lord Forbes came around the corner. "Ah, Mr. Sinclair – just the man I sought. We will not be taking a wagon – speed will be of the essence. We will not need a cook. Load enough dry provisions to last. If necessary – we can stop at a tavern on the way."

"Yes sir, Lord Forbes. It will be as you wish," said Malcolm. "Damn," he thought – a quick trip for almost 100 miles? That means a steady gallop. My arse will be hurting for sure… Ok…change of pace. Dried meats and breads, then."

Lord Forbes entered his home and yelled for Lady Mary. She appeared close to the staircase. "Yes Father?" she asked.

"Lord McAndrew and I will be gone for close to a fortnight. Would you like to show him a bit of our estate before dark? You should have a couple of hours to do so, provided you don't spend two hours trying to decide what to wear?" said Lord Forbes with a smile.

Lady Mary smiled back to her father. She was used to his jests by now. What she was wearing would work for riding—but gone for a fortnight? She didn't like that at all! "What I have on is good enough, Father," she said in a pretend stern voice… and started laughing. "I would be delighted to do so, Father. Perhaps I can take him to the bend in the river as the sun sets?"

"That would be a great idea. You can show him everything he can see from there – we own. Just in case he does need another reason to marry you, my love?" once again – said in jest.

Lady Mary pretended to pinch him… hugged him, and left to find Connor.

Lord Forbes pointed outside – so she went to fetch him. "Ahhh, Lord Connor McAndrew. My Father suggested we ride to my favorite spot for you to see while he attends to everything for your departure on the morrow."

Connor's eyes perked up when he saw her. "I would be delighted to do so, My Lady. I would gladly enter the gates of Hell provided that you were my guide, my Lady."

Lady Mary giggled… "It's much closer to Heaven, My love. I am sure you will love it as much as I do. I also have some news to tell you once we are there."

"News? Something you cannot tell me now?" he queried. "Hmmm? So now we will have secrets? I think I may like this side of you, my love."

Lady Mary laughed. "Let's get our horses ready and take a canteen. You will enjoy this! I am sure! Though we will have to hurry before the sun sets!"

They were quick to their horses. The Horse Master got their horses ready, and then they were off.

Lady Mary said it wasn't too far... and then took off in a gallop. Connor easily caught up. She then had her horse up at a full run. Connor kicked Shadow Bane, and he was running at full speed. It didn't take long for Connor to catch up to Lady Mary. He passed her and then slowed down... and passed her once again. That's when he saw it. Lady Mary was dead on. This view was breathtaking. The sun was beginning to set behind a bluff overlooking a river... with mountains as the backdrop. He was sure that no place on earth looked as beautiful as this. I would think that Lord Forbes would have built his house here...

"My Lady – this is by far the most beautiful sight... next to you, of course, that I have ever seen," said Connor.

Lady Mary said, "Follow me. There is a place where we can dismount and watch the sun begin to set."

Connor dismounted, tied Shadow Bane where he could munch on the green grass... and walked over to help Lady Mary Dismount from her horse. He held her once he had her with her feet on the ground and stared intently into her eyes... The intensity of his stare made Lady Mary a bit uncomfortable. She looked away. "I'm sorry, My Lady... I need to see the most beautiful eyes I have ever seen...and plant them forever in my memory."

Lady Mary blushed and said, "My Lord... those will fade as will any sense of beauty I have now. How will you feel then, My Lord?"

"It will never falter, my lady. That's a promise. Ever. Though I may one day be old, fat, and bald?" They both laughed at that.

Her father had built a bench where the sunset was best observed.

They sat quietly in each other's arms. Connor then reached up to kiss her, and she kissed him back passionately. This was a memory that neither attendee would ever forget. "I do love you, you know."

"I know." smiled Lady Mary. Now, for what I was going to surprise you with. Our wedding day has been set. It will be Saturday,

May 7. You should be back before May 3. That will give you a few days to rest before I wear you out on the evening of the tenth?" She said with a mischievous grin. "But alas – it is time to head back." They both sighed and headed back to the Estate.

In the meantime, everything was in a mad rush to get everyone and everything ready for their trip in the morning.

The cook decided to cook a rather hearty supper since biscuits and dried meats would be his Lord's fare for the next few days. The main course would be Goose, Beef, and Pork tonight—Lord Forbes' favorites.

Everyone sat down at the table for supper. Connor was seated next to Lady Mary. As far as he was concerned, no one else was at the table. The talk at the table was of the journey to come and the local gossip.

No whiskey or cigars tonight. It was already eight, and everyone had to be up early for the trip. So, off to bed for all.

Connor was surprised that he was escorted directly to Lady Mary's room. His nightshirt was on the bed, as was hers. The board was in the middle of the bed, making him smile. I guess the quickness of the wedding date created the need for more comfort between the two. There were water basins, a toilet – now that would be awkward.... towels – everything one would need to prepare for bed.

She quickly removed her clothes, except her shift. She looked over at Connor and said, "Well?"

"Well, My Lady, I am not quite sure what I am to do?" said Connor, blushing.

"I will show you, My Lord," said Mary with her eyes twinkling. She walked over and began to undress Connor. He was standing naked in front of her on the day of his birth. She walked over to the basin, got a washcloth, and bathed him. She started at his face, neck, and ears... then she kneeled, washed his feet and legs, and moved up to his chest, back, and abdomen. He had several tattoos. She had heard about them on military men who had been abroad. But she had never seen them. These were quite interesting. Even his family's crest was upon him. It would be interesting to know how they did that without the ink washing off... Then she washed his butt, turned him around, and exclaimed, "My Lord, you must be injured. There is a large swelling in front of me!" and giggled. She then washed that as well. Connor was not quite prepared for this!

Lady Mary then fully disrobed and asked him to wash her – to which he willingly complied. He proceeded to wash her as she did him. Starting with the face and neck, then on his knees for her feet..." Oh, LORD! DON'T LOOK UP! He told himself. Focus. Concentrate." He then moved to her back. "Oh God!" her breasts and then midriff. Then he washed her buttocks, turned her around to wash her front... She teased him more – and MOANED. F O C U S!

She giggled and got on her knees in front of him. "Honestly, My Lord. I must take care of this swelling. I can kiss it and make it so much better..."

"My Lady... as you can see – I want this as much as you – probably more. But our wedding will be on May 7. That is less than twenty days away. We have waited this long. We can surely wait twenty more days and do this right before God," said Connor.

Lady Mary sighed... she did want this. She wanted this now. But she would do as he asked. He wanted it too...as she grinned to herself. "Very well, My Lord. I will do as you ask."

She used the toilet, got her nightshirt on, and lay down on her side of the bed. Soon... she was breathing softly as she fell into a deep slumber.

Connor was on his elbow watching her... and listening to her breathe. Should he have taken advantage of the moment? No. He did the right thing. God would honor that decision. Besides – it would be less than twenty days. Be reached over and kissed her. She would be his soon.

Connor was awakened at six. He quietly got his clothes on. Lady Mary looked up sleepily. "Is it time for you to go already?"

"Yes, My Lady. I am afraid that it is," said Connor.

"You must kiss me before you go." She demanded. She reached up and grabbed his manhood – startling him... you make sure you do not have any swelling here until you return home!"

Connor laughed... kissed her hard... and let her know that would not be a problem. And... furthermore – since he had not ridden that far – ever – he would probably be too sore to do otherwise! Lady Mary laughed at that and rolled over to go back to sleep.

Connor grabbed his things and headed out the door. He could smell the bacon and coffee, and suddenly, he was starving. He went downstairs and saw Lord Forbes.

Lord Forbes asked, "Are you still a man of honor, Lord McAndrew?"

"Aye. I am My Lord. But I admit that your daughter is not making it easy!" exclaimed Connor.

"Get used to it, my boy. Nothing with that young woman is easy... and that will soon be your problem!" Lord Forbes laughed loudly... Connor did as well... with a bit of consternation?

Breakfast was eaten. Everything packed. They headed to the horses. Connor was introduced to the men. Then Lord Forbes brought another man to meet him – he was about 5'9" tall. Maybe 165 lbs. Reddish hair with a neatly trimmed beard and mustache. Lord Forbes said, "Lord McAndrew – a man in your standing must have a Steward. You will need to learn things as a Lord and possibly an Earl once the Kingdom is decided. This is Steward Colin Grant. He will be your Steward moving forward. He is a man to be fully trusted. He will learn to know you better than you know yourself. He will be a trusted ally and give you instruction and opinion – which will not always align with yours – but must at least be considered. Steward Colin Grant, meet your new Lord – Lord Connor McAndrew."

Steward Colin Grant bowed his head, looked up, and said, "I am pleased to meet you and honored to serve you, Lord McAndrew. I hear that you are quite an extraordinary man, sir. I am looking forward to what the future may entail."

"My Lord, the Pleasure is indeed mine, and I am truly thankful for this gesture, but are you sure I need a Steward?" asked Connor.

"My young future Son-In-Law... you have no idea. There is much to learn in being a Lord and doing it properly. Our very way of life relies on the proper order that is required to be set by the Lords of this nation. It is not a thing to be trifled with... understand?"

"Yes, My Lord," answered Connor. He then looked at his Steward. "I am pleased to meet you, sir, and look forward to getting to know you and how this relationship is supposed to work!"

"We're burning daylight – Mount up!" said Lord Forbes.

"You do realize it is still dark?" said Connor.

He was met with an intense look of disapproval. Of course... Connor laughed heartily... which even made Lord Forbes smile. "That little bastard is going to win me over yet!" Thought Lord Forbes. He then gave his horse a kick, and they were on their way.

Connor thought they would gallop for 20 miles and then rest and do this for five days to get to Lord Keith Lamont's stronghold. He found that the horses were held to a cantor or a trot. Shadow Bane did not like that at all. He wanted to run. It was a constant battle the first 5 miles, getting Shadow Bane to stay in the group. After 5 miles, the men stopped to relieve themselves, stretch, let the horses drink, and take a break before they would continue. Connor got off of Shadow Bane... "Oh Lord Jesus!!! Only 5 miles down? My arse and legs may never recover after this!"

This continued all day. They came across a tavern once they had reached the 20-mile mark and ate a fine stew for their evening meal with a rich dark rye bread to accompany the meal.... along with several mugs of Ale. Thankfully, that took a bit of the agony of the ride from his inner thighs and his arse. How he wished he had some Ibuprofen! Maybe he can invent that... Lord Forbes, his Steward, and Lord McAndrew, and his Steward got a room at the inn. There was not enough room for the rest, so they slept in tents.

Steward Sinclair was almost as sore as Connor – and was damned glad to sleep on a bed tonight. If you have the rank – then by God, use it...

Connor collapsed on his bed. He was exhausted. Steward Grant insisted that he disrobe, clean up, and then sleep – insisting he would sleep better. Lots of grumbling later, Connor was out – clean and in a nightshirt. He was not going to argue tonight. He was too damn tired.

Derek and Mac's day started differently. They met with the Carpenters first. To start this show – they have to have several complexes to perform the various tasks required to construct everything. It was decided that a building would be separated from them all – for the gunpowder. The one essential product was the most finicky and the most dangerous. Everyone should understand the risks associated with gunpowder. It's more unpredictable until it is the proper mix.

Each of the structures would have to allow a lot of natural light. Windows would be a very extreme luxury now – so that would have

to be included in the mix. They would be built like two-story barns –
40'x 80' x 16'. They would need four. While the construction is
taking place, the raw materials can be gathered. The goal would be
to provide the raw materials once the buildings are constructed. They
also decided that a smaller building, say 20' x 40' x 16', would be
for R&D.

But – before we begin – we need to build a real camp for our men
and get them out of tents. While they were waiting for Lord Forbes
and Lord Lamont to return – they could build temporary housing for
his men.

Derek and Mac met with Lt. Ross, Lt. Gordon, and Lt. MacLeod.
He wanted them to gather axes from the other camp and chop wood
for their barracks. Each would hold ten men. They would be bare
and have to add fireplaces if they stayed here long enough for the
winter. He also wanted to build a large meeting building and lodging
for him, Connor, and Mac. Over 1200 men in the next camp decided
to stay and help with the construction. If he could get all those men
to assist – they could have everything ready in a week at most.

In the meantime - That meant an ample space, a lot of lumber, a
lot of carpenters... the logistics in this time period were going to be
challenging. Derek contacted the Prince with the Radio. "Your
Highness!" ... he waited a few seconds and called out again, "Your
Highness? Are you there?"

All of a sudden, he heard, "Son of a Bitch! I can't get this bastard
to work!"

Both Mac and Derek cracked up. They understood the frustration
when technology didn't work correctly. "Your Highness – we can
hear you now. Just let off on the button on the microphone when you
are not talking."

"I think I have this now," said the Prince. "I must admit I do like
this."

"We're glad you do, Your Highness. We plan to construct the
buildings - on the outskirts of Inverness. We will also need to begin
the process of gathering laborers. We will need all of the lumber
mills to begin making a lot of lumber. How would you feel about
making a personal appeal in Inverness?" asked Derek.

"I will do whatever is necessary at this point, Lord McAndrew,"
said the Prince. We are committed – whether we like it or not. The
King would be coming for them. All of them. He had no choice but

to move forward. Scotland would win or die based on their decisions over the next few months.

"We also need to find a cave with bats... a lot of them. That is one of the most important parts of this journey," said Derek. "Perhaps you can find someone local who knows of a cave with Bats?"

"I will ask and see what I can find out," said the Prince.

"Do you know the Provost of Inverness, Your Highness?" asked Mac.

"Indeed, I do. Provost John Fraser. He is a Jacobite. Highly favored by the town. He was able to convince a few hundred members of the community to support us here in Culloden. I am sure he has already heard of the victory," said the Prince.

"Perhaps you can give a speech and try to get local involvement. If all of the Lords attended with you – it would be beneficial – especially since Lord Forbes is currently unavailable," said Mac.

"Also, Your Highness – we will build a bit more of a permanent camp for my men. Could we use some to assist with the 1200 or so volunteers with your men? The more that can help, the quicker we can get our camp built to focus on the rest of the work to come.

"Of course. You can use them all. That way, we can focus on what we need to move forward," said the Prince.

"Thank you, Your Highness!" said Derek.

"My Lords – I have a request for you. I know that the time I have truly known you has been minimal. I trust my instincts. I would very much like to have you both and Lord Connor McAndrew as part of my Inner Council. I have one requirement. You must be honest with me. I do not need 'Yes' men. I need truth, integrity, and the ability to counsel even if you disagree with my opinion. Would you be interested, gentlemen?" asked the Prince.

Both men answered at once, "We would be honored, Your Highness."

Derek added – "But, Your Highness, we must be able to be brutally honest with you. If you agree, I would be honored to do so."

"As would I," said Mac.

The Prince was excited – you could tell by the tone of his voice. "Very well, gentlemen. I will request the presence of the Provost of Inverness to meet with me and discuss a time to get the entire community to be in the town square, and I will ask him about caves. I would think he would know or at least know someone who does.

"You had mentioned buildings and other items that would be necessary to start the construction. We are currently on Lord Forbes' Property. This would be a good place to begin building what we need and even our army. It's centrally located, and the surrounding area has many resources available," said the Prince. "Plus, to be honest – I am not fond of big cities. I trust the commoners more than Royalty. Somehow, after this is done – something will be done to make their lot a little easier. Perhaps this wealth you discuss with new inventions can assist them with their needs. I know we cannot begin construction without Lord Forbes – but we can begin to gather what will be needed."

"Agreed, My Lord," said Derek.

"Very Well, Gentlemen – let's get this started!" said the Prince.

Chapter 28
Arduous

The worst of the "oh my God, I'm gonna die" soreness had left his legs, butt, and especially his inner thighs. "I thought I was in decent shape," thought Connor. Though he loved riding, this was far beyond anything he had ever done, and Shadow Bane's every stride reminded him of that fact. Of course – he could not show any weakness to Lord Forbes or any of his men.

"We are almost to Lord Keith Lamont's Castle – Toward Castle. It's just over the hill. We will be seen by then. With as many of us coming down the road – expect some company. They've been a bit paranoid since the Campbells all but wiped them out in the Dunoon Massacre. On June 3 – it will have been precisely 100 years ago," said Steward Grant.

Connor hated to admit it – but Steward Grant had been a godsend in keeping him going. Next time – I'm taking a Jackal, he decided.

They came up over the hill. Connor gasped. This was the replacement castle that Colin had talked about?!? He had also explained the massacre by the Campbells. To slaughter men, women, and children in their beds and then burn their castles and take even more prisoners to execute them later? I would think that would make for a long-term grudge.

Just as Colin predicted – it looked like two dozen men on horseback were racing towards them. Lord Forbes had the men stop and allow the oncoming force to approach them.

Lord Keith Lamont...looked like a rather stoic figure on his white stallion. His hair was gray, long – to his shoulders. His beard, black and gray, was maybe three inches long. He and his men had firearms at the ready if need be. Then Lord Lamont noticed Lord Forbes. "What the bloody hell are you doing here, old friend? Did Lady Forbes kick your arse out of the house? And with this rag-tag force to protect you?" He started laughing and then rode up to take his arm in friendship. It had been almost four years since he had seen Lord

Forbes. He had to give him shite. That would indeed be expected! "You realize that next month – it will be 100 years since the Campbells showed their sinister side with my family? If it would've been dark – I might have shot you – thinking they were going to try it again!"

"Ahhh, My Dear Lord Lamont – We would've waited until tomorrow! However, it appears your dull wit remains," he said with an exaggerated sigh, then clasped his arm tightly. "It's damn good to see you, Lord Lamont."

"Well... I'm guessing you didn't ride this far to shake my hand?" He motioned for his Steward. "Please take these gentlemen and put them up in the bunkhouse – make sure they are fed well and taken care of."

As they were riding away, Lord Lamont looked questionably at Connor.

"Lord Lamont, I am pleased to introduce Lord Connor McAndrew – my future Son-In-Law," said Lord Forbes.

"What?!?!" Exclaimed Lord Lamont. "You are going to let a mere mortal marry your precious Lady Mary?"

"I know'" said Lord Forbes with a remorseful look. "But he grows on you!" he said with a wink and a smile.

Lord Lamont looked at Connor and smiled, "Well, My Lord, if it's any consolation – that old bastard grows on you too!"

Connor looked at Lord Lamont and smiled, "Lord Lamont – I can tell you, and I are going to get along famously!"

That even had Lord Forbes smiling.

With the pleasantries spoken, they headed to the Castle.

It was a little after four in the afternoon. That meant a couple of hours talking and then supper. Connor was hoping to get everything completed and Lord Lamont on their side so that he could get back. There was so much work to do. Despite his sore arse – he wanted to get the conversation started. The reason they were there was not for pleasantries – but to gain a necessary ally. He wished to be blunt, as the military had taught him… but pragmatism kept him quiet.

They arrived at the Stables. The horse master took control of the horses. Lord Lamont explained the journey there and the one to come – to be sure and give them more protein than usual and some additional grains. Also – be sure to walk and stretch them –spoil them, and prepare them for the trip home.

The men then walked toward the Study. It would be Scotch, Cigars, and probably a very energetic conversation.

They stepped into a room of unparalleled luxury. No expense had been spared – from the deep stains, the exotic wood – from Mahogany, Rosewood, Ebony – weaving together with the delicate hues of Tulipwood, Zebrawood, and Padauk. The tapestries adorned the walls with intricate designs. The crystal scattered radiant light, casting a warm glow throughout the room.

Connor was stunned into silence. He finally broke the spell woven, "My Lord – this is the most beautiful inviting feast for the eyes – that I have ever witnessed – except for my bride-to-be," Connor said with a side look towards Lord Forbes – who simply rolled his eyes.

Lord Lamont had his guests pick out a drink of their choice. His selections included Scotch Whiskeys, Brandies, Gins, Rums, and Cognacs. He suggested the Cognac after Supper. He also had Ale, Beer, Wines, and Fortified Wines.

Connor picked out a whiskey that was a beautiful amber liquid. He swirled it around in his glass and sniffed it... smiled sincerely and sipped. The liquid had a warming sensation...it was whisky – but the flavor profile was unlike any he had ever had. This was good. Really good. He expressed that to his host. Lord Lamont smiled. Well... the young Lord knew good whiskey. That was a plus. Even Lord Forbes was impressed.

Lord Lamont was not one to approach any topic delicately. He knew that the discussion was important enough for Lord Forbes to come in person with the additional men – and it was evident that getting here had been a hard ride. "Alright, Lord Forbes – we have exercised all of the niceties expected between old friends. You have ridden virtually non-stop to get here. Your horses show the strain – as did Lord McAndrew's bowed legs in getting stiffly off his Stallion. Why exactly are you here?"

"Well, My Lord...you are as direct as usual. I'm not sure why I thought that would not have been the case today?" They both smiled at that. "Alright, My Lord. Have you heard of the battle fought in Culloden Moor with the Duke of Cumberland's Army against Prince Charles Stuart?"

"Rumors only, I'm afraid. Something about The Duke's men numbered around 10,000, and the Prince's men numbered around

6,000. The rumor is that Prince Charles won and only sustained 16 wounded and three dead. That seemed like a total fabrication – so I disregarded that information. That the Battle was won conclusively by the Prince – and I am assuming you gentlemen as well?" asked Lord Lamont.

"Actually, there were around 9500 British Troops and 6500 Scottish troops. The British were not defeated... they were annihilated. There were no survivors – including the owner of this ring." Lord Forbes pulled out the Duke's Signet Ring and handed it to Lord Lamont.

"That is the Duke of Cumberland's Seal... his... Signet Ring. There's no bloody way Lord Forbes! The Duke was an Arse – but he had a military mind and training that was quite unequaled," said Lord Lamont.

"And... Yet... he was the very first to fall at Culloden. By a single shot over 1000 yards away," said Lord Forbes.

Lord Lamont did what any logical person of the time would have done... He laughed...hard... "My Lord Forbes – such a fabrication will not help you trying to get me to align with your cause."

"First of all, ... We don't want you to align with us. But before we even go down that path – there is something we need to show you," said Lord Forbes.

"Lord McAndrew, please present your rifle and show them to Lord Lamont?" Connor brought the two rifles and the two pistols he had brought with him. He pulled the Magazine and cleared the chamber on each of the weapons.

"What are those?" asked Lord Lamont.

"These are the reasons why there were no survivors. It is not the firearm that took out the command structure – including the Duke. But it was responsible for killing the majority of the commanders and officers. Lord McAndrew led the attack."

Lord Lamont looked at Lord McAndrew with a grudging respect.

Connor spoke up – "I could tell you what it can do. Why don't I show you outside?"

"Very Well," said Lord Lamont.

Connor gathered the rifle and his pistol. He hated to blow through a magazine but thought it might come to that to gain support.

Connor asked if Lord Lamont had a target...maybe a bucket or something. He would need two targets. One for his pistol and one for his rifle. Or... would it be acceptable for Connor to use one of the white fence posts he could see that were at least 300 yards away?

Lord Lamont said, "Surely you jest. One of my fence posts over there?" He pointed generally in their direction.

"Yes, My Lord," said Connor.

"But first – let's start with this bucket here." Connor walked close to 50 yards away and put it on the ground. He walked back and turned his back on the target. He showed Lord Lamont the pistol and asked if he could hit the target more than once.

"With that?" Lord Lamont began to laugh... and then Connor went into action. He turned around swiftly and pulled the trigger. He hit the bucket, and it jumped into the air. He shot it again, and it flew back a few feet. He shot it again...and again... and again. He finally double-tapped it. Ten shots into the bucket. It was in pieces. Lord Lamont was flabbergasted.

He then pulled out his rifle. The range was a little over 300 yards. It would be an easy target. Before he began – "Would you care to wager if I can hit it from here? I would be willing to bet 100 Guineas that I can hit it at least five times. Lord Forbes? Would you cover for me until we return?" Lord Forbes nodded an affirmative.

"100 Guineas? To hit that post five times? From here? My Young Lord, you are quite ballsy. I would be delighted to take your money."

With that, Connor immediately raised his rifle... shot ten shots, and blew the post into splinters. He did not miss a single shot – and Lord Lamont knew it.

"That, sir, is the best shooting I have ever seen. Well worth 100 Guineas just for the exhibition," said Lord Lamont.

"Would you like to shoot them, My Lord?" asked Connor.

"Indeed, I would." Grinned Lord Lamont.

Connor showed him how to use the weapons. Lord Lamont brought the rifle up to his line of sight. Connor told him how to aim. He did so as Connor taught. He inhaled, then exhaled and held his breath. He fired at the post right next to the one that Connor had excoriated. He fired off three shots. He saw splinters fly. He had hit the post?!?! At 300 yards?!?! How?!?! This was a game-changer. This meant something for this rebellion. With these weapons, It was probable that Prince Charles would be the next King.

Connor then pulled out the 5.56mm and the 7.62mm shells and laid them next to each other. He picked up the 5.56 mm shell. "This, My Lord, is the shell that we just fired. This shell is a 7.62 mm shell. It is the ammunition that we use in our machine guns."

"Machine Guns?" Lord Lamont asked.

"Yes, my Lord. A machine gun. You have seen the damage that the 5.56 mm shell can cause. Now imagine this shell – the 7.62 mm – accurate to 800 yards. We have a machine gun – which can fire 700 rounds per minute. We are developing a firearm that uses this shell that can fire at a rate of at least 4-6 per minute for the firearm to be used by the Scottish infantry."

Lord Lamont was quiet for a minute as he realized what firepower was available to Prince Charles. That's a dangerous game to play. If the young Prince is a narcissist – the world will be unbearable and incredibly dangerous. "It's bloody Armageddon! No army could withstand this onslaught."

"That's correct, My Lord," said Lord Forbes.

"Then why do you need me? He can take what he will. There will be no sanctuary for anyone who finds himself on the receiving end of these weapons. None," expressed Lord Lamont.

"You are correct – but we do need you sir," said Lord Forbes. "Why? You ask? Because you took no side. You were neutral. Prince Charles needs to become the King of Scotland first. Scotland needs to be united. Then none can prevail. He needs an advocate that is known and respected by all. That would be you, Lord Lamont."

"But why should I take one despot over another?" asked Lord Lamont.

"For several reasons. The first is that he is going to need council. Godly council. If you are on his council – you can influence the direction we will go as a country. He needs you to speak with the other Scottish Lords and help us reach a consensus with Prince Charles as our King. He is not the man that many believe him to be. Why don't you come back with us and speak with him yourself? Form your own opinion. Make your own decision," said Lord Forbes.

"Lord Forbes – you are still a bastard. You knew bloody well that I would be going back with you even before you set out on this journey. Let's rest your horses tomorrow, and we'll head back the day after," said Lord Lamont. "Is that acceptable, My Lord?"

"Indeed. That sounds good," said Lord Forbes.

All the while, Connor thought, "My arse will never be the same." This was quicker than he anticipated.

Finally, Lord Lamont approached Connor with a small bag.

Connor looked at him questioningly.

"Lord McAndrew – it appears I have a balance due for a bet made in haste?" He handed Connor the bag. "It's the 100 Guineas, sir. My bet is paid."

Connor laughed and started to return it, saying, "My Lord, that is not necessary. The bet was made to prove a point and to encourage your participation. You may keep your money, sir."

"No sir – I am afraid not. I made the bet in good faith and will repay the same – in good faith. It's a matter of honor, sir," said Lord Lamont.

"Very well then," said Connor. "I will gladly accept your gold. Thank you. Let me know again when you wish to place such a wager!" laughed Connor.

"Oh, My Lord… I am a man of honor – but I am no fool!" exclaimed Lord Lamont.

As Prince Charles had requested, Provost John Frasier was at the camp early. Derek, Mac, and Lord Murray were there as well. They began to lay out the plans that they had for Inverness. If things went well – Inverness could be a central hub in a new Scottish Economy. The overall economy had been terrible since the Rebellion. Getting workers should not be a problem. They also asked about the Prince making a direct appeal to the town and appealing to their patriotism. The material needed was going to be a tremendous challenge. But they would find a way.

It was decided that the Prince would meet the townsfolk in two days' time at 1 pm to give the Provost time to let everyone know, and the town center readied for all to hear.

Derek and Mac were not excited once the actual date was set. There had been a brazen assassination attempt in the actual camp. There would be exponential risk in a town square surrounded by thousands of people. Having the Prince speak from the Jackal would provide a level of protection and should terrify any potential attacker.

The Prince would have rather spoken the next day. He understood the need for preparation. He also knew that because of that delay, the atmosphere would be like a street fair. But it is as it will be. "God grant me the words to move and begin to unite this nation." He wanted to get the construction in process. He wondered how things were with Lord Forbes and Lord Lamont. He wondered what the future would be – though he felt more confident with the role that he would play. Would he rule under the divine right of Kings as those who would be his peers? Or would he break out and do things differently? The conversations with Lord John Stuart strongly affected his overall demeanor. He could be remembered for being a King of the People when that did not exist. He could create a new Justice System – where Equal Justice under the Law...even for him – would mean something. He could prevent the American Revolution and maintain the colony. There is so much that he could change. He could be frugal and maintain the financial strength – not only of Scotland – but of the world. He could eliminate Central Banks... he could change the entire trajectory of the planet. It would be his choice.

Finding a trustworthy Council – now that would be a chore. This inner circle of Lords surrounding him now would be a step in the right direction. How many English Lords would perish in the battle to come? How would he begin to distribute the property? Could he get behind some Constitution? He knew many of the Bill of Rights Lord John Stuart discussed with him would be a non-starter. Not only in England as he conquers the nation – but even here in Scotland, where the aristocracy looked at themselves as God's Chosen. So much depends on how many decide to fight against him – and those that would be neutral or on his side moving forward. There is something about the McAndrew Brothers and Lord McKenzie. Their sense of duty, honesty, and integrity will allow him to speak freely and get the honest opinion of someone with a historical perspective – their advice could be invaluable.

He anticipated that Lord Lamont would not need as much convincing as Lord Forbes and Lord Murray believed. From what he had heard regarding Lamont, he was pragmatic- a bit hard-nosed – but practical. Once he saw a limited amount of firepower and could begin to be involved in remaking Scotland, he would have no choice. He also would be on his council. He had never met him – but he knew full well the reputation of the man – and his brother Kevin – would be valuable assets to the realm.

It is somewhat ironic. When he began this journey, he was in it for himself and the glory it would bring. The death and destruction had sobered him. The conversations with Lord Stuart had grounded him. Oddly – he wanted to make his father, James Francis Edward Stuart, proud. Even though his father was the rightful King – he had already told his son that he no longer wanted the throne –he wanted his son to have the Crown. If he only knew where they were and what had transpired. One day, he would. He would have his father return in honor as it should be.

He needed company. He got on the radio and asked Lord McAndrew and Lord McKenzie to join him for supper. They agreed. He then notified Lord Murray, Lord Gordon, and Lord Drummond for Supper. He needed friendship, frivolity, good food, and good company tonight. Perhaps he could get some music for the evening—something besides politics and gamesmanship. Reality would be there tomorrow. Tonight, good company was what was needed.

The Prince was correct. This is what was needed. He sat back and listened to the conversation. The bond that he was hoping for was beginning to develop. It was still apparent that Lord McAndrew and Lord McKenzie were trying to find their way. Their fantastical tales about the future engrossed them all. These metal machines that flew at 30,000 feet and could transverse the continent in hours rather than in months?!?! Or these "Automobiles" that could take one from Inverness to Lord Lamont in less than two hours? He chuckled to himself as he thought about the younger brother to Lord McAndrew. His arse is probably still throbbing. He mentioned that to his companions... not subjects. Lord Gordon raised a toast, "To Lord Connor McAndrew's Arse... may it ride well and feel well padded!"

The room erupted in laughter.

"In all seriousness," said the Prince. "There is one thing that I want you all to think about –how we can change the culture of the clans to begin to see themselves as Scottish first. A family – not enemies. That has always been our downfall. We fight each other more than our enemies – who exploit that fact. That is something that must stop."

Everyone agreed. The question is, "How"?

It was early morning, and there was light rain. Thunder rolled down the valley to Lord Lamont and Toward Castle. The Horse master had been up preparing the horses for several hours. Lord Forbes and Lord McAndrew had brought 12 additional riders. Lord Lamont would bring ten more. It would almost look like a raiding party as they prepared to ride to Inverness.

Lord Lamont felt uneasy leaving his castle this close to the 100th anniversary of the Campbell's slaughter. But alas - he had no choice. It was for his family's future…for his grandchildren.

All at once… the front door to the courtyard burst open. His granddaughter shouted, "You forgot to tell me goodbye, granda! How could you forget me?"

Lord Lamont told her he could never forget her – because she wouldn't let him! "But... do this… I will find something special to give you when I return – but only if you behave while I am gone!"

"I will, granda! You bring me a big surprise because I will be real good!"

He leaned down, gave her a big kiss and hug, and handed her off to his wife, where he gave her another kiss on her cheek. Then, he surprised his wife with one as well. "I love you both. I'll be back as soon as I can. Lady Lamont looked at her husband with worry in her eyes. She felt good about the prospects she and Lord Lamont had discussed the night before. But the journey and the times are just too dangerous.

With that, he mounted up, and they were off. The stage was set. The participants in the initial drama were cast. And the rain began to come down harder.

Chapter 29
Inverness

The big day for the Prince had arrived. He first went to Inverness Castle to begin his trip to the town square of Inverness. This is the beginning of his public persona that he must build. He was to give a speech in Inverness—the first of what will eventually be many. "I suppose this is a warmup," Prince Charles said to himself. His Steward had brought his Stuart Tartan and all that entailed.

He felt rather somber in preparation for this. There is no reason for solemnity. Instead, it will be a celebration of the defeat of the British and the Public announcement of the death of the Duke of Cumberland – the King's son.

He would have an entourage of men with him and ride his magnificent White stallion. The sight of the Jackal would be terrifying to those in attendance. They would need to get used to these machines. He had been in them several times- and his sense of wonder still excited him.

In the meantime, the chamber was dimly lit, with only a few candles. He, of course, was beginning to feel the excitement a bit more as the anticipation of what would be said began to wear on him.

First – he put out the Stuart Tartan. Its deep blue and green hues could be seen with the help of the candlelight – which permeated the area with a soft light reflected in his blue eyes. He stepped into it, and the sudden sense of the historical context of this moment struck him. The best artisan in Scotland crafted the pleats.

Next came a white silk shirt. Its sheen contrasted with the rugged look of the kilt. The fabric was cool against his skin. He slid into the shirt with the billowy sleeves, and the cuffs were gathered on his wrist. Each movement was deliberate. It was well-practiced and efficient. Next came the black belt that he cinched tightly. He had lost quite a bit of weight while in the field. The Prince fastened the

Kilt Pin. The motto was "Nemo me impune lacessit – which means "No One provokes me with impunity." He would have to be resolute with this now. He would be King and must be the part as his father had taught him.

Knee-high white hose, held by garters also in the Stuart Tartan, held them in place. Next came the polished black leather brogues upon his feet. Then, his dagger, which was handed down to him by his father, who had received it from his father.

He stood in front of the mirror. Even his Steward looked pleased. He felt the weight on his shoulders, and he, for the first time – realized he would be King. It was a sobering thought.

There was a knock at his door. It was time. He gathered his wits and made it to the door. All of the Lords that had supported him, besides Lord Forbes, who should be back in the next few days, were there to support him earnestly. As he made his way to the courtyard – the ones there – hundreds began to shout, "Stuart! Stuart! Stuart!" He smiled profoundly and felt very humbled and waived.

He mounted his horse at the head of at least 20 others – followed by at least 100 men from his army from Culloden. He wondered who had put that together...then he laughed. He knew. That would be Lord John Stuart. But where was he?

He mounted as did the others. The infantry behind him also had a pipe and drum corps, and they began to play. It gave him chills. Following everyone was the Jackal that he would be speaking from. He hoped the Provost had done an excellent job of spreading the information that the machine was nothing to be feared – unless you were on the wrong side of the conflict. And they began their procession and headed into town.

What he saw – warmed his heart beyond belief. Lining the road...were hundreds...thousands... of men, women, and children shouting, laughing, and waving to him. The Provost had indeed delivered!

They reached the town square. The Prince dismounted from his horse to the top of the Jackal as he had practiced. Everyone continued cheering. He waved at the crowd as they continued cheering. The Prince was handed the microphone.

At first, he mumbled into the PA. Derek showed him again how to depress the microphone and to speak into it. When he started, it was loud and squealed with a bit of feedback... that scared everyone into silence. Derek smiled up at the Prince and told him that it was okay and to begin speaking.

"Ladies and Gentlemen of Inverness."

Everyone was startled that they could hear what was being said!

Finally – the Prince began his heartfelt message:

"I stand before you today humbled and thankful for your genuine support. You have no idea how much that means to me. However, I also feel this is a solemn occasion, as there is much to do. As you have probably heard -we defeated the English Army at Culloden Moor. There were no survivors that remained – which is well. They offered us no quarter, and we replied in kind. But you must understand – that will happen to ALL enemies of Scotland. The days of robbing, raping, and murdering our kinsman are over." The applause and yells in support lasted several minutes before he could continue. "We are here today – not only as citizens of Inverness – but as the protectors of our children... of our precious nation." Again, the applause was almost deafening. "We stand here united – as freemen who will no longer tolerate the belligerence from our neighbors to the South!"

"As your Prince – I have witnessed your indomitable spirit... your unwavering and enduring determination. We have faced countless trials and tribulations for over a thousand years from those who would invade our shores. I say before our enemies – NO MORE!"

"Today – I come to you with a need, not as a rebel, but as a protector. My loyal subjects, we believe that the real usurper in London will once again launch an attack on our great nation. We believe that it will be larger than the last incursion. But we will not fear those that can be beaten."

"I said that I came here with a need. It is the need of Scotland as we begin to prepare for the onslaught that is to come. In this moment of crisis, I am asking you to lay down all blood feuds, take up the mantle of nationhood, and be a Scotsman first and foremost. For you know as well as I – that none can defeat us if we gather as one!"

Over the next few months, close to Culloden Moor – we will be building the facilities that we need to outfit the best Army in the world so that we can once again defeat the pretender and his cohorts on the battlefield. This is where we need you. We need you to help us achieve our goals. We need you for construction, we need artisans, we need chemists and alchemists, we need those that are

Blacksmiths... We need metallurgists... we need cooks and captains... We need those who know and can work in caves. We need anything that would help us build our future! We need your unwavering support. We need ingenuity. We need courage and dedication. Together – we can craft weapons of war that the world has never seen – to defeat George once and for all!"

"In this endeavor – we will pull from the strength of our community...from our history. This project will be a beacon of hope ... a symbol of our determination. A cry to the freedom that yearns in our hearts! The coming months will determine the future of our children. Whether or not we survive as a nation... As a people. You know as well as I that we are held in contempt by the English. Their air of superiority is repugnant and has made our lives intolerable. We must defeat the arrogant... those who would exterminate our people. We have the opportunity to build liberty and freedom for the first time in many generations. "

"What say you?!?! Will you join me?!?! Will you sacrifice for Scotland?!?!? Will you help the cause for freedom?!?!" The entire town erupted. They would be there. They would be the ones praised in history. They would be known... they would be appreciated. And BY GOD, HE WOULD GIVE THEM FREEDOM!!!

Derek then got on top of the Jackal. "I am Lord Derek McAndrew. We are determining the manpower needs. We need you to come out tomorrow at 8 am, here in the town square. We will need you to sign up to help. We need you to put down any skills or trades and be prepared to work harder than ever. But in the end – it will be worth it. Those that would hurt our nation or our cause will tremble before the strength and the power of our people... with the genuine help of Almighty God!"

The population of Inverness was close to 5,000... at 8 am, there were over 2,000 people in line in the square... The Prince, Lord Murray, Derek, Mac. Ross, Gordon, and MacLeod, as well as the Provost, were overwhelmed with the support.

A young woman was standing close and staring at the Prince. "Ah, Your Highness... it seems you have caught a lass's attention," said Lord Gordon.

The Prince looked up and over... he recognized her in an instant. The young woman saw his eyes... she was elated and terrified immediately. She froze. He smiled. He walked up to her... now she blushed... she felt so awkward... she could almost hear her mother who had died six winters past... "Mind your manners, girl." She immediately curtsied. "Your Highness! Begging your pardon, Sire."

The Prince walked directly to her... he bent slightly, took her hand, and kissed it... "Ahh... It's Mary, I believe?"

"Dear Lord in Heaven... Your Highness! I am sorry that I flirted with you and made you feel uncomfortable," said Mary.

The Prince laughed heartily... and Mary blushed even more. "I hope we treated you well and were not a burden?"

"You will never know, Your Highness, how much your generosity helped me and my family! We won't starve because of you! I had to find you and thank you... but I thought you were a merchant! I had no idea you were a Prince," said Mary.

"How did you know it was me?" asked the Prince.

"It was your eyes, Your Highness. I will never forget them... nor your overwhelming generosity." She curtsied again. "You will always be welcome at the Tavern," said Mary.

The Prince pulled her close to say something to her... "Lady Mary... I will need you to do me a favor, please."

"Anything you ask, Your Highness," said Mary.

"I like to visit Taverns. They allow me to hear what is on the minds of those that I would serve. If you see me as a Merchant – treat me like a Merchant. I will expect you to be just as bawdy as you were when we first met. Would that be possible?" asked the Prince.

"Yes, Your Highness. I can make that happen. I am eternally in your debt," said Mary.

"No, My Lady... it is I who am indebted to you," said the Prince.

Mary curtsied deeply. She thanked the Prince once again and was on her way.

Everyone looked at the Prince with concern and curiosity. He looked at them, smiled, and said not a word.

Finally, back to the task at hand. What was decided was that the leaders of the community would gather and organize the personnel to accomplish the priorities. Building the structures would be the first requirement. Building the foundation, Logging, digging wells for water – building a small town to start the process is what is required. The Provost began the process of organizing. He got the significant tradesman together. The biggest push would be to get the sawmills busy making lumber. Most of the buildings would be of log construction since the two small sawmills would be quickly backlogged to complete the buildings using only lumber. But for the finished work, producing the raw materials for the firearms, flooring, etc. – the sawmills needed to get to work.

The young and the old would take water and food to those working. They would help the cooks and do whatever small tasks they could do to assist. One hundred would build a tent to act as a communal dining hall. Fifty would be cooks and servers. No work was ever done well with a starving workforce. Six hundred would begin the earthwork necessary to get the building foundations in place. Feeding 2000 folks per day was going to take some logistics. Oh wait – that would be 3,000 or so. There are still 1,000 men from the soldiers who fought in Culloden.

Several teams would need to be sent out looking for Caverns. Several members of the Royal Highlanders were Cavers and had explored several here. Derek would have to get them together with some daring souls to see if they knew of or could find caves.

The rest, for now – would be lumberjacks. That meant everything from cutting the timber to getting it where it would be used. That would take teams of horses to get everything moved into place.

All of the construction would take place on the outskirts of town. It was decided that the buildings would benefit the community once the war footing was over.

It was getting late. Derek and Mac needed to check the structures in their camp. Derek wanted to find out who the Cavers were. It was all for naught if they could not produce modern gunpowder.

"What the actual Hell?" Said Derek when they came through the woods to see the camp. The men had been PRODUCTIVE. At the head of the camp were the larger structures that Derek and Mac had wanted to have for meetings and planning. Then, three distinct buildings were a bit smaller. Derek and Mac knew that they were for them and Connor as well.

Lined up across from each other were 26 Buildings – what would be the individual barracks for his men. There were even wooden latrines to make things a little more comfortable. They also had built a place to Muster. I probably need to begin Physical Training again. We can't have the men getting soft!

One thing they did notice while coming in was A large area in the clearing had been fenced in, with a significant water source. Horses. Lots of them were in the enclosure. Then he remembered what the Prince had said – that each of the men in the Company would get two horses, each with all of the tack. The men would have to decide which they wanted. I guess they could officially be called a Calvary? There are more issues with logistics. Hopefully, the Prince had sent someone who could take care of them.

Everything was framed out. The roofing will be added tomorrow. They had gone on a massive hunt, and several herdsmen had donated a few calves for a feast for all. Fires were starting. Friends were being made – from the old world and the new. This is how it needed to be. We could be separate – but integrated as well. Team cohesion would be required once the combat operations began.

That's when Derek saw him. Sergeant Robert Stewart. "Sergeant Stewart – would you come here, please?"

Sergeant Stewart snapped to attention. Derek smiled – old discipline dies hard. "Aye, sir?" he asked.

"You're a Caver, I heard. Is that correct?"

"Aye Sir. There're a few caves around here that I used to explore in detail," said Stewart.

"Do you think you could find them without a GPS in today's environment?" asked Derek.

"I believe so," said Stewart.

"I want you to get at least six men tomorrow and assemble supplies to find those caves. There should be a few locals from Inverness to assist you in the next couple of days," said Derek.

"What is that you need me to find," asked Stewart.

"Shite." Smiled Derek.

"Shite? Did I hear you right, sir?" asked Stewart.

"Aye – ya did." Laughed Derek. We need Guano: Bat Guano and a lot of it. The Potassium Nitrate from the Bat Guano is a principal ingredient that we will need for gunpowder.

Sergeant Stewart laughed at that. "Got it, sir. Three of my Caver buddies are with us here."

"Excellent," said Derek. "How long will you gather materials for your journey?"

"We could be ready in two to three days," said Stewart.

"Very well then...make it happen. Keep me informed if there is anything that you may need."

"We will need rope. Lots of it, sir. Torches or something to work accordingly. I know we need torches – ours and theirs. Probably a lighter or two in case we have to use flames. We'll also need to take a firearm and ammunition – as well as a couple of tents," said Stewart. "If I remember correctly, there is a Cave not too far from Inverness. Perhaps that will be an excellent place to start.

"I will get with the Prince and the Provost and see what we can find. Make your plans and let me know when you're ready," said Derek.

"Aye, sir," said Stewart as he went to tell Mac, John, and Alexander the news.

Mac and Derek settled by a fire. They had received some whiskey from Lord Murray. They hated to open it without Connor to share – but they were pretty sure he was wining and dining with the best - at least in between back-breaking rides. "Dear Lord, Mac, Look at all that has happened in only four weeks! I'm exhausted thinking about it."

"No doubt, Major," said Mac.

"Mac... do me a favor," said Derek.

"What do ye need, boss?" asked Mac.

"I need you to call me Derek. We're a long way from Afghanistan. You're not just the Sergeant Major now. You are Lord McKenzie. We are equals before man and God..." He started laughing. "What I'm saying, Mac-is you're the best and most loyal friend I have ever had. When we're not around the troops or anyone else that might take offense – please call me Derek."

Mac started laughing. "My Lord. Can't have a Noble pissed at me..."

Derek picked up a pinecone and threw it at him. They laughed and took a wee dram...or two... or three... watched the fire... and thought secretly of their home and loved ones they would probably never see again. Mac's heart ached. He so wished Annie was here.

"FINALLY!!! Home!" Connor loved Shadow Bane... but he would be okay if he didn't have to ride for a bit. It had gotten easier... but DAMN! Everything still hurt. He thought to himself – he must've turned his liver upside down with all of the damn bouncing..."

They rode into Culloden House – Forbes' Estate around 8 pm on May 3, 1746. Quite a crowd came rolling in with Lamont's men and their own. They were sent to a bunkhouse where the cooks would prepare a meal for everyone. Everyone was exhausted... except for Lord Forbes. He was energetic and ready to kick into high gear as the host of this gathering. He jumped into command mode once he dismounted in the courtyard. Stewards were jumping. Cooks preparing. All hands on deck for the arrival of another Lord and all that entailed. Baths were prepared, and clothes were readied. It was as if there was a gigantic mound of ants, and the mound was disturbed.

Connor dismounted and almost wanted to kiss the ground. Before he could turn around, he was nearly tackled by a raven-haired mad woman... he laughed. As did she. "Lady Mary – I am inclined to believe this manner of behavior is not too lady-like?" Connor asked with a smile.

"Aye. You're right, My Lord. I suppose I can act as an old proper woman if that would be your preference?" Smiled Mary.

"No, My Lady. It is my sincere hope that when we have been wed for 50 years, you will hobble up to me with your cane and attempt to jump into my arms then as well as now!" Laughed Connor.

"Aye, My Lord. Though I'll probably want to beat you with it if you stay this contrary?" Which elicited an even bigger smile from Connor. "I have SO much to tell you. We have had to move quickly with our upcoming wedding. We have everything just about set. I hope you're not disappointed with not having much to do with the planning part of this?" asked Mary.

"My Lady... as long as I am a part of the wedding night – I am sure I will be delighted with whatever the plans may be..." Connor smiled and then gave her a kiss for good measure.

All of a sudden, Lady Mary stopped and wrinkled her nose. "My Lord, you smell like the backside of your horse. Please go bathe. I must have been totally out of my senses rushing to you as I did!"

"And you know the smell of the backside of a horse... how?" asked Connor. Lady Mary blushed deeply and then almost became indignant... when Connor busted out laughing, and then she did as well.

Bath time was over, and dinner had been served – remarkable as always. It was time for the Study for the men and the Parlor for the women. The discussion will be quick tonight. It was late, and all were exhausted. A wee dram, Cigar, a few minutes of conversation and bed.

Lord Forbes poured for Connor and Lord Lamont. Connor sat back and listened to the two men talk politics moving forward.

"What do you want, Lord Lamont?" asked Lord Forbes.

"I've told you. I want rights. I want to live my life unmolested and taxed enough to pay for the government that we need – not taxed out of my property. I understand the need for a Monarch to have power – but unlimited Divine Rights of Kings is total Bull Shit. I'll not trade one tyrant for another. I've told you that. I also want some rights for the common people. They need to be able to have some rights to the land they've worked on and legal protections as well. If he wants my support to help him claim the crown – he will have to work with me."

"That's what I've been telling you, friend. He is more than willing to do so. He wants what is best for Scotland – and eventually for the United Kingdom," said Lord Forbes.

"That is what he is telling you. But we do the work. We do the paying. We do the fighting. We do the dying. I've fought my share. My family has paid with blood for generations. I'll just no longer do it unless the reason is justified," said Lord Lamont.

"Lord McAndrew – you have said very little," said Lord Forbes.

"My dear Lord Forbes," said Connor. "I am learning from the best. Why should I interrupt?"

"Do you jest?" asked Lord Lamont.

"No, my Lord. I do not. I have heard this all before. What we need is a Constitution. To make this government a Constitutional Monarchy."

"And what do you mean by that, young McAndrew?" asked Lord Lamont.

"I am utterly exhausted, and my thoughts may be clouded by this amazing whiskey that I have been presented with tonight... but I will do my best to explain. Are you talking just for Scotland – or for the larger prize, which is England itself?" asked Connor.

"Well," said Lord Forbes. "Let's discuss the larger prize – England itself."

"Very Well then, we would need to merge Scotland and England fully together – more than just the act of Union from 1707. They would have to be a completely united country. Then, we would establish a Constitutional Monarchy. In a Constitutional Monarchy, there are limits. It is a Monarchy that is bound by the rule of law – just as the Nobility... and the Commoner would be. It is an equal opportunity and equal justice for all," said Connor.

"Hmmm.." said Lord Lamont. "I am intrigued. Go on."

"In my honest opinion, there are certain rights that are given to us by God. Your station in life is based on who God decided to use as your parents. It's not based on anything that you have personally done – no achievements accomplished... you were blessed with being born at the right time, at the right place, with the right parents. That place of birth gives wealth and power – or starvation and want. I believe that for those who have wealth and power ... their responsibility is to protect the rights of those who do not have wealth or power. It would be a good thing if Prince Charles championed the rights of the nobles and the rights of the commoners. What type of compromises with the Nobility can be made that can give them additional rights, reduce taxes, and give rights to those that are baseborn? In essence – it is the defined rule of law that dictates behaviors and punishments – that are given out by judges and juries of the peers of the accused. I haven't been able to set it to paper. I believe that it is something that can be worked out to the benefit of all. What I see, gentlemen is that we are in a position to influence a future king. What kind of world will it be? Not only for us – but for our posterity. I can say that history has shown that things do not go well when the masses are mistreated for a long time. We are outnumbered, gentlemen. Heavily outnumbered. I would much rather be on good terms with so many – than to be overlords and adversaries."

Lord Forbes looked at the man that would be his son-in-law. "I am not so sure that I agree with all that you say. My initial response is to grab you by the throat and to stop what you say. Yet… there is merit to what you say. I think that a compromise would be acceptable. You are correct that we are vastly outnumbered. If all of those in Inverness wanted me dead and my lands spoiled, there would be nothing that I could do but take some with me. And that, My Lords – is what scares the bloody hell out of every Noble."

"Fascinating discourse, Young McAndrew. You now have my attention. If these are the advisors to a future King – I could support that train of thought and course of action," said Lord Lamont. "If we cannot be free – what is the very point of life? God has designed us for such a purpose – yet our society squashes any purpose – despite God's Design. There has to be room for compromise. If we find that, you can bet that I will wholeheartedly support Prince Charles as our King.

"Alas, My Lords and My Friends – I am exhausted. Would you be so kind as to show me to my bed chamber before I pass out here in the study?"

Everyone agreed. Everyone was exhausted. The future would indeed be an exciting discovery.

Lord Lamont was escorted to his bed chamber. Connor went automatically to Lady Mary's. She was in there awaiting him. "Ah, my love…it appears you have had an exciting journey. How's your arse?" She smiled innocently.

"Dear Lord, In Heaven… it was awful. Fortunately, it is much better now…though it is still tender. I've been in full combat situations where I did not feel as bad following," said Connor.

Lady Mary burst out laughing. "You do look exhausted, my love. Let's get ready for bed." She disrobed and bathed. Connor started to help – she waived him off, to his surprise. He started to do the same. "No," said Lady Mary. You wait.

"Very well, My Lady," said Connor.

When she was ready and in her shift, she walked over to Connor and began to disrobe him. She looked at the weariness in his eyes. "This won't take long, My Love." She washed his hair – it was getting longer. He now had the beginning of a beard. She liked the look. She washed him, paid particular attention to the large muscle groups, and massaged them. She laughed when Connor grimaced at a particular sore spot. She finished and put a nightshirt on him as well.

They went to the bed. The board was gone. Connor looked at her questionably. "Love – we wed Saturday. It's okay."

Connor then reminded her – "My Lady, I am adamant about our relationship until we are married."

"I fully understand, My Lord. If you notice – I have not been as forward as I have been in the past?"

"Indeed, I did. And I am thankful," said Connor.

They both got in bed. Lady Mary rolled on her side and snuggled close to Connor. He put his arm around her. This just felt right. Then he felt her backside push against him. His body reacted accordingly.

"My Lady, if you continue to do that, you will force me to turn over to sleep on my other side," said Connor.

Lay Mary laughed. "Aye, My Lord. I just wanted to make sure that you were still interested in me. It's been almost two weeks!"

'There is no way, My Lady… that I could ever NOT be interested." Replied Connor…

But before Lady Mary could reply, Connor's breathing evened out. His body jerked twice, and he started softly snoring….

Lady Mary smiled to herself. She leaned over… poor baby… he is indeed exhausted. She turned over and kissed him as he slept. She thought to herself. God had indeed intervened with this man coming into her life. She could not be happier. She pulled him close – feeling safer than she ever had in her life… and was soon asleep as well.

Chapter 30
Progress

Derek woke up ready to get to work. There was so much to do, and that unknown timeline of the King in London and when the invasion would come added more urgency to that preparation. Connor would be here soon if he were not already. He needed his help – but that wedding was coming up on Saturday. "I may as well face it… he won't be much help for the next few weeks. I haven't even met her yet. I need to remedy that before they marry," he thought.

So… what to do? It looks like the Officers here had everything under control. He would do a walk-through, then head to Inverness with Mac. He wanted to see that his plans were going to come to fruition. They could start where the building was to begin, see the Provost, and see how everything was developing. Progress is a strange thing. It can appear on the surface that everything is moving in the right direction – only to discover a flaw beneath that surface. Relax! You have a great supporting team – not only from your troops but also from the town.

He thought back to Connor. I wonder how it went with Lord Lamont. He wondered if Lord Lamont would get on board with everything and be able to see the direction in which they were moving. For some reason, Derek knew instinctively that Lord Lamont was THE KEY to the Crown of Scotland. He was glad Connor was there to participate in that discussion. Connor could be quite the salesman if he needed to be.

Derek stepped outside. The sun was beginning to rise. He could hear movement in the camp. Once the camp was constructed, he would have to take the troops to Inverness. This is home for now. Everyone needs to get acquainted. However, he would have to remind them again about Venereal Diseases and the lack of cures in their new home. Houses of ill repute would not be a good destination – no matter how badly they wished to do so. Perhaps Penicillin could be an invention on which they could work. There is so much room for innovation. Educational diversity within the camp would be huge for their continued success.

Mac came around the corner. "I thought I heard you stirring. What do you say we go for a run? I know we're not just sitting on our bums and doing nothing. But I also know the stress load is about to increase exponentially. We need to get in the habit of exercising. We may need to get everyone up for PT in the mornings. I feel like this is something we need to make into a habit. What do you think... Derek?"

"Damn! You know my name!!" exclaimed Derek.

Mac smiled at that. "Aye. Vaguely."

"And yes, you are correct. We do need to do that. Let's get through this week and Connor's wedding on Saturday. In the meantime – I am totally up for a run. Let's do it."

They took off running. It had been a while. They decided to run north through the woods. A couple of miles away, there was a pond. It would be an excellent place to run, get a drink from the creek, and head back. The air was thick with humidity. The temperature was pleasant, so it wasn't overbearing. Each man was lost in his own thoughts as they started with a brisk pace. They had run many miles together. This was not the first. Their pulses were rising. Their breathing increased. There was a deer trail they came across and followed it. It went up a bluff, and they could see the pond from above. That was their original plan. There was a farm not too far away from there, but they chose to bypass it. The pond was up ahead, and their pace increased. Derek was in the lead... Mac decided to challenge him..., and then the race was on. It was a full sprint. Derek was younger but was challenged by Mac. Faster. Mac started to pass him. Derek would have none of that. He picked up the pace even faster. They were about 100 yards from the pond. It was a run as fast as you can mad dash sprint now. Mac was ahead. Then Derek. Derek was a few paces ahead. Then Mac started to catch him. Harder. Faster. They were pushing each other. Derek got to the pond by only a couple of steps and then was forced to bend over to catch his breath. Mac collapsed upon the Heather... They both started laughing. "Dear God, Mac! I thought you were gonna kill me!"

"We're both getting fat and out of shape," said Mac. We definitely need to do this regularly. We've only gone a couple of miles. My lungs are in open revolt right now!"

"Aye! Me too!" Laughed Derek. "While we're here…let's take a swim. It's been a while since we've had a bath. You're starting to stink, I'm afraid!"

"Moi?" asked Mac. "Why do you think I've been making it a point to be upwind of ya? You're starting to smell like roadkill!"

They burst out in laughter. They disrobed, set their clothing on several large rocks, and jumped in the water. It was a bit chilly – but not as cold as they thought. Derek splashed Mac, and the water fight was on. They swam around a bit, then decided it was time to get back to camp. There was much work to do.

They headed towards where their clothing was. They were gone— even their boots.

"What the bloody hell? Where's our clothes?" asked Derek.

Before Mac could answer, Derek heard a feminine voice cry out…

"Well, Heather… what have we here? It appears that two gentlemen are frolicking in the water with no clothing to be seen anywhere?" said Helen.

Heather said, "I am astonished that anyone would be naked out here in the wilderness. Totally unashamed. You would think that a man of decency would make better arrangements for privacy, Helen."

Two women walked out from the woods. "Good morning gentlemen. It appears that you're in quite a predicament, I would say," said Helen.

"It depends on what you would call a predicament. It could always be an opportunity," said Derek. He and Mac were neck-deep in the water. "I would love to continue this conversation; however, we have much to do today."

"Perhaps you do. I have no doubt. But I am sure that clothes would benefit all involved?" asked Heather…laughing.

"May I at least get the names of the beautiful lasses that have absconded with our clothing?" asked Derek.

"I think we have a better bargaining position?" asked Heather. "Perhaps you could tell us yours first?"

"I am Lord Derek McAndrew and the ugly one to my right is Lord Ian McKenzie."

"Lords? Here? Now? I'm afraid that is a difficult story to accept," Helen said. "Besides, why would you have been running and not riding a stallion if you were a Lord?"

"Could it be we like to run?" asked Mac.

Helen laughed. "That is even more doubtful!" But because of your total unflinching look, I would guess that you believe the fancy… then perhaps you can have your clothes. But you will have to come get them." She smiled mischievously.

"Don't think we won't," said Derek. "We have been in much more difficult positions than these and have survived nicely."

Heather and Helen stepped back about 20 yards, laid the clothing on the ground – and stepped back further. "We'll wait then!"

"Only after you bless us with your names," said Derek.

"I am Helen, and this is my younger sister Heather," said Helen.

"Well, looking at your Tartan – then you're Ferguson's as well," said Mac.

"Indeed, we are. And you're trespassing on our land. Which is what got you into this 'situation.'" Laughed Heather. "Though I admit that I like your current state of affairs!"

"Well, now that we have been formally introduced, would you be so kind as to leave our clothes where you found them?" asked Derek. "We are trying to be gentlemen, and you're not making it easy!"

"No… I don't think we are so inclined," said Helen. "You are going to have to come get them."

Derek and Mac started towards the shore within a blink of an eye. Naked as the day they were born.

Helen shouted, "My Lords! The water must indeed be cold!" They watched the men come to get their clothes, and as they started to put them on. Then they took off running back home and laughing as they left.

"I think they like us," said Derek, laughing. "I'd chase them down, but I am afraid we have too much to do."

Mac agreed. "That's definitely a first. I thought women were supposed to be much more reserved now. Unless they have brothers, that would be a little less than ladylike, I think?"

Everything is on, and it's time to go back. The run was needed. And Heather… that was a lovely lass. He would have to meet here sometime. She would probably shite herself if he rode up with his stallion and proper attire…. Or even yet – a Jackal! She would probably faint on the spot! He made up his mind that he would indeed visit that farm.

They got back to the camp around 0830. Breakfast had already been served, and the men were already working. Fortunately, the cooks had saved them a meal. They were both famished from the run and their encounter.

They ate, then took a quick walk around the camp. A roof was being put in place on his "home." He was thrilled with the prospect of having walls and a window. If he just had a toilet and shower… Oh well… baby steps. They will have to invent that, too, he thought to himself.

"Alright Mac. Let's go see what our future King is doing, then head to Inverness," said Derek.

"Sounds like a good idea, Derek," said Mac.

They went to get their horses. Derek called, "Riogh! How are ya lad? It's good to see you, boy!"

"Well… I guess I will have to come up with a name for mine. I've been too busy to think about it. Connor has Shadow Bane, and you have Riogh. I'll have to think about it," said Mac.

They mounted up and headed to the Prince's camp.

Once they got to the Prince's Tent, Mac said, "Brendan."

Derek looked at him. "Brendan? Who would that be?" asked Derek.

Mac Smiled. "My horse's name is Brendan. It means 'Determined.' I think that fits. What about you?"

"Aye," replied Derek. "I like it."

Fiona popped out of the tent. "I'm afraid you missed him. He went to Inverness to check on the progress and to meet with the Provost."

"Very well – we will head there as well, then," said Derek.

"Which is exactly what the Prince said that you would say." Fiona smiled.

They mounted up again and were off. It was only a 30-minute ride.

They could see hundreds of people from a distance working on the foundations of the buildings that needed to be constructed. He knew that there were hundreds felling trees and preparing them to travel to the construction site. That reminded him – he needed to ask for a lot of rope and some volunteers to look for caves – or if anyone knew about caves that were not too far away – and especially if anyone knew where there were bats.

In the distance- he saw the White Stallion. The Prince would probably need to consider getting a Black Stallion. That white stallion was such an easy identifier– it would make it easier for assassins. Of course, the Provost was right there with him.

"It's about time you decided to join the fun, Lord McAndrew. I thought you would sleep the day away!" jested the Prince.

"As you know, Your Highness, we are doing a major construction project at our camp as well," said Derek. "Good Morning, Your Highness and Provost. It looks like things are coming along famously."

"Indeed, they are, Lord McAndrew. We are setting up the foundations for the buildings, as you discussed. We are also digging wells for water, as you requested. This will indeed be quite an undertaking," said Provost Frasier.

"No doubt about it," replied Mac. "You do realize this will make Inverness a very popular town? Are you ready? Once we are done – you may wish to plan for more infrastructure. I do not doubt that your population will probably double in the next year or two."

The Provost gulped hard. "Do you really think so?

"Yes, Provost. This is going to be the hub of a lot of different types of development. Your community is going to change the world. It would be best if you were prepared," said Derek.

"Provost. I have a need that I hope you can address. I need rope. Hundreds of yards of rope. I also need to know if your citizens have any experience in caves and if you are aware of any large bat populations that are close," said Derek.

"Bats? What do you need with those vile creatures?" asked the Provost.

"You are familiar with gunpowder, correct," asked Derek.

"Of course, I have muskets, so I am familiar with gunpowder."

"The Bat Guano can be refined into Potassium Nitrate, an additive we need to manufacture our ammunition. We will need tons of it to get the quantity we need for production," said Derek.

The Provost then mentioned, "I am aware of a few caves that should have bats – but I believe there are probably some roosting sites relatively close that may work as well – if all you need is the bat shite. I have some folks that could probably be a guide for your men. I can have them, the rope, and other materials that can be of use, a wagon, and a team of horses for you by tomorrow morning. Have your men meet me here at 8 am."

"That would be great and very much appreciated!" said Derek.

"What is the process so I can ensure we have what we need?" asked the provost.

"The first thing, of course – is to collect the bat manure. Then you mix it with water. You then pour it over a straw or something like that to filter out the solids. You collect the liquid, then set it in the sun to let the water evaporate. The crystals that remain are what we will need. Depending on the purity, you may need to mix it with water again to get the rest of the impurities to evaporate. That's one of the reasons we need water wells close to where we will be building."

"Ahhh... okay. That makes sense now. Thank you for that information. Now I know what else we will need to plan appropriately," said the Provost.

Provost John Frasier of Inverness had indeed been a busy man. This man was an organizational genius, thought Derek. He had put together work teams with a gaffer (foreman) in charge – each in teams of 20. Each of the five teams had a Supervisor in charge, and they all reported to him and his assistant – Jordan McGregor. Ten wagons with cooks were put together to feed everyone. Outhouses had been constructed. The daily wage was 2 Shillings for a laborer, 5 Shillings for the gaffer, and 10 Shillings for the Supervisor. This would put a little strain on the liquidity for the Lords financing it – but all of this was doable for at least the next year – and even more so once the sale of items produced could be accomplished.

The Prince asked, "Well, what do you think of our capabilities?"

"Impressive, Your Highness. And to be honest – I am totally amazed at the ability to get things moving so quickly. I must admit that when I looked at the time frame that we had hoped for in preparation, I was concerned that we may not meet the need. But with what I see here, with only three days in? It is truly miraculous." Derek responded.

"A change of subject, Lord McAndrew. I want to ensure that you know that your brother is to wed Lady Mary Forbes this Saturday." The Prince reminded.

"Oh shite! Oh – excuse me, Your Highness. I had totally forgotten!" said Derek. "I guess I should find out my responsibilities in the ceremony. I don't even know if I have any!"

"I found out last night that they made it back safely with Lord Lamont and his men in tow. I expect they will be contacting me today to set up a meeting with Lord Lamont tomorrow. I would like for you and Lord McKenzie to attend. Lord Forbes and your brother should be in attendance as well. I will also want Lord Murray, Lord Gordon, and a few other prominent men in my Council to attend two hours later. That way, if it gets heated, we can calm it down before the others attend. Perhaps then, you can discover your role in the nuptials," said the Prince.

"Excellent, Your Highness. We would be honored to attend," said Derek.

Lord McKenzie agreed as well.

Pleased with the progress, the men decided to head back to Camp Striker, as they called it…their home for now. Checking on Progress and letting the Cavers know their materials would be available to plan on leaving tomorrow to get to Inverness by 0800.

When the men arrived at Camp Striker, they sought out Sergeant Robert Stewart. They informed him that he must have his team ready to go to Inverness at 0800 tomorrow.

Several roofs were complete. He went to his "home" and noticed a mason building a fireplace. That would be useful as the weather progresses into fall and then winter.

Lord Forbes hammered his fist on Connor's door. "Damn son! Are you going to sleep the day away!"

Connor woke up with a start and looked at his watch. It was 1030! He had slept for over 12 hours! "Sorry, My Lord. This trip was harder on me than I thought. Give me a few minutes, and I will be down."

Lord Forbes laughed. "To be honest with you, lad – I only woke up an hour ago. Lord Lamont is just stirring. Dinner will be ready soon, and I knew you would be hungry. Lady Mary wanted to be the one to awaken you… I thought it would be more fun if I did."

Connor heard him laughing as he walked away. He definitely would have preferred waking with a kiss from Lady Mary! He stretched and groaned. He was still a bit sore. He needed to get up and meet with Derek and Mac to see where things were and what he needed to do to get plugged in. Although he knew that it was good for him to be a part of the team to pick up Lord Lamont – missing two full weeks of planning and the initial building of what was to be the future of the entire enterprise? He wasn't content to sit on the sidelines. He wanted to be in the middle of it all!

Mary then arrived and came in. Connor had gotten up and was beginning to use the wash basin. Mary had a cup of coffee for him. "Bless you, My Lady! You have no idea how much I need this!"

Mary laughed and laid back on the bed. Connor began to disrobe to put on his kilt and clothing for the day. Scars. Even though she had bathed him before, she had not noticed his scars. Of course, the lighting was much better in the daylight. He had been wounded several times. She began to look at him physically – as if for the first time. She could not wait to hear the stories – of the scars and the tattoos.

Connor was dressed. He bent over and picked up Lady Mary, and spun her around. He set her gently on her feet and kissed her firmly. "Now, I guess we must act properly. But today is Wednesday. Saturday will be here soon. You know I have no idea what I am to do?"

Mary laughed. "Just stand there and say what the Minister says to repeat. I think you can handle it… it will be much easier than handling me?"

Connor laughed at that… "Ahhh, My Lady. We shall see?" With that, they went downstairs. Dinner could be smelled at the top of the stairway, and Connor was starving suddenly!

Everyone was at the table when Connor and Lady Mary arrived. Connor held the chair for Lady Mary as she sat. Lady Forbes smiled at the gesture – and then gave a subtle scowl towards her husband, who no longer attended to her as Connor did to Lady Mary.

Lord Forbes announced to all that they would be able to rest today and would meet with the Prince the following day at 900 am at his camp. Following their meeting, they would meet with the rest of the Prince's Council. "Lord McAndrew, you will be attending. The Prince has requested your presence as well. For today, Lord McAndrew. You will be meeting with a Tailor for your wedding attire. He will have to work through the next few days to have it completed by Friday afternoon so that he can make any adjustments for you."

With that – the meal began. Small conversations, simple as everyone, looked to Lord Lamont to see what he had to say. The conversation was simple and cordial – more directed to the future wedding than anything else. Lord Lamont and Lord Frasier kept politics away from the table. That would be for another time. Connor thought of how right everything felt. He just wished that his parents could be here. Are they even alive in this timeline? Would they have learned of the disappearance of their sons? He gulped back the tears. Wow! That was not the emotional response that he anticipated. Connor excused himself from the table. Everyone looked on in bewilderment – but he left the room and walked outside for a few minutes. Deep breaths. They are ok. He knew it. God would not have brought them here to hurt his family. After a few minutes, he was okay. He walked inside and apologized. "When you have to go…sometimes you have to go." Everyone laughed it off but Lady Mary. She knew something was amiss. She would speak with him later.

A Steward walked into the room, bent down, and whispered to Lord Forbes. When he left, Lord Forbes announced that he, Lord Lamont, and Lord McAndrew were confirmed and would meet with the Prince on the morrow at 9 am. That meant the day would be a rest day for Connor – and he was glad of it. Connor felt like he needed to ride by himself. He needed some room to contemplate the new life thrust upon him.

When Dinner was over – he went over to Mary. He apologized in advance and said that he needed to go for a ride. To be by himself for a couple of hours. She understood. She had seen her father do that as well. The enormity of what was, in reality, happening struck Connor. It was more than a simple assignment in Afghanistan.

Connor climbed onto Shadow Bane and just rode. He let Shadow Bane choose the gate and the direction. Feeling the wind blow through his hair… the gallop… each step jolting him back to reality. He realized that he was almost at Camp Striker. He needed his brother. He needed family – at least for a few minutes. Once they reached the woods, Shadow Bane began to Cantor, trot, and then walk, catching his wind from the run. It was apparent that the run… the freedom… is what Shadow Bane lived for. Connor took him to the Horse Master and dismounted. Rest, water, then oats. Connor told him he must leave in the next couple of hours.

Connor found Derek. Derek said, "I'm glad you could trouble yourself to attend to those lower in rank." Derek was teasing him when he realized there was indeed something wrong. "Are ya getting cold feet? I've known ya too long. What's wrong?"

"Cold feet? Maybe a bit. But she is amazing, Derek. No. That's not the problem. It's everything else, Derek. Where and when we are. What we're doing. How we're changing everything. I started to hyperventilate during dinner. I just had to get out. None of them know what we know. I need to hear it from you. Are we doing the right thing?" asked Connor.

"It's a bit late to ask that question now, don't you think?"

Connor looked at Derek with pleading eyes…

"Alright. Yes. I seriously believe we are doing the right thing. Why would we be here otherwise? We have to trust in God on this one. We have no choice but to trust."

"I suppose you're right," said Connor. "I just wished I could call and talk to mum or da. To get their opinion on this whole situation."

"Aye. I understand, little bro. I miss them too. There's not much we can do about that – except live the life we have in front of us as well as we can – and be there for each other. Besides – you haven't said a thing about our new camp. Not a word about my new home. You also have one, though I doubt you'll be here much to use once you are married. I'm not sure Momma Forbes would let her daughter be with 150 men here at Camp Striker!" They both laughed at that.

"Alright then. Show me what all I've missed," said Connor.

Derek took him on the tour. Eight more cabins needed roofs—and 12 needed Fireplaces. There was a courtyard and meeting Cabins. Connor hated to admit it – but Derek had managed to pull this off quite nicely. Derek told him of his run with Mac – including Heather and Helen. Connor laughed at that. Cold water huh? And laughed even harder. Connor could tell there was some interest in Heather when Derek mentioned her name. It would be suitable for Derek to find a woman, too. That was the life that Derek wanted. To be a family man and have a farm. Who knows? But God.

Connor hugged Derek, gathered Shadow Bane, and returned to Culloden Estates. He hoped that Mary would understand. He felt that she would. He was going to have to begin the process of letting her know where he came from and what all of that entailed. Hopefully, she wouldn't think that he had lost his mind.

He arrived back at Culloden Estates – feeling much better about everything. Derek was a pain in the ass… but that's what brothers do. He was glad he wasn't here without some family. No one else could say that from his Company.

Lady Mary saw Connor arrive. "Are you okay, My Lord? It is almost dinner time. You have been away for some time. I was getting worried."

Connor jumped off Shadow Bane, scooped her in his arms, planted a kiss firmly on her lips – and let her know – yes. He was much better. Much better, indeed.

The morning got here quickly, thought Derek. He felt like he had just closed his eyes. He liked his new cabin. It did feel like a home. He was still missing the bathroom and kitchen, though. Today was going to be monumental. He hoped Lord Lamont was as reasonable and could be persuaded as Lord Forbes had suggested. He hoped there was a Plan B if this didn't work out as planned.

It was 0600. I wonder if Mac was up for a run? The sun was rising. No time for a swim today, though… he laughed. Why was he thinking about Heather again? She was beautiful, though he believed she could be a handful!

There was a knock on the door. A real knock! On an actual door! "Yes?" Derek asked.

"You up for another run?" asked Mac,

"Just shows you intelligent minds think alike. Yes. I am. I need to use the latrine and drink water before we go."

They took off on a run. It was a beautiful morning. The sun was beginning its westward journey. The temperature was perfect for this May. It seems it has not rained as much as he thought. He would enjoy the perfect weather while he could. Up and around the pond and back to Camp Striker. It was a 5-mile run. Funny… he was getting used to the English Measurements. It is definitely more cumbersome than the Metric System. But at least he had learned it as a kid. It would be a bitch trying to figure it out now!

Breakfast at 7. Clean up and leave by 8 to get to the camp before 9. He could feel the difference in his body. He had probably lost 20 lbs. since arriving and was in good shape. He was leaner. His hair was getting long. He was sporting a beard. He missed those at home… but they were becoming a distant memory. He honestly believed that in this timeline – they would not exist. That's the only way he could keep his sanity.

Before he knew it, he was mounting on Riogh. This was becoming easier. The past was becoming further away. At first, he had wondered if God had made a mistake by including him here and now. But he was beginning to understand. He was born 200 years too late. This felt as close to home as he had ever felt.

They arrived at 0845. Everyone rode up at roughly the same time. The gray-haired man… that must be Lord Lamont. He looked rather stern… like he was expecting a fight and wasn't afraid should it come to one. Of course, the niceties would come as everyone was introduced.

Lady Fiona met them at the entrance to the tent. The Prince would see them now. And so, it begins…

The Prince stood to greet his guests. Rather than worrying about a bow – he reached out and shook the hands of them all. It's funny how that simple gesture relaxed Lord Lamont. If this man who would be King was willing to shake the hands of the lower born – perhaps there could be a chance this might be the man to get behind as King.

First of all, Lord Forbes and Lord McAndrew – thank you for your harrowing journey to seek out Lord Lamont. And Lord Lamont… thank you, sir, for meeting me during this momentous occasion.

"We shall see, Your Highness. That being said, sir, I intend to be vocal and honest. I have no choice but to be blunt. Please do not see it as an affront to your position," said Lord Lamont.

"Lord Lamont. Understand this. I expect your honesty. Without your and my honesty back towards you – how can I ever wish to gain your support?" said the Prince.

"Very well. I will start it with a blunt question. Why, Your Highness, should I trade one tyrant for another?" said Lord Lamont.

There was a collective gasp in the room. The Prince laughed.

"You, sir, are who I need on my council," said the Prince.

"Wait. What? What did you say, Your Highness?" asked a flustered Lord Lamont.

"Lord Lamont. I do not have now, nor ever want sycophants on my Council. I need those who are willing to tell me what I do not wish to hear to be able to make a better decision. I cannot say that I will always agree with you – but I can tell you that your opinion will be heard. Do you see these men in here with us right now? Besides Lord Murray – who I wanted to wait until we had this discussion – these men are on my council. Have you ever known Lord Forbes to be a Yes Man?” asked the Prince.

“No, Your Highness. He’s a rather opinionated man for sure,” said Lord Lamont. All laughed at that comment.

The Prince continued, “Let me tell you a story that will, at the very least, get you to see things from my perspective. As a child, I had a commoner that was a friend. Commoner. I wouldn't say I like that name. We are ‘Noble’ simply because God gave us this life of privilege. This child that I grew up with was the son of our cook. I ate with him daily. We became good friends. I would sneak him food – he was always hungry. He got older, and one day – he was gone. I asked his mother where he was. She started sobbing. He had run in front of a noble that was on his horse. The horse threw the Noble, who broke his arm in the fall. Now understand. This child was ten years old. The noble got up with his arm hanging as it was broken. It was his left arm. He drew his blade and killed that child on the spot. No one spoke. There were no consequences. He was a base-born child. Why did it matter? When I heard the story – I was an 11-year-old child. And I swore before God – that if I ever became King – Justice would apply to all. I swear before you and before God Almighty now… That I meant it then – and I mean it now. More than ever.”

Lord Lamont sat down. Silent. Taking in all that had just been said. “I have but one question then. Would you support a Constitution that would limit your powers and limit the powers of the Lords while providing for basic rights for those without power?”

“Only if you would be involved in writing it. I might not agree with everything, but it would all be negotiable. I want you to understand this, Lord Lamont. I have the military capacity to seize absolute power should I desire. I am not aware if you know this, but in the battle of Culloden with the British and the Duke of Cumberland, there were no survivors, including the Duke. We could march on Edinburgh now, and no one could stop us. Do I say this to brag? No sir. I do not. It is a fact. Is it so, Lord Forbes?” Lord Forbes nodded in agreement. “But I choose not to. I want your support. I want the support of the Nobles. I want the support of the people. We have the chance to do this right. To give freedom and to end tyranny. We need you, Lord Lamont. We need to believe that we are a Nation. We are Scottish. Even above Clans. We are all of the same blood." The Prince put out his hand… "Will you be on my Council, Lord Lamont? Will you be a part of the history of our nation as we are separated from the tyrants that are the English?"

Lord Lamont…saw his hand… on its own… reach out and shake the hands of the man that would be King. "How on earth did you do that, Your Highness?"

The Prince laughed. "It is because I am being sincere, My Lord. I speak from the heart. I love this nation. I love the people. It is my responsibility before God to bring freedom to those that I would rule."

The other Lords came into the tent: Lord George Murray, Lord William Gordon, Lord John Drummond, Lord John Murray, and John O'Sullivan… they heard laughter, heard wine goblets clinking… and there were smiles on everyone's faces. They asked no questions; they knew the deal was made. Instead, they grabbed the wine and celebrated with the rest.

The Prince declared," I have taken the privilege of having dinner prepared early. From here, we will be going to Inverness. You will be pleased to see where we are in the initial stages of construction. It's truly amazing what these people can do when they have a single mindset. Perhaps that is a lesson that we can all learn?"

After dinner was consumed and an almost overabundance of wine was served, the men mounted their stallions and left to go to Inverness.

On the outskirts of town – it was easy to see that a great deal had been completed. The layout of the buildings and the leveling for the foundations had been done. The wells had been dug. The first loads of timber had been received. And there was the Provost – in the middle of all barking orders, pointing where the delivery of supplies was to go… There is a yell here. A smile there. It was organized chaos. It was easy to see why the Provost…well... why he was the Provost.

"Prince Charles – I am so grateful that you are here. We are preparing to lay the first stone for the foundation of the Main Armory. Reverend Finlay Cameron is preparing to say the invocation."

All of the men rode to the Armory. They dismounted. Everyone was assembled. The Provost thanked everyone for their dedication and hard work. That there was much to be proud of. He then asked the Prince if he would like to share some words.

"Indeed. I would," said the Prince. He stood upon the stage that was built for this moment. He would not say much. "Ladies and Gentlemen of Inverness. I know that you did not come to listen to me drone about all of the hard work and dedication that has been shown over the last few weeks… but you left me no choice. I am truly humbled. I am humbled and so very appreciative of that hard work and dedication. It is the beginning of a future that our children's children will celebrate. I know this is not much. But Thank you. Thank you for everything… and since I was unprepared for a speech… I will leave it to our Minister."

With that – everyone gathered laughed.

Reverend Cameron stood up before the congregants. "Almighty and gracious God, we are gathered here today to seek your Divine Blessing upon this place and all who are in attendance here today and all of those working for this endeavor. Where the tools of defense and protection will be fashioned. We ask for your guidance and protection over Prince Charles, his Council, and all who labor within and upon these walls. Grant them wisdom, skill, and a strong sense of duty as they craft the instruments of peace and security. May this armory stand as a symbol of our commitment to safeguarding our community… and our nation. May this foundation laid remind us of Christ, the Foundation on which we stand. We humbly ask you for your blessings upon this endeavor. Amen."

With that…the stone… was set where the foundation of the armory had been carved. Much fanfare was given to laying the foundation's first stone. There were probably 2,000 people in attendance. The dignitaries gave their speeches. The meal wagons had food for all. With the beautiful weather, the joy of those in attendance…, and the touch of Providence… it felt like the hand of God was blessing this undertaking…guiding us with divine favor every step of the way.

With that, the celebration began in earnest. Pipers were playing, dancers were dancing, children were running to and fro… but it only lasted a few hours. There was more work to be completed before the day was done. Once two hours had passed, wives and children were sent home, and the rest returned to work.

Derek and Mac were able to get with Lord Lamont. They asked if he would like a tour. Which, of course – he said yes. The Prince and the Provost attended as well. They allowed Derek to take the lead…to explain each building. What each would be dedicated to constructing a world-class armory and military machine – but how the tools could be fashioned to produce peacetime products and prosperity for the people of Inverness. Derek's passion and commitment were what Lord Lamont needed to see. He began to feel it. He could understand it. He could taste it. He wanted more…to learn more. This could indeed be what he had prayed for his children and grandchildren. But – this is a question that needs to be asked. So – he gathered his inner strength and asked… "Your Highness, I have a difficult question I must ask – but I am afraid I must do so."

"Please do," said the Prince.

"Your Highness. It is well known that you are, by faith, a Roman Catholic. Scotland is a Protestant Country. Presbyterian is the primary faith denomination that the majority of Scots believe in. The prayer that was prayed today was by a Presbyterian Minister. I also do not have to remind you of your cousin – Queen Mary Stuart – who was a Roman Catholic and the direction that went. Would you consider converting to the Protestant Faith as a Presbyterian?"

"Indeed, Lord Lamont. A necessary shot across the Bow. I intended to allow for the Freedom of Religion – as a right for all. I have had several months to discuss the possibility inwardly and what that would entail. Each time, I would vacillate between what I knew versus what I knew would become an eventuality should I become the King. So – Lord Lamont. The answer is an unequivocal, 'yes.' I know to do otherwise would plunge Scotland and perhaps England itself into a Civil War. That is not the goal or my mission in being here. What point would it be to win the nation and then lose it again by Civil War? I am more pragmatic than my cousin was – though I must admit, there is a lifetime's worth of instruction that I will have to unlearn and a new faith that I will need to learn. Is that an acceptable answer, Lord Lamont?"

The smile on Lord Lamont's face answered the question before a word was uttered. "Yes, Your Highness. This is more than acceptable. It matters, Your Highness. It matters a lot."

"Lord McAndrew and Lord McKenzie, would it be acceptable for Lord Lamont, Lord Forbes, and I to attend Camp Striker on the morrow? I want Lord Lamont to see your camp and what the future holds for our nation."

"Yes, Your Highness," said Lord McAndrew. "By all means."

"Now, my dear Provost. Would you please ask if The Reverend Finlay Cameron would be interested in converting a Roman Catholic Prince to his way of thinking?"

The Prince saw it. There was a distinct difference in the Provost. It was a tangible change in his demeanor. His decision to convert fully to the Protestant faith – he knew… would guarantee him the crown. The sooner he learned this faith and was able to operate in that faith… the sooner he would be able to build the trust of his subjects. He also knew there would be difficulties from the Pope – he was already prepared for those. If it came down to it, having Scotland as an enemy instead of an ally may be a direction the Pope would not wish to go.

Chapter 31
The Wedding

Lord Forbes was in a mood! Today was Wednesday! Wednesday! "You've had weeks to prepare for this! Why the hell are we having so many problems? Do you realize the Prince is going to be here and will be staying the night?!?! Is it possible once… just once… to get competent help?!?!"

Lady Forbes walked discreetly to her tirading husband. "Lord Forbes. May I have a word with you?" There was enough stress in the house without his explosive behavior. She was not going to have it. "You do realize that repainting and completely renovating the room that the Prince is going to sleep but a few hours in – IS THE PROBLEM… and YOU created that problem?!?! Why don't you check on the progress in Inverness and let me take care of the wedding? NOW!"

"I want it perfect, Love…" said Lord Forbes meekly.

"Don't 'Love' me. It will be perfect. Now GO!!!"

Lord Forbes decided not to push it. Besides – he needed to invite a few others to the wedding officially. He did not like long engagements – because he believed that would lead to sin. But four weeks in the middle of all this and the two weeks to get Lord Lamont may have been pushing it – even with a staff of over 100. And she was right. It was his idea to remodel the King's room AND repaint the whole house. What the hell was he thinking with less than a week to go? He stormed out of the house to maintain his dignity. He had his horse saddled while Lady Forbes fixed his mess. She was talented at doing so. Perhaps from so much practice? Well, at least that made him smile.

He knew to go to Inverness. There was no use going to the camp. The Prince would be where the action was. Lord Lamont would unfortunately miss the wedding as he was en route to meet with Dr. William Wishart – Principal of the College of Edinburgh and the Moderator of the last Assembly. If Lord Lamont could convince him of the need for an Assembly – the ties could be voted on and severed with King George, and a new King could be installed. Lord knows they had sufficient reason to do so.

When Lord Forbes arrived, he saw the Prince in the middle of everything, as expected – which is where a leader should be. He was growing to truly respect this man – even though he was much younger than he.

All of the foundations were being laid for each of the buildings they would need to begin the construction of the military material they would need. He saw load after load of timber and other materials coming in by wagon. God, this was going to be a drain on his accounts. They had better win quickly so he could recoup what he was pouring into this happening. Thankfully, he was not the only one carrying the load.

"Good afternoon, Your Highness," said Lord Forbes.

"Ahhh. Lord Forbes. It is good to see you. I expected you to be preparing for the wedding?" asked the Prince.

Lord Forbes said sheepishly, "My Wife ran me off, I'm afraid."

"Imagine that." Laughed the Prince.

"Well, Your Highness. I have not officially invited you and your entourage to come to my home and enjoy the wedding. I would like to officially invite you to join us at the nuptials of my daughter, Lady Mary Forbes, and Lord Connor McAndrew. We even have a place for you to spend the night or more, Your Highness. We would be honored to have you in our home." Requested Lord Forbes.

"I would indeed be honored, My Lord. I would not miss it for the world," said the Prince.

"Reverend Cameron will be officiating. Has he approached you yet about converting?" asked Lord Forbes.

"Indeed, he has, sir. I am in my second class. I am learning the process. It will take a month or two to understand it completely," said the Prince.

"I should have started with this," said Lord Forbes. "Lord Lamont is en route to see Dr. William Wishart – Principal of the College of Edinburgh and the Moderator of the last Assembly. If anyone can begin installing you as King, Your Highness – it would be him. He has the power to declare an Assembly. Once that has been declared, you must address the Assembly."

"I will be ready, sir. Of that, you can be certain," said the Prince. "I may get Lord McAndrew to bring a Jackal to Edinburgh. That would indeed get their attention."

Lord Forbes laughed… "No doubt about that, Your Highness."

"Have you seen Lord Drummond, Murray, or Gordon, Your Highness?"

"Aye. They went into Inverness to the Boars Inn. I am assuming they wanted an Ale and private conversation. They asked me to attend, but my place is here right now," said the Prince. "As long as they see my Stallion – they know that I will support them and work as hard as they to make this happen."

Which, of course, is why he didn't want to leave Culloden Estates, thought Lord Forbes. They don't work as hard or fast when I am not there… "I fully understand and agree, Your Highness. I will go to the Boars Inn and have an ale on your behalf. Lord knows I could use one!"

The Prince laughed at that.

Lord Forbes headed to the town. He saw Lord McAndrew also overseeing the construction. This man was as different to his brother as day to night – but he had also earned Lord Forbes's respect. He was fearless, loyal beyond measure, hardworking, diligent… a leader in every sense of the word….and of course, Lord McKenzie was with him as well. There was a presence of Lord McKenzie that drew people in. Lord Forbes wanted to get to know them both better. "Lord McAndrew and Lord McKenzie… Good Afternoon!"

Both men had shovels and worked just as intently as those around them. "Good Afternoon, Lord Forbes! I'm guessing you came to join us? I am sure we could find another shovel that would fit you nicely?" Laughed Lord McAndrew.

"I'm afraid not today," said Lord Forbes. "But I am glad that I saw the both of you. As you know – your brother is to marry my daughter on Saturday. I have not been able to invite you and Lord McKenzie to the wedding formally. So – You are now formally invited. You may bring a companion should you so choose. Please extend this invitation to Lord Ross, Gordon, and MacLeod. I do not know if I will see them prior to the event. This is being rushed beyond my level of comfort, I am afraid."

"We will be delighted to attend. And will also pass the invitation to the others," said Derek.

"Excellent!" said Lord Forbes. "I'm afraid I must leave you to your work. I have to meet with Lord Murray, Gordon, and Drummond. I believe a pint is calling my name at the Boar's Inn," said a smiling Lord Forbes…and he was off.

"I like Lord Forbes. I guess it's good since the marriage will connect us," said Derek. "I would really hate to be on his bad side."

"No doubt," said Mac.

"I have an idea," said Derek – with a glimmer in his eye.

"You know, sir…that look always scares the shit out of me when you say that with that look," said Mac.

"I don't know. This may turn into nothing – but you heard Lord Forbes say we could bring a companion?"

"Aye, and are you planning on paying for one? We seem to be a bit short of companions currently," said Mac.

"Aye…currently. You do remember Heather and Helen, don't you? The Ferguson sisters?" asked Derek.

"How could I forget? Do you remember they commented about the water being cold? I'm not sure they were impressed," said Mac.

"Perhaps. But perhaps they were? I have an idea," said Derek with a devious smile.

"Oh God, why do I believe I am going to regret this?" said Mac.

"It's about Dinner time. Let's go to the wagon and get a bite to eat. Then head to Striker. I'll let you know my idea when we get there," said Derek.

"Now?" asked Mac.

"Yes! Now!" said Derek.

"Well Hell," sighed Mac. "Let's do it. I'm hungry anyway."

Lord Forbes rode to Boar's Inn. The Hostler attended to the Lord and took the horse to the Livery, where it would be fed and watered.

Lord Forbes walked inside and saw Lord Murray and the others at a booth. Lord Murray looked up and smiled. "Why, Lord Forbes. What a pleasure to see you. I would have expected you to be rather busy at the home front preparing for the big day?"

"You know what happened?" said Lord Drummond. "The missus probably ran his ass out of the house, knowing Lady Forbes!"

That brought laughter to all and an embarrassed nod from Lord Forbes.

"With his pleasant disposition when he is highly stressed? Say it isn't so!" remarked Lord Gordon. Everyone laughed at that.

These men had known each other for years. They knew the good, the bad, and the ugly of each other's personalities and had experienced each unequivocally. That made everyone fair game for harassment.

"Your lovely bride did us a favor. As you know, we are funding a great deal of this venture. I have no doubt that it will be a financial boon for us as time progresses – but we may need to get a line of credit should this proceed for over a year," said Lord Drummond.

"I am okay as well for at least a year. The trade with England, of course, is non-existent. We may have to work on trading more with France than we currently do. We all had bumper crops last year – which helped tremendously. We may need to ask other Lords to get involved as we move forward," said Lord Gordon.

"I totally agree," said Lord Forbes. "However, you have seen some of the abilities of those who recently joined us. If we can boost the manufacture of many of their capabilities – we will be wealthy beyond all we can even dream of. That said, we could be Earls if we can maintain this ourselves. With our current arrangement, the Strikers get 25%, the Prince is in for 30% and we split 45%. It is unbelievable that the Prince would allow us such a large percentage. Usually, the Prince or Royalty would take 51%. Even he sees the potential for wealth."

"Here is the question that must be asked, gentlemen. And we must ask it now if we are to move forward. How far should we push this? Should Prince Charles become King Charles or maybe even Emperor Charles?" asked Lord Gordon. "We have much to lose should we make the wrong decision."

"You picked a hell of a time to ask that question." Laughed Lord Murray. We have known, fought, and bled with the Prince for nine months. We saw him at his best, and I believe at his worst in Culloden – where I believe our asses were to be handed to us – until the miracle happened. His father, by rights, should be King. We have seen the letter his Father penned that gave up that right to Prince Charles. I personally have seen tremendous growth in only the last 30 days. I genuinely believe he intends to give us more rights and reduce the level of power that Kings have traditionally employed. He loves the people he would serve, and they also love him. I will see this to the end with Prince Charles as King. I see no reason to do otherwise."

Everyone agreed. They got an Ale and drank to his honor. They now had to wait for the call for the Assembly. "I am confident Lord Lamont will get that to happen. You do realize that once Prince Charles becomes King Charles of Scotland – the battle is just beginning."

"Alright Lord Forbes. You have spent more time than anyone with those from the future. What are your thoughts?" asked Lord Drummond.

Lord Forbes began. "I have spent a great deal of time with Lord Connor McAndrew. I believe that he is like the others in leadership. He is uncomfortable in ruling – but he is comfortable in command. Ruling has to do with policy. Command has an underlying goal or purpose—a mission, so to speak. I am grateful to have him become my son-in-law. He is loyal. Absolutely fearless. His men love, respect, and would die for him." Lord Forbes told the story of Lord McAndrew with the 6 Bandits – even how he sewed up his Steward. He also discussed the level of honor he had conducted with his daughter – even in the bundling bed. That was something he could not say when he was betrothed. "His brother, Lord McKenzie, Gordon, Ross, MacLeod… all are solid like a boulder. Indeed – you saw how they reacted to the Assassination attempt when we first met them. I think once we start manufacturing and training for our troops, we will have no problem defeating England and anyone else that will get in our way. And furthermore… I would wager all that I own or will ever own – that we are truly… on the right side of history."

Everyone once again agreed. Now the conversation turned more to local politics, the size of the breasts of their current serving maid, their growing herds, their need for long-term planning… maybe finding appropriate daughters for the men from the future. The more they are attached to our area – the better it will be for us all.

Derek and Mac got back to Camp Striker. "Alright, Derek, what's on your mind?" asked Mac.

"Give me a minute first. I want to ensure we can make this happen now," said Derek.

"You know you have now reached the point where you are scaring the hell out of me," said Mac.

"Lieutenant Gordon, I need to know if we can have ten men up for a ride – smartly dressed in an hour. I would love to have the other Lieutenant's join us."

"Should we be armed?" asked Gordon.

"Only your blades and a pistol… this should be fun," said Derek.

Mac sighed… "Are you gonna tell me?"

"Aye. Do you remember how much the ladies doubted our stories being Lords and such?" asked Derek.

"Aye. I do," said Mac.

"I think we should get dressed up with an honor guard and meet the ladies' father – Lord Ferguson."

"And?" asked Mac.

"After the young ladies have squirmed a bit, apologized a lot – then see if they would like to attend the wedding." Beamed Derek with the most devilish grin Mac had ever seen.

Mac actually laughed. "Are you serious? Don't you think they would slit our throat after if given the chance?"

"Not in the least," said Derek. "Our charm will win them over. If not – the embarrassment will serve them right!"

Gordon returned with nine others, ready for an adventure.

Derek gave a quick description of what had transpired and his intentions. Everyone was on board… even Mac by then. He then told them to be dressed in their finest and be ready to mount up in an hour.

Everyone returned in an hour. All dressed up and ready to go. They mounted up and headed towards the farm close to the Pond, where Derek and Mac went for a swim. They got to the entrance of the Ferguson Estate and began down the road. They didn't charge in. They didn't wish to scare anyone. The entrance was quite beautiful. Ancient Oaks lined this portal to another world as they made an archway where sunlight filtered through radiantly.

The mansion, made from blocks of stone interlaced with Ivy, was stunning. Derek and Mac were riding at the head, looking at the exquisite workmanship… they didn't pay attention to the 20 men who appeared armed in their path.

"Good afternoon, gentlemen." Came a voice from the end of a portico. "How may I help you? This is not the road to Inverness."

Derek rode a few feet beyond the rest and introduced himself. "Good Afternoon, Gentlemen. I am Lord Derek McAndrew and here with Lord Ian McKenzie. We are here to meet Lord Ferguson."

Another voice said, "Without being rude, why would he desire to meet you?"

Derek said, "Because of his daughters."

Finally, a man appeared in front of them all. He was a powerfully built man in his early 50s with fiery red hair and a touch of gray in his beard and sideburns. Not a man to be trifled with. "You'll need to be more specific, sir. I have six daughters and four sons."

"That would be Helen and Heather," said Derek.

Derek heard the man say "Damn" under his breath – and smiled.

"Would you mind if we dismounted, Lord Ferguson? Asked Derek.

"Which of you had an issue with Helen and Heather?" asked Lord Ferguson.

"Lord McKenzie and I," said Derek.

"You and Lord McKenzie may do so. I sincerely apologize for the rudeness – but the times being that it is – one can never be too careful. And the rest of ya on horse – please keep your hands on your reigns. Every one of you has a musket aimed at him until I feel better about this unannounced meeting," said Lord Ferguson. "And for the two of you, I would appreciate it if you left your blades with my servants, who are coming to your horses now."

"Very well, sir. We are not here for trouble, I assure you," said Derek.

"I'll be the judge of that, sir," said Lord Ferguson. "First of all, I know your names. You are a part of what Inverness is calling the Saviors of the Jacobites."

Two men approached Derek and Mac. They both dismounted and handed over their blades. This wasn't what he expected…but for whatever reason, he did not feel his or anyone's life was in danger. Just a wise, extremely cautious man – especially considering a dozen men rode up unannounced.

Derek and Mac walked up to Lord Ferguson and gave a slight nod. Lord Ferguson gave them a nod back and bid them to follow him. There was a Veranda that overlooked the immense garden in the rear of the home. It was immaculate. The flowers – particularly roses, were blooming. The aroma was a sweet symphony of fragrances that worked together beautifully. Derek had to respond, "Lord Ferguson – your home and garden are beyond description. I truly believe this is as close to heaven on earth as possible."

"Thank you, Lord McAndrew, it is the culmination of generations of work. I did indeed add to it – but it is up to me to keep it for my children and their children. Now... we know you are not here to smell flowers, are you?"

Derek and Mac told their story. How Helen and Heather had stolen their clothing – and how they had to walk naked and barefoot over 50 yards to retrieve them while the women had looked and berated them the entire way. They tried to explain they were Lords to no avail. They thought now would be as good a time to prove their truth.

The more they talked, the angrier Lord Ferguson became. His face matched the fiery red in his beard. "HELEN!!! HEATHER!!! GET DOWN HERE THIS INSTANT!!!"

The young women ran to the Veranda, unaware of the problem or what had triggered their father's outburst. He NEVER yelled at them!

They stood in front of their father and curtsied. "Yes, Father," They said in unison.

Red-faced and trying to keep control, Lord Ferguson seethed. "Do you know these men?!?!"

"No, Father!" said Heather. "We have never seen them before!"

"Perhaps if they were wet and naked, you might recognize them?!?!?" Shouted Lord Ferguson.

Helen started to say something…, and then the realization and memory from the pond hit. Heather started to tear up…

"Do you have something to say to these gentlemen, whose honor you shamed?!?!" Scolded Lord Ferguson. "Do you not know they saved the Prince, and if they wanted to create problems for the family, all they would have to do is give the word?!?!"

"We're…we're sorry," said Helen.

Heather's head was bowed… "We should never have done anything like that. I truly am sorry, Gentlemen."

Lord Ferguson started to chastise his daughters further when Derek spoke up. "Lord Ferguson. We did want an apology from these young women, and it's been given. We rode here to prove our case before them as we told them we would. Of course, they did not believe that we would do so. You see, sir, we are men of our word."

"Now, everyone, please take a deep breath. This was not intended to ramp up so quickly. We are not angry or offended. We wanted to prove a point." The tension immediately eased.

"You see, Lord Ferguson, my brother, Lord Connor McAndrew, is to marry Lady Mary Forbes on Saturday," said Derek.

"I have heard I must be out of town on Friday and will not be back for a fortnight – so I will not be able to attend. But how does that bring you here? Asked Lord Ferguson.

"Well, Lord Ferguson. Lord Forbes informed me and Lord McKenzie that we could have a companion for the ceremony and feast following. Neither I nor Lord McKenzie know any other women – the closest thing we have to any relationship – is your daughters."

"You mean you came here to ask my daughters – the ones that tried to embarrass you – to go with you to your brother's wedding?" asked an incredulous Lord Ferguson.

"Aye! That was the entire purpose of coming here, My Lord," said Mac. "There was no other pretense of doing so. Please allow Helen to attend the Forbes/McAndrew wedding with me. I give my solemn word that I will be a gentleman with her honor."

Mac and Derek looked over at the women – you could almost audibly hear the relief in their eyes. Then they both started to smile.

At that moment…laughter began. Not a chuckle – but a hilarious uproar as Lord Ferguson began to laugh. He laughed until he was bent over laughing. He finally caught his breath and said, "Helen. Do you wish to go with Lord McKenzie?"

"Aye, father, I do," said Helen.

"And Heather," asked Lord Ferguson. "Do you wish to attend the wedding with Lord McAndrew, too?"

"Yes, Father, I would like to," said Heather.

"Gentlemen – I have ten children their dear mother has blessed me with. Do you see these gray hairs on my beard and in my hair? You need to understand that it is because of those two. You may take them at your own risk," said Lord Ferguson. "God… I need a drink. You are safe here now, Lord McAndrew and Lord McKenzie. You may send your men home if you would like. We will have a couple of shots of whiskey, and then I will need to get back to work."

"Ladies," said Derek. "We will be here to take you on Saturday at 1130 am sharp."

Heather and Helen winked and began coyly walking away when their father interrupted… "You know that I should take a strap to you both. I best not ever hear of anything like that again. Do you hear me?"

"Yes, Father," they said in unison and ran off to plan for the event.

Mac went to where the other men were still on their horses waiting. He thanked them and told Lord Gordon that he and Derek would leave shortly. He thanked them, winked, and said everything went according to plan.

The servant then gave Mac his and Derek's sword. Mac put his immediately into its scabbard and handed Derek's to him, who did the same.

They joined Lord Ferguson on the Veranda. A bottle of whiskey and three glasses were waiting for them. Lord Ferguson poured. Derek took the glass and smelled the aroma. He truly loved the nuance in good whiskey. Some had a vanilla or floral essence. Some were smokey with a caramel aftertaste. Either way – since coming here – he loved them even more. He sipped it and savored it. Mac did the same.

Lord Ferguson said, "You can tell a lot about a man by the way he drinks the nectar of the gods." He had served the drink in brandy sniffers, swirled it around, and took a taste. "A man that simply swallows without tasting is a man with poor character and poor judgment. A man who sips without exploring all that she has to offer – is a timid man – indecisive and cannot be trusted. A man who adds water – is a feckless, weak man. Now, a man who inhales, swirls, inhales again, and savors the flavors – is a man who embraces life. He is in charge of his environment. He can be trusted to do great things. I noticed you both chose correctly."

"Gentlemen," he continued. "We will need to talk later. I do not have the time since I will be going to Edinburgh to attend to business. I know of the battle that occurred. I know there were no survivors. I know what will happen and what we must do – soon. We will have to pick Prince Charles as King or King George. I believe

Prince Charles will get the nod, and then we will have the big fight with King George. Something tells me that you gentlemen will not be denied."

With that, hands were shaken, and a friendship started. Derek and Mac were on their way back to Camp Striker.

The days passed quickly. Everything that needed to be painted and remodeled was complete. The dress was finished on Friday night at midnight. Exhaustion ruled at the Forbes household – but at least the preparation was complete. Three hundred guests were planned. Now, they just needed the weather to cooperate. As Friday night came to a close in the Forbes house… Connor and Lady Mary collapsed in the bed next to each other. "Dear Lord," said Connor. "I am so glad tonight is not our wedding night. I would be inclined to kiss you, roll over… and go to sleep. After the wait, that would seem rather disappointing."

Lady Mary snuggled next to Connor. "If tonight were our wedding night… I would beat you to sleep." With that…her breathing became deeper, and she softly began snoring.

"I'll be damned," smiled Connor…" She did beat me to sleep. He kissed her on the forehead and was out as well.

All was quiet in the Forbes house – except for a few more servants finalizing the rest of the touches. A chair was added here… a floral arrangement was added there… The cooking was only beginning as quite the feast was planned.

The sun rose. Lady Forbes bounded out of the bed to the chagrin of Lord Forbes. Lord Forbes groaned, "It's just after six, love. Why so early?"

"Go back to sleep. There is still much to do, and we will be prepared," said Lady Forbes. "Besides, the wedding is at 3. Guests will be showing up by 1. That's only a few hours."

Lord Forbes put the pillow over his head. He had intended on sleeping until 7. Of course, that would not happen with Lady Forbes getting her first set of clothes on – her work clothes – before clothes for the actual wedding. "Dear God woman! Can you make any more noise?" He started to continue when he saw that look on her face. He quieted right down. There was no point in starting a fight this early.

Her clothes on – she reached down and kissed Lord Forbes on his forehead… "You are an ornery old man, yet I love you regardless." She laughed as she left the room.

She marched down the stairs, and the entire staff was there, ready to obey her every order. Most – if not all of the festivities would occur in the garden. The Pipers would be here at 12. The Minister will be here at 1. Servants were decorating anything that was not decorated with some flower or embellishment. The outside cooking area was a beehive of activity. She thought to herself – we have 300 invited and 700 attending to them? The six bakers from France were an extravagance. Fortunately, they were in Edinburgh – or it never could have happened. And Lord – the cost for alcohol. This wedding was going to cost a fortune. Her husband knew it and was not worried about it. Perhaps he knew some things that she did not. Ok… dammit. Focus on the wedding. Nothing else matters today.

Connor awoke to Lady Mary, naked and unashamed – had jumped on top of him… "Tonight is the night, My Lord. Do not drink too much. We have much to catch up on." And she kissed him deeply. Then giggled and jumped out of bed. Like her mother, she would don her first set of clothes to check and ensure all was ready. Connor – was clueless, as most men are; he just knew where to be and how the ceremony would take place – and then the food, drinking, and dancing would begin. He had learned a few of the Scottish Dances with Mary's urging. He laughed to himself when he realized that Hip Hop dancing would probably not be as well received here as opposed to his former life. He rolled over and went back to sleep. He did not doubt that he would need whatever energy he had available for Lady Mary tonight.

By nine am, the house was abuzz with activity. Breakfast was served, and it was simple. Porridge, Corn Cakes, eggs, smoked venison, and COFFEE – this would be needed today… then the race was on. Before you knew it – it was 11. All the preparations that could be made – were complete. The weather was lovely – as if God himself had prepared the day for the nuptials.

Lady Forbes took a deep breath and walked upstairs to put on her formal gown. Sometimes, she did wish she were a man. They were fucking clueless as to what went on to make everything work properly in these settings. They would all get there, eat, drink, enjoy the wedding, dance – most get drunk – and not have a fucking clue how it all came together. It takes us women to make things happen! She smiled to herself.

She had her gown made for her by the best seamstress in Edinburgh. She knew the only way to get the wedding dress for Mary completed, and her dress as well with this short notice was to have the seamstress and her team working at her home. It cost a lot, but when she saw the finished product, she knew that all the women would be jealous of her attire, especially the wedding dress. Of course, this is how it should be… especially Lady Catherine MacDonald. That Bitch. She would be jealous, for sure!

She pulled her gown, looked at it, and began to put it on. It was Silk…an Emerald Green to match the color of her eyes. Her tartan was worn as a sash. White lace and embroidery outlined her dress and showed off her figure – which was still really good for her age. A white cape would cover her and keep her warm if it got cool in the evening. All of the family jewels would be worn that night between her and Mary! Her Necklace and bracelet would be the emeralds that had belonged to Lord Forbes's mother. They were exquisite.

Lord Forbes entered the room to put on his attire. Before he could do so – he had to admire his wife. She was stunning. How she handled her duties and still managed to look this good was beyond him. He told her how beautiful she looked and kissed her smartly as she waved him away so she could continue to dress. He would wear a formal Kilt, a white silk shirt, a cravat with the Clan's colors of Green and White, and a silk vest topped with an Emerald Green Waistcoat to match his wife's dress. A sporran with the Forbes Family Motto "Grace Me Guide" on one side and the clan crest on the other. White Silk Stockings followed by shoes shined to perfection – a deep black that could double as a mirror. Finally – topped with cufflinks, his signet ring, a pocket watch, and a broach to complete the package. He looked in his mirror – he looked pretty damn good. His wife was lucky to have him, he thought to himself!

Lady Mary went to her room early. She had attendants that would help her dress. Connor was told he would have to dress in another room. He would not see her until she walked down the aisle…and would definitely see much more later… She giggled to herself.

Connor had received an unexpected surprise at 9 am. It was from the Prince. The note said – everything a true Nobleman needs for a wedding – from Prince Charles. Lady Mary had already picked out everything for Connor to wear. Prince Charles's gift, of course, would take precedence. He better have done well with his choices. She would hate to have to berate a future King at her wedding.

He opened the case in which it came. The McAndrew Kilt and Tartan – are made from the finest wool. A white silk shirt and Cravat are also in the McAndrew colors. Next came a white silk vest, followed by the formal coat. White Knee socks and black leather shoes. He was beginning to get nervous – when in walked Derek. "God, I'm glad to see you!" He got up and gave him a hug. "I thought I might have to do this alone. They have kept me so busy – I couldn't even get over to see you."

Derek laughed. "You little shite – you know you couldn't do this without me, and I wouldn't have missed it."

Lady Mary's attendants arrived. One began working on her hair. Lady Mary liked her hair braided – especially for dancing. God, she hoped Connor remembered what she had taught him. Her hair would have many braids with flowers woven in. Another was applying light makeup. She, of course, didn't need much. She didn't like the stuff anyway. The dress was pulled out for her to put on. White Silk with Pearls stitched over the bodice, with white lace and Embroidery to accentuate her figure. A long skirt and then a train, which could be removed after the ceremony. Her veil had incorporated her grandmother's tiara, with the diamonds still looking as new as they had many years ago.

Of course, she could not – nor would not forget "Something Old, Something New, something borrowed, something blue…and a sixpence in her shoe!"

She had borrowed a bracelet from her best friend, Catherine. A Garter – in the McAndrew Colors would be her blue.

Someone shouted it was 230. Damn! She had to hurry. Her attendants completed everything and had her ready at 305…

Connor noticed that everything Derek had on was new as well – but his shirt was the McAndrew Blue – also in silk. "A gift from the Prince?"

"You know it," said Derek. "So. Are you about ready to do this?" Derek said as he pulled out a flask – took a nip, and asked Connor if he would like one as well.

"Oh, Hell Yes!" said Connor. The burn as the whiskey went down hit just the right balance and began to calm him down.

"I don't know if you know it – but apparently, Mac and I will stand up there with you. Don't even think of running. If I can't catch you – Mac can!" said Derek. They both laughed at that. "Does your heart feel this is right?" asked Derek.

"More than you can ever know," said Connor.

"Very well then – let's get you married," said Derek. Mac was outside waiting. They walked down the stairs and were escorted to where the ceremony would take place.

It was then that Connor noticed the crowd. He had heard the pipers and the music coming into his window – but he had been so focused on what he was doing that he didn't even hear the crowd as they began to assemble. Who would have thought that a Prince would be at his wedding? Who would have thought that he would be marrying into nobility and proclaimed a Lord himself? "Da... damn... I sure wish you and Mum could be here."

The Reverend was up there. Lord Forbes had reminded him they did NOT need a two-hour church service to begin the wedding. But where was Lady Mary?

Finally, Lady Forbes was escorted to her seat. Lord Forbes then escorted Mary to stand next to Connor.

Connor felt weak in his knees. Dear God – she was the most beautiful thing he had ever seen. He had to remember after the ceremony that he would add a sash in the McAndrew colors to show the combining of the families by their marriage.

The Minister cleared his throat. "Who gives this woman in matrimony to Lord Connor McAndrew?"

Lord Forbes said, "Her mother and I." Lord Forbes handed Mary's hand to Connor and walked away to be seated with his wife. He looked at his wife and then rolled his eyes as he saw she had started crying.

The Minister began: "Dearly beloved, we are gathered here in the sight of God and these witnesses to join this noble lady, Mary Forbes, and this Lord, Connor McAndrew, in holy matrimony. Lord McAndrew, do you take Lady Mary Forbes to be your wedded wife, to have and to hold from this day forward, for better or worse, for richer or poorer, in sickness and in health, to love and to cherish, till death do you part?"

Connor said, "Aye. With all my heart and mind, I do."

The Minister continued, "And Lady Forbes, do you take Lord Connor McAndrew to be your wedded husband, to honor and obey, to have and to hold from this day forward, for better or worse, for richer or poorer, in sickness and in health, till death do you part?"

Lady Mary said, "Yes. With all my heart, mind, and strength, I do!

The Minister then said, "May the Rings be presented as a symbol of your unending love and commitment.? Lord McAndrew, repeat after me. With this ring, I thee wed, and with all of my worldly goods, I thee endow. In the name of the Father, and of the Son, and of the Holy Spirit."

Connor said, "With this ring, I thee wed, and with all of my worldly goods, I thee endow. In the name of the Father, and of the Son, and the Holy Spirit."

The Minister then looked at Lady Mary," Lady Mary, repeat after me. With this ring, I thee wed, and with all of my worldly goods, I thee endow. In the name of the Father, the Son, and the Holy Spirit."

Lady Mary repeated, "With this ring, I thee wed, and with all of my worldly goods, I thee endow. In the name of the Father, the Son, and the Holy Spirit."

The Minister then began with a short message. Neither Connor nor Lady Mary would remember any of it. They heard nothing of it. They didn't hear the message. They didn't hear the blessings. They didn't hear the final prayer – they were too busy staring into each other's eyes... sharing the hopes and dreams that their future would bring. Finally, they heard, "Lord McAndrew – You may kiss your bride."

Connor lifted her veil and kissed her deeply as she did him back. The applause erupted. At that point, Connor pulled out the McAndrew Sash and put it over Lady Mary to announce the joining of the clans. The Minister said, "Your Highness, Nobles, Ladies and Gentlemen... In the presence of God and these witnesses, I now present to you Lord Connor McAndrew and Lady Mary McAndrew as husband and wife. What God has joined together – let none separate!"

Lord Forbes stood up and shouted, "Let the festivities begin! We have a large marquee set up for our feast and for dancing after. Please head in that direction so we can get the celebrations started."

At that point, the Pipers, drummers, and other musicians began to play. It was time to feast, drink, dance, and enjoy life!

The feast was lavish. Traditional Scottish dishes of haggis, neeps, and tatties. Roasted meats of lamb, beef, and venison with many rich gravies and sauces. Root Vegetables were abundant, along with barley dishes and a variety of bread. Scots desserts of Shortbreads, cranachan, and clootie dumplings. With the French Bakers, there were petit fours, cakes, eclairs, Macaroons, and Profiteroles covered in caramel and chocolate sauce.

Whiskey, Ale, Wine, and Brandy abounded—more than enough for all. Even the servers were able to enjoy the bounty.

Reels, jigs, and dancing from everyone. Even the Prince was able to get a dance from the bride – and Connor remembered all of the dances. Lord Forbes and Lady Forbes showed their skills, too. Connor laughed – it was apparent that Lord Forbes had been hitting the whiskey, and Lady Forbes had been nipping on the Brandy!

Finally… it was time to escort the Bride and the groom to their wedding chamber. A red ribbon was tied around their arms as they were hoisted from the ground, carried to the top of the stairs, and gently let down in a new room that was larger than the last – and would be theirs. Derek looked at Connor and asked him if he needed any advice on what to do from there. Connor respectfully declined. The door was opened, and the couple was pushed into the new room alight with candles… Bawdy songs were sung all the way up the stairs…and then all the way back down.

Soon… it was just Connor and Mary, alone at last. Mary looked at Connor and could tell he had much to drink. "You didn't have too much to drink?" asked Mary.

"Not at all Mary. There is no way that I would ruin tonight. "He had her stand up, and he undressed her. She did the same to him.

A crowd began to gather beneath the window and egg them on. Lady Forbes looked up and could see the naked shadow of her daughter as Connor was kissing her breasts. "Oh, Hell No! You get away from that window! All of you!" She got one of the servants to knock on the door and discreetly tell Connor that everything could be seen as a shadow from the window and blow out the candles or get in bed like normal couples do on their wedding night!

The servant got to the door and knocked. Connor said, "Whoever is out there had better have a damn good reason for knocking!" The servant explained what was happening and that everything was being seen from below. Connor thanked the servant, moved away from the window, and put out some of the candles, which was good since Mary had just gotten on her knees in front of Connor! The shadow looked huge!

Finally, they were lying in bed. Connor was on top. "Well, my Lady…my wife… are you ready?"

Yes! More than ever!" she moaned. When he entered her, at first, she felt a pinch and a little discomfort – then felt…better than her mother described it. She tried to be discreet. She tried not to be loud. But she couldn't help herself. Everyone heard her outside and made bawdy sounds, much to her mother's chagrin.

To her credit, Lady Forbes moved the Pipers outside where her daughter could not be heard!

The dancing continued through the night. Derek and Heather got along famously, as did Mac and Helen. This was their beginning, as it was for Connor. They each were allowed to share beds with the same bundling boards that were successful with Connor and Mary. They were successful here, as each couple was able to talk privately. To get to know each other and see if this would be worth pursuing. They each decided that it would be and fell into a deep sleep. There would be many hangovers the next day. But this would be the wedding spoken of for years. Lady Forbes had, indeed, outdone herself.

With Connor and Mary? After 3 am and the 4th time Mary's screams of pleasure awakened Lord Forbes, he walked to the bedroom and knocked loudly, asking Mary to cover her face when she reached her ecstasy so at least the rest of the house could sleep! Automatically, Mary said, "Yes, Father!" and then busted out laughing. Sleep then finally came to all.

Chapter 32
Exploration

Sergeant Robert Stewart, Privates Ian Calhoun, John Munro, and Alexander MacKay started to Inverness. They had gathered what they could that would work in their endeavor… to find Bat Shite… Stewart laughed at that despite himself. Though he fully understood how important that was to the overall success of this undertaking. The last cave they had hiked close to Inverness was on the Isle of Skye. Fairy Glen Caverns. Some areas had not been explored. They didn't have long at the time – so they didn't go deeper. If Stewart remembered correctly – it did not become popular until the 19th century. But that was close to 100 miles away. That would be a trip by horse and wagon. There was a nature preserve close by as well. What was it? Merkinch Local Nature Preserve, if he remembered correctly. They had explored that and had found some cliff areas that might work. They would go there first unless the folks in Inverness had a better idea. The more he thought about it - the more daunting the challenge became!

The first stop was the Horse Master. They had talked to him the previous day and asked him to pick out four horses that he felt would help them accomplish their task. Two of the four were experienced horsemen. The other two would have to figure it out on the way. Of course, those two had taken a few drunken rides on camels in Afghanistan – so this should be easy!

They had canteens, torches, rifles, pistols, shovels, and duffle bags to carry the Bat Guano back to camp. They did have some rope, Carabiners, Quickdraws, and a few other climbing tools – they were to be used if they had to make a surprise attack against the Taliban. Who would've thought they would be here and now?

They mounted their horses. Stewart and MacKay had the experience with horses. Calhoun and Munro – well – it showed that they had not. Of course, the ones with experience were more than happy to give the others crap about their lack of experience. The

Horse Master was an expert instructor, so he had them somewhat comfortable as they departed for Inverness.

They met at the Provost's office at 0800. True to his word, there were ropes, pick axes, axes, a wagon, and more, and six eager young men looking for an adventure. They were about to have one. They told the provost where they were going. He had heard about a cave, but no one had wanted to go exploring. Too many witches, demons, and other monstrous apparitions would be found there – he knew it. Once the Provost expressed that sentiment – it was thought the six young men – might change their minds. Stewart spoke up and said they would not have to go in if they did not want to do so. They loosened up a bit and decided to go anyway. Introductions were made: The three brothers were Craig, James, and Thomas Alexander. Then, Angus McFadden, Shamus Sinclair, and finally, the youngest at 16 – Clinton McCollough. After a quick bite to eat, they were off, and biscuits and dried meat were added to their wagon.

Stewart asked those from Inverness if they knew of any areas with bats. There was a place Northwest of Inverness close to Beauly Firth, where they had seen them while camping one night. It was there they decided to go first.

There was an old road there, so it didn't take long. If they could find Bat Guano there – it would make their lives much easier since it was so close. It was decided that two of the men would fish for dinner so they could make the most of their rations and make them last as long as possible,

The weather felt more like an early Spring Day in Scotland. It was damp and a bit rainy. But everyone's spirits were up. The groups would split in two so they could cover more ground. This resembled the area that Stewart had been to over 240 years in the future. Without the roads and bearings – it wasn't easy to tell. But… they had to start somewhere.

Angus let Stewart know there was a Ferry to get across the Firth to an area where he had seen a lot of bats a few years ago. He told him it would take a few days to get there. There were cliffs on the other side of Dingwall. Excellent thought, Stewart – that gives them another place to go that would be close.

The day they got a bit warmer. The rain stayed as a constant reminder that the task would be arduous. They made camp. Stewart thought they would give it a few days here before crossing to

Dingwall. Something about that area made him feel a bit more confident in the area around them.

Once the camp was set up, Shamus and Angus would be the fishermen. Stewart and Calhoun took Craig and James, while Munro and MacKay took Thomas and Clinton. They loaded up with rope and material in case they did get lucky. Each chose a different direction and said they would meet up at 6 pm back at their base camp.

The first thing Stewart did was go to the Firth and then turn back around. He closed his eyes… remember, lad. Think! They headed inland for about an hour. What the bloody hell was the name of that place?!? Craig…. Phadrig! That's it! He saw it in the distance. It could not have been over a mile from their position. They moved towards the Craig. They climbed to the top – probably less than 500 feet or so. Once there, they moved towards the Northwest side and headed about halfway down. He recognized the area! There was a large indention where he would be in 240 years! What kind of Déjà vu would that be called? He thought to himself.

Stewart and Calhoun grabbed a pickaxe and hit the area, and a large hole opened before them. Craig and James gasped! They had been up here hundreds of times and had no idea such a place existed! It was black as midnight going straight down. Stewart asked Craig and James who wanted to be the first to go in. They both said, "Hell No." – without equivocation. Stewart and Calhoun laughed. Stewart then dropped a rock to see if he could gauge how it was. He never heard it hit the bottom. "Hmmm, that was unexpected," he thought.

Stewart got their torches, ropes, and carabiners and tied one end of the rope to a tree close to the hole. Stewart would be first. He shined his torch in and saw them… "Oh God, how he hated these… they were not dangerous… just creepy as hell." The wall was pulsating with thousands of Daddy Long Legs. He had no covering or hard hat to keep them at bay. That meant the bastards would be crawling all over him. He took a deep breath, plunged in, and tried not to scream as he was bombarded with them by the thousands. Craig and James saw that occur and were further convinced they made the right decision!

Calhoun followed Stewart in with the same urge to scream as he went through the pulsating arachnids. He found Stewart about 30 feet down on a narrow ledge. "Do you smell that?" asked Stewart.

Calhoun wrinkled his nose. There was a faint smell of ammonia. That was a good indicator of bats in the area. The goal is to get there and to NOT be overcome by the odor. Noxious gases can be fatal.

They dropped down to another ledge about 70 feet down. The hole continued down – but across from the ledge, there was a large opening. The smell of the ammonia was coming from there. They jumped across the ledge and saw an opening ahead. A light came in from above, about 100 yards from their current location. They yelled above what they saw and would untie their ropes and return in a few minutes.

They had to stoop to crawl through the area to the larger room. The smell was strong, but the air circulation made them comfortable continuing.

Stewart was so intent on the light shining in front of him that he neglected to see the hole in front of him. His right foot went down, anticipating a solid floor, only to be met with empty space. He tumbled down, yelling suddenly and grabbing anything he could cling to! Down he went – until he hit roots that had grown through the hole from a tree at the surface about ten feet down. That slowed him down – just as the rope tied from him to Calhoun became taught. They had fashioned a harness – but it was simplistic by design. The sudden stop tightened around his torso. Calhoun did all he could to brace for the impact. He was also nearly pulled into the hole but managed to hold on.

Stewart was hanging, thankful to be alive. What a rookie mistake. Rookie mistakes kill! Damn! How he managed to hold onto his torch – he would never know. He was able to look at his current predicament. He was actually hanging upside down, tangled in roots and his rope. He took an inventory – his right bicep hurt - probably pulled it. No cuts or anything broken. He yelled to Calhoun and thanked him for saving his dumbass life. He also told him it would be a challenge to get back up. It was probably a 30-foot drop he would have to climb with an injured bicep. Damn!

He was able to right himself after some extensive effort. He then took another look with his torch… and that is when he saw it! A vein… a HUGE Vein! Of Gold!!!! They were rich!!! But wait… who could know? No one but his mates. He would tell them about it later. In the meantime – he had to get out of this mess.

He worked it out with Calhoun that he would climb a step every time Calhoun would pull. Slowly and steadily, he was able to get higher and higher until he was finally out. Exhausted – but alive. That had been entirely too close. Climbing back up was going to be a bitch – but he had been through worse.

They decided to continue. They made it to the opening above. It was a large chamber… and there they were. Bats. As many as they needed? Probably not. But enough to at least get the party started. He scooped a bunch into the backpack that he had brought. He also sorted out those beetles that ate the stuff. Nasty! They creeped him out as well. He would send one of the Inverness men back to the Provost to ensure this got to the Major. Along with the instructions on how to get here, they would look for larger populations of bats before they came back to camp. There was probably another way out, but after the harrowing moment a bit ago, he decided to wait another day.

The two made their way back to the ledge without any further incident. Stewart told those above they would have to help pull him out since he had injured his arm. Calhoun would come out first so the three men could pull Stewart back to the entrance.

Calhoun made it up, and then it was Stewart's turn. He could use the left arm that had hurt a bit. It was starting to throb a little. Thankfully, he brought a medical kit just in case they needed it. I won't need the morphine – but Advil will help with the inflammation.

Once everyone was apprised of the events, James and Craig looked at the two. They were a muddy, mangled mess that smelled absolutely terrible. You both look and smell like you have been rolling around in a Privy exclaimed James!

They laughed and made it back down to the camp. Four Ibuprofen and a couple of shots of whisky, and Stewart felt better. Craig decided to leave in the morning and then head back. He should be back by the afternoon. In the meantime, that would give a bit of additional time to look locally for more bats.

Munro and MacKay had limited success. They found small colonies of surface bats – but nothing worth writing home about.

Now Angus and Shamus? They had a great day of fishing. They had three huge salmon. When everyone returned to camp, they had already cleaned them and had a fire going. They looked up, and

Calhoun and Stewart... wrinkled their noses and shook their heads. "Damn, Lads! Have you been swimming with the devil or what? You smell like Shite!" said Shamus.

They both laughed and headed towards the Firth to bathe. The water was bloody cold...but it felt good to get the grime off and to remove that horrible stench from the ammonia in the bat guano. They cleaned their kilts and set them out to dry.

When they got back, the fish were done. These boys knew how to cook. Just the basics. They had left the fish whole after gutting them. They had found some green hazelwood branches to act as a skewer and rotisserie. They used a combination of peat and oak to make the fire. The flames and the smoke combined to create a simplistic but perfect meal for those in attendance.

After further discussion over the fire, Clinton would leave first thing in the morning and get the Guano to the Provost. He would then meet them at the point where the Ferry was set up. Angus was convinced that the cliffs where he described would be the amounts they would need.

"That was amazing!" said Stewart, and everyone agreed. They all gathered around the fire. Stewart looked up at the stars. It was so clear. The Milky Way was hanging like a tapestry. Countless stars are hanging... calling out to those to see... you are but a pinprick in the universe... but you matter – more than you will ever know.

The morning came. Clinton was up before the sun was. He wanted to get the guano delivered and back to the point of meeting with his companions before they did. He was the youngest and would not let them wait on him. He always felt like he had something to prove. That drive made him want more than he used to think would ever happen in Inverness. But with these new events changing everything – maybe – for the first time in his life – he was right where he needed to be. Using Bat Shite to make better gunpowder. Who would've ever thought? He wanted to be in the middle of it all. Maybe one day, he would even meet the Prince.

He came charging up to the Provost's office just as he arrived. "Clinton? What are you doing here? Is everything alright?"

"Yes sir, Provost. I was asked to get this to you so you could get it to the Major... I mean Lord McAndrew. We found some – enough to get started. It's on the backside of Craig Phadrig. Stewart left a mark he said would be easy to find. He said once you get about 100 feet deep, you can smell it – but to be careful about halfway in; there's one hell of a drop, so make sure you don't fall in like he did. Oh – he's okay, by the way… But I gotta go. We're going across the Ferry to the other side of Dingwall. I gotta meet them at the ferry and don't want to be late."

"Alright, Clinton, I got this and will get it to Lord McAndrew. I'll let your mum know where you're headed," said the Provost.

"Thank you, sir. I'll see you soon!" With that – Clinton was off.

The Provost bent over to pick up the backpack. It felt heavy…and then it hit him. The smell was atrocious. This would sit outside his office until he could get someone to deliver this to Camp Striker.

Clinton had his horse at a full gallop. It wouldn't take him long to get there. He could see his destination straight ahead… and Son-of-a Bitch… how did they beat him there? Well… it looked like they were getting there. He came sliding up. The horse was lathered, so he walked a bit to cool him off while they waited for the Ferry to carry them over.

The ferry arrived. It was a flatbed boat. There were six men to row them over to the other side. It was large enough for all – including the wagon – to make it in one trip. Clinton saw Stewart give the man 2 Guineas. He had never seen that much money in his entire life. He was sure it didn't cost that much. Clinton didn't know that Stewart also paid for the return trip – in case he didn't make it back.

They landed close to Charlestown. They did not need to stop there, so they continued to Dingwall. They would stay at an Inn tonight before heading to the area that Angus had spoken of.

They got to the Inn around 5 pm. Stewart thought A bed, bath, and a good stew would be good. He spoke with the innkeeper. He only had three rooms left – so they would have to share. When he offered an extra Guinea – he amazingly found an additional room. The innkeeper took care of their horses. Stewart gave extra money for the horses to be fed and groomed well.

Once they were unloaded and in their rooms, they came down for Supper. Just as Stewart hoped – there would be a hearty beef stew, some good ale, and a couple of pretty serving maids. They flirted heavily with the men… especially Stewart. Everything in him screamed, "Yes!" However, the Major's discussion of VD and not having penicillin made him reconsider. No Venereal Diseases today, thank you!

After they finished their stew, they sat by the fireplace and drank a few more pints before heading to bed. He had a hot bath he had purchased. The water had been prepared. The bath was small, but hot water sounded like a gift from heaven. He disrobed, and it felt indeed heavenly. What he didn't expect was for one of the serving maids to come in to scrub him. She walked in like she owned the place. Her name was Agnes. A pretty redhead that was at the top of her game at flirting. She had him stand up so she could scrub him. And she did so – starting at his back. Bragging about how muscular he was… that he was a beautiful specimen of a man. She turned him around to scrub his front as she wanted to see what his condition was at the time. She washed everywhere but there – saving it for last. She lathered up her washcloth and giggled as she began to clean him… then stroke him. She rinsed him off…and before he could say a word… she was on her knees in front of him. Her lips wrapped around him. Everything in him said, "Stop!" …he did say "stop" … but it came out as "Oh My God." It had been so long…it didn't take long. She squealed in delight as he tensed up and then erupted. "I knew you needed me love. I didn't realize how much!" she giggled. She dried him off. She kissed him for good measure. He then handed her a Guinea – 10 times what it usually costs. But he didn't care. She offered more at that point. He politely declined. What he had received was more than enough and more than he expected.

He wrapped his kilt around him… and walked weak-kneed to his room. He lay in bed, and in 30 seconds – he was out for the night.

The following day, both he and Calhoun were even happier than usual. Come to find out – Calhoun had a bath and received the same treatment from Gweneth. They would have to remember this place on the way back!

They went in for breakfast. It was hearty. Eggs, beef, potatoes, and bread. A pint to start the day, and they were off. Angus said it would be a half-day to get there. That should be perfect. Hopefully, they would see a bat colony as they prepared to feed for the night.

Angus said a road would take them to Glensgaich, and then they would go North from there. They started around 8 am. The path to Glensgaich was easy to navigate. Finding a trail wide enough for the wagon was more of a challenge. It took them a couple of hours – but they finally found one that would accommodate them all. They got to the entrance of the canyon around 4 pm. Stewart fully understood now what Angus was saying. This looked like a bat paradise. Stewart and Calhoun pulled out their binoculars and did a sweep of the cliff facing. There were at least four different holes that looked to be entrances to a cave—good places to start. In the meantime, while the camp was set up, Stewart and Calhoun would continue to sweep the horizon for signs of a swarm.

It was right at 6 pm – about 30 minutes until dark. Calhoun saw it. Not over the cliff face… but on the huge Hillock to their rear. They saw what appeared to be a black cloud coming into view. It was a shapeshifter… a tornado of bats flying in a clockwise circle going higher and higher… there had to be over a million bats!!! Of course, it excited the men from Camp Striker. The men from Inverness were terrified!

"Holy Mary! Mother of God!" Exclaimed Shamus.

"You're not Roman Catholic! Why are you praying to Mary?" shouted Angus.

"Do you not see those demon spawn?!?!" said Shamus.

Even MacKay started laughing at this spectacle. These men were on their knees, thinking it was an apocalypse! "Lads! That's what we came here to find! Those are bats! Not Demons!"

Shamus cried out, "Are ye sure? You're not fucking with me?!?!"

"No, Shamus. He's speaking the truth. Thanks be to God! That is what we needed to find. Tomorrow, we find their lair!" said Stewart.

Shamus was a bit embarrassed. He didn't like the thought of a lair. These fucking Scotsman are nuts!

The evening flowed quickly. Dinner and then bed came shortly after.

Stewart was up before daylight. The sun could not come fast enough. He wanted to see where these bats came from. It had to be a vast cavern.

They saddled their mounts. After seeing what came out of the lair, Shamus and Angus decided to hunt for their food… instead of becoming those vile creature's meal.

Stewart and MacKay took the lead. They brought as much rope as possible and extra batteries for their torches. They left the camp at first daylight. They decided they would take it easy as the climb would be steep. They should have brought a drone. They headed West and would see if they could approach the back of the hillock, then head South to complete the climb. It looked to be about an 8%

grade for over a mile before they could swing South. Going direct was at least a 15% grade. That was too steep for a horse and rider with all their gear.

It took about an hour to get to the top of the ridgeline of the hillock. They could see a giant hole just before reaching the mound's top. It was a good 12% grade to the top to get there. They decided to dismount their horses and lead them. It took another two hours of strenuous hiking until they broke over the top, and it leveled out. Stewart figured they were at 2,000 feet. This was nothing like the peaks in Afghanistan… but a challenging hike nonetheless. He stopped for a minute and looked around them… he took a minute to pause and catch his breath…the view was breathtaking.

To the North… it was a quilt of emerald green and heather covered slopes. Hills and valleys interplaying with the eyes and drawing you in. To the East was a Valley… like a silver ribbon plunging through the rugged terrain. The wildflowers exploded, adding vivid color and texture to God's canvas… alas… they weren't here for sightseeing… that's when he saw it. A large black eye the size of a man staring at him. He looked through his binoculars and saw the entrance they were seeking. After another 30 minutes, they were standing outside of an entrance to a cave. At least 6 feet around. He shined his torch inside, and it disappeared into the blackness of the cave.

The horses were secured between two trees. There was plenty of grass to eat so that they would be content. Next, a rope was secured to a large tree at the entrance for those inside. The Alexander brothers decided they would brave the cave this time. That meant seven would enter: Stewart, Calhoun, MacKay, Munro, and the three brothers – Craig, James, and Thomas.

All of the Strikers had electric torches. The brothers had made theirs from pine saplings covered in pitch and wrapped with hemp. Everything needed to be conserved, so one of the Striker torches would be used up front, while the pine torch would be used in the rear. They had no idea how long they would be down. They weren't there to explore this time. They needed to find the nesting area for the bats.

It was apparent from the beginning that the Alexander brothers were having difficulty overcoming superstition. Every noise, drip, trip, or splash would cause some nervous response. Craig was probably the worst, with nervous laughter or cursing beneath his breath.

They had traveled in close to 100 feet, moving steadily down. Until now, they had been able to stand. Now, they would have to crawl on their knees. Craig was the last one in, and he held the torch. James didn't appreciate him getting so close to his ass. "Dammit, man! You're gonna catch me arse on fire! You need to stay back a bit!" said James.

"You worry too much." Laughed Craig. "Though from my point of view… it would probably make it look better!"

James just grunted… then farted in response.

Then it happened. Daddy Long Legs… Thousands of them started a mad dash up the tunnel. Stewart disturbed them as he pushed through. The Strikers saw them, closed their mouths, and powered through. All Thomas saw was a vague outline of Munro's ass in front of him. He felt the little bastards and instinctively did the same. James did likewise. But Craig? He had allowed for some space between him and James so he wouldn't burn him. He had looked down for only a second… he looked up again… and screamed at the top of his lungs!!! Thousands of the arachnids were charging a 360-degree field of vision… directly at him. He flailed… he kicked… he screamed again… he lashed out with his torch and caught James's Kilt on fire – who fortunately had the presence of mind to put it out.

"You stupid Bastard!" Yelled James. "They are fucking Daddy Long Legs. You're being a fucking little girl! Act like a man before I have to beat your arse! You get me with that fucking torch again… I'm going to tell ma you disappeared in the Caves!"

Craig stopped his screaming. He swallowed hard and got his wits about him. Deep breaths. What the bloody hell? He had never been this skittish before. He was fucking scared, and it made no bloody sense. His inner voice won out when it told him his family's future depended on him to complete their mission.

Now that Craig's meltdown was controlled – Stewart continued down. They had traveled another 300 feet when they reached the tunnel's end. Stewart looked out and saw they were going to enter a small Cavern. The Stalagmites and Stalactites created this eerie shadow effect with the interplay of his torch. It was about a four-foot drop to the floor. He jumped down and was followed by the rest. Everyone was in awe of what they saw. The room was rectangular.

Maybe 30' long, 10' wide, and a gradual increase in height – from 10' to 15' at the end. You could make out an exit at the end of the Cavern. As they reached the exit – Stewart stopped and brought everyone in to see. Right at that exit… was a hole over 3' in diameter. He shined his light into utter darkness. He took a rock, dropped it into the hole, and counted… 1…2… 3… 4… 18. It took over 18 seconds before you could hear it hit below. That means it was over 300 yards to the bottom.

With a stern warning, he told them all… "Caves are amazing. There is much to see and much to learn. But they are a fickle mistress. If you make one miscalculation – you will die. If one of us falls into this hole – they will die. There is nothing anyone will be able to do for you. You will remain buried where you hit. No one will be able to retrieve your body. Do you understand?"

Those who were Cavers already knew this mistress. The Alexander brothers once again questioned their decision to come… and had a new profound respect for the men who guided them.

They carefully moved around the hole and entered another chamber. When everyone passed the hole… Stewart told them to watch. He turned off his torch… there were long, slender strings that glowed a cool blue light. This cavern was tall, maybe 75'… and looked otherworldly. Stewart shined his torch on the floor, and everyone jumped. It was as if the floor was alive… it was moving with insects… beetles… scorpions… centipedes. That was it. That was all Craig could stand. He took off in a blind run… and fell directly into the hole he had been warned about.

James yelled, "NOOOOOOOOOO!!!"

Stewart shined his torch down. Craig was holding onto a root for dear life! James reached down and was just able to reach his fingers… not enough for a grip. He inched down further. Munro grabbed his feet! It still was not enough. Craig's hands were slipping. He looked up, imploring James to reach further… but realized that James was also putting himself and others in danger.

Craig steeled himself. He looked up at James. "I'm sorry. Tell Mum and Da I love them, and I love ya all here today."

James cried out, "I'm almost there, lad! Don't give up!"

And then Craig let go… falling without a sound… until they heard the sickening thud from below.

James and Thomas were beside themselves. They started grabbing ropes in an attempt to save their brother. "Craig!!" They shouted into the hole, and the only reply was silence.

In a surprise shock to James – Stewart grabbed his arm, threw him against the cave wall, and shoved his elbow into his throat. That was saying a lot since James was at least 8" taller and outweighed him by 50lbs. It was so sudden it shocked Thomas into quiet as well.

"Shut the fuck up and listen to me! I'm a Sergeant, and I've led men I loved into battle, and they died! You can mourn - later. If you go down there, you will join him. We can't get you out! How would your mum and da feel about losing you all?!? Craig let himself fall rather than risk losing you, too. Honor his sacrifice!" Shouted Stewart.

James bared his teeth to him and pushed back against his elbow in his throat… then came to his senses. He collapsed against the wall and resigned his brother to his fate.

"Now listen to me," said Stewart. "We have a mission to complete. I want you two to turn around, tell the others what happened, and return to the base camp. I have a feeling we will find what we need soon. Get your head screwed on straight. You're not out yet. Okay?"

"Aye. We'll do that. Thank you," said James.

"Thank you for what?" asked Stewart.

"For getting my wits right about me," said James.

Stewart grabbed the bear paw of a hand with both hands. "I'm sorry for your loss, lad. He died with honor."

With that, they lit their torch, and James and Thomas headed to the exit after carefully avoiding the giant hole that took their brother. James swore to himself that one day, he would come back and get Craig for a proper burial.

Stewart blamed himself for this disaster. He should have never allowed them to go with them. His men had countless hours of caving experience. These men had none. Well, they could do nothing about it now but complete the mission.

They got to the end of the chamber. It was 2 pm. He knew it would not be long before the bats began exiting for their nightly hunt. So, he pushed forward. There were two exits before him. Which one? He stood in the doorway to the next exit to see if he could feel or hear anything. Nothing. There was no breeze as he had felt throughout the cavern so far. He went to the other doorway. There it was. The breeze to his back. This had to be the way. The tunnel was wide as it continued to descend. He got to the edge… and then looked up in wonder. The Cavern was immense. He shined his torch above. There were millions of bats! He was shocked that he couldn't smell the Guano. Then it dawned on him. There must be another large opening that pulled the smell downwind of them. 3 PM. Damn! They needed to get out before the bats swarmed on them!

They left and were moving at a much faster pace. They knew the primary danger and would avoid it when they got there. 4 PM! Faster! They hopped up the four feet where they had been just hours before. They were on their knees now. 0430… out of the mouth of the cave. They mounted their horses and began to get away. 0445… they saw the first bats shoot out of the mouth of the cave! Damn! That was close. Their mission was a huge success! They had enough Bat Guano to last for 100 years!

The mood was somber as they came down to the base camp. When they got there, supper was ready. Angus and Shamus came through again. A Red Deer had been cooking low and slow over the campfire. Stewart was going to speak with the Alexander brothers… only to find out they had left to tell their Mum and Da a few hours earlier. He couldn't blame them. He had lost many men in combat… and they were all senseless. Even though he didn't know the lad… this one stung. He was too young.

They had only been gone a week. It felt like it had been a month. They spent a few days trying to find the other entrance, to no avail… and decided to head back home. Home. What a concept. This, indeed, was home.

They broke camp at 9 am and headed to Dingwall. They got there around 2 pm. They checked into the Inn and headed to their rooms. There were four rooms on the third floor. They got them all – Stewart would have a room to himself. It was early yet. They decided to explore Dingwall Castle—anything to forget their lost comrade temporarily.

You could see the castle Southeast of the Town. As the hooves echoed on the cobblestone – it became evident even from afar that the castle was ancient. The castle loomed ahead… a sentinel overlooking its protectorate. Its gray stone walls showed evidence of conflict. The scars were deep. The battles must have been fierce…but eerily abandoned.

From there, they went to the market square. It felt good to be around people… reminding all of what was essential and needed protecting… what was genuinely worth fighting, and perhaps – even dying for. Stewart just listened and watched. It was 0330 pm. Everything would be closing up soon. They wandered into the square and were immersed in a symphony of practiced choreography of enticement to the day's wares. Angus, Shamus, and Clinton went directly to the hatmaker and tried on some Tricorn hats. Some were quite plain in various colors. Others were more ornate and made from different materials, such as wool, beaver, leather, and silk. The young men were interested in the Beaver Pelt Tricorn hats… but were more expensive than they could ever afford. Stewart had been given 100 Guineas to take on their expedition. To date, he has only spent 15. The Hatter saw the interest. Stewart stepped up to the table. He asked the Hatter what they cost and was told 1 pound and 10 Shillings. Stewart said he needed 10 of them, and the age-old haggling battle began. Stewart was up to the challenge – the Hatter even invoked his poor old mother and starving children in the midst of the battle, and Stewart would have none of it. 10 Guineas – 10 Beaver felt Tricorn hats. Period. Or he would walk, leaving the Hatter 10 Guineas lighter. In the end… after the Hatter proclaimed he should get the Sheriff since he was being robbed… he acquiesced. The exchange was made.

Everyone received a hat… as a memory of the brief, successful – yet tragic expedition – including one for the mum of Craig Alexander and his sacrifice. Angus, Shamus, and Clinton were as children receiving their first taste of chocolate in Afghanistan, thought Stewart… and he smiled. They would wear their hats with pride walking through Inverness.

They got back to the Inn in time for Supper. Ale…another hearty stew, two roast chickens, and a thick brown bread. As you would think, Agnes and Gweneth paid particular attention to the men at the table.

Stewart brought the women to the side and told them there would be hot baths for all – just like the last time… and he paid them in advance. He would be curious about how young Clinton would handle one of these women… he quietly laughed to himself.

He announced to the table that everyone smelled terrible and that he had paid for bathes for all. Angus, Shamus, and Clinton all groaned in disdain. They had no idea.

It was finally Clinton's turn. Stewart, Calhoun, Munro, and MacKay stood outside the door listening. Agnes came with the last bucket of hot water… "You boys should be ashamed of yourselves." She smiled, walked inside… and closed the door. Before she closed the door, they could see him inside the tub. He looked like a drowned whooped pup.

"Alright, lad – I need you to stand up," said Agnes.

"Wait. What?" asked Clinton.

"I need you to stand up so I can wash you, lad," said Agnes.

"Thank you. That's okay. I can wash myself," said Clinton nervously.

Agnes put on the charm. You could tell by her voice. "Trust me, lad, you can't wash yourself as well as I can." You heard her clothing drop to the floor.

That was followed by a muffled yell…followed by a scream and a large "SPLASH!!!"

Clinton marched out of the room, soaking wet with his clothes covering his private parts… "YOU! YOU BLOODY BASTARDS PLANNED THIS!!! DIDN'T YOU?!?!?" He yelled. And he marched indignantly to his room.

The men looked inside to see a naked Agnes looking exasperated in a very undignified pose with her butt in the air, trying to get out of the tub. The men lifted her to make sure she was okay… Agnes started laughing… the men followed uproariously, gasping for air…. Followed by an even angrier "Fuck You All!" coming from Clinton's room.

Stewart paid her another Guinea. "Love… that was worth the price of admission!" She smiled at him and hugged him. "Until next time, sweetie!"

The morning came early—a big breakfast, then on to the ferry. Clinton was unusually quiet and subdued. Angus asked him if he was alright.

"You know damn well I'm not! I'm to be wed to Sarah next Spring! Did you think I would give up my honor for a whore!?!?" shouted Clinton.

"Lad. She was only going to kiss it. You would've lost no honor," said Shamus. And they all started laughing once again, to Clinton's dismay. "Just don't tell your mum. She won't let you go with us again if you do." And the laughter began again.

They got to the ferry safely to the other side… and were back in Inverness by noon. They were at the Alexander's by 1. Stewart knocked at the door with his hat in his hand. James answered the door. "Hello, Stewart. You missed the funeral. It was two days ago. It was hard not having a body to bury, though. But it's funny what you remember when there's time to do so."

"I can only imagine," said Stewart. "Is your mum and da here?"

"Aye," said James.

The entire family came out of the house.

Stewart looked at each one… the grief was almost overwhelming. He went to the wagon and pulled out the Tricorn Hats. He gave one to James and Thomas. He then walked up to Mrs. Alexander. Her eyes were red and puffy from crying. Her heart was broken. Stewart handed her Craig's hat. "We got one for Craig as a remembrance to the family. The three corners represent the Father, the Son, and the Holy Spirit. The hat is a cover – a protection for the wearer as he will also protect you. The material is of fine quality – and worth much – even as your son. He sacrificed himself rather than allowing anyone else to get hurt trying to rescue him."

She grabbed the hat and pulled it fiercely to her breast. "Stewart. That's your name, correct?"

"Yes ma'am. It is," said Stewart. "I'm so, so, so, sorry." As tears began to flow.

"I want you to promise me… no… I want you to swear to me. I don't care if it takes you the rest of your life – I want you to swear to me that you will get my boy from the depths in which he fell and bring him to get a proper burial." She looked at him fiercely.

"But ma'am…" protested Stewart.

"SWEAR TO ME!" insisted Mrs. Alexander. "You will not leave him in the hell in which he fell. Do you hear me?! SWEAR. TO. ME."

Stewart looked down…and then looked her in the eyes… "Yes, Ma'am. I swear it. By God's strength, I will make it happen in my lifetime."

With that… she collapsed into his arms. Sobbing uncontrollably. Her family came and gathered her and took her back into the house.

James stayed behind. "No one blames you, Stewart. You tried to warn everyone. I'll not hold you to your oath. You did all that you could do."

Stewart looked James in the eye… "I swear I will do my best to make it happen."

"I know," said James. He grabbed Stewart and hugged him…had tears in his eyes… and shook his hand. "We still have much to prepare for, I'm afraid."

"Aye, Lad" … that we do.

Chapter 33
Diplomacy

Prior to leaving, Lord Lamont met with Lord Forbes one last time. Lord Forbes, of course, had been distracted by the upcoming wedding. He fully understood why time was of the essence and that Lord Lamont needed to move quickly to get the Assembly set up and established. Lord Lamont was able to get the Duke of Cumberland's Signet Ring, and Lord Derek McAndrew was able to loan him a pistol, a full magazine of 9mm ammunition, and one each of the various types of ammunition that would be available as firepower to defeat the Pretender in London.

Of course, the purpose of the trip to Edinburgh was to inspire Dr. William Wishart to call an Assembly. He was in agreement that an Assembly be called and that Prince Charles Stuart be named King of Scotland before he could take his proper place as the King of all of the United Kingdom. A proper Declaration of Independence would be a good start. He would have ample time to consider such a document on the ride to Edinburg. They had plenty of reasons to declare independence from that arrogant ass as a King. He thought to himself that he genuinely hoped that Prince Charles was the man he professed to be. If not – he would kill the man himself.

There were 10 of his most trusted men with him to travel to Edinburgh. It was over 150 miles there. It would take ten days to get there without killing the horses…

They left on Thursday, 7 May 1746. Hopefully, they would be in Edinburgh by Sunday, 17 May 1746, so they could meet with Dr. Wishart on Monday. Gathering an Assembly would take at least two months from the announcement. He had known Dr. Wishart since they were students together… when he believed he would be a Minister rather than a Clan Chief… Before the plague had killed his Mum, Da, and older brother. That was over 30 years ago. They had seen each other several times over the years. He wished they were back in the innocent days of debating Biblical Theology.

There would have been an Assembly if Prince Charles had lost. That is what was anticipated. He knew the Nobles now had learned that Prince Charles had won the Battle of Culloden – though the details would be missing. They, indeed, would be anticipating some call to action with that new detail to throw into the mix.

Of course, the snakes, the Campbells, were probably conspiring to create some mischief to give them an upper hand. "Stop thinking that way! You will poison the possibility of unity… so that your grandchildren won't have to learn or experience such treachery. Understand this, old man – you will not under any circumstances allow personal animus to negate the ideal from occurring."

One thing he enjoyed about long trips by horseback was that one could get lost in one's thoughts. History remembered. Futures planned. Besides the occasional breaks, riding at a Cantor didn't allow much in the way of conversation – you only had your thoughts to keep you company.

Sixteen. 1710 – still barely into a new Century. At University in Edinburgh. The city was larger than he could have imagined. William Wishart. Yes. He remembered him as they were the same age. He was shy… kind of gangly. His eyes, though. They would pierce you to your very soul when he looked at you with conviction. The debates on the Doctrine of Predestination, the Nature of the Eucharist, proper church governance, and Apologetics were but a few of the topics debated. He really missed those days. The weight of responsibility had weighed heavily on him over the years.

It had been almost five years since he had seen William. He was sure William would have preferred the Theological rather than the Political Realm that seemed to constantly be battling us Scots for hundreds of years now. And the bloody English! Why couldn't they just leave us the hell alone? They and their arrogance. They claim to be followers of Christ – yet all other races and peoples are but tools to be used in their exploitation of us all. And their use of money and debt to enslave has to be the most ungodly notion of all!

Another day of riding and another day of thoughts. He was 22 and was to be an Assistant Minister in Inveraray. He was preparing to accept the position and begin the move when he got the news. His mother and father had the Plague. He got home as quickly as possible… but it was too late. They and his oldest brother had succumbed to the devil's spawn. He had missed the burial as well.

He remembered the pouring rain as if God and His Angels had broken down in tears for the loss. He went to the cemetery… and saw the freshly dug graves… he fell on his face in the mud and begged his parent's forgiveness for not being there when his family needed him and swore that would never happen again. He was bitter with God. Angry actually. He had wanted to serve the Almighty and took the ones he loved the most. Little did he know that the tragedy would bring about everything he lived for today.

He remembered her as a little girl –six years his junior. He had ignored her as any that much older would do. Once he recovered from the death of his loved ones, he traveled to Inveraray to explain to the Minister why he would not be able to become the Assistant Minister for the Church. After that difficult discussion with the Minister, he stopped to explore the market center and take his mind off the difficult times he was facing. He was looking at the leather goods stores and bumped into her. Margaret MacLauchlan. My, how she had grown up! He smiled, even now thinking about her. She instantly recognized him, knew of his situation, and expressed her concern sincerely. She even hugged him, which was inappropriate, but he needed that simple gesture. God would understand.

God definitely understood. Four months later – they were married. With six children and twelve grandchildren, God had blessed the union. This is why he was here now, preparing to work diligently to depose the King and install another. The Lord indeed works in mysterious ways.

It was Sunday, 17 May 1746. He was correct in his timing. Of course, it was pouring down rain, as to be expected. They were coming from the East and could see the outlying city of Edinburgh. The population was over 50,000 and so much larger than any area he had ever been to – except London twenty years prior. God… how could anyone live in such a crowded city? He loved his private, small population centers where people and families truly mattered.

There was what he was looking for… The White Hart Inn. It wasn't luxurious, but they were good at what they did. Their clothing would be cleaned and dried before the morrow; the meals would be simple but hearty. The Ale or Whiskey would be as warm as the fireplace – which would be roaring. He would have his own room and a bath to go with it. His men would share a room. Their horses would be well tended at the livery. He wanted them well-fed since they had been traveling constantly with little time for grazing.

It had been ten years since he last stayed here. He closed his eyes. It smelled the same. It was oddly comforting. There was nothing odd about it. His home had extremely extravagant materials, but they were all simplistic in their design. He liked simple and unpretentious. He liked tradition and continuity. Some would call it boring. He called it comforting and consistent – values he highly appreciated.

After their meal of roast lamb and beef stew, he ordered a bottle of whiskey for his men. He informed them he would be leaving early in the morning and for them to enjoy some time to themselves – but that there would be hell to pay if they got into so much as a hint of trouble.

The hot bath did wonders for his aching joints. Getting older was not for the faint of heart. Once dried… he made straight for bed. He knew that unannounced – he would have to get to the College of Edinburgh early even to see Dr. Wishart. No doubt, an appointment during the day would be impossible, and of course, Dr. Wishart would want some elaborate meal to entice him for the meeting later.

The true weight of why he was there made sleep come slowly and then filled with dreams that pointed to doubt and fear – which he rebuked. He decided to pray. He got out of bed… his knees creaked… he welcomed the hard floor on his knees – the pain, in a weird way, meant he was committed to the path that God lay before him. "Almighty and merciful God, Thou who art the sovereign ruler of all creation. I humbly beseech Thee to hear my supplication. Grant me, wretched man, that I am, your divine guidance and protection. May your divine wisdom illuminate my path – and the paths of those who would rule. In your infinite mercy, grant me success in my mission, should it be according to thy Will. With utmost reverence, humility, and devotion. Amen."

Amazingly, he finally fell asleep and slept soundly.

He woke at six and dressed in his station. He would not put up with a disagreeable administrator who would not allow him access. Too much was riding on this for an arrogant and ill-mannered child to create a problem and delay the meeting.

An extensive breakfast and an Ale prepared him for the meeting. Then he was off.

He arrived at the campus at 730 am. None were in Dr. Wishart's office yet, so he waited outside his office. Perfect. There he was, coming to the door. Of course, his nose was pouring over some letter of import, and he nearly ran into him before he looked up. It took him a minute to determine who was standing before him, but when Lord Lamont smiled – he did so as well!

"Why…why Lord Lamont! What! It is so good to see you! It has been way too long, my friend!" said Dr. Wishart.

"Yes, My friend. I fully agree. It's been at least five years. The time flows like rapids in an angry stream," said Lord Lamont.

"Follow me into my office before anyone else arrives. I may have 20 minutes to converse with an old friend before I have meetings all day today. Would you be available for dinner to converse longer and privately this evening?" asked Dr. Wishart.

"Why, of course, my friend," said Lord Lamont as he reached out to help Dr. Wishart with the three volumes of books that he had in his hand. All three on Apologetics. Why was he not surprised?

They stepped into the opulent office that was in place for those who were held in high esteem within the University. Once Dr. Wishart had everything in place, he looked at his old friend. He was dressed in formal attire. Damn. That meant it would be official in its capacity rather than a talk between old friends.

"My friend – you appear as Lord Lamont – not simply Keith Lamont – my friend and confidant. I guess this conversation will be more formal than catching up on old times?" Questioned Dr. Wishart.

"Aye. You are astute as always, my friend. I have much to tell you of Culloden and the current state of affairs," said Lord Lamont.

"I am aware that Prince Charles defeated the Duke of Cumberland. Some said that there were no survivors – including the Duke. But you know how ridiculous rumors can be." And he laughed at his trip down into the realm of the impossible.

Dr. Wishart noticed that Lord Lamont did not laugh. He also noticed that Lord Lamont gave him a ring. He looked at it closely. And his breath left him. He fell onto his chair. It was Duke Cumberland's Signet Ring. The only way to have that ring in his possession would be for someone to take it off of the corpse of the Duke. "Well… I suppose there could be some truth to the rumor?"

"My friend, you have no idea. I do not know if God intervened or what occurred exactly. I only know that Prince Charles lives, that none survived, and the weapons at Prince Charles's disposal make him certain to defeat the Pretender in London – no matter how many he sends to try to defeat him. William. No army on this earth can defeat Prince Charles. I have seen a small portion of what he has – and he is changing Inverness into a military arms behemoth."

"Aikman's at precisely 6 pm, my friend. We will have much to discuss. If what you say is true… it may be time to call an Assembly," said Dr. Wishart.

"I will be waiting," said Lord Lamont. He left the doctor to his thoughts. Of course, he picked the most expensive and pretentious place in Edinburgh to have a meal. That will be at least 10 pounds for a meal! That is outrageous! But he would do it. And he would pay – gladly if this got the Assembly process started.

Lord Lamont arrived early, dressed in his finest. This irked him – but he paid the Mistress of the establishment a pound to seat them in a quiet corner so they could have a discussion instead of having to yell above the crowd to converse. He also brought each piece of ammunition and the 9mm pistol to be shown at the table. He had no time to waste since he knew the process took time.

Precisely at 6 pm, Dr. Wishart was escorted to his table. This was usually the table that Lord Lamont would have chosen – as he valued his privacy and did not like flaunting his wealth. So, he was not surprised. It was secluded, with just the right feel of warmth and ambiance, without all of the crowd noise that would be in the main hall. Dr. Wishart would have preferred being in the crowd where his face and, of course, his excellent taste – would have been seen by all. That said, this was probably not a conversation that would need to be heard by others.

Lord Lamont stood and reached out his hand and clasped Dr. Wisharts. "It is so good to see you, old friend. I could not help but see your books this morning on Apologetics. Are you still trying to discover where you were wrong in our debates?" said a smiling Lord Lamont.

"Not hardly, old friend – you figured that out decades ago. There's no point in bringing that up again. It would appear as if I were gloating!" said a tremendously smug Dr. Wishart. "Besides, it would be as fencing with an unarmed man. That would not be fair, now would it?" asked a precocious, smiling lifelong friend.

"Alas, some things never change. Well played, sir," said Lord Lamont.

"I have taken the liberty of ordering our meal. I even paired them with your favorite wines," said Lord Lamont.

Dr. Wishart looked aghast. "How do you know my tastes have not changed in the last five years?"

"Have they?" asked Lord Lamont.

"Well, of course not – but how did you know? Am I that predictable?" asked Dr. Wishart.

"Oh, William, my dear friend – in the finer things – no. You have not changed, and you are totally predictable. You know what you like. As do I!" said Lord Lamont.

Their waiter was a veteran. He knew the proper attention to detail, with the perfect flamboyant flair to entertain, and delivered the food with the precision of a watchmaker.

First, the Appetizer, A Lobster, Crab, and Shrimp Bisque accompanied by a Chardonnay. The silky texture is lightly peppered with a subtle garlic aftertaste. Wait! What was that? Paprika... on the back end. Like a creamy seafood butter... the bright acidity of the Chardonnay with its citrusy notes was a perfect blend.

Then, the first course – a grilled salmon, spiced simply with salt, pepper, and lemon, and smothered in butter. With the oils from the salmon and butter, a Riesling was served.

Dr. Wishart was a single man. His wife had passed away 30 years ago, with the birth of their first child. Neither had survived and after their burial, Dr. Wishart had given his life to his profession. The conversation was lively as the two were able to catch up on what had occurred over the last five years of their lives.

The Main course – several different selections of lamb, from the delicate ribs, a shank... and then the Crown. Immaculate in its presentation, frenched, with a red wine gravy. Roasted potatoes of diverse colors, buttered asparagus, and Onions drizzled with drippings from the lamb as it roasted. The wine? A Burgundy from France, of course! The complexity of the meal – even appealed to Lord Lamont. Lord Lamont decided the political discourse would begin over dessert.

Three hours later – dessert was served. A fresh berry trifle – layers of sponge cake, custard, berries, and topped with a fresh cream. Nothing but a Port would work with such a dessert.

Dr. Wishart's eyes sparkled, and his cheeks were rosy from the food and wine consumed. He was as merry as a man could be apart from the embrace of a lovely woman. He had no idea how the direction of the conversation would turn.

Before Dessert was served, Lord Lamont set out the 7.62 mm shell for Dr. Wishart to see. Dr. Wishart picked it up and intently looked at it – from the tip to the base. Top and bottom. He could make nothing of it. Lord Lamont then set out the 9mm along with the magazine. Once again, Dr. Wishart and his unquenchable curiosity were in full bloom. He began to ask a question – when, of course – the trifle appeared –much to his annoyance – which even surprised him.

Dr. Wishart set down these foreign implements, consumed the Trifle, and drank the port – more out of duty than preference. He wanted to know what had been presented to him.

The dessert was finished. The plates were removed. A good brandy was set before them to finish the evening meal.

Once again, Lord Lamont pulled out the 7.62 mm and then the 50-caliber shell, followed by the 9mm. He didn't say a word. Much to his displeasure – Dr. Wishart understood that he would have to express his interest in discovering more. He also knew once he found out what these were – intuitively, he knew that he would go along with whatever Lord Lamont needed him to do. He had gotten too old and easy…

"Alright… what the bloody hell are those." Asked Dr. Wishart.

"Those, sir, are ammunition for firearms," said Lord Lamont.

"You mean for a musket?" asked Dr. Wishart.

"No sir. New weapons about which you would not even remotely know. This shell… is a 50-caliber ammunition. Listen to this – it has a range of over 2,000 yards!" said Lord Lamont.

"Bullshit," said Dr. Wishart. That is physically impossible.

"So, you say," said Lord Lamont. He then picked up the 7.62 mm shell. "These are what decimated the calvary and the Dragoons of His Majesties Army. Hundreds of these rounds were fired per minute. Not a soul survived. Twelve firearms were used to destroy the Cavalry and the Dragoons."

He then picked up the 9mm shell. "You see this little thing? Lord Connor McAndrew – whom you do not know but was wed Saturday to Lord Forbes' daughter. Six highwaymen accosted him and Lord Forbes' Steward." Lord Lamont pulled out the Browning – unloaded, of course! And allowed Dr. Wishart to look at it and feel the weight of it.

"What is that?" asked Dr. Wishart.

"That, sir, is a pistol that fires thirteen rounds as fast as you can pull the trigger - without reloading. As I was saying, Lord McAndrew and Lord Forbes Steward were assaulted by six men – all armed with pistols and blades. Lord McAndrew killed four and wounded severely a fifth – while Lord Forbes Steward killed one with his pistol." Lord Lamont then pulled out the magazine and unloaded each shell – just as Lord Derek McAndrew had shown him to do. "This weapon – is accurate to seventy-five yards – as small as it is –is far more superior and deadly than the smooth bore muskets. Do you understand, sir – everyone… every single soul – including the Duke – was killed in less than fifteen minutes of fighting!"

Silence.

"There is no military in the world as strong as Prince Charles is currently. They are currently working on a rifle that can be loaded 4 to 5 times per minute with an accurate range of 200 to 300 yards. With 10,000 of those rifles, England would belong to Prince Charles," said Lord Lamont.

"What do you need me to do?" asked Dr. Wishart.

"I, sir, need for you to call for an Assembly—all of the Earls, Lords, and leadership of our nation. Prince Charles must be able to speak to them all and make the case for the Scottish Crown. He knows if he wanted it – he could take it. He chooses not to do so. But hear me on this – what is astounding are the conversations that we have had… he truly loves the people. He loves this nation. He wants to govern by the consent of the governed," said Lord Lamont.

"Do you want to hear how I started the conversation with Prince Charles?" asked Lord Lamont.

"I'm all ears," said Dr. Wishart.

"I explained that I was going to be blunt – then I asked him- 'Why should I trade one tyrant for another?' "Said Lord Lamont.

"You WHAT?!?!" said a surprised Dr. Wishart.

"It's a legitimate question, and I needed to hear his answer," said Lord Lamont.

"Well?" asked Dr. Wishart.

"Well, what?" asked Lord Lamont.

An exasperated Dr. Wishart said… "You know damn well what I meant."

Lord Lamont laughed. "Aye. I did. After I asked him that question – there was a 'gasp' from everyone in the room. And do you know what Prince Charles did? He smiled. "You'll never guess what he asked me right after I asked him that."

"I'm waiting." Declared Dr. Wishart.

"He bloody well asked me to be on his council! Then he said, 'Lord Lamont. I do not have now, nor ever want sycophants on my Council. I need those who are willing to tell me what I do not wish to hear to be able to make a better decision. I cannot say I will always agree with you – but I can tell you that your opinion will be heard.' "Declared Lord Lamont.

"You are not jesting? You are indeed telling me what he said and how he reacted?"

"Aye, my old friend. As much as I enjoy your company – you need to know – I rode from my home to Inverness in the last month. I then spent a couple of days observing Prince Charles and what he was building. I then spent ten days riding here to speak with you. This needed words spoken – not words written. I would not have even made this much effort without believing the man and the cause he represents. So yes. I am telling you exactly how he reacted." Explained Lord Lamont. "So… what say you, My dear friend? Will you call for an Assembly?"

"My Petition will go out tomorrow. I am convinced," said Dr. Wishart. "Shall we drink a toast then?"

"I thought you would never ask," said Lord Lamont. "My Dear friend Dr. Wishart, tonight we have shared not only this fine meal, memories of a faded past, but what will become a profound moment in the history of our Country. Your wisdom and conviction in supporting the cause of Prince Charles have stirred my conviction even further. So... Here is to the future of Scotland, where justice and freedom shall reign… and the only rightful King we shall acclaim. May the Assembly choose wisely and proclaim the legitimate heir as King of Scotland. Raise your glass, my friend. For tonight, we toast to hope, unity, and the promise of a brighter country. For our progeny and ourselves – we have started the foundation of our own country! May God Bless Scotland and Long live our future King!"

With that, the bottle was emptied. Never in his life had Lord Lamont felt such an optimistic view of what the struggle would be once the difficult part was past. His father once told him that the greater the struggle – the greater the prize. For his children and grandchildren… they would indeed have a country of their own!

Chapter 34
Innovation

Derek woke as he had since Lord Lamont left – almost a month ago. Would this be the day that he would return with the news? Prince Charles becoming the King of Scotland was an essential part of the plan – especially in gaining international acceptance – not only for the King of Scotland – but the same acceptance for the eventual defeat of The Pretender in London.

He heard a knock on his door. It would be Connor and Mac. Against Lady Mary McAndrew's wishes – Connor now stayed at Camp Striker Monday – Friday. There had been so much accomplished but so much left to do. Maybe it was selfish – but he believed that he AND Scotland needed Connor now more than his new wife. The knock was more insistent.

"Yes?" he shouted.

"Sir. Are you awake?"

Derek knew that voice. It was Sergeant Josh Douglas. "Yes. I'm not out of bed yet. Come in."

"The Captain asked me to get you up and at 'em. You've been called to meet with Prince Charles as soon as possible. Connor and Mac are getting ready. Breakfast will be waiting for you," said Sergeant Douglas.

"Aye." He rolled out of bed while the Sergeant left the room. He was quickly dressed. In 10 minutes, he was with Mac and Connor having breakfast. Fifteen minutes later, they were on the way to Camp Charlie, as they started calling it. He still found it interesting that Prince Charles stayed in the camp. Every Noble in and around Inverness would love to have the ear and favor of the man who may be King. Which, of course, is why Prince Charles would have none of it. He fully understood the childish jealousy that seemed to surround virtually every Noble – especially if it was perceived that one was getting more attention than the other. Derek had to admit that he wanted Prince Charles' favor – but it was not for benefit or financial gain. It was to improve the business and the lives of those around him. He wanted his men to be taken care of. He wanted Scotland taken care of. He wanted honor and integrity in government. Why was that so hard?

They rode up to the tent. Lady Fiona met them. She seemed… giddy. Surely, it was too early to be drinking…he laughed to himself.

"Lords, I am so glad to see you. I am sure you will also be happy when you are told," said Fiona.

When they entered the tent, Lord Lamont was sitting across from Prince Charles – and laughing – that was a good sign.

"Lord Lamont! You've returned!" said Mac.

"Indeed, I have," said Lord Lamont. "Will you take me on a tour of the businesses in Inverness today?

Mac said, "Why, of course, Lord Lamont."

Prince Charles interrupted, "Lord Lamont. Would you be so kind as to stop delaying the point of asking these gentlemen here this morning?"

"What is the date today?"

"Friday, 3 June," said the Prince.

"Your Highness, you have been asked to appear before the Assembly on Tuesday, 4 July 1746, at 9 am to present your case as King of Scotland. They will convene on 1 July 1746 in Edinburgh! We did it, Your Highness!" Smiled an obviously tired Lord Lamont. "The rest will be up to you and what we can accomplish before then. I will be going, along with every other Lord and Clan Chief."

"Well, Gentlemen, we have accomplished the impossible – truly by the Grace of God. I do not doubt that we will prevail!" exclaimed the Prince. "Now, my dear friend Lord Lamont – do you need rest? Or would you like to see what we have been able to accomplish in the last five weeks?"

"To be honest, Your Highness… I am exhausted… but I would not miss this for the world!" said Lord Lamont.

The Prince smiled, "Excellent! Lords McAndrew and Lord McKenzie – would you be up for giving a tour?"

The three lit up… "Absolutely, Your Highness!" exclaimed Mac. "Lord Lamont – you will not believe your eyes! One of our gunsmiths has even fashioned three prototypes of the firearm we wish to mass produce!"

With that, they gathered their horses and headed to Inverness.

When everyone rode up – The Provost rode out to meet them. Lord Lamont was stunned. There ended up being six huge buildings. There was one to produce the rifled steel barrels for the "762." The Scots are calling it the "Liberator." One is for putting the "Liberator" together. The one furthest from there is a gunpowder producer. Another is for the ammunition. It will produce the 7.62 mm shell made entirely from Brass. It will be able to change to whatever caliber we wish to produce. One is for producing the Bio-Diesel to fuel the Jackal and the Mastiff. The last – is a miscellaneous building for research and development. The first business order is assembling the steam engine to produce a locomotive.

Each structure was larger than any local builder had ever constructed. The mathematics of the engineers worked wonders. All six of the structures were built to the same specs. They were 75'x100'x20' – more than large enough to complete their goal and to be prepared by the following Spring should King George decide to invade. This would allow more innovation than anyone had hoped or dreamed.

Lord Lamont wanted to see this prototype. Lord MacLeod was found inside tweaking what had been his invention. This prototype was a work of art. The carvings on the Stock named it The Liberator. Lord Lamont showed the workings of the firearm. He then asked Lord Lamont if he wished to fire it – which was a "Yes" with a large smile.

There was a practice range. The targets were at 100 – 400 yards. Lord MacLeod brought 10-7.62 mm shells. He explained that they were already producing the ammunition. As a matter of fact – he would be using some of the shells produced here.

Lord MacLeod showed Lord Lamont how to load the firearm by pulling on the opening lever. The barrel opened. The shell is then inserted. Once inserted, the barrel is closed. The trigger is then pulled – which causes the hammer to strike the primer, firing the shell downrange.

Each step, Lord Lamont followed. He then pulled the Liberator into the firing position. He was instructed on how to use the iron sites. He focused on the target, then pulled the trigger while aiming at the 100-yard target. "Plink" – it hit the target. Lord Lamont was stunned. He opened the lever, removed the spent cartridge, replaced it with a new cartridge, and then aimed at the 200-yard target. "Plink" … this brought a big smile. That distance was enough to win an engagement against the strongest military in the world. He repeated the process, aimed at the 300-yard target… "Plink.". "Son of a Bitch! I hit that?!?" expressed Lord Lamont. "Well, now I have to try the 400-yard." He repeated the process, squeezed the trigger… and missed. He tried it one more time and hit low and to the left. He received one more shell to try one more time. Lord MacLeod suggested aiming just above the plate. Lord Lamont opened the lever, removed the spent casing, replaced it with the new shell, aimed, and fired! He hit the target at 400 yards! "I want one of these!" Exclaimed Lord Lamont. "We will need to take one of these to the Assembly!." His smile was contagious.

"Now, take me to where they are producing the gunpowder," said Lord Lamont. They walked the 200 yards to the gunpowder building. Lord Macleod explained that they were digging out the bat guano in a cave quite close to Inverness. They had to dig out much of the cave to turn it into a mine. It looked like there would be more than enough to get everything started. They had sent some engineers to one that was further to begin the process so there would be no lapse in production.

"To produce the Potassium Nitrate for the gunpowder, the bat guano is mixed with water, and then the solids are filtered out. The water is then evaporated. It took a while to figure out the best method for filtration with what we had, especially in the amounts that we needed. We built a frame and attached it to a linen cloth on one side. We use 12 inches of shredded hay as a filter medium and have it sandwiched between another linen cloth. The liquid flows into a trough where it evaporates and leaves this… Potassium Nitrate crystals," said Lord MacLeod.

"Now, the dangerous part is over here. This is where we mix the ingredients to make the gunpowder. Typically, the mixture would be 75% Potassium Nitrate, 15% Sulfur, and 10% Charcoal. We have found 72% Potassium Nitrate, 17% Sulfur, and 11% Charcoal works the best. It works exceptionally well in our environment," said Lord MacLeod.

"Why is the mixing the dangerous part?" asked Lord Lamont.

"If it is not mixed in the proper proportions – it's unstable – so it can blow up. If there is static electricity – it can blow up. If there is a flame – it can blow up. We make sure everything is grounded to prevent static electricity. If you notice – we have No Smoking and No Open Flame signs everywhere," said Lord MacLeod.

"This is truly fascinating," said Lord Lamont. "So, how do you produce the ammunition?"

Lord Connor McAndrew took over for Lord MacLeod. "There is a foundry in Inverness. They are producing all of the brass they can for us. Let me show you here." Connor escorted him to the ammunition building. "One-half of this is for the production of the shell and the casing and primer for the shell. The other half is where they are loaded and prepared for use. The Primer was the most difficult challenge." Connor picked up a shell and showed the parts to Lord Lamont. "Making the primer fire consistently was the problem. The initial mixture had a 1 in 4 failure rate. Totally unacceptable. From where we are now – the failure rate is about 1 in 25. It still needs to be adjusted for what we would consider acceptable."

"We have put together a different way of manufacturing. Instead of one person being responsible for the total production of the shell, we have different groups of people responsible for each stage of the production. Over here is where the brass comes into the facility. It is immediately taken to our foundry, where it is melted for use. This group is responsible for producing the molds for the molten brass. Each mold produces 50 rounds. When they complete the mold, it is taken to the foundry, where the molten brass is poured. Once that step is complete, it is taken to the next room, where the brass is cooled and released from the mold. From there, each shell is polished – that's the most labor-intensive portion of the process. From there, it is taken to the Ammunition Loader, where the shell and the gunpowder are inserted into the casing for the final product. We are currently doing up to 1000 rounds per day. By the end of the month, we should have up to 2000 rounds per day. The goal is to produce 10,000 rounds per day," explained Connor.

"10,000 rounds per day?!?!? Is that even possible?" asked Lord Lamont.

Connor smiled. "No doubt," he said with confidence.

"Have you tried any of these shells in your equipment yet?" asked Lord Lamont.

"Yes, My Lord. You just used homemade ammunition from this foundry. We want the capability and quality to improve a bit more. But as you have seen, they work in the Liberator," said Connor.

"Indeed, I did," said Lord Lamont. "So, where are we on the production of the Liberator?"

Lord McKenzie answered this question. "As you saw, we have a prototype that works how we want. We are developing a better way of developing the barrel – which is time-consuming – especially the rifling portion, which we need for accuracy. Right now, we only can produce around ten rifles per day. They are each individually made with the parts that have been produced separately. The barrels are all made with steel that we receive from another foundry in Inverness. Each of the Foundries is expanding to meet our demand. Our goal is to be able to produce 100 rifles per day, with the possibility of doubling that if my idea works. We are working with the Foundry to be able to produce the rifled barrels. Should that happen – then the capabilities are increased substantially."

"Now, what about the fuel for your Jackal and Mastiff?" asked Lord Lamont.

Lord Derek McAndrew said, "Let me show you here. Now be prepared – it smells terrible there. We are making a product called 'Biodiesel' – which we need for fuel. Fortunately, we have chemical engineers who are more than capable of making this happen. The first step is to render the fat into a liquid and add Potassium alkoxide to the heated fat while stirring. See the large vats? That is what is happening there."

Lord Lamont interrupted, "Dear God, it does smell quite awful."

Everyone laughed, and Derek continued, "The next steps are essential. You must stir until the reaction is complete. Then, you let it cool. There is a byproduct called glycerin that settles to the bottom. The glycerin can be used in various products – like soap, food production, and industrial lubricants – so it is not wasted. Then, take the top layer – which is the biodiesel. Filter out the impurities, and it is ready to go. We are still experimenting with the best ratios. We can store this and take it with us in combat. We have tried it in one of our vehicles. It smokes a bit, which means we must adjust our equipment – but it works. And that is what is important."

"Now – what are you doing in that building?" asked Lord Lamont.

Derek was excited about this one, "We have several steam engines that we are working with to determine how to increase and improve production on all fronts. I am a Mechanical Engineer, as is Connor. This is what fascinates us. The potential is truly unbelievable. I won't go into this yet – but perhaps you would like to see what we are doing in there?"

"Absolutely," said Lord Lamont.

As Lord Lamont stepped into the building, he was assailed with monstrosities he had never seen before – 4 steam engines—one in each corner. Three were in various stages of construction. One, however, was complete. "We just got these in last week," said Derek. "We have only just begun to explore their capabilities are… how they work, what the horsepower is, and what we can do to make them accomplish what we desire. Transportation is high on our list, in addition to dramatically increasing production levels and the ability to generate electricity… wait until you see what can be done with electricity! Our world is on the cusp of change like you cannot even imagine!"

Lord Lamont was stunned. This was accomplished in only five weeks. What on earth will they be able to produce in a year? I have never been so proud and excited to be a Scotsman in my life. We need to get the crown settled. The Campbells better not fuck this up… They will be the last Clan to get these updated rifles.

"Well?" asked the Prince. "What do you think, Lord Lamont?" You could see his level of excitement… his eyes told the story. He knew. His ambition was going to be fulfilled. He had a month to get prepared. And By God – he would be ready.

Chapter 35
Edinburgh

Wednesday, 29 June 1746

Tomorrow, the Lords are to leave for the Assembly. So much has been prepared for this trip – even how the trip will be accomplished. Instead of being on horseback for ten days or more, it has been decided to be bold. We will be using 2 Mastiffs for a road trip. Yes…when they arrive in Edinburgh - it will scare the populace. But the point is to make a statement. These should do quite nicely. Then they will return. As mysteriously as they arrived.

So much has already been accomplished. Anything short of miraculous doesn't even begin to give a legitimate description of all that has transpired in the last month. We are up to 30 rifles per day, 2,500 rounds of 7.62 ammunition per day, and 100 gallons of Biodiesel per day. The primer failure was down to 1 in 100. One thing that our electrical engineers have been working on – is developing electrical power from waterpower with the River Ness. There is a lot of potential on that front. The Prince and his entourage will arrive in a couple of Mastiffs on July 3 to be prepared for his speech to convince the Lords of the necessity of the Crown. Reconciliation and uniting the clans was paramount, with the ability to convince all that any enemy that attempted to conquer Scotland would be squashed – no matter their numbers.

Lord Lamont will be opening the Assembly after an introduction from Dr. Wishart. He was looking forward to expressing his point of view. He was not looking forward to the political wrangling. Especially since he understood the strength of their firepower and the ignorance that each had regarding that firepower. The Duke of Cumberland's body would be shown sometime there before being dispatched to the King of England with a powerful statement of independence – almost a dare to attack.

Derek planned to have a solid contingent to protect Prince Charles. There would be ten heavily armed Strikers to protect the contingent. He, Connor, and Mac would be a part of that contingent.

Lord John Stuart of Grandtully arrived unexpectedly. He had not been seen in several weeks. "Lord John Stuart! It is so good to see you, my old friend!" said Prince Charles. "It is as you have predicted – except I think it may be even better than I could have anticipated!" Prince Charles clasped his hand and then pulled him into a hug. One that would be unexpected from a future King. This is what was becoming enticing to all that were around him. Any arrogance or haughtiness that may have been a part of who he was when he arrived had been completely eradicated from his persona with all that he had seen and worked with in Inverness. He was indeed a changed man… for the better.

One change his father would disapprove of… was his conversion to Protestantism – especially as a Presbyterian. He had made his public profession of his faith and his denunciation of the Roman Catholic Faith – including of the Pope. It felt liberating. He felt more in tune with his faith and belief system since coming under the tutelage of Reverend Finley Cameron. He could dive into this Jesus and these scriptures and had spent many hours just reading and reveling in the simplicity of the Bible – God's Word. He would be a ruler like David – a man after God's heart.

"So…Lord Stuart. Will you be coming with us to the Assembly?" asked the Prince.

"Aye. I wouldn't miss it for the world," said Lord Stuart. "You're going to need me there," he said matter-of-factly. "You are also going to need to bring an armed guard."

"Lord Derek McAndrew already informed me. If you noticed – I said informed… He didn't give me much choice." Laughed the Prince.

"He is right, Your Highness. And you will need it. I have seen it. But not to worry – it will all pass in your favor," said Lord Stuart – with a twinkle in his smile… "So do not fret. It is how I knew it would be – and you are indeed the right man for the task before you. I will want to speak with The McAndrew and McKenzie, however."

"Very Well," said the Prince. I will make it happen.

All of Inverness was awash with excitement. This Prince, who would be their King, had built a relationship with all –rich or poor.

He had helped those in need. He had encouraged those who labored to bring all that was an idea to fruition. He had warmed and was kind rather than aloof when all this started. All had marveled at what God could do with this man – and were excited for the future. They knew it would be far from easy – but with the tools being developed – they knew that the world would change in their favor.

It's July, and the evening is warmer than usual. The Tavern and the folk attending this night are excited about the prospects for the future – especially with the possibility of Bonnie Prince Charlie becoming King Charles Stuart. The fireplace roars, cooking the meats and roast vegetables for the evening meal. The Tavern had prospered more than ever before. Agnes and Beth joined Mary and Anne. The building had been enlarged to entertain almost 100 folks at a time! They had even hired cooks!

The Barkeep, though his usually gruff self – had a smile this night. He had met and had gotten to know the Prince. The Prince would even sneak in occasionally for an Ale or some of the good Whiskey. He even had talked about renaming the Tavern to "Charlie's Place" once he became King.

Mary and Anne had the ebb and flow of the Tavern in their very blood. They knew instinctively who needed another Pint and who wanted seconds for their meal. Agnes and Beth were struggling to keep up – but the tips were so good – they kept smiles on their faces as they began to learn those that frequented the Tavern Daily.

John – the Blacksmith and the foundry owner- ordered drinks for the crowd. "To Prince Charles… they purveyor of all of this abundance. I don't think it's ever been this good in Inverness!"

"Aye," said the Barkeep. "I would not be surprised if our town doubles by the end of the year. The new manufacturing businesses are growing tremendously. Has anyone seen the new rifles?"

"I have," said Shamus. "You wouldn't believe how far they can shoot… and not miss! I heard of a man that shot a target at 400 yards!"

"That's Bull Shit!" said James. "That or an exaggeration! That's better than anything anyone in the world has! Even King George himself doesn't have that with his best troops!"

"All I know is what I've been told," said Shamus. "But it's my Uncle who told me. He isn't going to lie to me."

"No offense, Shamus. That sounds truly impossible," said James.

"No offense taken," said Shamus. Though my uncle would whup your arse if he were here." Everyone laughed at that.

"Someone said they had these carriages that required no horse. And that they sounded like a bellowing bull when you heard them."

John said, "All I know is that I have to look everywhere to make the steel for his rifles. They have me doing this thing they call "Rifling," – which is why they call it a rifle. They say it makes it more accurate."

Mary asked Agnes, "Have you seen some of the Striker boys? My, that's a handsome lot. They're so bloody serious, though."

"Aye," said Agnes. "I might have to start seeing about delivering some Ale and whiskey to their camp. Who knows what kind of secrets they could tell? Especially with what we have to work with?" With that – she protruded her breasts – and had Mary laughing uproariously!

Mary said, "Well – you are the one without a mate. I'm pretty sure my man would not take that so well!"

John was talking to Clinton. "Do you see what Prince Charles has done for our town? There's life like I've never seen before. I wonder what will happen if he becomes King. Will he remember us? Or choose Edinburgh and move everything there?"

Clinton said, "You've heard him and the Provost. They act like best friends. I can't see them pulling everything away from here with everything that we've been able to do! This is going to be a business paradise! You can bet money on that!"

Mary leaned over. "You know I served him a meal at that table right over there! He was polite. I thought him a merchant. I may have flirted a bit too much to be proper." Laughed Mary. "But it was fun… and he left me a whole Guinea as a tip!"

"More money than sense!" teased the barkeep.

"He's supposed to be in Edinburgh on July 4 to make his case for the crown and uniting the clans," said Thomas. "It's going to take some work for that. The bloody Campbells fought for our enemy!"

Agnes looked at Beth and smiled… their feet would be sore before the night was through – but their pockets would be complete. God was good…and finally, their lives would also be good!!

Dinner for Prince Charles would be a quiet affair as most of his peers had already left for Edinburgh. Three hours sure seems ambitious! He smiled when those loud bastards made their way to

Edinburgh, especially when they deposited their contents at the hotel where they would all be staying.

The attendees were Lord John Stuart, Lord Derek McAndrew, Lord Connor McAndrew, and Lord McKenzie. Supper was simple. Wine and cheese for an appetizer, roast mutton, roast vegetables, dried fruits with honey, and wine for dessert - Prince Charles's favorite.

Derek looked at the Prince. "Your Highness, you have changed a great deal."

"Indeed, I have Lord McAndrew. Would you like to know why?" asked the Prince.

"Very Much so, Your Highness," said Derek.

"Because sir – for the first time – in my entire life… I am content," said the Prince. "If it were not my duty to become King – I believe I would become a farmer.

"A farmer? Really? Why?" asked Lord McKenzie.

"This is going to sound strange. But I love the smell… the dirt… creating and cultivating life. So much of a Prince or King's life is spent in the destruction of life. I want to see it flourish!" said the Prince.

"Perhaps, Your Highness, you will one day have the opportunity to help a nation flourish?" said Connor McAndrew.

Dinner was brought and eaten. It was a low-key, intimate conversation. One of friendship and trust… until… Lord John Stuart spoke up. "It is only the five of us, and initially, I was only going to keep this quiet. However, this is a critical discussion you must prepare for. As you know, there is an English Garrison in Edinburgh. Major General Sir John Cope is the commanding officer. There are 400 men in the garrison. He was informed yesterday that Your Highness was to be in Edinburgh and that you would meet him in combat at 3 pm tomorrow. He will wait in a clearing where he and his men plan to capture you.

It was deathly quiet as Lord Stuart continued. "Once he sees the vehicles approaching, his first inclination will be to charge. There will only be six officers on horse. The rest will be infantry. I will be with you to let you know when we are coming up on the clearing. Then you will unleash Hell on the British, and there will be no survivors. The general's body will need to be presented to the Assembly."

Derek smiled. "Well, with that information, things will change regarding our transportation plans. We will need to take 4 Jackals in addition to the Mastiffs we will be riding in. We can have two in the front and two in the rear. Can you tell me anything about the clearing?"

"The clearing is about 2 miles to the West of town. You will want to turn to the left as soon as we get there. You will see him in formation with his men preparing to fire. Once you begin speaking, he will hold off for a few seconds after you finish. You must be prepared to fire immediately when he says, 'Make Ready! Present!' At that point, the infantry will aim their weapons in preparation to fire. Don't let them fire, and all will be okay," said Lord Stuart.

"Very well then," said Derek. "The Jackals will group with the Mastiffs moving to the rear. I will prepare a loudspeaker and be on one of the guns on a Jackal. My brother will also wish to be on a machine gun. Probably Lord McKenzie as well. We will make that decision when we are prepared to leave. Now that Supper is complete and I have this new information, we must retire to ensure we are prepared. Your Highness, please be ready to leave at 10 am. That will allow for any potential mishaps and for us to make our 3 pm appointment with the General. Our quiet little ride will be a little more adventurous than anticipated. Thank you, Lord Stuart, for bringing that to our attention. We could've accomplished the same task with the Mastiffs, but it would be overkill, and we cannot replace the 50 Caliber Ammunition yet."

"Good night, My Lords. Tomorrow awaits," said the Prince.

As the men were riding back to Camp Striker, Connor brought up Lord Stuart. "I am thrilled that he is on our side – but he gives me the creeps. I'm still having the issues from our dream before we got here from Afghanistan! How does he do that?"

Mac said, "Sir, I have no clue – but I'm glad he can for us now."

As soon as the men returned to Camp Striker, the orders were given to prepare four jackals in addition to the Mastiffs. "Three Hundred Rounds per gun should be sufficient to care for our dear General," said Derek. "I want Sergeant Douglas in the Mastiff with the Prince – well armed and ready in case something gets out of hand."

Connor and Mac both agreed.

They planned the action one more time before retiring for the night. They would arrive in the clearing. The Mastiffs would move to the rear as the vehicles turn left. Derek would then announce to the General that he was trespassing and give him the opportunity to unconditionally surrender.

Everyone knew how that would end. It's too bad for the British Regular – just following orders to their demise. It seemed ridiculously unfair to have the Mastiffs and the Jackals against these men now – but he would appreciate that advantage for as long as possible.

Sergeant McKenzie fell asleep and awoke with a start. Lord Stuart was in his dream again. This time as he truly is – not the pretense of an old Clan Chief. Mac welcomed him, and they were again transported to the fire. There was some excellent whiskey and simple conversation. It was interesting that Lord Stuart was asking historical questions. It was said that Ian was the company's historian – which was indeed the case. He could give detailed accounts of many wars involving the Celts –back to Hadrian's Wall - and the wars with the Romans. Lord Stuart then asked personal questions… about his life in Afghanistan… about his personal life… about his Annie… and for some reason, it hit him like a ton of bricks – that he would never again see her sweet smile… taste her kiss… or hold her. Dear God – what he would give for a simple hug right now.

Lord Stuart had known that he had struck a chord with McKenzie – and he did it on purpose – for two reasons – the first was that he knew McKenzie needed that release. Mac had kept it bottled up for way too long. The second was even more critical to him… he needed to know his temperament. He needed to know this man intimately. He wanted to "feel" and understand his emotions… his drive. What motivated him to get up and go through his day? What did he see, and how was he reacting to his current circumstances? If his long-term plans were any indicator, they would work together a great deal.

McKenzie began to wake up, realizing it had all been a dream – but it felt so real. His face drew as he remembered the dream and the details of the conversation. Mac knew that the conversation had indeed been real. What had their conversation been about? What was Stuart trying to learn? What was he fishing for? Well…enough about that. He had to finish packing soon and prepare for what was going to be a combat situation in only 8 hours.

It seemed unfair. Muskets against machine guns – but this was war. He would take every competitive advantage he would have. What was that Patton had said in WW2? Something along the lines that the goal was not to die for one's country – but to make the other Son of a Bitch die for his? That would happen a lot today and for the foreseeable future. He was packed up, locked, and loaded. He would lead one Jackal, Derek and Connor would each have their own, while Lieutenant Gordon would have the other. Lieutenant Ross would command one of the Mastiffs, and Sergeant Douglas would command the other. He met with Derek, Connor, Ross, Gordon, and Douglas for breakfast. They would have a hearty meal, which might be a while before supper.

Once done, they gathered all of the men that would be on this journey. Derek, Connor, and he each expressed the importance of their mission and what they anticipated when they got to that clearing right before Edinburgh. They also decided that since the British would no longer need the Headquarters, all would stay there tonight instead of trying to find accommodations. It would be a safer position for the Prince as well.

Everyone saddled up as they started each of the 4 Jackals and the 2 Mastiffs and left to pick up the Prince and Lord Stuart. Each man had his assault rifle with four magazines of ammunition and his side Arm with three magazines of ammunition. Definitely overkill – but it is far better to be safe than sorry. Derek had everyone put their military uniforms on – including their body armor. They were more comfortable wearing when going into battle, and Derek would not take any chances with his men or the Prince.

They rolled up into the Prince's camp right next to the tent. There was more luggage than anticipated, but is having the proper clothing for a Prince to become King an essential part of the equation? Since the Prince would be in a Mastiff, there would be little opportunity for Derek to converse with him. Derek let the Prince know about staying the night in Edinburgh Castle – since the British would no longer need it after today. The Prince laughed at the irony. "Yes, Lord McAndrew. The Castle at Edinburgh would be delightful accommodation this evening. Should I thank you now for making the accommodation available? Or should I wait until the arrangements have been confirmed?" asked the Prince.

"Let's wait until we have confirmed the reservations, Your Highness." Laughed Derek. Besides, he didn't want a hoodoo on the conflict to come.

They got away closer to eleven. It was later than what Derek wanted, but it would still be before the 3 o'clock meeting with General Sir John Cope.

It was a beautiful summer day as they began their trip to Edinburgh. All the gunners decided to ride next to their weapons in preparation for the combat. It felt "Normal" to what their previous lives had been in Afghanistan – except the weather and the scenery were so much nicer – and there was no concern for IEDs!

Derek had time for frivolous thoughts. He felt the wind blowing and allowed himself time to look at the beautiful landscapes that enveloped him—rugged valleys, breathtaking mountain views... flower-covered meadows. A couple of the bridges were too narrow and frail to allow the Mastiffs and Jackals to cross, so the streams and rivers crossed through the beds of those streams and rivers. Good thing these things rarely got stuck! But the smells. They are what reminded him of home. The heathers almost smelled as sweet as honey. The Pine – the Scots Pine… made him want to pull over to inhale the butterscotch vanilla scent.. how he loved the woods.

Getting to Edinburgh had taken a little longer than he had anticipated. Derek looked at his watch. It was almost 3 when he heard a honk behind him. It was the Mastiff with the Prince and Lord Stuart. Lord Stuart pointed just ahead. Derek nodded. He told his gunners to Chamber a round and be ready to move as planned. They slowly moved up to the clearing, as Lord Stuart had described. There they were. The British. They held the higher ground, but it would not matter.

Just as planned, Derek's Jackal took the lead and veered left. Connor followed him, as did the other Jackals. The Mastiffs rested behind the Jackals, but gunners were ready with the 50 Caliber if necessary.

The four Jackals had a commanding view of the Battlefield. Derek got on his PA System. "Major General Sir John Cope. If we were in a Pub, I would probably buy you a beer, and we could talk about politics. Unfortunately, we are not. You are here to take the True

King of England and Scotland forcefully. Unfortunately, we cannot allow that to happen. So here are your options, sir. You can unconditionally surrender immediately, or in two minutes, you and your entire Regiment will be dead. If you act aggressively, we will rain down Hell upon you immediately."

You could feel the disdain from the British Officer. He told his men to "Make Ready" – the first step in preparing the Musket to be fired. It would then be followed by "Take Aim" … those were the last words ever spoken by the General.

Derek ordered his men to "Fire!" – and fire they did. Derek and his other gunner, along with Connor and his other gunner, had the East Flank, while Mac, his other gunner, and Lieutenant Gordon, with his other gunner, had the West Flank. Derek opened on the General and his staff, who immediately fell to the ground – a bloody testament to his arrogance. He then turned to his east and opened fire fully automatic. Men fell by the hundreds, breathing their last as they attempted vainly to at least return fire.

"Mother Fucker!" Connor yelled. "That Son of a Bitch Shot me! Or at least I think he did. Fuck, that hurt!" He looked down at his body armor, and sure enough, there was a .75 flattened lead ball that had hit him squarely in the chest. If he did not have his body armor – that would have been a fatal shot! He squeezed the trigger in the direction that the shot came from. He would have the satisfaction of killing the bastard that had just shot him.

Once Derek heard Connor resuming firing, Derek did the same. It took less than two minutes. In less than two minutes – every British soldier and officer breathed their last. Derek ordered everyone to cease fire. All of a sudden, it was eerily quiet. There were no groans from the wounded – for a groan would indicate there was life… and none was available.

Prince Charles and Lord Stuart exited their Mastiff to look at the battlefield. The carnage reminded the Prince of the Battlefield at Culloden. He was once again astounded by the power these men wielded so effectively. He looked up to the sky and thanked the Almighty that these men were Scots on his side and not on the other. As discussed, the General's body was retrieved, rolled into a blanket, and tied to the front of the Mastiff. It was 0310 pm. All of this had taken less than 10 minutes.

Several men on horseback came rushing up to the battlefield. Derek met them and told them, "This is what happens to the enemies of Prince Charles Stuart and Scotland." The men eyed him warily with his uniform and battle dress and their equipment. Then they asked if they could see if there was anything valuable they could find on the battlefield. Derek told them to take whatever they needed. There would be over 400 muskets, gunpowder, swords, and other items that would be put to good use by Scotsmen – rather than the invaders. They did not have the time nor desire to do so. They had the General, his personal weapons, and other identifiers. He didn't care about the value of the rest of the loot.

Everyone loaded up, and they headed to the Edinburgh Castle. The Gate had been left down, and the group parked in the courtyard. The Prince and Lord Stuart were asked to stay in the Mastiff until the castle was cleared – which would take a while.

The 24 men split into small squads, and as they prepared to move forward, they were met by two dozen surprised Brits. The Brits were told to surrender. When it was apparent they would not do so, the SA-80 did the trick. The 5.56 mm efficiently accomplished the task it was designed to do as the British fell to the ground. There would be attendants – mainly Scots, taking care of the Castle.

Derek called his men back to the Jackals. He got on the PA System and called out for any British to Surrender – that no harm would come to them. He then announced in Gaelic that the British Regiment would not return, that the General was dead and that if they still needed employment, their true King would appreciate their help. He also announced in English and Gaelic that any that were not in the courtyard in ten minutes would be counted as an enemy and killed on sight.

Slowly, people began to come out. First, it was a trickle…then it was by the hundreds. There were roughly 500 support staff here at the castle. There were no more British on site. Those who had attempted to fight were dead. Each group was split into approximately 25. Only Gaelic was spoken. Each of them was asked simple questions in Gaelic, and soon, it became evident that there were roughly 53 Englishmen who had worked in the support staff – Clerks, guards, administrators, and personal attendants for the officers.

They were terrified. The Prince walked up to them and spoke to them in English. "I am Prince Charles Stuart—the rightful King of Scotland. You are here on behalf of the invaders. I could execute you all by right and custom, and my conscience would be clear. However, I will be the King of England in less than a year, making you my future subject. Shall I treat you as my enemy? Or as my future subjects?"

With that – every one of them took a knee.

Prince Charles smiled. "Excellent. Do you need further employment? Or would you like to go home? It is your choice. All of you have levels of expertise that I will need. If you wish to serve me here, it would be appreciated. That being said, if you wish to go home, you will not be accosted. You will be given whatever horses and wagons are here, and you will be allowed to leave. I would advise leaving under cover of darkness early in the morning and getting out of town before daylight. I cannot guarantee your safety any other way."

Eighteen decided to remain employed at the castle. This had been their home for far too long. They did not wish to return to England. That meant there were thirty-five who wished to leave. The Prince spoke with the Horse master of the Castle. Arrangements were made. It was decided that horseback would be the preferred method of all leaving, so the horses were picked out and would be ready by 3 am.

Now that had been worked through, everyone swore allegiance to the new Prince, and all welcomed him. The Prince made it a point to welcome everyone there personally. He had new attendants who volunteered to assist him in his new quarters. It was a celebratory atmosphere as every party member was generally hailed as heroes.

The British Flag was unceremoniously cut down and cast to the ground. The St. Andrew's Cross flew proudly…and everyone began to notice.

Derek and Mac finally had the opportunity to ask Connor about what happened to him on the battlefield. Connor pulled up his shirt. A bruise already formed the size of a fist with a knot in the middle right under his right shoulder. Connor looked at Derek and said, "I will never argue with you or doubt you when you tell us to wear Armor. That fucking hurt. I would be dead now without the body armor. And next time – don't fucking wait until they say 'Aim' before we fire on the bastards!" Yep – Connor was going to be okay.

At 6 pm, supper was ready. The richness of the food available astounded even the Prince. The officers enjoyed the finer things. Fine Ports, Wines, and Whiskeys prevailed. All the men that accompanied the Prince were also treated to the bounty – though warned about overindulging in the alcohol for tomorrow could also be filled with surprises.

Guards were posted, and the Gates were closed. Finally… a Royal was at the Royal Palace in Edinburgh. It was the first of many changes to come.

Prince Charles was to speak to the Assembly at 9 am. He had a good idea of what he was going to say. He was not going to write it down. He was going to speak from the heart. What he had to say would be considered Revolutionary… not just with Independence from King George… but even more regarding the Rule of law's future.

Chapter 36
Airson Alba - For Scotland

Lord Lamont was set to speak at the opening. He was to speak at eight am and Prince Charles at nine. The Initial Vote would be one hour after the Prince spoke. If it were a simple majority in favor of the Prince, he would be crowned King. He had argued, cajoled, and debated for countless hours since this began on Friday. Of the 362 in attendance, he was confident in 49%. The fucking Campbells were trying to derail everything with their candidate that had no legitimacy whatsoever. Their division and their allies have maintained division within Scotland for hundreds of years. They would see their folly. He had seen the weapons that could be arrayed against them. Rumor had it that the British Contingent here in Edinburgh had already experienced the Jackals and the Mastiffs. There was even a rumor the Prince had spent the night in their Quarters in The Royal Castle of Edinburgh.

It was seven am. He had a good breakfast and was ready to get this done and the King in place. So many things needed to be addressed before the war with England began. God, how he hated politics!

He dismounted from his horse, taken away to be fed and pampered all day. He would almost rather trade places with the horse.

Deep breaths…and smiles. And so, it began. Handshakes, encouraging words… pleas for unity… financial opportunities… what about English Lordships and Properties? Greedy bastards – the lot of them. Of course, there would be English Estates available – especially when they send their large army, and they are utterly devasted.

Finally – it was his time. He said a short prayer to himself before beginning the speech. "Heavenly Father, Thee alone knows what this will mean or the future this will bring to my beloved country. We have been through so much already; I beseech thee in thy mercy to allow this to be of your divine will. I pray that you will speak through me as thy divine will is engaged and brought to fruition. Amen.”

He calmly and quietly walked up to the lectern. Not a word was spoken as the audience felt the gravity of this day… of this decision. No matter what was decided, Scotland would no longer be the same.

“Lords and gentlemen, esteemed members of the Assembly,

“Today, I stand before you, not as a fervent Jacobite or a staunch loyalist. Today, I stand as a humble Scot, a Lord of this land, who has witnessed firsthand the winds of change that have swept through our beloved homeland. With great pride and profound conviction, I call upon each one of you to unite behind a cause that transcends loyalty to a family or clan. It is a cause that represents the very essence of Scotland, a cause that calls for a brighter future, a cause that places power not in the hands of a monarch alone but in the collective will of the Scottish people.”

“Before us will stand a man whose name is known far and wide – Prince Charles Edward Stuart. A man who, in the wake of the Battle of Culloden, has proven his commitment to Scotland and its people. Many of you may have known him as the arrogant aristocrat who once sought power for his own glory. But times have changed, and so has he. His transformation is nothing short of remarkable, and it is this transformation that gives me hope and the courage to stand before you today.”

“The Battle of Culloden, my friends, was not merely a clash of armies but a turning point in our history. It was a battle that saw our fellow Scots, armed with knowledge and new weapons, stand together with unwavering resolve. It was a battle that ended in a resounding victory. A victory that saw no British soldier left standing on the battlefield. It was a battle that should serve as a reminder that when Scots unite, we are an invincible force.”

“But let us not forget the lessons of the past. Victory on the battlefield is just one step towards a free and prosperous Scotland. We must now harness that spirit of unity and turn it towards the path of nation-building. We stand at the precipice of a new era, an era in which we can determine our own destiny, an era in which we can establish a constitutional monarchy that safeguards the rights and freedoms of every Scotsman.”

"Prince Charles Stuart has recognized the need for change and to break free from the shackles of old traditions that have held our nation back. He envisions a Scotland where the rule of law prevails, where justice is blind to one's birthright, and where individual rights are not just empty words but living principles. His commitment to these ideals is genuine, and it is time for us to embrace this opportunity to shape our nation's future."

"I, Lord Keith Lamont, was once neutral in this conflict, hesitant to take a stand. But I have witnessed firsthand the transformation of Prince Charles, and I have come to believe that he can lead us towards a Scotland where our clans, families, and people can thrive. I stand before you today as a testament to the power of change, as evidence that even the most neutral among us can be moved by the winds of progress."

"My fellow Scots, today, we have a choice. We can continue to dwell in the past, clinging to old rivalries and divisions, or step into a new dawn united in purpose and vision. We can choose to support Prince Charles Edward Stuart as our king, a man who understands the needs and aspirations of our people, a man who has shown his dedication to our cause. He even has cast away the Roman Religion and disavowed the Pope – he has embraced our faith – which explains much of the change that has come upon him."

"Let us not be bound by the chains of history but rather inspired by the possibilities of the future. Let us unite the clans, not in blind loyalty to a name, but in pursuing a brighter, fairer, and more prosperous Scotland. Together, we can build a nation that we are proud to call our own, a Scotland that stands as a beacon of hope and progress for future generations."

"I urge you, my fellow Scots, to cast aside old grudges and seize this historic moment. Let us declare Prince Charles Edward Stuart as our rightful king, not as an act of blind faith but as a conscious choice for the betterment of our beloved homeland. Together, we can forge a new path, and together, we can make Scotland truly great."

"Thank you, and may God bless our noble cause and great nation."

There was quiet. The applause was more than tepid. Not as he had hoped – but he believed it to be a majority.

That's when he heard it – and smiled. It would be the mighty roar of the Mastiffs and the Jackals bringing the man who would be King.

The very walls vibrated. You could see surprise and then fear as the noise came closer.

"My Lords and Gentlemen: the noise you hear is our Prince's arrival. It is part of the equipment and weapons that we have at our disposal. It is why Scotland will be free if you allow it." With that, Lord Lamont stepped down from the Lectern.

The Prince suddenly walked in as if he owned the place. His confidence was electric. He fit the persona… the aristocracy was ingrained in his demeanor… it shook the very room. His bodyguard with these new weapons surrounded him, which no one had ever seen before.

Several men were carrying a wooden box… a casket? The crowd began to murmur. Prince Charles walked up to the Lectern as one of the guards unceremoniously dropped British Major General John Cope's body onto the floor. There was a collective gasp from all in attendance.

"Lords and Gentlemen of the Assembly. My Countrymen…. I am Prince Charles Edward Stuart. I am the legitimate heir and the rightful King of Scotland and Britain. Before me, you see the results of all that would attack our country. The body that was thrown onto the floor with disdain was Major General John Cope. The previous resident in the Royal Castle of Edinburgh. He and his 400-500 men tried to stop me from arriving yesterday on the West side of Town. You probably heard the battle as it began but were surprised at the rapid fire and the quickness that the battle was resolved. I had at my disposal twenty-five men against their 400-500, and the English were soundly defeated – in fact, I slept at the Royal Castle last night… The man in the casket is the Duke of Cumberland – the Pretender's son. I have his signet ring should anyone wish to check the authenticity of my claim. Of the over 9,000 men who fought with him - not one of the enemy survived. As will be the policy for all that would invade our country."

"We have a unique opportunity in history…now…right now… to end the rape and pillage of our people and our lands. Our chance…now…right now…to stop being the chattel of a foreign usurper… Our chance…now… right now… to be the freemen that our Creator has meant for us to be… to express our rights as we choose, rather than those dictated from a foreign power."

"If we unite – then we will finally have a country of our own."

"Why is that important to me, and why should you care? That is a great question. I am not sure if you are aware, but I am no longer a Roman Catholic. I have seen the light of truth, which has overcome the spirit of deception. The Bible says that David had a heart after God's own heart. That is what I wish to achieve. I desire to serve as opposed to being served. Not only have I embraced the Protestant Faith… while in Inverness, working to build the engines that will offer so much to our nation – and the world… I had the wonderful opportunity to get to know and work with the people of Inverness… I got to talk to them- not as a King to a Commoner… but as a man to another man or woman. I heard their hopes, dreams, and struggles. I have also had the opportunity to speak at length with Nobility and Clan Chiefs… true, intimate discussion. I had the opportunity to sweat alongside them… to laugh with them… to cry with them. You see, My Lords and Gentlemen… my life… by the Grace of God has truly changed course. Arrogance has been replaced with the need to be humble. The pursuit of pleasure has been replaced with the pursuit of truth… of building a nation that we can be proud of…because of that – I am proposing the following should I become King."

"I am proposing that Scotland become a Constitutional Monarchy… where rights and freedoms are declared in the Rule of Law… even my rights as a King will be subject to the Rule of Law." There was a rumble of approval… Prince Charles noticed this and continued.

"There will be branches of government that will have to be decided upon, but this is what I propose: It will be similar to the English system of Government. The King will be the Head of State. The Parliament will be the House of Lords, made up of the Nobility, and a House – made up of those elected into power by the citizens. Those Houses will make the laws of the land. As the King, I will have a right to Veto the legislation if I find it repugnant…" There was a roar of disapproval. "Let me finish…" he continued, "But the Parliament will have the right to override my veto – we will have to agree on the percentage of both houses that would be required to override my Veto." That was met with a roar of approval. "And finally – there will be a Judicial Branch that will interpret laws that contradict the Constitution and make them null and void. I propose a Judiciary for the Nobility to execute judgment and negotiate disagreements – to eliminate the need for clan wars." That provided a standing ovation that lasted a full two minutes."

"Here are the rights that I propose for the Nobility: 1. Property Rights so your ancestral lands – your property be protected except in acts of treason. 2. Participation in the rule of law with a House of Lords as discussed previously 3. Judicial Autonomy - rights for you to rule over your estates 4. Preservation of Titles and Hereditary Privileges."

"For Rights for the Common Man – 1. Equal protection before and under the law. 2. Freedom of speech. One should be able to speak one's conscience freely – without fear of reprisal. 3. The ability to appeal being removed from lands they farm to an impartial judiciary. To protect from arbitrary confiscation or seizure. 4. Religious Freedom. We have killed and tortured too many that disagree with a particular religion. We should all be free to worship how we believe we should. And 5. The right to bear arms. It should be the right, and the responsibility of each citizen to be able to utilize arms in self-defense and defense of our nation should invaders arrive at our shores."

"And finally… limitations to my rights as King: 1. I must work within a Constitutional Framework. I cannot make arbitrary rules or laws. They must be voted up by the Legislative Bodies previously discussed. 2. There will be checks and balances within the branches of our government – to create tension between the branches to ensure that the rights of our citizens are preserved. 3. Oversight by the Parliament. Especially when it is regarding taxation and any declaration of war. 4. There must be regular assemblies. One cannot govern if one does not gather regularly to oversee what is necessary for the welfare of our citizens. And finally – I cannot arbitrarily go to war. There must be an underlying reason. It must be in the interest of Scotland to do so – or in defense of our great country. Territorial ambitions cannot be the impetus for a war – unless our Parliament declares war against another nation."

"And finally – we must coin our own currency. We cannot allow a Central Bank system to steal our wealth at our expense – to leave us as paupers as they steal every copper from us!"

"We can operate as a Constitutional Monarchy to ensure the freedoms that our ancestors only dreamt of. Together, we can build a nation to be envied and copied globally – with the military might to protect our nation and our interests if necessary. It's there. It is within our reach. I can see it. I can taste it. A life in which our children and grandchildren will forever thank us.

"So, what say you? Would you be free?" There was the beginning of a roar of approval. "Would you determine your destiny as opposed to being ruled over by a foreign power that would subjugate you, steal from you, and bankrupt you?" The applause was increasing in intensity. "Would you dispatch any enemy that would attack us to the pit of hell where they belong? Are you ready for Scotland to take its place among nations?"

"This is a decision given to you by God – a chance truly of a lifetime. So once again, I ask you… WHAT SAY YOU?!?! Shall I…by God's Grace and Providence… be your King?!? Will you take your place as leaders among nations?!? WHAT! SAY! YOU?!?!?"

The entire room erupted in a cacophony… a maelstrom of cheers… applause… and thunderous approval. The deafening clamor … the roar gave a resounding "Yes," … a testament to the profound impact of his words. Scotland would have a King. And it would be Prince Charles Edward Stuart.

Prince Charles stepped down, and Lord Lamont stepped back to the podium. "Now you know, my Lords, why I changed my mind and supported this man as King. We will break for 30 minutes and return for our vote." 362 Attendees thought Lord Lamont. One hundred eighty-two would be enough. The Prince would be the King – but he really needed a mandate. He needed at least 300 to win all of Scotland. One hundred eighty-two would leave too many doubts.

Prince Charles withdrew into a Mastiff. Lord Stuart, Derek, Connor, and Mac joined him. Lord Stuart had a huge smile on his face. He felt confident. In fact, he reached into a leather box – when had he managed to get that on board? He gently opened the container. He pulled out five glasses and a bottle of Madeira. Prince Charles' eyes lit up… "I supposed my speech was acceptable?"

Lord Stuart continued to open the bottle and pour. Once everyone in attendance had a glass, Lord Stuart began, "Your Highness… your speech was more than acceptable… it won the crown. That was extremely well done, sire!" Everyone agreed. "Here is to your Crown, Your Highness. May you govern as David and truly be a "man after God's Own Heart!"

"Hear-Hear!" said all of the men in unison.

Now, the wait would begin as the count would be taken.

Lord Lamont chose a secret ballot to protect all that were in attendance. He knew there could be shenanigans and that a potential disloyal subject could hide themselves by being anonymous. But it seemed the best way – especially if it took multiple votes – to start the voting process. It was simple. Either an "Aye" or a "Nay" would be sufficient. The ballots were handed out.

Fifteen minutes later, the ballots were distributed and returned. The ballots were brought to Lord Lamont. They would be counted in front of everyone. Each ballot would be shown to all as each was counted.

1: Aye
2: Aye
3: Aye
4: Aye

.

.

.

.

312: Aye
313: Abstain
314: Abstain

.

.

.

358: Abstain
359: Aye
360: Aye
361: Aye
362: Aye

Lord Lamont sent for the Prince.

Prince Charles approached the podium. Lord Lamont said, "On the first Ballot, Your Highness, The Count is 318 Ayes, 44 Abstains, 0 Nays. The Assembly has spoken, Your Highness. You will be installed to your rightful station at 10 am on July 5, 1746, here, on this platform, where you will be Crowned as King Charles III. Are there any objections, my Noble Lords? Hearing none. We will reconvene tomorrow in this Assembly at nine am – as Scotland begins a new era!" The room resounded in thunderous applause!

Prince Charles stood at the exit… and made it a point to shake every hand and thank everyone as they left the auditorium.

Prince Charles returned to the waiting Mastiff with his friends and bodyguards. That's when it hit him. The enormity of the undertaking is coming to fruition. His father would be proud. However, what was in his mind currently was to make the Father… the Almighty, proud of him and his actions. He was determined to do the right thing for the right reasons. He knew that tomorrow was only the beginning.

Derek asked the obvious question, "Who do you think were the ones that abstained?"

Lord Lamont laughed, "You bloody well know who. It was the Campbells and their sycophants. They were the biggest backers of the current Pretender. They were hedging their bets."

"Perhaps," said the Prince. "Perhaps not. What I know is that I am going to have to govern them or eradicate them. They are too strong to do otherwise. My sincere feeling, especially when I shook the hand of the Clan Chief – is that they will do what is in their best interest – followed by what they perceive to be in the interest of Scotland. As long as I know what motivates them, I can act or react accordingly. It's those that smile to your face with a dagger in your back in which we must tread lightly."

Lord Stuart said, "That is a great assessment, Your Highness. It will take time, but they will become an ally."

"I still wouldn't trust the bastards," said a defiant Lord Lamont.

Price Charles laughed at that remark. "Time will tell, my friends."

Chapter 37
King

Word had gotten out. They knew. Everyone knew. Prince Charles Edward Stuart was going to be crowned. Despite the Monstrosities in the Mastiffs that terrified most – everyone wanted a glimpse. A smile. A gesture.

Against the better judgment of all inside the Mastiff – Prince Charles stopped the Mastiff and crawled up to the gun turret. He started waving and smiling. Initially, there were just a few hundred… but the closer they got to the Royal Castle – the hundreds turned into thousands. The Bells from the church towers began to ring triumphantly. It took just over ten minutes to get to the Auditorium this morning. It took two hours to get to the castle.

'Finally,'… Derek thought. 'This was a security nightmare.' All he wanted was to be surrounded by the Castle Walls, having a decent supper, and collapsing in the bed. But he also knew that would not happen as quickly as he hoped. Everything they had been working toward was coming to pass tomorrow. So why was he nervous? One shot or blade could destroy everything – and Prince Charles was still young enough to think himself bulletproof.

That is when they saw them… literally, hundreds of the staff had come out of the castle to welcome him. They all knelt and swore allegiance to the man who would be king on the morrow. Ewan Douglas, the lead Steward of the Castle, stood before them all.

"Repeat after me: I, (State your name), solemnly swear my allegiance to King Charles III as the rightful monarch of Scotland, Chosen by Almighty God. I pledge to serve him and his heirs faithfully all of my life, defend his realm, and uphold his authority. So help me God."

Prince Charles was truly humbled. He walked over to all of them and had them stand. He shook everyone's hand. He spoke kind words to all. His ability to relate to anyone and to speak comfort were gifts not generally endowed with those that would be King.

Prince Charles thanked them all – and then let them know their position was secure. He also informed them that they would all receive a 25% increase in their pay rate – which brought cheers from all.

Supper was subdued as everyone was exhausted from the day's events. Of course, everyone knew that tomorrow would be even more eventful. Lord Lamont still had a massive smile on his face. The Prince knew how instrumental Lord Lamont was in getting him this far. He would indeed be rewarded.

Everyone enjoyed the quiet before the work truly began. Prince Charles could not take his mind off what needed to be completed in Inverness. My place is there while we prepare for the eventual invasion force. Of course, he knew that a Constitution would take time. He would also ask the Lords to write a Declaration of Independence from England.

The easy part was the construction and planning phase of this entire process. It would be nothing compared to the governing part. He would need strong advisors, which he did have by God's Grace. There would need to be some political appointments to his Council. He would have to be highly discerning. Like Lamont – he wasn't feeling the need to be entirely forthcoming to the Campbells. He knew he would be able to win them over to his cause. It would just take time to do so.

After some whiskey, dessert, and cigars, everyone agreed that bed and sleep could not come soon enough.

Prince Charles retired to his quarters, as did the others. Prince Charles collapsed on his bed to be there for only a few minutes. He awoke at 6 am the following day! He quickly left bed and had his servants draw a hot bath for him. "Damn!" he said out loud to himself. "I can't be late to my coronation!"
He opened his door to a servant waiting…" It seems I slept instead of bathed last night," he said with a smile. "Would you be so kind as to have a bath drawn? Make it hot. I will need it today and probably another this evening!"

"Yes, your Highness." Everything erupted in the castle. The future King was up, and it was time to get ready. He had decided already what to wear – it would not be the apparel of Nobility… it would be the dress of those he would serve. He would not wear the Tartan of the Stuarts. It would be one that he had designed. Royal Blue will be used to designate Royalty as the background color. Yellow symbolizes Nobility, leadership, and hope for the future. Green symbolizes Scotland – her strength, renewal, and character. Finally, white – to symbolize purity and a clean slate…hope is what he wished to represent.

The bath was done, and his attendants helped him to dress. His white silk shirt was first. His especially woven Kilt was next, with a belt to keep it in place. Silk Stockings in place with a garter. The Ghillie Brogues, followed by a Sporran. His silk jacket was next. His primary accessory was to be a sash with Scotland's Motto: "Nemo me impune lacessit" – "No One Provokes Me With Impunity" – and by God's Grace – he meant that more than any would understand.

He looked in the mirror. Simple yet elegant. He was satisfied. This would work.

It was seven, and he met the others for breakfast. When everyone saw him, applause erupted. The Prince smiled. Derek, Connor, Mac, and Lord Stuart took their place at the table. There was nervous laughter amid the conversation. The enormity of the cause weighed heavily upon them all.

At last, it was time to leave. All the men would be going – including the Jackals and the Mastiffs. The Prince would not be exposed to any inkling of danger as far as Derek was concerned. God, he just wanted to go back to Inverness!

The crowds were lining the streets to the Assembly. It appeared they had gotten used to the motorized equipment. They still gawked as it went by, but at least they didn't run from them.

They arrived. The Two Jackals in the Front, the two Mastiffs in the Middle, followed by the last two Jackals. All of the men exited their vehicles. They were at their finest as well. However, they were heavily armed. It would not bode well for anyone to show any mischief to the Prince today! Finally, the Mastiff Doors were opened. Lord Lamont was the first to exit, followed by Derek, Connor, Mac, Lord Stuart …, and finally, the Prince. Everyone bowed in respect. He was escorted into the Assembly. Derek sincerely hoped that the Prince, whom he had come to know, would continue as the Prince became the King.

The Preparations that could have been made on such short notice were completed well. A Crier had already been through Edinburgh announcing the Coronation of Prince Charles. As part of the Royal

Entrance, the Lords of the Ten Largest Clans and the city leaders gathered around the Prince and escorted him with a great deal of fanfare into the Assembly Hall. Trumpets were blaring for the precession. Prince Charles beamed. He was indeed made for a time like this.

For the Religious Service, Prince Charles thought it would be fitting for Reverend Finlay Cameron to conduct the ceremony. There was going to be an entire anointment ceremony. Prayers were prayed, and a sermon was given – of course, it was regarding King David and being a man after God's heart. The weight of that responsibility. He even discussed David's sins and how they drastically affected his subjects – from the census to Bathsheba. The responsibility of the Crown must always supersede the desires and ambitions of the one wearing the crown. Finally, Prince Charles was anointed with oil. At that point, all of the Clergy walked up to the Prince and placed their hands upon him, and each asked for God's blessings upon him, that his reign would be long, that his enemies defeated, and for his children to be many. At that point, the Protestant Archbishop of St. Andrews walked to the throne where Prince Charles was sitting. He placed his hands and prayed over him for wisdom, mercy, grace, and peace. He decried that the Stone of Destiny was in England and charged Prince Charles III to bring it home where it belonged and that, once again, he could be crowned on the Stone of Destiny as he should be. Prince Charles was then given an oath to recite:

"I, Charles, by the will of destiny and the people's aspirations, do at this moment pledge my solemn oath and fealty to the ancient realm of Scotland as your rightful King. I accept this mantle of leadership, bound by duty and honor, to guide our nation toward prosperity and unity.

With unwavering dedication, I promise to protect the rights and liberties of our subjects, uphold the laws of our land, and govern with justice and compassion. In the face of challenges and triumphs, I shall be the guardian of Scotland's heritage and the champion of her people.

On this day, as I ascend to the throne, I accept the great responsibility bestowed upon me with humility and grace. May my reign be marked by the enduring bonds between King and country, and may the spirit of Scotland forever thrive under my stewardship."

The Archbishop then held the Crown and placed it gingerly upon the head of Prince Charles Stuart. He then gave him the scepter and made the proclamation.

"Hear ye, hear ye, assembled nobles and subjects of Scotland, on this momentous day, we gather to proclaim a new era in the annals of our kingdom. By divine right and the will of our people, we announce the ascension of Charles, rightful heir to the throne, as King Charles III of Scotland."

"With solemn reverence and gratitude for the blessings of providence, we declare that the ancient crown has found its rightful head. This noble monarch, chosen to guide our realm through trials and triumphs, is anointed and consecrated in the name of our sacred land."

"May his reign be marked by wisdom, justice, and compassion. As the guardian of our traditions and the shepherd of our people, King Charles III takes up the noble mantle of leadership with the promise to protect the liberties and prosperity of all his subjects."

"We beseech divine favor upon this coronation and, more importantly, his reign, asking for strength, wisdom, and guidance in the coming days. With our resounding acclamation, we salute and honor our new King and unite in Scotland's spirit under his benevolent rule... Long live King Charles III!"

The audience erupted, "Long live King Charles III!

It was time for the Lords to kneel and swear Fealty to the new King. Lord Lamont chose to be the first.

"I, Lord Keith Lamont, by the grace of our ancestors and the loyalty of our clan, do hereby swear my solemn and unwavering fealty to you, King Charles III of Scotland. I pledge my allegiance, sword, and the honor of the Lamont Clan to your rightful reign. With steadfast devotion, I commit to stand by your side, defend your realm, and uphold your authority. As the shepherd of our people and the guardian of our traditions, I will strive to ensure the prosperity and unity of Scotland under your benevolent rule. May our loyalty be unshaken, and may our bonds remain unbreakable."

Each of the Lords and Clan Chiefs followed in line to swear the same commitment… until it got to the Campbells. Archibald Campbell, the 3rd Duke of Argyll, nodded to the new King. "Your Highness, you know that our clan supported King George in the Jacobite Rebellion that has brought us here. While I respect your military victories and what has brought all of this to this conclusion, I cannot at this time swear fealty to you."

"Traitor!" "Hang them all!" "You're no Scotsman!" "Fucking Bastards—A ll!" were the screams from the crowd.

Lord Archibald Campbell continued, "There are more than enough here to do all as they say. We could be with a noose around our neck in only a few minutes – yet I still would refuse to swear fealty to you now. That doesn't mean forever – it means now. You see, Your Highness – I know King George. I have seen him and have spoken to him on numerous occasions. I know the resources that are at his disposal. I know his temper and how he will react when the rumors of his son's death are confirmed. He will call up 100,000 experienced troops that are currently in Europe. He will order blockades to prevent supply or aid from other countries. He will hunt you and all who support you to the ends of the earth to exact retribution." He looked at the audience, "You would be wise to understand that is what will happen because of what happens here. I am the leader of our family, your Highness. I will not bring about the end of my clan because of an emotional appeal."

"That being said, Your Highness. I am willing to see what you have described. I would meet you in Inverness, where your camp and production facilities are located. If you can convince me that you will have the capacity to not only take on but defeat the strongest military the world has ever seen – then I swear to you before God Almighty – that I will swear fealty to you – and be the most faithful of your subjects. Today is July 5 – let us meet in Inverness on August 8. Are you acceptable to that? Are you indeed willing to do what it takes to unite the clans?"

King Charles stood up and smiled. He walked over to Lord Archibald Campbell, a man that he towered over by at least 6." Lord Campbell, to his credit – did not flinch. "Your terms are accepted. I will meet you in Inverness on August 6. But understand this – if there is any treachery found within – you and your clan will no longer exist. Do we have an understanding?"

"Yes, Your Highness. Completely," said Lord Campbell.

The fealty ceremonies continued as other clans swore fealty to the new King. Finally, it was finished.

King Charles then stood and thanked all in attendance – even the Campbells. He acknowledged all that had happened. He explained his hopes and dreams for Scotland. Finally – he charged them all to commit to producing a Declaration of Independence for the Crown in England. He expressed that this declaration needed to be made to the world to justify their independence from the Crown. He also charged them with writing a Constitution. He then explained that he would be in Inverness while they accomplished that task as he had to prepare for the confrontation with King George.

As King Charles III stood, and everyone bowed. They stood tall and shouted, "Long Live King Charles III!" Over and over.

Then, the feasting and drinking began. King Charles drank port and sipped whiskey. He would not allow himself to get drunk. There was too much riding on this. He would use Solomon's wisdom in this situation.

It was dark as the celebrations began to wind down. King Charles had shaken more hands than he had ever before. Each clan jockeyed for position to gain his attention and, therefore, their influence. God, how he hated politics – but it was a necessary evil. He could not govern the nation without them.

Finally, the day was done. It was time to return to the Royal Castle – a place that would be his home once the preparations had been made for the battle to come. Once the Pretender was defeated and became King of all of Britain, he planned on making this his permanent residence and only be in London when necessary.

They arrived at the castle. It was only 8 pm, but it seemed so much later. Everyone was still excited from the day's events – but exhausted from those same events. It all seemed surreal to the now King Charles III. He wanted a quiet evening with his friends…and friends they were. He knew that he could indeed count on them to be faithful and true, and he would also be to them.

The King had found the Withdrawing Room or Privy Chamber in this castle. A private, comfortable room where he could be with friends and council. There was an extensive bar. The General had immaculate taste. Derek, Connor, Mac, Lord Lamont, and Lord Stuart were having a quiet conversation planning for the future when there was a knock on the door. "Come," said the King. Ian MacDougal, the Lord Treasurer, came inside. The King had met him briefly the day before.

The King asked, "You are here quite late? Is there a problem?"

"No, Sire," said the Lord Treasurer. "But there is something that you must see, and it cannot wait. Now that you are King, it is proper for me to disclose this to you and to show you privately."

"You may speak openly to all in attendance. I owe them my life and trust them with everything," said the King.

"I am sure that you know that every Castle has a treasury – especially for paying expenses for a garrison?"

"Yes. I am aware that is the case," said the King.

"Well, Sire, there is more to that here. There were only 400 troops left here to guard the treasury because 1,000 were taken with the Duke to try to locate you and your men. When they did not return as promised, the General began to ask for reinforcements to take their place – which was not forthcoming as anticipated. The King responded that once the Jacobites were found out, the General could have 1,500 men there to assist."

"To assist in what?" asked the King.

"Well, Sire, two distinct treasuries are in this castle. The one for the garrison…and a private one held by King George," said the Lord Treasurer.

"Oh? Please go on," said the King.

"Well, Sire… the amount in the Treasury for the garrison is 10,321,486 pounds and 6 Shillings," said the Lord Treasurer.

There was a collective gasp in the room.

"But that's not all Sire. In the vault for King George, there are 27,827,618 pounds and 12 Shillings!"

King Charles jumped up and said, "Show us!"

The Lord Treasurer guided them to a vault in the basement of the Treasury Chamber. A lantern was brought for light as they descended into the basement. It was pitch black, where the light did not touch. It took some time to get there as it was on the bottom floor. The doors were thick wrought iron and heavy wood. The Lord Treasurer had the key to the locked door. He opened it to find more wrought iron and more locks. Finally, they arrived in the inner chamber. There were two distinct rooms. Each had massive stores of gold within. But one room was colossal. It was full of gold coins and gold ingots! There were precious stones as well.

King Charles stepped into the room and began to laugh. "Gentlemen… You do realize that our war against the English and modernizing Scotland… will be financed by the King of England?"

"Lord Treasurer – I am assuming this vault is secret, and only a few know its origin, amount, and location?" asked the King.

"Yes, Your Highness," said the Lord Treasurer.

"Here is the first thing that I want you to do. I want each employee here given 100 pounds from the Garrison Treasury. And you, sir – I want you to have 500 pounds for being diligent and handling the affairs quietly as they should be done. This should take care of you and your family quite well. In the meantime, I would like you to continue your position for me. Is that acceptable?" asked the King.

"500 pounds?!?! Yes, Sire. It is very much acceptable and highly appreciated. And Yes! I will stay and do as I have always done – and even better this time," said the Lord Treasurer.

They returned to the Privy Chamber, and the Lord Treasurer was thanked again and dismissed for the evening.

Everyone sat in silence for a few minutes. Finally, Derek spoke up…" We must leave some of our men to protect this wealth."

"I fully agree," said the King. "The 10 million pounds will probably fund all that we need. The other is the emergency fund. Derek, Connor, and Mac, I agreed to split the funds with you and your men at 30%, making the Striker Team a 25% shareholder in our company. Would it be acceptable to you and those here to make it 10% for this stake so that we have the available funds to prosecute this war and fund the growth of the innovative technologies?"

Derek looked at the others, and they nodded. "Yes, Your Highness. That is perfectly acceptable. The total would be over 3.5 Million pounds! That will make us all wealthy beyond belief! We will not be greedy in our time of great need."

"Here are my thoughts," said the King. "We will take your 3.7 million pounds and an additional 5 million pounds from the 16 million that are a part of the garrison's funds. We will leave the rest here under the protection of your men until we can get a proper contingent here. I wish to repay the Lords in Inverness for their investment in the modernization project. The last time I heard, over 500,000 pounds had been spent. They will also appreciate repayment much sooner than anticipated with a good profit."

"And finally, my friends. It is time to return the body of the Duke and the General to the King in the South. I intend to write a letter explaining that I am now the King and that he nor his army will be allowed to Trespass into Scotland on pain of death. He will not take that well and plan earnestly for an attack here. I wish to meet them in Falkirk—where William Wallace lost and the negative history that occurred there. I intend to change it to a positive memory. Thoughts?" asked the King.

Mac said, "Your Highness… those funds invested will mean everything to the future of Scotland. We will be able to afford the best and the brightest in getting everything constructed. We still must focus on the weapons of war – as we all know that King George will definitely attack. It is only a matter of time. We also have a good idea of where he will come. We will be prepared. We will be ready. It is almost time to get our soldiers back to train. The English will not know what hit them and will never attempt to subjugate us again!"

"I'll drink to that," said the King. He held his glass high, as did the others. "This will be the story of the ages! Our Children's children will celebrate what we do here now. On the morrow, I will write to Old George and send the bodies to their final resting place. It will be interesting to hear what transpires in Jolly Old England."

Chapter 38
Missive

"**S**O How vexed should I make Old George?" thought King Charles. "I'm thinking incensed would be the proper amount." He brought out a Parchment. He would not allow another to write this for him. This will be of my own hand for that son of a whore…

"My Dear King George:

It appears that your attempts to capture or kill me have not worked out too well for those who attempted to do so. It is with such sorrow that I am sending you my condolences as well as the remains of the Duke of Cumberland and Major General Sir John Cope. They died bravely, as did all of the men under their command. The rest of those departed souls are in a mass grave. I am afraid they did not have much of a chance against the skill and the bravery of the Scottish men that put them out of their misery.

If you have not heard, I have been anointed and crowned as the King of Scotland. As such, it is my responsibility to protect the people of Scotland, and I will do so. I am writing to inform you that any invasion on your part will be violently opposed, and no quarter will be given to any such invader. You would be wise to focus on your European equals instead of your betters in Scotland.

However, I do wish to offer my sincere thanks. I had no idea you had such a treasury in the Royal Castle in Edinburgh. That money will do a great deal in providing the funds for our defense.

In conclusion, this is a warning. You would be wise to stay on your side of the border. I will not guarantee your safety should you decide otherwise.

With True Sincerity,

Charles Regis"

With that, a team was dispatched with a wagon, and a letter describing the wagon's contents were those of the Duke and the

Major General. They were to be left in the City of York in a visible location, so they would then be taken to London and from there to the King.

From there, it took several weeks to get to London. Those assigned to the task were not overjoyed with the prospect of presenting this to the King of England. Ten weeks later, the motley crew arrived at St. James Palace – the residence of the King of England.

They pulled up with the wagon to where the guards were stationed. They promptly left the wagon and left hurriedly on their horses. They were NOT going to be the ones personally giving the body of the son to the King of England. And the letter that was sealed…sealed by the King of Scotland? Oh hell no. They did their duty, and they would get the hell out of town and back to York.

The guards walked up to the wagon and saw two caskets. There were two letters. One was sealed by the King of Scotland? The other was penned by the Duke of York.

"Your Majesty.

The bodies of my brother and that of Major General Sir John Cope were left at our gate anonymously. It appears that the Jacobites have inflicted more damage than we expected them to be able to accomplish and have placed Prince Charles Stuart as King of Scotland. There was a letter sealed to you only, so we sent the bodies to London, where they could be honored. We are thoroughly preparing for war with Scotland, anticipating what you want to accomplish moving forward. We are awaiting your command.

You Majesty's dutiful and obedient son,

Edward"

The King of England knew there was a problem. It had been too long since he had heard from his son. He had dispatched riders – but none had returned. He read the letter from his son – the Duke of York. He felt weak in the knees, knowing that these heretical bastards had killed his son.

He finally opened the seal from Charles. He read it once… then reread it. A fire burned inside that was unlike any anger he had ever felt. That arrogant son of a bitch was going to be captured and Drawn and Quartered! And fucking Scotland would be burned to the ground!

He yelled at his Steward… "GET ME THE SECRETARY AT WAR – HENRY FOX – NOW!"

The Steward scurried away. In 30 minutes, a thoroughly disheveled, out-of-breath Secretary at War arrived to meet the King. The King did not say a word – which frightened the Secretary. He only handed him the letter received by the King of Scotland?!?!

He read the letter; "Shit" came out of his mouth unexpectedly. "I'm sorry, your Majesty."

In an even-toned but livid growl – "Do you think for one fucking moment after reading that, that I am concerned ABOUT YOUR VOCUBULARY?!?!? Let me tell you something, Fox. I want action. I want you to recall and prepare 100,000 men to march on Scotland by May next year! We will burn it to the ground and draw and quarter their new King. Do you understand?!?!?"

"Yes, Your Majesty. I fully understand," said Secretary Fox. "I will make it happen." And he promptly left the King to begin recalling troops from France and Europe. The logistics of this were going to take time. He shook his head… "What a fool this new King must be."

With that, the King was left to his thoughts. He did not care… he had felt anger towards adversaries. But this newfound feeling was HATE. He would strangle this son of a bitch's neck with his bare hands!

END OF BOOK 1